Cursed Bones

Sovereign of the Seven Isles: Book Five

by

David A. Wells

CURSED BONES

Copyright © 2012 by David A. Wells

Edited by Carol L. Wells

This is a work of fiction. Characters, events and organizations in this novel are creations of the author's imagination.

www.SovereignOfTheSevenIsles.com

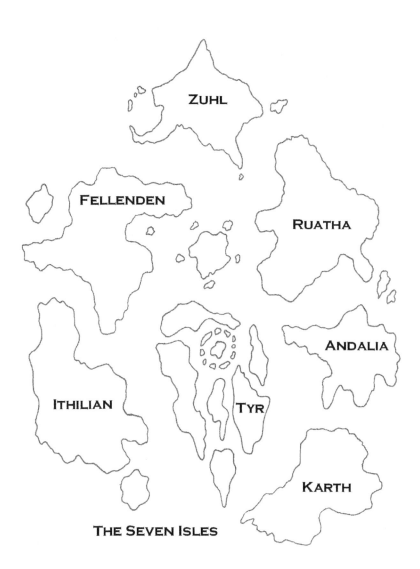

ZUHL

FELLENDEN

RUATHA

ANDALIA

ITHILIAN

TYR

KARTH

THE SEVEN ISLES

Cursed Bones

Chapter 1

Isabel woke with a start, her heart hammering in her chest, her hand instinctively going for the hilt of her dagger. Once she realized where she was, she eased herself back onto her bunk and swallowed hard against the rising lump in her throat. She'd been dreaming again, the same dream she'd had for the past three nights, the dream, or rather the nightmare, where she killed Alexander.

A tear slipped down her cheek. She'd left him. The only man she'd ever loved, the best man she'd ever known, and she'd left him without even saying goodbye, without giving an explanation … nothing. And yet, she knew deep down in that calm place where reason prevailed, that she'd done the only thing she could have done. The dreams were proof of that. Proof that Phane's dark magic was working within her, working to subvert her free will and turn her against the people she loved.

The solution was painfully simple and even more painfully difficult. She couldn't afford to be around the people she loved anymore. As lonely a thought as that was, she knew it was the only way to protect them. More importantly, it was the only way to protect their common cause from her own inevitable betrayal.

She put her hand on her stomach and stared into the darkness of her stateroom as she swallowed back another sob.

It was one thing to face an enemy, to stand and fight, even against insurmountable odds, but this was profoundly different. It was so insidious. In the days since she'd left the dragon isle, she'd begun to carefully observe her own thoughts, scrutinizing each for its authenticity. Did it originate from within her own mind? Or was it planted there by Azugorath?

Phane's dark minion was the immediate cause of her suffering, but the Wraith Queen was really just a symptom of a much larger problem.

Phane.

She meant to kill him.

The moment she'd left her wounded husband in his Wizard's Den, she knew her course. It was the only path open to her. She couldn't stay with Alexander, even though she longed to be with him. She couldn't go home to Ruatha lest she become a danger to her friends and family. She couldn't go to Ithilian or to the fortress island for the same reason. The only place she could go without endangering those she cared about was to her enemy.

Her intent was resolute—honed to a razor's edge by desperation and a furious rage simmering in the pit of her belly.

That left the how.

Phane was more than a match for her in any kind of direct confrontation. She had to beat him at his own game. She had to deceive the deceiver. Only subterfuge would give her the opportunity she needed.

A little flutter of fear chased the pangs of loneliness and loss from her belly. She'd never been a very good liar. Surely, Phane would see through any direct effort at deception. In order to work, her ruse would have to be subtle and artful.

But how?

No matter.

She'd been turning these thoughts over and over in her mind for days, pondering all of the possibilities, but in the end, she decided that circumstances would dictate her tactics. Things would become clearer as she got closer to her target.

A soft knock at the door disturbed the darkness.

"Yes?" she said, quietly.

"We've reached the coast of Karth, Lady Reishi," Captain Kalderson said. "We're holding half a league from the surf."

"How long before dawn?" Isabel asked.

"Couple of hours."

She sat up and took a deep breath. It was time.

Captain Kalderson was waiting for her when she opened the door to her stateroom. "It's not too late to set a new course, My Lady," he said.

"Thank you, Captain, but I'm afraid you're wrong."

"At least let me send a squad of men with you."

"No, you'd just be sending them to their death."

"What about you, Lady Reishi? What's to stop the Regency soldiers from killing you the moment they lay hands on you?"

Isabel shrugged. "Phane wants me alive." She handed the captain a letter, sealed in wax with the medallion of Glen Morillian. "As soon as I'm away, make haste for Ruatha. Land at Northport and personally deliver this letter to Commander P'Tal in Blackstone Keep."

"He'll skin me alive for letting you go into harm's way alone," Captain Kalderson said, taking the letter and inspecting the seal before tucking it into his shirt.

"You have your orders, Captain. Now, show me to my boat."

***

Even this far south, the night air was cold. Her face was red from the stinging, wind-whipped spray coming off the surf, as well as from the exertion of rowing the little dinghy to shore. Another wave caught her, pushing her toward the shallows, rocking her back, then forward, before passing beneath her and setting her boat on an even keel once again. The shadow of Captain Kalderson's ship was lost in the predawn black.

Isabel was alone … well, almost alone. Slyder was nearby, as always. Her boat ran aground in the surf. She steadied herself as she hoisted her pack and gathered her resolve, then stepped into the water and dragged her boat toward shore.

After securing the dinghy just inside the jungle that hugged the beach, she built a small fire and ate breakfast while her clothes dried. She didn't worry about the light of the fire attracting the enemy. If they found her, so be it. If they didn't, she meant to find them.

She wasn't sure how Phane would react to her arrival, especially since she wasn't bringing him the Sovereign Stone, but she was confident that he wouldn't kill her, at least not right away. He wanted to use her against Alexander, and besides, she was a valuable captive if nothing else. Phane would keep her alive to use as leverage, probably offer her in exchange for the Stone. Regardless, his machinations would work against him. He would take precautions, no doubt. But she would find a way to circumvent those precautions and land a killing blow.

One way or another, she would see Phane bleed.

Slyder landed, cocking his head at her quizzically. She scratched him under the chin.

"It's just you and me now."

He leaned into her affections.

She sat quietly, staring into the flames and pondering her future as the orange glow of her fire gave way to the light of dawn. Her clothes dry, she strapped on her pack, checked her sword in its scabbard and set out into the jungle.

It was a different kind of forest than the Great Forest of Ruatha, but it was a forest nonetheless. The trees reached high into the sky, shading the undergrowth and providing a framework for the multitude of climbing vines that seemed to thrive in the warmer, wetter climate of Karth. The canopy above was an intricate network of vegetation, teeming with life. Birds and small mammals woke with the dawn, filling the air with sounds of countless jungle denizens starting their day.

Isabel kept Slyder low and close as she carefully threaded her way through the dense undergrowth. She wasn't sure where she was going but reasoned that she'd find a road near the coastline. From there, whatever passed for civilization on Karth couldn't be too far.

She'd walked for nearly an hour when she heard a noise in the jungle that didn't fit. Frozen in place, her ears straining, she waited. The instant she heard it again, she linked her mind with Slyder and directed her familiar to the source of the noise.

Her forest hawk came to rest on a tree limb overlooking a young boy buried to his armpits in sand. Using Slyder's eyes, Isabel plotted a course to the child and set out, cautiously and quietly. When she stepped into the clearing, a dog challenged her. He was big, built very much like a wolfhound, standing three feet at the shoulder. He had a long snout and powerful jaws, and he was very unhappy with Isabel's presence.

The child was now nearly up to his neck in sand. Isabel might have been more concerned by his plight if she hadn't been preoccupied with the dog. She reached out with her mind and touched the animal, soothing him and gently gaining control of him. He sat down with a barely audible whimper.

"Will you help me?" the boy said. "Please?"

Isabel started toward the child without hesitation. He looked to be about ten years old, and had dark eyes, black hair, and a swarthy complexion. She could see fear in his eyes but also determination. He meant to live.

"No! Stop!" he said. "You'll just get stuck too."

Isabel stopped, perplexed.

"Get a stick or a vine and pull me to you," the boy said.

She looked down and saw her feet sinking into the sand. Sudden realization flooded into her mind. She remembered Wizard Kallentera telling stories about the quagmire sands of Karth that could swallow a horse without any trace. When she looked behind her and saw a safe spot within reach, she quickly sat down and worked her feet free. Then she found a stout fallen limb and laid it out across the sands to the boy.

Nearly half an hour later, he came free of the muck, scrambling onto solid ground, breathing heavily from exertion and fear.

"Thank you," he said. "I was looking for my dog and I got so worried about him that I wasn't watching where I was going until it was too late. Figures … he found me a few minutes after I got stuck."

Isabel smiled at the child. He was covered from head to foot in mud, but his eyes sparkled with a mixture of inquisitiveness and mischief.

"I'm Isabel. What's your name?"

"I'm Baqi. And this is my dog Kolo."

"Hello, Baqi. Can you tell me about your village?"

"It's not far," Baqi said, pointing off into the jungle. "Mama will be worried if I don't get home soon." He looked down at the mud drying on his clothes and shook his head. "She won't be happy about this either."

"Are there soldiers in your village?" Isabel asked.

Baqi frowned, nodding. "Used to be we were left alone, but now the soldiers always want to know what we're doing. Mama doesn't like them, but I'm not supposed to talk about it. You won't tell, will you?"

"Of course not, but I do need to go see the soldiers," Isabel said. "Could you take me to your village? I promise I won't tell anyone about you and Kolo."

"All right, just so long as Mama doesn't find out. She doesn't like me talking to outsiders," Baqi said.

"I won't tell her if you won't," Isabel said.

"The village is this way," Baqi said, pointing into the jungle again. "Once we get close, I'll go around to the other side so people don't see us together. Nothing personal. You seem like a nice person, but I don't want to get in trouble."

"Sounds good to me," Isabel said.

"So where are you from?" Baqi asked while they walked.

"I come from Ruatha," Isabel said.

"I don't know that village," Baqi said.

Isabel smiled. "It's not a village. It's an island and it's a very long way away."

"Did you come through the ancient gate?" he asked. "I heard it came to life and a giant monster came through and killed a bunch of Regency soldiers." He looked at her expectantly.

"No, I came by boat," Isabel said, smiling at confirmation that Alexander's gift for Phane had arrived.

"Oh," Baqi said, the light of excitement fading from his face. "Someday I want to go through the ancient gate and explore other lands. Mama says it would

be too dangerous, but I can handle it. I already know how to survive in the jungle."
He looked down at the mud caking his clothes and grimaced. "Well, mostly, and
that was Kolo's fault anyway."

Isabel heard voices off in the distance and stopped.

"We're getting close to the village. It's right over that way. Well, it was
nice to meet you," he said with a boyish smile, then turned and disappeared into
the jungle.

Isabel heard him say, "Kolo, don't you wander off again. I'm already
going to be in enough trouble for getting so dirty."

She waited for several minutes, listening to the distant voices of the
villagers and steeling herself for the encounter that was coming, the challenge she
was about to make to the soldiers. She was betting that Phane had made
preparations for her arrival, that his soldiers had standing orders to escort her to
him. If they didn't, things might go badly.

Once she was certain that Baqi had had plenty of time to make it safely
home, she set out, moving cautiously. The undergrowth started to thin, giving her
a glimpse of the timber wall surrounding the village. It was made of stout, twelve-
foot wooden poles pounded into the ground and tied together. Isabel could see an
open gate at either end of the wall and two Regency soldiers standing guard in the
village watchtower.

She took a deep breath and stepped out into the fifty-foot swath of cleared
jungle surrounding the village. It didn't take long before the soldiers in the tower
noticed her.

"You there, stay where you are," one shouted while the other rang a bell.
A dozen men poured out of the village, approaching her with weapons drawn.

The moment the warning bell tolled, Isabel began casting her shield spell.
If Phane hadn't given orders for her arrival, she intended to be ready for anything.
The soldiers fanned out around her. She stood her ground, her head held high, and
waited.

The largest of the bunch pushed his way through the cordon of men and
stopped several feet outside of sword range. He was easily six and a half feet tall
with a barrel chest and broad shoulders. He crossed his arms as he appraised her.
A series of scars ran across the back of his right arm that looked too even to be
anything but self-inflicted.

"Might be the men could have some fun with you," he said, smiling
lewdly, broken and stained teeth showing behind his lips.

"I doubt they would enjoy that as much as you might think," Isabel said,
ignoring the dozen soldiers ogling her. "Are you the commander of this garrison?"

"No," he said, "I'm the sergeant. The lieutenant is inside the walls,
preening himself or something about as useful."

His men laughed. Isabel ignored them, focusing on the sergeant.

"Take me to him."

"I don't think I like your tone," he said. "You're an outsider here. You'll
answer my questions and then I'll decide what to do with you."

Isabel could see some of the villagers peeking through gaps in the wall.

"This will all sort itself out much faster if you'll just take me to your commander," she said.

"I think maybe you need a lesson in manners first," he said, motioning to his men with his head.

Two men tried to grab her from behind but her shield stopped them a foot short. She muttered the words of her force-push spell, blowing the sergeant eight feet backward onto the ground, then drew her sword.

"This is unnecessary," she said into the stunned silence.

All of the men surrounding her stopped for a moment, unsure of what to do until the sergeant growled, "Kill the witch."

They rushed in unison but their weapons were easily deflected by her shield. She bowled another man over with her force-push. Thwarted by her magical defenses, two soldiers tried to knock her down by holding either end of a spear and rushing her. It smashed into her shield, knocking her back a few feet until she stabbed one of the men in the leg and he dropped his end of the spear.

"Stop this or I will start killing you!" Isabel shouted.

The sergeant had regained his feet. "Too late for that, Witch," he said as he approached, preparing a mighty downward attack with his two-handed sword.

Isabel started casting her spell. Moments later, just as the sergeant brought his sword overhead, she unleashed her light-lance, burning a hole through his chest and dropping him at her feet, dead.

The rest of the men became far less certain, backing off and raising their shields.

"You'll pay for that, Witch," one of them said.

"Can I assume that you're in command now?" Isabel asked.

He looked to the others for support. They were only too happy to have him do the talking, given the fate of their previous sergeant.

"I am," he said, puffing up a bit past the fear in his eyes.

"Good, send a man to fetch your commander … or join your sergeant," Isabel said, raising her hand toward him. "Your choice."

He flinched, then shouted impatiently at one of the soldiers, "What are you waiting for? Go get the lieutenant!"

The man hesitated for a moment, looking first to Isabel and then back to the new sergeant before hurrying away toward the walled village.

Isabel waited silently with a dozen men standing nervously in a loose cordon around her. She didn't have to wait long before a Regency officer came from the village, with the soldier sent to fetch him trailing close behind.

He appraised the situation as he approached and wary anger started to build on his face. "What is the meaning of this?" he demanded as he stopped in front of Isabel, his fists planted on his hips. "My man told me you're a witch, but I've met one of the witches, and you're not even close to pretty enough to be one of them."

Isabel filed that little piece of information away for future scrutiny and fixed the lieutenant with her flashing green eyes. "My name is Isabel Reishi. You will assemble an honor guard and escort me to Prince Phane at once," she demanded.

A little of the color drained from the lieutenant's face. When he noticed the cauterized hole burned through the chest of his dead sergeant, his face went whiter still.

"Lady Reishi, you have my most sincere apologies for any mistreatment you've suffered at the hands of my men. Prince Phane has issued strict orders to all Regency forces on Karth that you are to be treated with the respect accorded a queen and brought to him at once. He has been anxiously expecting your arrival."

Isabel inwardly breathed a sigh of relief mixed with trepidation. Phane was expecting her. She knew he had ways of gathering information, so it could be that he'd been watching her, or it could be that he knew Azugorath's darkness was overpowering her free will. Either way, her plan suddenly became very real. Her resolve hardened. The only path to salvation lay through Phane.

"How long before a suitable honor guard can be assembled for the journey?" she asked.

"First light tomorrow at the earliest, Lady Reishi," the lieutenant said. "I'll need to summon men from a nearby garrison to ensure your safety. The jungle is dangerous, all the more so with the insurgent threat."

"Explain," Isabel said. She'd decided to play the part of a queen, even if it wasn't in her nature to be so demanding.

"When we invaded under Prince Phane's command, Karth's army melted into the jungle without much resistance. Since then, they've been waging a war against us from the shadows, never standing to fight, bleeding us a nick at a time. We'll be most vulnerable on the road, hence the need to summon additional troops."

"Very well, Lieutenant," Isabel said. "Show me to my quarters while you make preparations."

The rest of the men were clearly unhappy with the turn of events, but nonetheless, they obeyed the lieutenant's orders, sending riders to the closest village to gather more men for the journey to the Regency headquarters.

"I'm Lieutenant Febus, commander of the garrison here," he said as he escorted her into the village. "You can have my chamber for the night, Lady Reishi. It's the most comfortable and secure room in the village."

Isabel nodded absently, taking in the people of the village. They lived in a state of terror, scurrying from the path of the soldiers, never daring to make eye contact with any of the men from the Regency. They were a subjugated people, broken and cowering in fear of their occupiers. A few cast furtive glances her way, appraising the newcomer and likely wondering if her arrival would change things.

She nearly spoke up when one of the soldiers kicked a woman, knocking her to the ground and spilling her freshly washed laundry into the muddy street because she didn't get out of his way fast enough. Several of the other soldiers laughed at the shaken woman scrambling to collect her laundry without giving any further offense. Isabel kept her a face a mask of indifference while her emotions roiled within. She reminded herself that she couldn't risk her ultimate goal by going to the aid of a woman who wasn't in any real danger ... but the behavior of the Regency soldiers galled her.

Just as she arrived at the barracks building, she caught Baqi looking at her from a hiding place under a wagon. She met his eyes and shook her head ever so slightly, warning him to stay where he was. He frowned but nodded and remained hidden.

The lieutenant's quarters were obviously confiscated from the village elder who had once guided the people of this little community. The decorations and furnishings were carefully crafted with great attention to detail and pride of workmanship. Isabel got the impression that most of the art was made by the hand of the man who had once lived there. She wondered if he was still alive.

"I'm afraid it's not much," Lieutenant Febus said, "but it's the best we have to offer so far from civilization."

"It'll do," Isabel said, sniffing and wrinkling her nose. "Send a meal and hot water so I can get cleaned up."

"Of course, Lady Reishi," Febus said, bowing as he left.

Chapter 2

The dream had her again. She was standing over her husband, preparing to plunge a dagger into his heart, unable to stop herself. Her eyes snapped open and she realized someone was on top of her, pinning her down with her blanket and covering her mouth so she couldn't call for help ... or cast a spell.

His breath was sour and hot. She felt the coarseness of his unshaven face when he slowly licked her cheek. Panic threatened to claim her, but she shoved it aside and called up the rage she would need to cast a spell, if she could only speak past the hand clamped over her mouth.

"You killed my brother out there today. Febus says we have to take you to the fortress, but I have a few ideas of my own."

He pushed his knee between her legs, forcing them apart. Thankfully, the blanket was still between them, but it also held her arms pinned to her sides, rendering her nearly helpless.

"They tell me you're a witch," he said from just inches away, his breath foul and acrid from too much to drink. "I'll just have to make sure you can't say anything," he said. "Should make it easier to have my fun with you without drawing attention, anyway."

He stuffed a filthy sock into her mouth, then tied it in place with another. Isabel fought the urge to vomit.

"That ought to do it," he said, sitting on top of her, using his knees to keep the blanket firmly in place, pinning her to the bed. She could almost see him smile in the dark before he hit her across the face with an open hand, then he swiftly backhanded her across the other side of her face.

Isabel stopped struggling and went limp, closing her eyes and reaching out with her mind, searching for an animal to call to her defense. Kolo was sleeping at the foot of Baqi's bed. She called to him, rousing him with a start. He came bounding out of Baqi's quarters, running through the night.

The soldier hit her again, and again.

"I thought you'd put up more of a fight than this," he said. "I'm kind of disappointed. Can't imagine what Phane would want with you."

The door burst open and Kolo leapt at the man from behind, clamping powerful jaws on to his neck and pushing him over onto Isabel. She drove the dog on, commanding him to bite down even harder, crushing the man's neck and killing him where he lay on top of her. She heard bones snap, followed by footsteps coming toward her quarters.

She pushed the man off of her and rolled out of bed, pulling the gag from her mouth and drawing her sword. She was muttering the words of her shield spell when Lieutenant Febus entered, followed by three soldiers.

"Lady Reishi, we heard a commotion," Febus said.

"One of your men tried to rape me," Isabel said, her shield firmly in place. "You told me this chamber was secure."

Febus swallowed, looking from the dead soldier to Isabel.

"I'm so sorry," Febus said. "I gave strict orders that you were to be treated with respect, but this man is brother to the man you killed outside the wall."

"So he said. His disobedience cost him his life."

Baqi burst into the room. "There you are, Kolo. I told you not to run off in the night." He stopped suddenly, looking around at the soldiers, at Isabel, and at the corpse, before stepping in front of his dog.

"Kolo didn't mean any harm," he said. "You have to believe me."

"Your dog killed a man," Febus said, drawing himself up and looking down at the little boy. "We can't have dangerous animals roaming the village at night."

"Lieutenant Febus, this dog saved my life," Isabel said, not wanting to reveal her power over animals. "You will leave the child and his dog alone, is that understood?"

"Yes, Lady Reishi," he said, somewhat deflated.

"Go on home, Child," Isabel said to Baqi with a wink.

"Lieutenant, remove this corpse, post two men at my door, and leave me."

"By your command, Lady Reishi," he said, motioning to his men to carry the dead soldier from the room and bowing on the way out.

Isabel sighed as she sheathed her sword and sat down on her bed. It seemed that the Regency had discipline problems. She curled up with her dagger and drifted off into a fitful sleep.

Breakfast arrived while she was strapping on her armor. When she emerged from her quarters, the honor guard was preparing to depart.

"Ah, Lady Reishi, we'll be ready within the hour," Lieutenant Febus said.

"Very good, Lieutenant. How long will the journey take?"

"A week to ten days, depending on the weather and any threats we might encounter along the way," Febus said. "The jungle is dangerous, home to many powerful predators, so we'll be preparing a fortified encampment each night."

"I trust you'll take the necessary precautions," Isabel said.

                                    ***

The first two days were uneventful. Isabel found herself alternately thinking about Alexander, wondering how he was and fretting over the way she'd left him, and marveling at the sheer volume of life surrounding her. The Great Forest was vibrantly alive but the jungle was full of activity. All around her, the residents of the jungle went about their daily business of surviving, largely ignoring her and the two dozen soldiers cautiously traveling through the thick underbrush that was trying to swallow the road whole.

At night, the soldiers erected a hasty fence of sharpened timbers, lit several fires, and posted four guards to watch the darkness, lest it sneak in and run off with one of their sleeping companions.

By day, they rode along the narrow road, the jungle crowding them from either side. The soldiers were wary, nervous even, but Isabel found the place enchantingly wild and beautiful. She'd always liked the untamed quality of the Great Forest, but it was slow to reclaim ground that man had conquered. Here, the thick vegetation was in a hurry, it wanted the road she was riding on and sometimes it didn't seem to be willing to wait for her to pass.

Toward evening of the third day, Slyder caught her attention. She tipped her head back and linked her mind to his, looking through his eyes, but a moment too late. Three gorledons sprang from the lush green and pounced on the three men in the lead of the column, knocking them from their terrified horses. Then they grabbed each man by a limb, swinging them screaming over their shoulders, impaling them multiple times on the row of bone spikes running down the length of their backs. It all happened so quickly, one moment they were simply traveling, the next, three men were vanishing into the brush to become dinner for one of Karth's more unpleasant predators.

To his credit, Lieutenant Febus didn't give chase. He simply ordered that the frightened horses be brought back into the column, and the honor guard moved on, albeit with some grumbling from the men.

At that point, Isabel decided to take a more active role in the security of the detachment. She had assumed that these men, having grown up on Karth, living their whole lives in the jungle, were better suited to assess the dangers surrounding her, but they didn't have her gifts. While she couldn't control a magically created creature such as a gorledon, she could watch the jungle through Slyder's eyes and keep any natural predators at bay.

The men treated her with a mixture of disdain, fear, and barely concealed hostility. She was responsible for killing two of their number and she was also the reason they'd had to leave the relative safety of the villages they were occupying.

Several times over the course of the journey, Isabel detected a jaguar stalking them and sent the animal harmlessly away. Once, a giant snake, easily thirty feet long, was poised on a tree limb above the path, preparing to take one of the men, but she commanded the animal to remain still and hidden. They passed by without incident.

By the fifth day, the magnificent beauty of the jungle had faded into the background. She was acting as a silent scout and protector for the men who were supposed to be protecting her. She realized that the jungle was altogether more hostile than the forest, and it required a whole different set of knowledge to traverse safely, knowledge that she had yet to acquire.

In the early afternoon, she was idly thinking about Alexander when she felt a sharp stinging sensation in the side of her neck. With a rising sense of alarm, she looked for the source as a feeling of numbing cold began to spread. Another sting, this time in her forearm, followed by more numbness. Frantically, she tried to call out a warning, but her voice wouldn't work. Her horse went down and she landed hard, paralyzed and helpless, staring down the road at ground level.

The men of her honor guard fell quickly, their horses toppling as well. Lieutenant Febus lay on the ground several feet from her, immobile, but from the fear in his eyes, still aware. Isabel saw a small dart in his neck.

Then the men came, emerging from the jungle, as if, just a moment ago, they were a part of the brush and canopy itself. They moved with fluid grace and deliberate menace, lifting each man by the hair, looking him closely in the face and then cutting his throat while they stared into his dying eyes.

One who was dressed more elaborately than the rest picked up Lieutenant Febus by the hair, stared him in the eye and casually cut his throat. Before he dropped the Regency officer, he turned and looked Isabel in the eye, then smiled.

A moment later, the world went black.

Chapter 3

Isabel slowly started to wake, struggling to focus her mind past a haze of pain in her head. She rubbed the grit from her eyes, but they burned terribly when she opened them. Her tongue felt swollen and she felt an intense thirst. She sat up, trying to work up enough saliva to swallow, her head reeling from the sudden movement.

She was in a dark room with only a sliver of dim light cutting through the black. She steadied herself with one hand while rubbing her eyes with the other until she could keep them open long enough to look around. In the dim light, she could see that she was in a small room formed from a natural cave. A stout wooden wall and door occupied one side.

Fighting to clear her head, she began to assess her situation. Her weapons and armor were gone. Her pack was missing as well. She was sitting on a pallet covered with straw. The only other items she could see were two buckets, one on either side of the door. She crawled to one, jerking her head back from the foul smell, then to the other. Cautiously she dipped her hand into the dark bucket and felt the cool touch of water. Slowly, deliberately, she slaked her thirst, taking care to remain silent lest her captors become aware that she was awake.

She sat back and closed her eyes, linking her mind with Slyder. He was perched atop a tree in the jungle looking down into a little village secreted in a box canyon. Several cave entrances surrounded the dozen or so huts at the center of the hidden community. Men were coming and going, many looked and acted like soldiers, though few wore uniforms.

She withdrew from Slyder and spent several minutes just breathing in an effort to quiet the hammering in her head. She assumed that the poison darts that had rendered her unconscious were responsible for the pain and dehydration she was feeling. After a few minutes, her head began to clear.

Muffled voices filtered through the door. She stood carefully, testing her legs and balance before attempting to take the few steps to the little slit in the door that was the room's sole source of light. Beyond was another cave, larger and occupied by three men, all armed and wearing armor.

She stepped back and started whispering the words to her shield spell, calling on her anger and focusing her mind the way she'd done countless times in the past … but this time, something was different.

The rage wasn't there.

She forced the spell and made a connection with the firmament, opening herself to the source of creation, but only for the briefest moment. The firmament called to her, beckoning with the promise of infinite possibility, and she wasn't angry enough to resist.

It felt like she was falling.

She slammed the link shut, staggered by the implications of what had just happened. Without rage, she couldn't defend herself against the pull of the firmament, couldn't cast her spells.

She sat down and recalled all of the hardships that had been inflicted on her and her loved ones over the past several months. Worked at bringing them to the front of her mind so she could feel the injustices done to her, but try as she might, the anger wouldn't come.

Her mind was clear but her emotional intensity was somehow blunted. She could understand the rightness of feeling anger for the things that had been done to her, to Alexander, to the world, but she couldn't *feel* the anger the way she needed to. Without that emotional control, she was powerless as a witch.

She swallowed hard. First she'd been deprived of her connection to the realm of light, a gift of such magnitude that she considered it her greatest power, valued it above all things save Alexander's love. Now her emotional control, necessary for a witch to access the firmament, was gone. The things she valued most were being taken from her, one by one. She felt Azugorath scratching at the edge of her psyche, promising power and purpose.

She calmed herself and thought of Alexander, thought of her love for him … but it too was blunted. Losing the anger was one thing, but losing her ability to feel the deep and abiding joy that her love for Alexander created within her was too much. She thought she would cry, but the tears didn't come either. The pain of her loss was blunted as well.

She could still feel … just not intensely. Her eyes narrowed. This was too specific to be an accident. Either it was a side effect of the poison or she'd been drugged. If she'd been drugged, then her captors knew about her magic and had the means to counter it.

She carefully searched the little room for a weapon but found nothing except the two buckets. After drinking again, she stood and pounded on the door, then stepped back and waited. There was some commotion from beyond, then the door opened. A swarthy-looking man, muscles toned from routine exertion, stood in the doorway and appraised her.

"You're a prisoner of the House of Karth," he said. "If you try to escape, you'll be killed. Otherwise, we'll treat you honorably."

Isabel quickly assessed her options and decided that attempting escape right now was unwise. She needed more information about her captors before she chose a course of action.

"Very well," she said. "I wouldn't know which way to run anyway."

The guard cocked his head quizzically, as if he hadn't expected her response.

"Can I have something to eat?" she asked.

He nodded, motioning to the table occupying the center of the guard chamber. A tray with a variety of tubers, berries, and fruits sat on the table, the remnants of the guards' meal.

Isabel wasn't bashful. From the grumbling in her stomach, she suspected she'd been unconscious for days rather than hours. The food was surprisingly good, but before she'd eaten her fill, another man entered, followed by the third guard.

This man was tall, easily over six feet, but not muscular like the guards. He was lithe and wiry as if he'd spent his days moving through the jungle. His hair was jet black, his complexion golden brown, and his eyes were dark and brooding. With a gesture, he dismissed the guards and sat down opposite Isabel, absentmindedly selecting a piece of fruit from the tray as he scrutinized his prisoner.

She held his gaze for a moment and then went back to eating. For several moments neither said a word, they simply shared a meal in silence. Once he'd finished his piece of fruit, he took a drink from a nearby flagon and sat forward.

"I am Trajan Karth. My father has summoned you. It will be a journey of several days. If you attempt to escape, you will be killed."

"Yeah, I got that," Isabel said around a mouthful of food.

He smiled curiously. "I would know why you have been summoned."

Isabel shrugged as she took another tuber from the plate. It had the texture of a sweet potato but wasn't quite as rich.

"Perhaps if you told me your name, it would shed some light on my father's interest in you."

This time it was Isabel's turn to smile, though without any hint of humor. "I'm Isabel Reishi," she said, punctuating her statement by taking a big bite of tuber.

Trajan's eyes narrowed and he tensed ever so slightly, like a cat preparing to pounce. "I wasn't aware that Phane had taken a woman," he said.

"Oh, he hasn't, or at least he certainly hasn't taken me," Isabel said, washing her mouthful down with a long drink of warm ale from the nearest flagon. "My husband is Alexander Reishi, formerly Alexander Ruatha. From the looks of things, your father didn't get the warning Alexander sent him in his dreams."

Trajan had been listening intently, clearly trying to discern the veracity of her words. His eyes went wide.

"My father did receive a warning," he said, "but he chose not to heed it until it was too late. My mother, two brothers, and a sister were lost in that attack, an attack that my father said could never happen. Fortunately, Erastus, our house man-at-arms, was paranoid enough to make preparations, and my father, sister, and I survived."

Isabel looked down at the table and nodded sadly. "I'm sorry for your loss," she whispered. "There's been too much suffering since Phane woke."

"On that count we agree," Trajan said, "but I'm still confused by a great many things. Why were you with Phane's men if your husband sent us warning against him?"

"My husband and I are at war with Phane," Isabel said. "But, for a number of reasons, Phane believes that I've turned against Alexander, so he's issued orders that I'm to be treated with respect and brought before him."

"And then what?"

"And then I intend to kill him," Isabel said.

Trajan stared incredulously, then burst out laughing.

"I hate Phane as much as anyone," he said, once he'd contained his mirthless laughter, "but I'm not fool enough to believe he would let you get close to him if you were any threat."

Isabel shrugged. "I guess it's all a matter of perception. He believes that I'm his puppet, a tool he can use to undo my husband. That belief will allow me to get close enough to strike."

Trajan shook his head. "He'll kill you."

"Perhaps," Isabel said quietly. "But I have nowhere else to go."

"Why?" he asked.

Isabel hesitated, unsure of how much she should reveal.

"He's infected me with his dark magic," she said. "Even now, it's working to subvert my free will and turn me against everything and everyone that I love."

Trajan sat back, staring at her intently.

After a moment, Isabel decided she had a few questions of her own. "Why doesn't my magic work?"

"So you admit to being a witch," Trajan said, sitting forward again.

Isabel shrugged. "Of course I'm a witch. I'm a triumvir of the Reishi Coven."

Trajan frowned in confusion, appraising Isabel intently before speaking again. "Magic is forbidden on Karth. It has been since the end of the Reishi War. My father heard reports that you used magic to kill a man. That's why we were sent to capture you."

"If the House of Karth outlawed magic, then how have you stood against the Regency for so long?" she asked.

"The Regency also prohibits magic," Trajan said. He paused, staring at the table as if weighing how much to tell her. "Only the witches of the Sin'Rath Coven possess magic on Karth," Trajan said, "and they are widely believed to be a myth—a story parents tell their children to make them behave."

Isabel stopped chewing and stared at Trajan, her mind working furiously to understand the implications of his statement. "But you know otherwise," she said.

"Yes, the Sin'Rath are very real," he said. "I do not trust them, yet they hold great sway over my father." He stopped as if he'd said too much.

"Trajan, I can help you kill Phane, but I need to know what I'm dealing with here. Did you capture me at the behest of this Sin'Rath Coven?"

"I believe so," he said. "The order came from my father, but he has been working very closely with the coven since the Regency attacked and scattered our forces into the jungle."

Isabel leaned forward intently. "Why won't my magic work?" she asked again.

He regarded her for a moment before nodding as he withdrew a vial from his pouch.

"The jungle contains a great many plants," he said. "This is nectar of the malaise weed. It diminishes a person's emotions. It's commonly used to aid people grieving for the loss of a loved one. My father's orders were very specific. You are to be dosed with malaise-weed nectar once per day. I don't pretend to understand why, but I was told that it will prevent you from using your magic."

She sat back in her chair and breathed a sigh of relief. At least the loss of her magic was only temporary.

"Why don't you trust the Sin'Rath?" she asked.

"I will tell you a story," he said. "Some years ago my eldest brother spoke harshly of the Sin'Rath. He told me how he resented the influence they held over our father and how he intended to reject their counsel once he ascended to the throne. Then he went to meet the witches for the first time." Trajan paused, lost in thought.

"He returned a changed man. He was enamored with them, spoke of their great beauty and wisdom, pledging to work hand in hand with the coven for the greater glory of Karth. My brother was not prone to sudden changes of mind; he was a very deliberate and thoughtful man. But one meeting with the Sin'Rath and he was under their spell."

"So you've never met them," Isabel said.

"No," Trajan said, shaking his head. "My mother forbade it. I believe she secretly hated and feared them, though she never spoke openly of it. I'm to meet the Sin'Rath for the first time when I arrive with you," he said as he stood.

"I need to think about everything you've told me. If you truly are Phane's enemy, then perhaps together we could bring him down. There will be more time to talk on the trail. We'll leave within the hour. Your equipment will be returned to you, but your weapons will not."

"Fair enough," Isabel said. "What about my armor? The jungle's a dangerous place."

He appraised her for a moment before nodding.

Chapter 4

Trajan and his twenty men moved through the jungle with the same kind of ease that Isabel could travel through the Great Forest. They picked their path intuitively, selecting a course that meandered through the dense underbrush to make the trek easier while diminishing any sign of their passage.

Two men escorted Isabel at all times, always careful to guide her safely through the jungle, often correcting her course and pointing out potential dangers. Of course, their true purpose was to prevent her from escaping, but she didn't care since she had no such intention. She had nowhere to go and no idea how to get there. Her course was set. She would speak with the King of Karth. Things would become clearer after that.

During the journey, she peppered her escorts with questions, trying to learn all she could about the jungle, its many plants, both dangerous and medicinal, and its animals, both the ones she was familiar with and the more exotic creatures that roamed the dense wilds.

Each day, Trajan made her drink a cup of tea laced with a drop of malaise-weed nectar to inhibit her emotional intensity and render her connection to the firmament too dangerous to access. She accepted without protest, although she did complain about the bitter taste.

On the third day of travel, Trajan dropped back from the front of the group, dismissing Isabel's escorts with a gesture. They faded into the jungle, while remaining close enough to come to his aid should the need arise.

"My men tell me you're full of questions," Trajan said.

"I grew up in a forest," Isabel said. "I can tell you a thousand things about that forest that a casual observer would never know. Your jungle has sparked my curiosity, so I ask a lot of questions."

He chuckled. "One could spend his whole life walking the jungle and learn something new each day. We have shamans who study their whole lives, passing their lore to the next shaman-in-waiting, and yet there are always things they do not know."

"Earlier this morning your men prevented me from walking beneath a particularly beautiful tree," Isabel said, "instead, steering me in a wide path around it, but they wouldn't tell me why."

Trajan nodded. "I instructed them to avoid revealing anything that you could use as a weapon. In this case, I believe they were taking that instruction a bit too seriously. That kind of tree is favored by yellow-spotted frogs."

"You've lost me," Isabel said. "What's dangerous about frogs?"

"These frogs in particular secrete a potent toxin on their backs and bellies," Trajan said. "One touch and you would die within minutes unless the antidote was administered quickly."

"What's the antidote?"

"Oddly enough, it's the milk from vines of that very tree," Trajan said.

"See," Isabel said, "that's why I ask so many questions."

Trajan chuckled again.

"I have a friend who would love this place," Isabel said. "He's an alchemist, and if you think I ask a lot of questions, he would hound you day and night … unless you made him something to eat, then he'd only ask questions between mouthfuls."

"I'm not familiar with that word, alchemist," Trajan said.

"An alchemist mixes potions," Isabel said. "He's a type of wizard. His magic allows him to make powerful concoctions, provided he has the right ingredients."

Trajan frowned and fell silent. Isabel waited for him to speak again, simply keeping pace as they wended their way through the jungle.

"Magic is forbidden on Karth."

"Why is that?"

"It has always been forbidden, ever since the Reishi War."

"So you've said. But why?" Isabel asked. "The Sin'Rath use magic. Why are they allowed to when no one else is?"

Trajan frowned again but said nothing. Isabel let him brood over his answer. He was silent for a long time before he spoke again.

"I don't know," he said quietly enough that only Isabel could hear him. "I have often wondered about that very question."

Isabel nodded to herself, pieces of the puzzle falling into place. She only had a rough outline, but it was slowly filling in.

"Have you asked your father?"

"No."

She sensed tension building within the young crown prince of Karth, so she let the line of questioning go for the time being and simply enjoyed the beauty and novelty of the jungle.

"I'm surprised you've kept up with our pace," Trajan said some time later.

Isabel shrugged. "This last year has been … arduous," she said. "I've traveled a lot—fought a lot. I'm stronger now than I've ever been."

Trajan stopped dead in his tracks and whistled a birdcall. His men fell silent, frozen in place, blending in with the jungle in an instant. Isabel stopped as well, tipping her head back and linking with Slyder.

He'd been flying through the canopy, keeping a careful watch over Isabel while remaining undetected. She saw the threat in an instant. A jaguar was stalking them, crouching in the jungle brush and creeping toward one of the men on the outside of the group. She brought her mind back from Slyder, debating with herself about the best course of action. She could leave the big cat to the soldiers or take control of it. If she controlled it, she could keep it a secret or she could reveal the power she retained in spite of the malaise-weed nectar.

She decided to be bold.

With a thought, she linked her mind with the cat's and imposed her will on the powerful jungle predator.

"It's just a cat," she said to Trajan as she began strolling toward it. "Here kitty, kitty."

The jaguar was a full-grown male, easily eight feet from nose to tail and more than two hundred pounds of graceful power. The men cautiously formed a circle around Isabel and the cat, poised to strike. She stilled them with a gesture as the black cat strode up to her and nuzzled her belly. She returned his affections by scratching him behind the ears. After a moment, he rolled over onto his back, exposing his belly for her to rub.

She smiled, kneeling next to him to oblige, eliciting a deep, rumbling purr from the cat that filled the stunned silence. She looked up and smiled at Trajan, holding his dark eyes purposefully, as if to say "I know something you don't know." She stood and the cat rolled to his feet, rubbing against her side.

"I think I'll call you Shadowfang," Isabel said.

"How?" Trajan said. "How is this possible? I was assured that the malaise-weed nectar would prevent you from using magic."

"And where do you suppose those assurances came from?" Isabel asked pointedly. "The Sin'Rath, maybe? Looks like they were wrong."

She looked around at the mixture of fear and awe on the faces of the men surrounding her, weapons still at the ready.

"He won't hurt you, any of you," she said. "In fact, he'll ensure that other predators remain at a distance while we travel."

"You expect us to travel with a jaguar?" one of the men asked.

"I do," Isabel said.

"No," Trajan said.

"Would you try to kill him?" Isabel asked, facing Trajan.

"No," he said. "The jaguar is our family crest. The House of Karth holds them sacred."

"Well then, I don't see the problem," Isabel said as if they were discussing what to have for breakfast.

He stared at the cat for a moment before nodding slowly. "I do not like magic," he said, "and I'm coming to understand why it has been forbidden—this is not natural."

From that point on, the men looked at Isabel differently, almost as if they were wondering if they had somehow become her prisoner and not the other way around. Shadowfang ranged out around the group, chasing off any other predators that were lying in wait. The days ran together until Isabel wasn't sure how many had passed when they finally arrived at their destination.

Trajan led them into a crack in a large stone that in turn led into a narrow ravine completely covered over by the jungle. Isabel commanded Shadowfang to remain in the area but to fend for himself, avoiding humans, until she returned. The ravine went deeper and deeper until Trajan stopped and unlatched a secret door fashioned to look like part of the rock face of the ravine wall. The door opened into a passage.

From there, the journey took another two days. Isabel used Slyder to keep track of which way they were traveling so she could keep both the hawk and the jaguar moving in the right direction. The passages were dark and dank, sometimes natural stone, other times cut from bedrock. When they finally came to a well-fortified stone door, Isabel instructed Shadowfang and Slyder to take up residence in one of the larger trees nearby.

The door opened to a roomful of soldiers all arrayed before it, shielded by fortifications and armed with all manner of heavy weapons, crossbows, and ballistae.

"Prince Trajan, you are a welcome sight," said a man wearing a uniform with emblems of rank.

"Thank you, General Rashford," Trajan said. "It's been an arduous yet relatively safe journey."

"Your father will be greatly relieved to hear you've arrived," Rashford said. "He'd never admit it, but he's been worried about you since he sent you to apprehend the witch."

Isabel cleared her throat and fixed the general with a glare.

"General Rashford, this is Isabel Reishi," Trajan said, letting the import of her name sink in. "She claims to be at war with Phane."

"Is that so?" Rashford said. "We'll see about that. Your father wishes to speak to her. I'll send word of your arrival at once."

"Thank you, General," Trajan said.

He led Isabel through the fortifications that defended the cavernous entrance to the House of Karth's secret base of operations. Many of the soldiers guarding the room glared at her with open hatred. Isabel ignored them.

Once through the cavern, Trajan dismissed all of his men save four. Two led the way while the remaining two brought up the rear. Isabel focused on the layout of the underground complex, trying to remember as much of her route as possible.

Trajan remained silent while they walked, until the men leading the group began to turn down a narrow corridor.

"No, we'll go to my quarters," he said.

"As you wish, My Prince," they said in unison, turning instead down a wider, better-lit corridor.

Several minutes, and a confusing maze of turns later, they arrived at a nondescript door. The two guards standing to either side opened it without a word and Trajan strode inside, inviting Isabel to follow him.

Isabel stopped a few steps inside and surveyed her surroundings, nodding her approval. The room was well appointed but not lavish, more serviceable and comfortable than ostentatious. She believed one could learn a lot about a person by how they lived. Trajan didn't seem interested in impressing people with possessions.

"Please, sit," he said, motioning to a comfortable set of chairs separated by a small table. "Would you like some tea?"

"Yes, thank you," Isabel said, easing into the chair. It had been a long journey and she was tired and sore. It felt good to simply relax in a well-padded chair.

Trajan prepared the tea himself, another promising sign as far as Isabel was concerned, but as he was bringing the tray to her, the door burst open and a dozen men filed in with weapons drawn.

Trajan stopped, facing the door calmly as his father entered behind his royal guard. The King of Karth was an older man, his jet black hair salted with grey and his paunch a little too big for his slim frame. His eyes were intelligent and inquisitive, yet ever-so-slightly furtive, as if he was always hiding something. Isabel decided she didn't trust him and again wished she had Alexander's sight.

"What is the meaning of this, Trajan?"

"Hello, Father," Trajan said with a genuine smile. "It's good to see you."

The King of Karth stopped abruptly and took a deep breath as Isabel stood up.

"Lady Reishi, may I present Severine Karth, my father and the rightful King of Karth. Father, this is Isabel Reishi, wife of Alexander Reishi, Phane's sworn enemy."

Severine frowned while he scrutinized Isabel.

"They told me you were a witch," he said gruffly, yet with an air of relief. "I'm glad to see they were mistaken." He gestured to his royal guard and all but one filed out into the hall, closing the door behind them.

"Had you ever met a witch, Trajan, you would understand why I entered as I did," Severine said. "It's not safe to be alone with a witch that you are not allied with."

Isabel's mind raced. She was missing something, some vital piece of information, but she didn't understand her situation well enough to even ask the right questions, so she decided to wait in the hope that things would become clearer with time.

"I believe you're mistaken, Father," Trajan said. "I witnessed Lady Reishi charm a jaguar and command the beast to range out ahead of our party, clearing the path of any predators."

Alarm returned to Severine's visage. "Did you give her the malaise weed as I commanded?"

"Every morning," Trajan said. "I prepared the tea myself, measured the malaise-weed nectar and watched her drink every drop."

"They told me it would inhibit her magic," Severine muttered, as if to himself, doubt creeping across his face.

"There are many forms of magic, Lord Severine," Isabel said. "Some of the magic at my disposal is limited by the malaise weed while other magic is not. I tell you this in good faith because I believe we have a common enemy and my hope is to forge an alliance with your house so that we might stand together against Phane."

Severine scrutinized her for a moment before nodding to Trajan to bring the tea as he took the chair next to Isabel's, motioning for her to sit.

"Why should I believe you?"

"My husband sent the warning that saved your life," Isabel said. "He sent word in your dreams that the Regency would attack on the new moon."

Severine stared at her intently before swallowing hard.

"I did not heed that warning," Severine said. "Were it not for an abundance of caution on the part of Erastus here," he nodded to the man by the door, "we would have all died that day.

"Very few people knew the content of that message. Your knowledge of it lends some credibility to your claim of friendship, yet there is much more I must know before committing to an alliance."

"I understand completely," Isabel said. She proceeded to recount many of her experiences from the past year, leaving out key details that might be used against her or Alexander, but presenting a true and mostly complete account of their fight against Phane. Severine and Trajan listened attentively until she was finished.

"I hate Phane," she said. "I came here to kill him myself, but I would welcome any help I can get."

"You weave a most compelling tale," Severine said. "I will take steps to verify some parts of your story but I'm inclined to agree that an alliance would be in both of our interests.

"On another matter, tell me more about your magic. I take counsel from a coven of witches and they are very different than you. So much so, that it's hard for me to believe that you are indeed a witch."

"I underwent the mana fast with the Reishi Coven last summer," Isabel said. "Since then, I've been learning about my power, refining my connection to the firmament and honing my skills of visualization and emotional control."

He sighed and then frowned. "I don't mean to be indelicate, but how is it that you're so plain-looking. Please understand, for a normal woman you're quite beautiful, but for a witch you are, well, homely."

Isabel was dumbfounded. She'd been called many things in her life but 'homely' was not one of them. She opened her mouth as if to speak, then closed it again, at a loss for words.

"Please forgive me, I don't mean to give offense," Severine said when it was clear that Isabel didn't have an answer. "I have much to consider, Lady Reishi," he said as he stood. "Trajan will attend to your quarters. For the time being, your movement will be restricted, I hope you understand."

After Severine left, Trajan sighed deeply, closing his eyes and shaking his head. "I apologize for my father's bluntness," he said. "He's accustomed to speaking his mind."

"I'm more puzzled than offended," Isabel said.

"I'm sure it has something to do with the Sin'Rath," Trajan said. "Hopefully, things will become clearer after I meet with them. For now, I'll take you to your quarters. I'm sure you're tired."

Chapter 5

Isabel woke in the dead of night. She'd been provided with comfortable quarters and was only too happy to sleep in a bed after days on the road.

There were two men stationed outside her door, ostensibly to protect her, but in truth to prevent her from leaving. She was a prisoner ... again.

In the darkness, she smiled. The last time she'd been a prisoner, things had turned out for the best. Perhaps she could repeat her victory over the Reishi Coven with the House of Karth and add yet more strength to Alexander's cause.

Suddenly, she froze, daring not to breathe when she heard a sliding sound as if wood were scraping against the floor. A glance told her that the door leading from her chamber was still closed, a thin crack of dim light leaking through from the hallway. Isabel strained to hear. A gentle rustling came from across the room. She took inventory of her surroundings from memory, searching for a weapon. The nearest, most likely candidate was a pitcher of water on the washbasin near her bed.

Fluidly, she tossed the covers back and rolled to her feet, striding calmly but purposefully through the blackness to the basin, reaching out to feel for it in the dark, but she misjudged and knocked the stoneware pitcher to the floor. Momentary panic rose in her throat as she whirled to face the unknown intruder ... but no attack came.

"Please do not be alarmed," a gentle voice said from the darkness.

"Is everything all right, Lady Reishi?" a guard asked from the hall.

Dim, greenish light spilled out of a vial of liquid held high by a woman standing across the room.

"Please do not alert the guard," she whispered. "I come with a warning."

The woman was in her early twenties, and quite beautiful, with golden skin, lustrous jet black hair and soulful dark brown eyes. She carried herself with poise and confidence, yet she was clearly afraid.

"Everything's fine," Isabel said to the guard. "I just knocked over a pitcher when I was trying to get a drink of water."

"I'll send for a maid at once," the guard said.

"That won't be necessary," Isabel said. "I'll clean it up myself."

The woman motioned toward the water closet. Isabel smiled and motioned for her to go first, never turning her back on the intruder. She was curious about the woman and how she'd gotten into the room, but she wasn't about to trust her until she'd earned it.

"I'm Ayela Karth," she said, "youngest in my family."

"I'm Isabel Reishi. Why are you here? And how did you get into my chambers?"

"I come with a warning," Ayela said again. "Do not trust the men ... any of them."

"Why not?" Isabel asked, frowning.

"I believe they're under the spell of the Sin'Rath," Ayela said, looking about nervously as if someone might hear her.

"I keep hearing about these Sin'Rath witches," Isabel said, "but no one can tell me anything about them except that they exist. Who are they?"

Ayela swallowed hard and looked down, composing herself. She was shaking like a leaf.

"I saw one once, though they do not know it," she said. "I was very young and I found a peephole into a chamber where my father went to receive their counsel. He stood before her as if she was a queen, treated her like a man treats a woman that he's courting, as if she were beautiful beyond words. But what I saw was a monster. I still have nightmares about her, and I'm quite certain that she would have killed me if she'd discovered my presence."

"I don't understand," Isabel said. "Why do you think your father was so enamored with her if she was so ugly?"

"I don't know," Ayela said, shaking her head slowly. "What I do know is that I've never seen anything so dark, so wrong, or so frightening. Not until I saw the things Phane sent against us on the night the rest of my family died."

Isabel's mind raced. "You mean the Sin'Rath are demons?"

"I think so," Ayela whispered.

"Have you told your father or your brother about your suspicions?"

"No," she said. "Every man who goes to see them is changed somehow, they come to believe the witches are working for the betterment of Karth and our people, they suddenly change their opinions on a host of issues and begin to work toward new goals. My father always issues a bunch of orders right after he takes their counsel."

Ayela paused, wiping a tear from her cheek with a trembling hand.

"Now Trajan has gone to see them and the same thing has happened," she said. "He's my best friend. I know his heart better than any. Before he went to meet with them, he confided in me that he intended to reject their counsel and demand that they stop meddling in the affairs of the people of Karth."

She shook her head sadly, another tear sliding slowly down her face.

"When he returned, he spoke only praise for them. He said the one he met was the most beautiful woman in the world. He said he understood why Father thought so highly of their counsel, even though they cost us our family.

"My father brought the warning he received in his dreams to them and they told him to ignore it, they told him it was just a dream, they told him that the Regency would not attack … but they did, and half my family died, not to mention countless thousands of innocent people. Now my brother has fallen under their spell and I have no one else I can trust."

She placed a small vial of clear liquid on the counter.

"This will counteract the effects of the malaise weed they've been giving you," Ayela said. "You must drink it all at once and it will take a minute or so for it to take effect. Once it does, the malaise will vanish."

"Why are you giving me this?" Isabel asked.

"Your husband sent the warning that saved my life, saved my father and brother," she said. "I can't trust anyone here; the witches have their fingers into everything and everyone in this fortress. I don't know what they're planning, but I do know they're up to something since you've arrived."

"I've offered your father an alliance against Phane," Isabel said. "It could be that they've decided to accept my offer and they're just making preparations."

"You could be right," Ayela said, "but things have a way of happening in the background, when no one is looking, after my father speaks to the witches. Please don't tell anyone about this conversation, and remember, don't trust the men ... any of them."

"What will you do?" Isabel asked as Ayela stood to leave.

"Try to save what's left of my family," she said. "This passage opens by pressing here," she pointed to a stone that blended in with the rest of the wall. "Use it only at great need. If they discover you're missing, they'll probably kill you on sight when they find you."

She smiled sadly at Isabel in the dim light and whispered, "It's good to have a friend." And then she was gone and the hidden passage closed behind her.

"Yes, it is," Isabel whispered to herself, looking at the vial of clear liquid she'd been given. "I just hope you're not really an assassin."

***

She woke to a knock at the door. A maidservant entered with a tray of breakfast, an assortment of unusual foods collected from the jungle. She sampled them all and found the few she liked before eating her fill. Trajan arrived several minutes later as she was sipping her tea.

"Good morning," he said with a broad smile, "I trust you slept well."

"A bed always beats a bedroll," Isabel said.

"I have good news," he said. "The Sin'Rath have agreed that my father should form an alliance with you. With your help, they think we can defeat Phane once and for all." He was almost giddy.

"I thought you didn't trust the Sin'Rath," she said.

"Oh, that was just foolishness on my part," he said. "I met Clotus last night, she's one of the witches my father takes his counsel from." He smiled boyishly. "My father told me they're beautiful, but I had no idea. She was stunning, easily the most beautiful woman I've ever met."

Isabel tensed slightly and her awareness sharpened.

"They want to meet you," he said. "It's unheard of, they never speak to women, never, but they want to meet you. Today. It's such an honor for you. Don't tell anyone I said this, but I think they're going to invite you into their coven."

Isabel said nothing while her mind raced. She was suddenly feeling very uneasy, but she was hopeful that the opportunity to form a meaningful alliance still existed.

"I look forward to it," she said when she realized Trajan was looking at her expectantly. "Hopefully, together we can come up with a plan to strike back against Phane," she added.

"I have to say," Trajan said, "I feel better about our situation today than I have since this war started. We've been living under a truce with the Regency for decades. Sure, we've had occasional border disputes and even a few battles, but mostly we've been at a stalemate. Once Phane's gone, we can get beck to normal, to the way things are supposed to be."

Isabel frowned but held her tongue.

"Everything's going to be all right now. You'll see," he said as he left, bowing with a flourish.

His behavior was so out of character that Isabel felt a chill creep up her spine. She didn't know what to expect from the Sin'Rath but she was starting to dread meeting them. Even with her magic, she was no match for a whole coven. So the direct approach was out. That left subterfuge, not her strong suit.

Chapter 6

The guard took off her blindfold.

"We're here," he said, pulling open a large oak door.

She'd been led through a confusing maze of passages, up stairs and then down, until she was thoroughly lost under the stone of the hidden underground fortress. Trajan had told her that the Sin'Rath were very security-conscious, so she wouldn't be allowed to know how to find them within the mountain ... that he didn't even know. A fact that didn't seem to bother him, but one that did bother Isabel.

In the short time she'd known Trajan, he'd shown himself to be cautious and inquisitive, prone to gathering information before making decisions. Since his meeting with the witches, he'd come to trust them implicitly, laughing off any questions about their intent and accepting their guidance without hesitation.

Isabel looked into a roughly circular room, carved out of a cave. The walls rose at a steep angle until they fell away into shadow. Around the edge of the room, a magic circle was carved into the floor. Each of the magic symbols etched into the stone appeared to be filled with dried blood. Sunlight streamed into the room from a hole in the cave ceiling far above, filling the well of the room with light while shrouding the balcony above in impenetrable shadows.

Isabel stepped into the room, her eyes adjusting to the sudden brightness. As she surveyed her surroundings, the door closed behind her and the bar was dropped into place. Scattered about the floor were the remnants of people ... a scrap of clothing here, a piece of bone there. Fear started to build within her. She thought about the draught given to her by Ayela but rejected the idea ... at least for now.

A rustling noise came from above in the shadows—it sounded like a dozen or so people filing into the balcony. She waited.

"You are from the Reishi Coven," a raspy voice said.

"Yes," Isabel said.

What followed made her blood run cold. The balcony erupted into a chorus of barking, snarling, mewling, and howling. It was almost animal in nature, but darker. When the cacophony of beastly noises subsided, another voice spoke, this one cloying and sweet.

"We have an agreement," she cooed, "your coven is not welcome here."

"I was unaware of any such agreement," Isabel said, a bit confused. She wondered what Magda might know about the Sin'Rath.

"We should eats her," a guttural voice barked.

"Yes, we should eats her," a mewling voice agreed.

"No!" the raspy voice said. "She may prove useful."

"But I'm hungry," the mewling voice said.

A snarl from one side of the chamber followed by a menacing growl from the other silenced the mewling voice.

"Why are you here?" the raspy voice asked.

"I've come to kill Phane," Isabel said.

Again the balcony erupted into chaos—howling madness filling the air.

"Silence!" shouted the raspy voice. The howling turned to mewling and then grudging silence.

"We hates him," the mewling voice whimpered.

"What makes you think you can kill Phane?" the raspy voiced asked.

"Yes, he is most powerful," the cloying voice said.

"He thinks he's turned me into his puppet," Isabel said, struggling to keep the trembling out of her voice.

"Puppet?" the mewling voice asked with rising alarm. "What if she's been sent to bait a trap for us?" her question trailed off into a petulant whine.

The raspy voice ignored her. "Why would you be his puppet?"

"He's summoned Azugorath," Isabel said. "Through her magic, he's trying to subvert my free will." She decided the truth was in order. From the sounds of things, she didn't want to risk being caught in a lie.

The chamber erupted again, but this time the majority of the noises were more whining and whimpering than barking and howling.

"Mother's sister is in the world?" the mewling voice whined.

Several other voices growled at her viciously.

"Silence, you fool," the raspy voice said.

"She can't be trusted," the cloying voice said.

"No, not with Azugorath's tendril in her," the guttural voice said.

"We should eats her," the mewling voice said.

"Not yet," the raspy voice barked.

Isabel didn't like where this conversation was going. "We both have the same enemy … Phane," she said.

"We hates him," the mewling voice said.

"We should eats him," the guttural voice barked.

"We will," the raspy voice said.

"I can get close to him," Isabel said.

"Then what?" the guttural voice barked.

"I drive my dagger into his heart."

"No!" the mewling voice wailed. She was immediately silenced by several snarls and growls.

"What about the Goiri?" a very reasonable voice asked.

"No!" the guttural voice barked.

"Too dangerous," the raspy voice said.

"We could sends her," the mewling voice said.

"How much do you want to kill Phane?" the reasonable voice asked.

"He's driven a wedge between me and my husband and cut me off from everyone I love. I would rather die than become the thing he wants me to be."

"She sounds committed," the reasonable voice said.

"I am," Isabel said.

"The Goiri may be the only way," the reasonable voice said.

"No," the cloying voice said, "there's another way—a doppelganger spell."

"Yes," the guttural voice said.

"It could work," the raspy voice said.

"But who would go?" the mewling voice asked. "Not me."

"I will," the cloying voice said.

"If you fail, he will kill you," the reasonable voice said.

"If I succeed, then Mother will be free," the cloying voice said.

"You fool," the guttural voice said.

"You reveal too much," the raspy voice said.

"No matter," the reasonable voice said, "we need only keep her alive until the task is complete."

"Then we can eats her," the mewling voice said.

"Yes, Sister," the reasonable voice said.

"We are agreed then?" the raspy voice said.

A chorus of barks and snarls followed. As the Sin'Rath filed out of the balcony and left her alone in the room, Isabel stood stock-still, trying to make sense of what had just happened.

Nearly an hour passed before she heard the bar being lifted.

The door opened and a creature that should not exist entered, smiling wickedly. She had dark grey skin ... one eye a smoldering red, the other a sickening yellow, both with the irises of a cat ... pointed teeth, the left canine extending past her lower lip, leaving a festering welt where it rubbed. Her long dark grey hair was patchy and stringy, coated in grime. Two-inch horns protruded from her forehead, curving toward one another. She was hunched over, her right shoulder and arm grotesquely larger than the left, both hands ending in long fingers tipped with razor-sharp black talons. She walked with a limp, each step revealing a barbed tail whipping back and forth behind her. Despite her contorted features, her face was perfectly formed, with high cheek bones and perfect bone structure. The contrast between the beauty of her facial structure and the grotesqueness of her body only served to heighten the sense of wrongness that radiated from her in undulating waves.

As Isabel stared in revulsion at the creature that stood before her, the balcony filled up with the rest of the coven and the door was closed once again.

"I'm called Clotus," she said in a cloying voice. "They won't believe you. They don't see me as you do, and besides, they belong to us."

Isabel swallowed hard, facing the monster. "What do you intend to do?" she asked.

"We will cast a spell to make me look like you," Clotus said sweetly. "Then I will go to Phane and take his magic and his life."

The balcony erupted in a fit of barking madness.

"It would be unwise to answer any more of her questions," the reasonable voice said.

"Yes, begin the spell," the raspy voice said.

The voices cloaked in shadow above began to chant—guttural, dark and animalistic noise reverberating around the cave. Isabel waited, wondering what to expect. She didn't have to wait long. A blob of spinning darkness, illuminated by flecks of sparkling purple, began to form in the air between her and Clotus. It grew in size as it spun faster and faster until it split in two with only a thread of darkness between the two halves. Very quickly the thread elongated as it spun, until a blob of darkness engulfed Isabel and Clotus at the same time, surrounding each of them with dark magic.

Isabel couldn't breathe, coldness seeped into her very soul as the black magic worked within her. She watched in horror as Clotus transformed into a perfect likeness of her, right down to the color of her eyes and the shade of her chestnut-brown hair.

The magic abruptly faded and Clotus smiled.

"You see, I am now you," she said in Isabel's voice. "Phane will welcome me into his fortress and then he will fall to me."

Her smile widened and she looked up to the rest of the coven. "This one is special," she said. "I can feel the darkness within her. With the proper preparation and motivation, I believe she could summon Mother."

Madness erupted from the shadows above.

"How can this be?" asked the reasonable voice.

"Yes, how?" said the raspy voice.

"She has a connection to the darkness within her," Clotus said. "I can feel it through the link." Her eyes narrowed and fear ghosted across her face before she snarled, "She also has a connection to the light, though Azugorath has blocked it."

"She may be more valuable than we first thought," the reasonable voice said.

"Yes," the raspy voice said. "We will think on how best to use her. For now, Severine will keep her prisoner here until we decide how she can serve us."

There was a barking agreement from the rest of the coven.

Clotus knocked at the door and a guard opened it.

"Yes, Mistress," he said, seeming to know she was one of the witches, even though her appearance had changed.

"Take this one back to your King. See to it that she remains here as our guest until we call for her again."

Chapter 7

Lacy ignored the knock at the door of her cramped little stateroom. She'd been at sea for less than a day and she'd already spent most of the voyage leaning over the gunnel, vomiting into the ocean. The cold sea air had burned her face raw, so once she was certain her stomach was completely empty, she retreated from the harsh, late autumn day to her room where she was trying, unsuccessfully, to suppress her nausea.

Drogan had followed her around the ship, silently watching over her, as he had since they had first met. She tried not to think about his master. Phane was still defined in her mind by the stories she'd read. It was difficult to believe that history had been so perverted, twisted, and distorted that the whole world believed Phane was a monster when he was really the true champion of the Old Law.

She wanted to believe—desperately needed to believe—that he had come to save her people. Without help, the people of Fellenden would suffer immeasurably at the hands of Zuhl's brutes. Reports of an army marching against the barbarian horde, flying the banner of the Reishi, gave her some measure of hope that help had arrived. Was it too little? Was it too late? The sad answer for far too many of her countrymen was yes.

Tens of thousands had already perished, maybe more. The thought of it made her nausea threaten to send her into convulsions again, even though there was nothing left for her stomach to heave.

The knock came again, this time more forcefully.

Drogan looked at her, then at the door. When she ignored them both, he sighed quietly. The sea journey didn't seem to faze him in the least.

"What is it?" he said.

"I have a meal for you," a strangely familiar voice said through the door.

Lacy swallowed hard against a threatened convulsion.

"I'm not hungry," she managed.

"I am," Drogan said, getting up and going to the door.

A grimy, weather-worn sailor stood at the threshold with a tray of food.

Drogan nodded his thanks and took the tray, turning to put it on the little table bolted to the floor across from the bunk beds. In an instant, the sailor was through the door with a short, stout club in hand.

Before Lacy could muster a warning, he brought it down hard on the back of Drogan's skull. The big man went down with a thud, lying still, though still breathing. Lacy sat up on her bed and drew her dagger.

Flashing her a wicked grin, the sailor closed the door and threw the bolt, then spun back toward her, pointing the stout little club in her direction. "Let's you and I have a chat."

His voice sounded so familiar.

"You have something I need," he said. "Give it to me and I'll let you live … for now."

Realization slammed into her—he sounded just like Wizard Saul did after the thing made of darkness entered him.

"You're a quick study, girl," the sailor said, smiling at her expression. "Did you really think a little water would stand between me and my prize?"

"You're Rankosi," Lacy said, the tip of her dagger shaking as she pointed it toward the creature that had been hunting her since the day she'd recovered the little black box.

"Yes, I am … now give me the keystone."

"I don't know what you're talking about," she said.

"Come now, Child. You've had it since the tomb. That box may be able to hide the keystone from others but not from me. Now hand it over."

Lacy stood, shaking her head slowly, keeping her dagger pointed at the sailor.

"If you kill this body, I'll just take another. Perhaps that one," he said, motioning toward Drogan. "I doubt he could resist me, considering the master he serves."

"My father entrusted me with this. I won't fail him."

"Oh, but you already have. You're all alone on this ship, in the middle of the ocean … with me. There's no one here who could ever hope to master me. Even if I fail to get my prize with this body, there are many others I can use."

"No," Lacy said. In that moment she was sure of just one thing—in his moment of greatest need, her father had entrusted her with this one task and she would not fail him while she still drew breath.

She lunged, driving her dagger toward his gut, but he was quick, too quick. He brought his club up, hitting her on the inside of the forearm, sending her dagger skittering under the table. She gasped at the sudden pain of the blow. Her arm didn't feel broken, but she couldn't make her fingers work.

The sailor crashed into her, driving her into the lower bunk, pinning her into the corner. His breath was rank and he smelled of sweat and brandy. His face was just inches from hers as he stared her in the eye, darkness and hate dancing in his gaze.

He seemed to master himself and then spun her around, shoving her awkwardly, face first into the corner so he could hastily bind her hands, tightly looping a piece of cord around her wrists, adding to the pain in her arm.

With a heave, he dragged her from the bunk and tossed her roughly onto the floor. She fell hard, knocking the wind from her and adding a bruised hip to her injuries.

"Let's see, these must be your things, yes?"

Lacy didn't answer.

He took up her pack and dumped it out on the table, carelessly tossing her possessions onto the floor until he found the little black box wrapped in a square of cloth. He set it on the table and carefully unwrapped it, taking pains to avoid actually touching the box itself.

"Pity I don't still have the wizard," he muttered. "His talents might have been useful right about now."

After a few moments of looking at the seamless box from every angle, Rankosi hauled Lacy to her feet and roughly sat her down on the bench facing the table.

"Open it."

"I don't know how."

"Try."

"My hands are bound."

He unwound the cord from her wrists, setting her hands to tingling.

"Open it!"

She clenched her jaw and shook her head.

He put her hand on the table and raised his club over it. She whimpered, clenching her eyes shut but still shaking her head.

Bones shattered as he brought the club down on the back of her hand. She cried out, pain like nothing she'd ever felt coursing up her arm, filling her shoulder and chest, ripping through her flesh and threatening her very sanity. In the back of her mind, in a place she didn't even know existed, she thought about all of the people on Fellenden who'd suffered similar torture, or worse. Before this moment, she didn't know that anything could hurt so much. She gasped for breath, pain threatening to overpower her consciousness, but her resolve held firm.

"Open it!" Rankosi demanded in a harsh whisper.

"No!" she shouted through tears and torment.

He grabbed her broken hand and squeezed.

She gasped again, agony flooding into her as broken bones scraped together. Darkness closed in around her and she drifted off into peaceful oblivion.

***

Pain returned before consciousness did. She was floating in that halfway place between sleep and wakefulness, pain surrounding her and engulfing her until she came fully awake with a start, gasping and whimpering at the sudden onslaught of torment from her broken hand.

"Ah, you're awake," Rankosi said, "seems I might have hit your friend here a bit too hard. He's still out cold. So where were we? Ah yes. Open the box!"

"I can't," Lacy whimpered. "I don't know how."

"Try."

"No."

"You're stronger than I would have thought," Rankosi said. "Perhaps I'm going about this all wrong."

He drew a knife and carefully, slowly placed it at Drogan's throat. "He's nothing to me but a body. Open it or I'll kill him."

Lacy swallowed and shook her head.

Rankosi smiled wickedly and his arm started to tense.

"Stop!" Lacy said.

"Yes?"

"He didn't do anything to you."

"What does that have to do with anything?"

"He doesn't deserve to die."

"What does *that* have to do with anything?"

"This is between you and me, leave him out of this. He can't hurt you, he's totally defenseless."

"Yes, he is. Now open the box or he dies."

Lacy struggled to regain her feet, wincing when she started to use her broken hand for leverage. She staggered to the bench and faced the little black box. Her father had entrusted her with this task, she couldn't let him down, yet a man's life hung in the balance. What would her father do? What would he expect of her?

He'd always taught her to value life above all else. She closed her eyes tightly, tears slipping down both cheeks as her resolve faltered.

Tentatively, cautiously, she reached for the box with her left hand. It felt cool to the touch. She tried to lift the top of the box as if it had a lid with hinges, but nothing happened. She picked it up and carefully looked it over for any sign or seam, but found nothing. She slammed it against the table—still nothing.

"I don't know how to open it," she said, hanging her head.

Rankosi stared at the box for several seconds.

"Place your hand on it and think of it opening," he said. "See it open in your mind."

Lacy did as he instructed.

Nothing happened.

Then it started to glow. She snatched her hand back, staring in wonder at the symbol that had become visible on all sides of the box.

Rankosi smiled in triumph.

"Place your hand on the box and say the word: Ruminoct."

"What does that mean?" she asked.

"It means: Open. Now, do as you're told."

She reached for the box again, her hand shaking visibly, and spoke the ancient word.

For a fraction of a second she felt like it might open, but then it recoiled as if it sensed her duress. The little box went suddenly dark and lifeless.

Rankosi snarled in anger, raising his club to brain her in sudden fury, but then mastered himself just as quickly.

"What does he know that I don't know?" he muttered to himself, staring off into the distance. "He could have simply killed the girl and had the box delivered to him, yet he chose …"

Drogan rolled over, drawing a dagger in a single smooth motion, and plunged it into the heart of the sailor, killing him in an instant. A faint black shadow drifted out of the dying man, floating up through the ceiling.

Drogan staggered to his feet and nearly fell again as he found the bench.

"How badly are you hurt?" he asked, burying his face in his hands.

"My hand is broken," Lacy said. "He hit you really hard."

Drogan nodded, gently prodding the lump on the back of his head. "Give me a minute to get my bearings and I'll see if I can do anything for your hand," he muttered.

She nodded, looking helplessly at her broken hand.

A few minutes later there was a loud pounding at the door.

"Open up in there," an angry voice said.

When they didn't immediately respond, the pounding grew louder.

"Open up, right now!"

Lacy looked at Drogan, then at the corpse on the floor as the door burst open and two men entered, followed by the captain.

"I heard a scuffle," a sailor said. "Came to you with it straightaway, Captain."

Lacy thought the voice sounded familiar.

"I'll not tolerate murder on my ship," the captain said.

"But he was possessed," Lacy protested.

The captain eyed her with a confused frown.

"I've heard a lot of excuses in my time, but that's a new one on me. Take them to the brig. We'll sort this out once we're sure they can't do any more harm."

***

They spent the night in cold, cramped cages that shared a wall of bars. Dinner was a moldy piece of bread and a cup of water. Lacy was miserable. Her hand throbbed with pain that wouldn't let her sleep. The guard ignored her pleas or threatened her when she didn't relent.

Drogan just curled up on the floor and went to sleep. She didn't understand him, but she had to admit to herself that she was glad he was still with her, even if they were locked in cages.

Morning came and two men hauled her out of her cell to face the captain. They took her to a little room and sat her roughly in a wooden chair. The captain and first mate sat behind a table facing her. Both guards took positions behind her on either side of the door.

"Do you have anything to say for yourself?" the captain asked.

"The man came to our quarters and attacked us," Lacy said, holding up her broken hand as evidence. "He was possessed by a creature that's been hunting me for weeks."

"Possessed?" the first mate said. "By what, a shade?" he laughed.

"I don't know," Lacy said. "He tortured me and threatened to kill Drogan."

"She's crazy," the first mate said.

"Perhaps," the captain said. "You killed a good sailor. He just brought you a meal, now he's dead. Justice must be served."

"I say we hang them and be done with it," the first mate said.

"I'm inclined to agree," the captain said. "Unless you can explain yourself more ... rationally, I will pass sentence."

"Could be she's someone important," one of the guards said, "fine stitching in her clothes and all, good steel in her blade, and she paid in gold."

Lacy's mind raced. She thought she almost recognized the voice of the guard, but she was far too afraid of hanging to do more than grab hold of the lifeline.

"My name is Lacy Fellenden, Princess of the House of Fellenden. I've been sent by my father on an urgent mission to speak with King Abel Ithilian. If you kill me or my companion, *you* will face justice, Captain."

The first mate guffawed, but the captain eyed her carefully.

"Not that I believe a word you've said, but I think I'll leave the dispensation of justice to the constable at port. It'll be another few days. Until then, I hope you enjoy the accommodations."

Chapter 8

Time passed. Lacy lost track of day and night in the poorly lit hold. Pain was the only constant. Her hand was useless, but that didn't stop her from trying to use it out of habit, only to remember a moment too late when the constant aching flared into sudden agony. Her only consolation was that the captain had ordered her belongings locked in a strongbox near her cell. At least she knew where the black box was.

Imprisonment gave her time to think, to recall every word of her conversation with Rankosi. He said that the box contained a keystone, to what she had no idea, but the fact that he wanted it was enough to ensure that she would go to great lengths to prevent him from getting it.

He showed her how to open it, told her the ancient word that she needed to speak, yet it didn't open when she tried. She played that moment over and over in her mind as well. She couldn't explain it with words, but it felt like the box was sensing her duress, like it chose to remain closed because she was being coerced.

The implications were staggering.

The proof was in the fact that Rankosi hadn't returned, even though she was certain he was still onboard. If the box couldn't be opened though coercion, then she had to choose to open it. That meant he would try to trick her. It also meant she was safe, in a manner of speaking anyway. Rankosi wouldn't kill her if he still needed her to open the box.

Rankosi had also spoken about Phane, at least she assumed he was referring to the Reishi Prince. From the sound if it, Phane wanted the contents of the box as well, but he knew something about it, something that Rankosi didn't.

She fell asleep, playing the encounter with Rankosi over in her mind yet again and woke with a start. The muffled sounds of shouting and fighting filtered through from the upper deck. She and Drogan shared a worried look, each straining to hear what was happening.

Moments later, the hatch opened and soldiers began to stream into the lower hold where the brig was located. They were big men, brutish-looking, dressed in furs and armed with simple yet effective weapons. Lacy recognized them at once—Zuhl's soldiers.

"Ah, there you are, Princess," the man in the lead said. He was easily six and a half feet tall with a close-cropped black beard, bald head, and dark menacing eyes.

"I'm Commander Kahl," he said. "Lord Zuhl has been looking for you."

Lacy's blood ran cold. Her face went white and she nearly fainted. All these weeks of running had come to this. Zuhl had captured her at last. She didn't know why the ruler of the island to the north wanted her so badly, but she was certain it wouldn't be good.

"Transfer them both to the brig on our ship," Commander Kahl said, "and be sure to secure their possessions. Lord Zuhl is particularly interested in one of the items she's carrying."

"What of the rest of the passengers and crew?" the man to his right asked.

"Kill them all and sink the ship," Kahl said. "We have what we came for. Once the prisoners are secure, set course for Crescent Bay."

Lacy whimpered when they roughly locked the shackles around her wrists and she nearly screamed when the soldier grabbed the chain between them and dragged her from her cell toward the steep stairs leading to the upper decks. She watched in helpless horror as the rest of those aboard the refugee vessel were casually slaughtered by Zuhl's brutes while she was led to the brig aboard the enemy warship. Men jeered and taunted her as she passed them, laughing at her predicament and speculating on how Zuhl might go about interrogating her. By the time the cold steel bars clanged shut on her new cage, she was totally dispirited. She'd failed her father, and she was probably going to die a terrible death.

Lacy Fellenden curled up on the pallet in the corner and cried herself to sleep.

***

Abigail sat atop her horse, looking out over the snow-dusted valley at the husk of Fellenden City. It was a cold, late autumn day. The first snow had just started falling from a bleak grey sky. The air was still and cold—the city in the distance looked the same.

They had been marching for weeks, thousands of soldiers guarding thousands of refugees. People from all over Fellenden were coming home to the central city of the entire island, the place that once, long ago, had housed the royal House of Fellenden. Now, it was a broken shell of its former glory, yet it was the best place for Abigail's army to shelter during the winter. Centrally located on the Isle of Fellenden, it gave her strategic options if Zuhl or Phane should choose to attack during the winter, an unwise choice, yet not beyond reason for either tyrant, considering how little they valued the lives of those who served them.

The weather had been cold and clear for most of the journey. Only in the last few days had the sky clouded over. Abigail had prodded her army to move faster, hoping to reach shelter before the inevitable snows began to fall. The soldiers could handle the faster pace, but the refugees could not. They trailed behind the bulk of the army for leagues, struggling to carry all that was left of their possessions to their new temporary home.

"General Markos," Abigail said, "send half the heavy cavalry forward to scout and secure the city and the other half back to ensure we don't lose any stragglers in this snow."

"At once, Lady Abigail," General Markos said, saluting, fist to heart, before wheeling his horse and tending to his orders.

"I doubt we'll get everyone inside before dark," Anatoly said. "Not even sure it would be wise."

"I concur," Magda said. "Zuhl is not above leaving a few nasty surprises in his wake to discourage those who might pick the bones of his conquest."

Abigail nodded, trying to gauge the time of day from the uniformly bleak sky.

"We'll make camp on the outskirts and move into the city in a careful and orderly manner," she said. "After bringing these people all this way, I don't want to blindly walk them into a trap."

Conner rode up, trailed by two Ithilian royal guards. "Scout riders just returned," he said. "Irondale has fallen without a fight."

"Blasted cowards," Torin said, biting off his words.

"Could be they're biding their time," Anatoly said, "waiting for the right moment to strike."

"Either way, Zuhl's brutes have a warm place to sleep for the winter," Abigail said. "At least we know where they are."

"General Kern reports that the Rangers have done some damage to the enemy forces but not enough to make a difference," Conner said. "He's starting to lose men and horses to the cold. The snow started falling a week ago farther north and hasn't stopped since."

"Recall him at once," Abigail said. "We're at a stalemate until spring."

"For any significant operations, I'm afraid you're right," Magda said, "though there are still some things we can do to make life uncomfortable for our unwelcome guests."

"I'm all for that," Abigail said with a sidelong grin, "but let's see to these people first before we go poking Zuhl in the eye."

***

A week later they'd cleared the city of the wild dogs and other unpleasant scavengers that had taken refuge in the ruins and they were beginning to rebuild. Abigail made the defenses a priority. Even though she knew that stone walls were no match for the kind of magic Zuhl could bring to bear, she felt better knowing that the people would breathe easier when they were surrounded by a stout wall and heavy Iron Oak gates.

A large portion of the Fellenden family keep had been shattered beyond repair, but part of it was salvageable. Abigail had taken that section as her command post and quarters for herself and her command staff. A single tower still stood on one corner of the keep. Abigail ordered that it be fitted with a guard house and a warning bell. The manor was cold and foreboding at first, but after a few days of work, it started to take on the lived-in feel of a home.

She had taken simple quarters that had probably been occupied by a servant before the attack, but they were close to the master bedchamber that she'd converted into a council hall and strategy room.

Several days after the last of the refugees had been moved into the city, Abigail assembled all of her advisors around the council table. She sat at the head of the table with her sword belt hooked over the corner of her chair. While she felt relatively secure within the keep, she wasn't about to let the Thinblade out of her sight.

"I've received word from several of the other territories," Torin said. "I estimate another three to four legions are prepared to join our forces. Zuhl's defeat at the shipyards has heartened many who thought all hope was lost. While there are few on Fellenden who have any real battle experience, many are eager to join the fight now that we have a fighting chance."

"With our losses at the shipyards, these new additions will bolster our forces to about twelve legions," General Markos said.

"That should be more than enough to drive the barbarians out of Irondale and into the sea," Conner said.

"We've received reinforcements from the fortress islands," Corina said. "My wing now stands at ninety-seven Sky Knights, including seventeen witches. Additionally, Bianca has cleared the northern fortress island and established a base of operations there. She is prepared to assist and is already running scouting operations. And Cassandra reports that the wyvern-breeding program is moving ahead and the new class of Sky Knights is ready and awaiting the next hatching."

"General Kern should arrive within the week," General Markos said. "Quarters have been set aside for the Rangers, and we've already made preparations for stabling their horses. The latest supply shipment arrived from Ithilian today so we should have enough food to last through the winter."

"Any word from Ruatha?" Abigail asked.

"I'm afraid not," General Markos said.

Abigail nodded, pursing her lips. Winter had set in, blanketing the majority of the Isle of Fellenden with over six inches of snow and effectively ending any significant military operations. She had turned her attention to the more mundane, yet vitally important tasks of rebuilding Fellenden City and sheltering the soldiers and refugees under her care.

She was running through the checklist of matters to address when the alarm bell tolled. She looked to Captain Sava, who was standing guard along the wall of the big room. He nodded and sent one of his Strikers for a report. Before the man could reach the door, a roar shattered the early evening.

Only one thing could make such a fearsome noise.

A dragon.

The air in the room dropped precipitously as the ceiling crystallized, freezing solid, icicles forming in seconds.

Everyone stood. Magda, Corina, Sark, and Dax began casting spells. The Strikers drew swords and raised shields as a soldier burst into the room.

"A dragon attacks!" he shouted as the arched ceiling shattered, sending blocks of stone raining down.

Anatoly grabbed Abigail and covered her with his body as he shoved her under the table. A rock the size of a man's head crashed into his back, knocking him unconscious and pinning Abigail underneath him.

Magda's shield flickered into being, followed a moment later by a force-push spell that shoved a section of ceiling the size of a wagon back against the wall, saving Conner and Torin from being crushed.

Sark turned to wind, barely escaping as several stones crashed into his chair, leaving nothing but splinters.

One Striker managed to deflect a stone with his shield, suffering a broken arm in the bargain. Another took a direct hit to the head. His helmet was undamaged but the force of the blow broke his neck, dropping him to the floor, dead in an instant.

Sava raced to Abigail, shield raised overhead, and took a position over her and Anatoly to protect them both.

Corina staggered back as a large section crashed into her shield, exploding into smaller stones that clattered to the floor.

Dax cast a spell that caught a dozen or more stones that were falling toward him, stopping them in midair, blue sparkling light dancing over the surface of each, then with a wave of his hands, he tossed them harmlessly against the wall.

Abigail worked to free herself from Anatoly, rolling him over and frantically checking his breathing. She could hear gurgling as he struggled to draw breath.

"Help me get his armor off," she said to Sava.

She gasped when she saw the extent of the damage. The right side of his upper back was crushed, shattered ribs sticking out and bright red blood flowing freely. She sobbed as she fumbled with her jar of healing salve, scooping out nearly all of the contents and spreading it liberally on his back, then gently rolling him onto his side so she could pour a healing draught down his throat.

When she looked up into the sudden silence, she saw that General Markos and two of the Strikers had been killed by the falling debris. The general was crushed under a section of stone that would have killed a horse. He'd died almost instantly. Several Strikers were down, a few were struggling to get back up, some would never rise again.

"Call for a healer," Abigail commanded.

One of the Strikers nodded and raced off.

"We have to get you out of here, Lady Abigail," Sava said.

"I'm not leaving him," she said, kneeling next to Anatoly and cradling his head in her lap. She felt the knot in her stomach tighten when she saw the bright red blood on his lips. He was hurt … badly. Then she heard another roar, and though not as fearsome as a dragon's, it had a similar quality. She looked up and saw a dozen or more creatures descending into the room.

They were a mixture of man and dragon, each standing eight feet tall with pale blue scales like those of a snake covering their entire bodies. They had bright golden eyes, horns that swept back from their dragon-like heads, and a ridge of spikes running down their backs. They were thin and sinewy, but looked inhumanly strong. Blue batlike wings, a long bone-bladed tail, sharply clawed hands and feet completed the nightmare.

One landed on the table in front of Abigail, its claws gouging into the wood. Captain Sava stabbed at it, but his blade was turned aside by the hardness of its scales. It backhanded Sava, sending him tumbling to the floor, then grabbed Abigail by the arm and started to launch into the air.

She grasped the hilt of the Thinblade just as the creature thrust with its wings, slipping the blade free of its scabbard and slashing up toward the monster. The Thinblade cut cleanly through the beast's arm and wing, sending them crashing to the ground amidst an inhuman shriek of pain from the half-dragon, half-man.

Abigail rolled to her feet as Sava and two of his men converged on her, forming a cordon of protection with their dragon-plate shields raised high against the threat descending on them.

Another beast landed in the center of the shattered table. It reared back and breathed a cone of icy air at Magda, coating her shield with frost. She seemed to be chilled by the attack, but her shield protected her from the brunt of it. Her spell came quickly, sudden anger flashing in her eyes … a blue pinwheel of force materialized in front of her, then moved quickly toward the dragon-man, catching it in the midsection and cleaving it cleanly in half. Three of its brethren shrieked in fury at the loss of one of their own.

Another flew over Torin and Conner, breathing a gout of frost on them, chilling them to the bone and sending them to the ground, shivering. They were both still alive, but completely incapacitated by the numbing cold. Corina released a light-lance spell at the beast, burning a hole through its chest. It crashed to the ground and never moved again.

Sark caught two of the creatures in a whirling vortex of wind and carried them up and out of the chamber into the dark of night.

Another of the beasts grabbed hold of one of the Strikers with its taloned feet and carried him several dozen feet into the air before dropping him to the ground. He crashed into the stone floor and fell still as death.

Mage Dax was feeding power into a ball of lightning that was forming between his outstretched hands. It was growing in size and intensity when a blue dragon landed on the edge of the hole in the ceiling. It was beautiful and terrible all at once. Abigail saw similarities between this one and Ixabrax. Its rider looked down into the room with calm, almost detached calculation.

Zuhl.

"Take the girl," he commanded as Dax released the ball of lightning at him. Zuhl directed his staff toward the streaking, crackling ball of electrical power and instantly formed a half-shell protective shield in front of him. The lightning struck it with thunderous force, shattering the shield and hitting the dragon square in the chest. The dragon reared back and looked like he was preparing to breathe frost into the room, certain doom for them all, but Zuhl commanded him to stop and they launched into the darkness.

Three of the dragon-men landed around Abigail. All three breathed frost at her and her cordon of Strikers. They all fell in a shivering mass. Abigail had never been so cold. It penetrated into her bones, paralyzing her with numbness. The nearest dragon-man grabbed her and launched into the sky. She held on to consciousness even as the Thinblade slipped from her grasp, burying to the hilt in the stone floor.

At the same time, two more dragon-men breathed frost at Magda and Corina, forcing them to defend against the attack long enough for the beast carrying Abigail to escape. She watched the ground fall away as the beast gained altitude. It flew to Zuhl, perched atop the guard house on the last remaining tower of the fortress.

"Very good," Zuhl said as he took Abigail and secured her over his saddle in front of him. He whispered a few words and she felt suddenly warmer, though she was still unable to move. Zuhl pulled a fur blanket over her and launched into the sky, followed by the remaining nine dragon-men.

The last thing Abigail saw before she lost consciousness was Mage Dax launching a bolt of lightning at the trailing dragon-man. It hit the creature, lighting it up with crackling power, then arced through the night to another and another and another and another after that, burning a hole through the chest of each as it leapt from one to the next, each falling from the sky in turn.

Chapter 9

She woke in a round room with a single barred window and a trapdoor in the floor. She was lying on a pallet with several furs covering her. The air was cold … she could see her breath in the dim light streaming through the window. Aside from the pallet and furs, the room was completely empty. She checked her boots and found her knives were gone.

She was defenseless.

Still wearing the clothes she'd been dressed in during the meeting with her advisors, she stood and wrapped a fur blanket around her to ward off the chill air. From the tiny window, she could see the ocean below, bleak and foreboding, low clouds blanketing the world to the horizon. Light snow was sporadically whipped into a frenzy by sudden gusts of frigid air.

She went to the trapdoor and tried to open it but it held fast, as she knew it would. She knocked on the door, but got no response, so she sat back down and tried to think of a way out of her predicament.

An hour later, she heard the sound of boots on stone from below, followed by the scraping of metal on metal, and then the trapdoor opened. One of Zuhl's brutes eyed her with a menacing grin and grunted while motioning for her to follow him.

With a sigh of resignation, Abigail wrapped a fur around her and followed the big man down the corkscrew staircase to the level below. There were four guards in the chamber. Each stared at her in open challenge—she ignored them.

The brute led her through the halls of a keep until he came to a large set of double doors, which opened to a sparsely furnished and somewhat cold room, though warmer than the little tower room where she'd awoken. Zuhl sat at a table with an assortment of foods arrayed before him, all served on fine porcelain dishes.

"Good morning, Lady Abigail," he said, dismissing the soldier with a gesture. "I trust you slept well."

She scanned the room, looking for a weapon or an opportunity to escape, anything she could use against Zuhl, but found nothing. She decided to be bold. The temperature of the room didn't warrant the fur blanket, so she shrugged it off, letting it fall to the floor without a second look. Then she walked to the table and sat down.

"Well enough, considering," she said as she took an empty plate from a stack and started piling food on it.

He almost smiled, but not quite.

"I have a number of questions for you," he said. "Most are simply matters of curiosity, a few are of strategic importance. You will answer them all, one way or another."

Abigail shrugged as she took a big bite of biscuit dripping with blackberry jam. "Maybe," she said around a mouthful.

He stopped and looked at her, not a simple glance, but really looked at her as if seeing into the essence of her being. Abigail was reminded of Alexander and the way he could look into a person and assess their true nature.

"What were you thinking when you jumped from your wyvern and attacked me in midflight?" Zuhl asked, his penetrating gaze searching her face intently as he awaited her answer.

"I was thinking it was the only way to kill you," Abigail answered, preparing another biscuit.

"The odds of success were so slim as to be improbable," Zuhl said. "Failure was almost certain death, yet you didn't hesitate. Why?"

"I told you, it was the only way," Abigail said.

"I don't understand," Zuhl said, shaking his head slightly, a deep frown creasing his pale brow.

"What choice did I have?" Abigail said. "No one else had any chance at all against that dragon. I was the only one who could do what needed to be done, so I did."

"You could have retreated, you could have sued for peace and offered terms for a truce, you could have ignored the dragon and focused on the land battle, you could have sent your Sky Knights against me, you could have surrendered, or better yet, you could have stayed on Ruatha where you belong, yet you chose to engage me when you are clearly not my equal."

"I cut you in half, didn't I?"

"That you did," Zuhl said. "I must admit, I would have been more cautious had I been aware that your brother had given you the Thinblade, another perplexing development. Why would he do such a thing?"

"He didn't think he could be both the Sovereign of the Seven Isles and the King of Ruatha at the same time."

"Why not?" Zuhl asked, leaning in with great interest. "Not that I accept his claim as sovereign mind you, but I'm very curious about his motivations. Were I in his shoes, I would never relinquish either the Sovereign Stone or the Thinblade."

"No, I don't suppose you would," Abigail said with a little smile.

"Why would he?"

"It created a conflict," Abigail said. "He couldn't rule Ruatha as king and still expect the other island kings to accept him as sovereign."

Zuhl's frown grew even deeper.

"Power is not about seeking the acceptance of those you rule, it's about imposing your will upon them, whether they like it or not," he said.

This time it was Abigail's turn to shake her head. "You don't get it, do you? He doesn't want power any more than I do … he just wants to live his life and be left alone."

Zuhl stared at her as if trying to reconcile two versions of reality that couldn't coexist before shaking his head in frustration.

"Back to your reasons for engaging me," he said. "My questions for your brother are best saved for him, should we have the pleasure of a conversation before I claim victory over him. Why would you risk your life when you had such little chance of success?"

Abigail put her biscuit down and fixed Zuhl with a glare. "Because I'd committed good people to a battle that they were going to lose as long as you were riding Ixabrax. Killing you was the only way to save them from defeat ... and the only way to get to your ships."

Zuhl shook his head again. "Your motivations escape me. I don't understand why you would risk your life for the safety of your subjects—their place is to serve you, your place is to command them, not die for them."

"You have it exactly backwards, Zuhl," Abigail said. "My place is to serve them, to protect them from the ambitions of tyrants like you."

"I don't comprehend you at all," Zuhl said. "Things I don't understand make me uneasy."

"Good," Abigail said, punctuating her statement with another bite of biscuit.

He glared at her for a moment before composing himself again and beginning a new line of questioning.

"You mentioned Ixabrax. Why didn't you kill him? Why set him free? How could you know that he wouldn't turn against you the moment you cut his collar?"

"I didn't," Abigail said with a shrug, "but I trusted my instincts and it paid off. He sank one of your ships for me."

"You gave up your one chance to strike on a hunch?"

"Yeah, I guess I did," Abigail said. "I met a dragon once before ... she was a magnificent creature. It turned my stomach to think of her in a collar like Ixabrax, so I cut him loose."

"You take great risks without due consideration of the consequences," Zuhl said.

"I've heard that before ... from my father no less," Abigail said. "Tell me something, why are you doing this? What do you want?"

"I want what everyone wants, immortality and the worship of every living soul," Zuhl said.

Abigail stared at him, mouth agape for a moment before she burst out laughing. "You've got to be kidding," she said, still laughing.

"No, I'm not," he said, looking somewhat offended by her impertinence. "Don't you want to live forever?"

Abigail frowned and cocked her head to the side for a moment. "Huh, I hadn't really thought about it. Death is just a part of life, part of the natural cycle. Don't get me wrong, I don't want to die, certainly not anytime soon, but I've always known my life would end someday."

"What if it didn't have to?" Zuhl asked, leaning in again. "What would you do for the chance to live forever?"

"I don't really know," Abigail said.

"I do," Zuhl said. "I'll do anything I have to."

"I guess that's the difference between us," Abigail said. "There are some things I love more than my own life."

Zuhl looked down at his plate, shaking his head again.

"Why did your brother commit the bulk of his forces to defending Fellenden?" he asked, changing the subject abruptly.

"Because your barbarians were killing innocent people," Abigail said.

"But Fellenden is nothing to you or your brother," Zuhl said. "Phane is your enemy. He's attacked you again and again, yet you declare war on me when I've done nothing to provoke you. Again, I don't understand."

"It's really very simple, Zuhl, you were hurting innocent people and we had the power to stop you, so we did."

"When doing so puts your own people in jeopardy? Even now, Phane is building his strength in Warrenton. When the spring thaw comes, he'll overrun your forces and his Lancers will be free to wreak havoc throughout northern Ruatha, all while your forces are mired in Fellenden."

"Alexander's looking at the bigger picture," Abigail said. "If we'd permitted you to build your fleet, we wouldn't have had a chance in the long run. He made a sound strategic decision with full knowledge of the potential consequences."

"Perhaps," Zuhl said, nodding slightly. "At least such an explanation is based on reason, more so than some of his other decisions. Where is he now?"

"I wish I knew," Abigail said, putting her biscuit down. "He was going to talk to a dragon, last I knew, but he could be anywhere by now."

"Tanis? The bronze dragon who rules in the Pinnacles?"

"No, Bragador, on Tyr," Abigail said.

"The chromatic dragons—why would he go to them?" Zuhl asked. "They're even less interested in the affairs of men than the bronze dragons."

Abigail realized she'd said too much. Zuhl didn't know about the Nether Gate, and she had no intention of being the one to tell him.

"Isabel's been infected by one of Phane's minions," Abigail said. "Alexander's gone to collect the ingredients for a potion that will heal her." A half-truth made for a better lie than an outright fiction.

"He sends his sister to wage war against me, leaves his home to fend for itself, and ventures off to bargain with a dragon to save his woman?" Zuhl scoffed. "I find that hard to believe. No man worthy of being called a Lord would make such poor strategic judgments. There must be more—he must have another purpose."

"If he does, I don't know what it is," Abigail lied.

Zuhl scrutinized her closely, his eyes narrowing before he nodded.

"Your brother has a gift for seeing colors," Zuhl said. "As I understand it, his magical vision offers him insight into the nature and intentions of others. Quite a powerful skill. When I learned of it, I developed a spell that accomplishes a similar result, though through very different means. I cast that spell just before you arrived. Up until now, you have answered my questions truthfully, but you just lied to me. Why?"

Abigail smiled and sat back, picking up her glass of juice. "There are some things we'd rather you didn't know," she said.

He almost smiled, although without any mirth. "Naturally," he said. "No matter. Once we arrive at Whitehall, I will have you interrogated properly. You will tell me everything I wish to know, and I assure you it won't be pleasant."

"You can torture me if you like," Abigail said, "but it won't do you any good." She tried to remain calm even as she quailed inside. The prospect of torture was terrifying.

"You just lied to me again," Zuhl said.

"Did you really expect me to answer all of your questions?" she said.

"Of course not," he said. "As for torture, that's such a crude means of persuasion, and not entirely reliable. No, I have a far more effective method in mind. You see, in the northern wastes of the Isle of Zuhl lives a most remarkable creature. Those who live in the area call it an ice slug. Harmless creature, but the slime it exudes has a most powerful effect when imbibed. It seems to release all inhibitions, eliminate all guile, and induce a state of mind that is utterly incapable of lying. So you see, there is really no point in attempting to deceive me, as I will have the answers I seek."

"Maybe ... but not today," Abigail said.

"Very well, perhaps another line of questioning is in order," Zuhl said. "What did Alexander find in the Stone's Wizard's Den?"

"I have no idea," Abigail said. "I haven't seen him in a while. Truth is, I didn't even know he'd gotten into the Wizard's Den yet."

"Fair enough," Zuhl said. "I have reason to believe there is a book of great interest to me, either in the Stone's Wizard's Den or the sovereigns' library within the Reishi Keep. I intend to make a trade with your brother ... you for that book. Provided he delivers it to me before the winter solstice."

"I don't know what you're talking about," Abigail said, "but if this book you're looking for is where you think it is, I doubt Alexander will ever give it to you."

"Fortunately, I have a contingency," Zuhl said. "I'm a firm believer in backup plans and redundancies. If I don't receive the book by the solstice, then I will consume your life force in my yearly rejuvenation sacrifice. Either way, I get something I need."

Abigail swallowed hard, trying to calculate how many days remained before the shortest day of the year.

"You have just over three weeks," Zuhl said. "That should be more than enough time. Not to worry, I've already sent word to your forces. I trust they will relay the message with haste."

A thousand questions and concerns vied for attention within her mind but one rose to the top of the list. "What's so important about this book?"

"Ah, I'm glad you asked," Zuhl said. "I must say, Lady Abigail, I'm enjoying our conversation immensely. There's no one on the entire Isle of Zuhl who would dare to address me so casually, so simply. I find it refreshing ... novel even.

"I am very old, seven hundred and twenty-eight years old, to be precise. Over the centuries, I have collected a great number of very rare works, many unique. I'm especially interested in the journals of wizards. You would be surprised the things you can learn about magic from the musings of long-dead wizards.

"One in particular has haunted me for centuries. A wizard named Jacinth. He was the lead assistant to Malachi Reishi in his research laboratory. He spoke of a spell that Malachi was developing in his last days, a spell that Jacinth had helped him create, a spell that I simply must have. Jacinth wrote that he watched Malachi pen the spellbook himself and saw him store it away inside his Wizard's Den. He called it the 'Lich Book,' a spell of such potency that Malachi killed all of the researchers who helped him develop it once it was complete, even Jacinth. The last entry tells how Malachi permitted Jacinth to take a poison that would kill him painlessly in honor of his years of loyal service.

"This book contains a spell that is the key to true immortality, and I must have it."

"And you think Alexander is just going to give it to you?"

"He will if he values your life," Zuhl said. "If not, then I'll find a way to take it from him."

"I doubt it," Abigail said. "Just for the sake of argument, how is this immortality spell supposed to work?"

"Therein lies the genius," Zuhl said, sitting back comfortably. "The spell transfers one's life essence into a phylactery, a specially prepared item designed to store a soul, while animating the now dead body with the person's awareness, will, and power. Through death, eternal life is found. It's perfect. Since your body is already dead, it can never be killed. Not only would this spell grant immortality, but near invulnerability as well. It is the god-maker spell that I have been searching for all my life."

"If Alexander actually has this book, and he has any idea what it does, I guarantee he won't trade," Abigail said.

"Perhaps not," Zuhl said, standing and placing a vial of slightly blue liquid on the table. "This is dragon draught; it will ward you against the cold."

"What cold?" Abigail asked, suddenly wary.

"We're leaving Irondale for Whitehall," Zuhl said. "You'll ride with me on Izzulft. I assure you, the journey will kill you without the dragon draught."

Abigail hesitated, looking at the vial, then at Zuhl.

"I can have that rather large man who brought you here make you drink it if you prefer."

She scowled at him but quaffed the potion with a sigh of resignation. A chill flowed into her, filling her with a coldness that seemed to encompass her entire body, yet without discomfort.

He led her to a battlement where Izzulft was waiting and shackled her to his saddle before mounting up behind her and launching into the cold grey sky.

Chapter 10

"Jack, come quickly," Chloe said, "he's starting to wake. I can hear his thoughts again."

"Go easy, Alexander," Jack said. "You've been through a lot. There's no rush."

Their voices sounded far away, muffled. He couldn't open his eyes but he was starting to see things anyway. It didn't make any sense. Nothing made any sense. Confusion swirled inside his cottony mind. Consciousness slowly started to take hold, thoughts began to form, pushing aside the gauzy feeling in his head.

He mumbled something unintelligible, then realized his tongue was swollen and dry. Someone drizzled cool water into his mouth. He struggled to swallow, working the muscles of his throat to overcome the scratchy dryness. More water allowed him to swallow, but he choked, coughing weakly until someone helped him sit up.

Images of his surroundings were becoming clearer. He was in a room. It looked familiar. Jack and Chloe were there with him. A small dragon sat at the foot of his bed, resting her chin on the footboard and looking at him with big, golden eyes.

Someone put a cup to his lips. He grabbed it and tried to tip it back, but the hand holding it resisted.

"Slowly," Jack said. "Drink a little at a time."

The voice sounded familiar. A small swallow sent him into a coughing fit. As soon as he regained his composure, he reached for the cup again. His vision was sharper now, even though his eyes were still closed.

"All right, Alexander, lie back and try to get some rest," Jack said. "Now that your fever has broken, you need to sleep."

He wanted to protest, tried to resist, but the hand gently pushing him back into the bed was too strong for him, and he couldn't seem to form words. Moments later, he was asleep.

***

Alexander woke feeling groggy and thirsty and hungry. He tried to open his eyes but they were crusted over with dried tears. Carefully, gingerly, he started to rub them clean, but before he could get them open, the room around him came into clear focus. Jack was there, sleeping in a chair next to his bed. Chloe was there as well, sitting on the back of another chair, watching him intently. The dragon was there too, sleeping at the foot of his bed.

He cleared his throat and worked up enough saliva to swallow. Chloe buzzed into a ball of light and floated down in front of his face.

"Can you hear me, My Love?" she asked out loud.

"Chloe, what happened? Where are we?" he mumbled.

"You were stabbed through the leg," Chloe said.

Jack woke and sat forward.

"My head's so fuzzy," Alexander said.

"You've been in a delirium for over a week," Jack said. "Lady Bragador said your wound became infected, causing a fever that nearly killed you."

"Bragador?" he mumbled. "Dragons … We're on Tyr."

"Yes," Jack said.

"Where's Isabel?" Alexander asked.

"We'll talk about that later," Jack said, after an uncharacteristic hesitation.

Reality slammed back into Alexander. His mind focused as the events leading up to his current predicament played out in his memory. He sat up, ignoring the stab of pain in his leg, and his vision sharpened. He could see more clearly than he'd been able to see since Shivini blinded him. His all around sight was more detailed and vibrant than he remembered it.

"Jack, tell me where Isabel is," Alexander said.

Jack sighed. "She left. We're not sure where she went."

"What?! Why would she leave? How did she leave? We're on an island!"

"She took the ship," Jack said, answering the easiest of his questions.

"I don't understand," Alexander said. "Isabel wouldn't leave me like this."

"She left to protect you, My Love," Chloe said. "The darkness within her was becoming a danger to you. So she left."

"What aren't you telling me?"

Chloe buzzed into a ball of light and started flying in a circle in front of him.

"Tell me, Little One."

She stopped and hovered in front of him. "The night you were wounded, you slipped into a fitful and feverish sleep. I woke to find Isabel standing over you with a knife in her hand, poised to strike. Her eyes were vacant and empty, like she wasn't really there, wasn't in control of herself. I cried out for her to stop and she came to her senses. When she realized what she was about to do, she became distraught, frantic. She looked so afraid, My Love. She left that night, saying she couldn't be trusted anymore by those she loved."

"Why didn't you stop her?!" Alexander demanded.

"How? I'm three inches tall," Chloe shot back. "Besides, I didn't want to stop her. She'd become a threat to your life, and I knew you wouldn't be able to bring yourself to admit it. We both love you, Alexander. And we both did what we must to protect you. She left and I let her go. What's more, I'm proud of her for what she did. Leaving you hurt her, but she did it anyway because staying would have hurt *you*."

Alexander started to get up, but the stabbing pain in his leg stopped him cold. He gasped at the sudden intensity of it, breathing in short, quick breaths for a moment while he regained his senses. The wound was bad. He wouldn't be going anywhere anytime soon.

"Take it easy, Alexander," Jack said. "You'll tear your wound open."

"I'm sorry, Little One," Alexander said, through the pain. "I didn't mean to blame you."

"I know, My Love," Chloe said. "Isabel will come back to you. I know it in my heart."

"I hope you're right, Little One."

Anja sat up and put her head on the footboard, her tail flicking about excitedly.

Alexander looked at the baby dragon, so gangly and uncoordinated, yet beautiful, a promise of power to come.

"Anja? Is that you?" he asked.

She nodded enthusiastically, her tail flicking back and forth.

"She hasn't left your side, except to feed," Jack said, "and then only at her mother's insistence."

His senses finally intact, Alexander surveyed his surroundings. He was lying in a bed in his Wizard's Den. Hector and Horace were both there, silently watching over him, one guarding the door, the other sitting at the table. Outside the door was the cavern where he'd fought the pirates, recovered the Tyr Thinblade, saved Anja, and been stabbed through the leg by a wraithkin's dagger.

"How long have I been out?" he asked.

"Ten days," Jack said.

"I need to get to my magic circle."

"You'll tear your wound and set your recovery back by weeks," Jack said. "Bragador made me promise to keep you from getting up. She spent hours applying heat to your wound to kill the infection. Without her, you'd be dead. Just stay in bed and heal."

"I need to find out where Isabel went," Alexander said, choking back a lump in his throat.

"What if we put a circle around your bed?" Jack asked. "Would that work?"

Alexander thought about it for a moment. He'd seen magic circles of all different sizes—the only constants were the seven symbols carved between the dual circles.

"I don't see why not," Alexander said.

"Good," Jack said. "You lie back and relax. Hector, Horace, and I will make a magic circle in the middle of the floor, then move your bed inside it."

The three men worked, while Anja nosed about, trying to figure out what they were doing, but mostly just getting in the way. Alexander carefully inspected each symbol as they drew it on the floor, using the symbols inlaid in gold on his meditation table as guides. Once the circle was complete, they carefully carried Alexander's bed into the center of it.

Before he could begin his meditation, he had an odd sensation … a knowing came over him. Bragador was coming. Moments later, she entered the room in human form.

"Anja, it's time to feed," she said as she entered. "Ah, Alexander you've woken. You had us all worried for a time there."

"They tell me you saved my life," Alexander said. "I'm in your debt."

"Careful, Alexander," Bragador said. "Dragons take debts very seriously."

"As do I," he said. "Thank you. For helping me and for sheltering us."

"Perhaps we're even," Bragador said. "After all, you did save my troublesome daughter." Anja frowned until she saw the genuine smile Bragador gave her. "It seems she's been spending all of her time here when she should be feeding and learning how to fly."

"Anja, I'll be fine," Alexander said, gently stroking the baby dragon's brow. "And I'm not going anywhere. You can come see me later."

She nuzzled his foot and then followed her mother out of the Wizard's Den.

"I'll be back in a while, Alexander," Bragador said. "We have much to discuss."

"I look forward to it," he said as she disappeared around the corner of the door. Then he turned to Jack and asked, "Has anything else happened that I need to know about?"

"Not really," Jack said. "Since Isabel left, everything's been pretty quiet around here. We're a good distance from the dragons' main chambers so they haven't come around much, except for Bragador and Anja. Mostly we've been watching over you and hoping you'd wake up."

Alexander nodded, then turned his thoughts to the state of the world when he'd arrived at the Spires. Battles were raging all around the Seven Isles. There were so many things he needed to do and so much he didn't know. And he'd failed in his quest to recover the keystone. From the pain in his leg, he knew it would be weeks, maybe even months, before he would be strong enough to travel. He decided to use the time wisely.

"I'm going to look in on Isabel," he said, "maybe have a look around the Seven Isles while I'm at it. I'll probably be a while."

"If you have a chance, could you see how Abigail's doing?" Jack asked.

Alexander nodded with a smile, then laid back and closed his eyes. It took some time to overcome the dull throbbing pain in his leg, but eventually he was adrift on the firmament. It seemed different somehow, more familiar.

With a thought, he was floating in the cabin of a ship at sea. Isabel was sleeping fitfully in the bunk. For several moments, Alexander just watched her sleep, grateful that she was all right but saddened that she felt it necessary to leave his side. He still didn't quite understand. They belonged together; she knew that as well as he did.

He slipped into her dreams and found himself in his Wizard's Den, watching Isabel stand over his restless body. She was dreaming of the night she'd left. Her eyes were vacant and distant, her hands held a dagger raised over his heart. She brought the dagger a few inches higher, preparing to strike, and then she stabbed down, hard. Just before it plunged into his heart, she woke, ejecting Alexander from her mind.

He found himself floating in the cabin once again, watching her in the darkness as she cried herself back to sleep. He felt so helpless. She was all alone and Phane's magic was claiming her free will. He could only imagine how scared she must be, but he was coming to understand her decision to leave. He tried to put himself in her position, asking himself what he would do to protect her under similar circumstances. She'd done the only thing she could have. That left him with the question of where she was headed.

He rose up through the ship, high into the sky, until he recognized the shape of the island she was sailing toward. The shock of it was so intense that he snapped back to his body and sat up with a gasp. Pain from his wound stabbed into his leg, causing him to gasp again. Then he gently lay back down, focusing on his breathing until the agony subsided.

Jack was lying on the next bed over, staring at the ceiling. He turned to Alexander but said nothing.

"She's going to Karth," Alexander said quietly. "I wish I knew why."

"I can think of two possibilities," Jack said. "Neither is going to be easy to hear."

Alexander turned to Jack, frowning.

"Either she's under Phane's power or she's going to try to kill him," Jack said.

Alexander sighed, nodding. "I don't think he has control of her yet, but I saw her dream—it won't be long before he does."

"I'm sorry, Alexander," Jack said.

"Me too."

He closed his eyes and focused his mind. He knew where she was and that she was safe, that was enough for now. Several moments later he was floating on the firmament again. This time he thought of Abigail and found himself over a vast army on the march. They were escorting thousands of refugees toward Fellenden City. Abigail looked anxious but well enough. Anatoly was riding next to her.

With a flick of his mind he was at the ruined shipyards. They'd been totally burned to the ground. Huge burial mounds marked with Reishi, Ruathan, Ithilian, and Fellenden banners gave silent testimony to the losses she'd sustained. The thousands of barbarians scattered haphazardly across the battlefield, left for the scavengers to pick at, gave Alexander some measure of hope that Zuhl's horde, while formidable, wasn't invincible.

Next, he visited Blackstone Keep. He was alarmed to see people carrying lanterns for light. The magic of the Keep was failing, and quickly. Without its protections, it was just stone, easily destroyed by magic.

Alexander went to his message board and saw two messages. The first confirmed his fears. It read, "Keep's magic is failing." The second read, "Stalemate in Buckwold—Phane's forces growing slowly."

Alexander found Kelvin in his workshop. The large room was lit with a number of brightly glowing stones suspended from the ceiling by string. He was busy creating more of the glow stones, presumably for use by others within the Keep.

With a flick of his mind, Alexander was in Buckwold. His father's men had built a formidable-looking berm wall that stretched from the ocean to the foothills of the Pinnacles. It looked sufficient to blunt the initial assault of the

Lancers, but it probably wouldn't hold for long once the enemy decided to attack. He thought of Warrenton and the world flickered by for an instant, then he was over the captured city. Lancers were camped all around its walls, and ships flying the Andalian banner were docked in port. Phane was managing to get some of his men through the blockade. A closer look revealed that two wizards stood guard atop towers overlooking the port. Any attack by the Sky Knights would be met with significant resistance.

Next, he went to Crescent Bay. Zuhl had his seven enormous ships docked in his port and was busy finishing construction of his fleet. Ice floes were already blocking passage into or out of the port, so Alexander breathed a sigh of relief. Zuhl would be unable to move troops until the spring thaw. At least he had time.

He opened his blind eyes and looked to Jack with a smile.

"Abigail is well. She's marching toward Fellenden City, and the shipyard is destroyed."

"Thank you, Alexander," Jack said. "I've been worried about her."

Alexander stopped, frowning in puzzlement as the sensation came over him again.

"Bragador and Anja are coming," he said.

Jack looked at him quizzically, then at the door. Several moments later, Bragador entered, trailing Anja behind her.

"Hello Alexander, I'm glad you're awake," Bragador said.

"Please, come in," he said, motioning to a chair.

"Thank you," she said, drawing the chair closer to his bed. Anja put her chin on the foot of his bed, looking at him with her big, golden, catlike eyes. "As I understand it, your wife has left. Had we known of your ship, we could have stopped her."

"I know, but it's probably best you didn't," Alexander said. "She's succumbing to Phane's magic." He stopped, swallowing the lump in his throat.

"I'm sorry to hear that," Bragador said. "We tried to find the pirates who stole the keystone, but they slipped past us in the night, no doubt with the aid of magic. It seems that Phane will have his prize."

"That leaves only one keystone," Alexander said, "and I think I know who has it."

"Perhaps we could be of some assistance in that regard."

"I thought you didn't want to get involved," he said.

"We don't," Bragador said, "but it may be necessary. If what you say about this Nether Gate is true, then it cannot be allowed to fall into the wrong hands. And the fact that Phane sent his agents to steal from us is incentive enough to work against him."

"What did you have in mind?"

"If you'll tell me where the final keystone is, I will send a dragon to retrieve it."

"As I said, I think I know where it is, but I can't be sure," Alexander said. "I believe the Princess of Fellenden is attempting to take it to Ithilian. She's not the enemy, but the man she's traveling with may be. My magic tells me he's evil, but I don't think Lacy is aware of his true purpose."

"Where can we find them?"

"They were in the south of Fellenden when last I looked," Alexander said, "but they could be anywhere by now. I'll have to look again."

"I'll wait," Bragador said. "We're anxious to rectify the situation."

Alexander closed his eyes and took a deep breath. It took several minutes before he was free of his body again. He thought of the young woman with strawberry-blond hair and his awareness coalesced in the hold of a ship. She was sitting on a pallet in the brig with a thin, raggedy-looking blanket wrapped around her and looking miserable. Alarm coursed through Alexander as he took in the scene. She was a prisoner and she was wounded.

He looked to the next cell over and saw the man she'd been traveling with … the man without a conscience. A frantic search of the room revealed that the little black box was stored in the footlocker against the wall, along with the rest of their belongings.

Puzzled, Alexander began to systematically search the ship. His alarm grew when he saw the banner of Zuhl flying on the mainmast. The men manning the ship were all big, brutish soldiers, wearing furs and carrying crude, but effective-looking weapons. Then he saw something he didn't expect, something that nearly made him lose his focus—a wraithkin. He would recognize the colors of Phane's created agents anywhere, man mixed with darkness.

But why would Zuhl have a wraithkin aboard?

It made no sense.

He searched more carefully, scrutinizing the men, one by one. When he saw the Regency crest tattooed on the arm of one of the men, his puzzlement grew. Phane and Zuhl wouldn't be in league with each other. Zuhl would never agree to it and Phane would double-cross Zuhl the moment the opportunity presented itself.

As he was floating there, trying to solve the mystery, a sailor walked straight up to him, as if he could see him, and smiled.

"Hello, Alexander," he said, his voice not quite human, his colors altogether inhuman, "so nice of you to visit."

"Rankosi?"

The sailor's smile broadened.

"The keystone is nearly in my grasp," Rankosi said, "and there's nothing you can do about it. All I have to do is wait for Phane's ruse to play out," he said, motioning to the rest of the crew, "and I'll have my prize. What's that? Oh, I almost forgot … you can't speak."

Rankosi walked away laughing.

Chapter 11

Alexander rose into the sky until he could see the ship. It was sailing in a circle in the ocean between Ithilian, Fellenden, and Tyr. He returned to his body, confused and disturbed.

"I can say for certain that she's on a ship in the open ocean due west of here," Alexander said. "The rest is less clear."

"How so?" Jack asked.

"The ship is manned by Regency soldiers pretending to be Zuhl's barbarians," Alexander said. "Lacy is in the brig. There's a wraithkin onboard. And the shade is there as well."

"The shade is on that ship, with the princess and the keystone?" Bragador asked, slightly alarmed.

Alexander nodded, frowning.

"Why hasn't he taken the keystone?" Jack asked.

"That's a very good question," Alexander said. "Maybe it has something to do with the box. Mage Jalal said he couldn't see the keystone, even though he was able to locate the other two. Maybe the box won't open for the shade."

"Mage Gamaliel might know more," Jack said.

"Probably," Alexander said. "I'll see if I can send him a message."

"For now, its location is sufficient," Bragador said. "I'll dispatch Aedan to retrieve Princess Lacy and the keystone at once."

"Who's Aedan?" Alexander asked.

"He's the dark green dragon that met you when you first arrived," Bragador said. "He's well suited to the task."

"Lacy is innocent in all of this," Alexander said. "Please don't harm her."

"Of course," Bragador said, getting up to leave.

Anja looked at her, then back at Alexander before curling up at the foot of his bed and closing her eyes.

Bragador stopped at the door, frowning slightly at her daughter before she left.

Alexander stared at the ceiling while the frustration of his predicament built in his gut. The world was fighting a war that he was supposed to be leading and he was helpless to act. He'd failed to retrieve the keystone … for the second time. And Isabel had left him. The last remaining shade was aboard the ship with the third and final keystone, his last chance to quickly end the threat of the Nether Gate, and he still didn't understand the game Phane was playing.

Why send soldiers pretending to serve Zuhl to capture Lacy when he could have just as easily brought her to Karth in chains? Alexander had too many questions and too few answers.

Then there was Siduri. He didn't know what to make of him, didn't know if he should believe him … and yet he did. As fantastical as his story was, Alexander believed every word of it, and that scared him even more. He wanted to talk to Jack about the first adept but that would only give rise to questions within the inquisitive mind of his friend, questions that he couldn't answer.

He needed counsel, so he decided to turn to the only people he could trust to remain absolutely silent about his experience—the sovereigns.

"I'll be a while," Alexander said, as he touched the Sovereign Stone.

He briefed the Reishi Council thoroughly, leaving nothing out since he last spoke to them. He told them of the contents of the Wizard's Den, the trip to Tyr, the addition of the Reishi Protectorate to his ranks, the destruction of Zuhl's shipyards, the seven ships that managed to escape, the battle with the wraithkin and the pirates, the recovery of the Tyr Thinblade, his wound by wraithkin dagger, Anja, the loss of Mindbender, his uneasy alliance with Bragador, finding the blood of the earth, and his disturbing conversation with Siduri. Finally he told them about Isabel. He saved that information for last, not because it was the most important item on his very long list, but because it was the most painful.

When he finished, he sat back and hung his head, Isabel's absence once again threatening to overwhelm his composure. He understood why she left, might have done the same if he were in her shoes, but none of that undid the empty feeling it left inside him.

The table was silent for several moments.

"Much has transpired," Balthazar said.

Alexander nodded.

"Perhaps we should set aside those things about which we have no insight to offer," Balthazar said.

Alexander nodded again.

"The destruction of Zuhl's shipyard is a victory," the First Sovereign said. "His escape with seven ships is a defeat. The recovery of the Tyr Thinblade, your wound, the newfound loyalty of the Reishi Protectorate, and Isabel's decision to leave require no counsel. That leaves a long list of things we can offer you advice about."

"May we start with Mindbender?" Constantine asked, sitting forward with interest.

"Sure, but I'm not sure there's much to discuss," Alexander said. "In fact, I'd add that to the defeat column."

"I'm not so certain," Constantine said.

"Nor am I," Darius said. "Please describe the destruction of the sword in detail."

Alexander told them about the battle with the pirate wielding the Thinblade, how he'd been distracted by the crossbow bolt to the shoulder at just the wrong moment, how the ancient, sentient sword had been cleaved in two, and finally, about the lights that played across the cavern walls before seemingly soaking into him.

"You say the light expanded to fill the cavern?" Dominic asked.

"And then collapsed into you?" Constantine added.

"That's the way I remember it," Alexander said.

They looked at each other.

"If I might," Balthazar said. "A phrase from your conversation with Siduri caught my attention. He said 'a link with source requires a place to reside.' Is that correct?"

"I believe so," Alexander said. "What are you getting at?"

Balthazar looked to his son Dominic, who nodded. Then to Constantine, who nodded as well.

"It may be that the magic of Mindbender, or more precisely, Benesh Reishi's link with the firmament, now resides within you," Balthazar said.

"How can that be?" Alexander asked.

"The ways of magic are not always clear," Balthazar said. "We're still not certain on the specifics of how Benesh created the sword in the first place."

"One of the books we found in his tomb detailed a process for transferring a wizard's link with the firmament to an item," Alexander said. "The wizards said they thought an arch mage could be stripped of his link, which could then be used to create an item capable of allowing its wielder to command the firmament with the same level of power as the wizard who gave it his power."

"If that's how he created Mindbender, it explains why he died," Constantine said. "Without his link, the aging process would have overtaken him relatively quickly."

"It may also explain how the link transferred to Alexander," Dominic said. "Under normal circumstances, a link with the firmament is bound to a specific wizard or witch. In order to transfer his link to the sword, Benesh would have had to ensure that the link didn't dissipate the moment it was separated from him. He would have had to harden it, if you will, in order to protect it long enough to become one with the sword. How he accomplished such a thing is beyond my understanding, but it seems from your description that the link contained within the sword sought out a suitable place to reside once the sword could no longer contain it."

"So what do I do?" Alexander asked.

"Guard that book carefully," Balthazar said. "Its potential is difficult to ascertain, but Phane or Zuhl could probably find ways to use it."

"It's in the care of the Guild Mage," Alexander said, "He's studying it to see if we could make use of it. But getting back to Mindbender. Do you really think I have the sword's powers?"

"Probably not exactly," Constantine said. "While our understanding of the adept wizard is limited, we do know that you developed specific capabilities after surviving the mana fast. You may manifest the same talents the sword gave you or you may develop completely new capabilities, provided our speculation is accurate."

"The only way to know for certain is to experiment," Balthazar said. "I recommend you proceed with caution and deliberate care. This is uncharted territory."

"That certainly gives me something to think about," Alexander said.

"Be aware of anything different about your magic," Balthazar said. "Pay careful attention to the details of anything you experience differently than before."

Alexander cocked his head to the side and frowned, suddenly realizing that things had been slightly different with his magic.

"I used my clairvoyance before coming to consult you," he said. "The firmament felt somehow more familiar. I can't really explain it, but I felt more at home, more at ease. Also, my all around sight is sharper."

"Given your wound, you will have plenty of time to experiment," Balthazar said. "I recommend you spend some time every day using your clairvoyance. Attempt to use it in ways you haven't before. Look at the very small and the very large, explore the inner workings of the substance around you at the smallest level you can, see the entire Seven Isles as a whole, look within yourself and attempt to penetrate the realm of light. Stretch out with your mind and see what you find."

"I will," Alexander said. "I already have a lot to do on that score. There are a number of conflicts brewing that will flare as soon as spring comes. I want to provide my people with all the information I can before the fighting starts."

He stopped, staring at the table for a moment.

"This may be nothing, but twice now I've felt a knowing sensation prior to Bragador's arrival. It's not like the precognitive experiences I've had in the past, but more like a subtle awareness of the moments to come."

"Take note of any more such experiences you have," Balthazar said. "Study each one in detail, look for commonalities. Above all, determine how accurate your predictive abilities are. Such a power is formidable beyond words, provided it's reliable and accurate. Otherwise, it could very easily lead to your doom."

"I hadn't considered that," Alexander said.

"Perhaps we should spend some time discussing the dragons," Demetrius said.

"I concur," Balthazar said. "You said that a dragon was born near you, that you were the first person she saw when she emerged from her egg."

"Yes," Alexander said.

"Dragon mothers are very careful with their eggs," Balthazar said. "The first being a dragon sees will be imprinted on the beast for its whole life. This young dragon will have loyalty to you above all others. Her mother is aware of this, and no doubt, unhappy about it. Take great care, Alexander. Dragons are fiercely protective of their own, especially their young."

"I had no idea," Alexander said. "Anja spends all of her time nearby, but I just thought she was young and curious. What should I do?"

"Encourage her to follow her mother's guidance," Balthazar said. "Bragador knows better than any what Anja needs. Tread lightly, offer friendship but encourage her to assimilate into her own community. As for Bragador, take her counsel seriously and don't make any promises that you aren't willing to keep. Dragons have long memories and will always collect on debts owed."

"That leaves Siduri and the blood of the earth," Constantine said.

"Indeed," Balthazar said. He fixed Alexander with a very direct look before proceeding. "I am inclined to recommend that you refrain from using the blood of the earth."

The other sovereigns nodded in agreement, save Malachi, who started laughing.

Alexander ignored him. "How will I save Isabel without the potion?"

"I don't know," Balthazar said, "but the warning given by Siduri and the manner in which he appeared and disappeared cannot be taken lightly. Had I been aware of his existence, I would have reached out to him. That he never chose to contact me or any of the other sovereigns, yet chose to warn you in this matter, is of great significance."

"He's clearly a being of transcendent power," Constantine said. "The very idea of residing within the firmament for millennia is difficult to grasp, but the ability to manifest physically at the location of his choice and then melt back into the firmament is profound in the extreme. He may be the single most powerful creature alive in the world today. His guidance should be given serious consideration."

"His experience with the darkness is of vital importance as well," Dominic said. "Firsthand dealings with the Taker are unheard of. No wizard would be foolish enough to attempt such a thing … unless they were driven by abject desperation. The result of his bargain is instructive."

"I have no intention of making a bargain with the Taker," Alexander said.

"I didn't mean to suggest that you did," Dominic said. "I'm referring to the origin of the shades. That they were made by the Taker suggests that they could be unmade by him."

"But why would he do that?" Alexander asked, intrigued by the possibility.

"The darkness and the light operate according to their own rules," Balthazar said. "It may be that the fulfillment of Siduri's bargain could bring the shades to an end."

"You're saying that if Siduri died and surrendered to the Taker, the shades would be unmade?"

"I'm speculating," Balthazar said.

"How can I confirm your speculation?" Alexander asked, sitting forward.

The table fell silent until Malachi started laughing again.

"What do you know that could help me end the shades forever?" Alexander demanded.

Malachi shrugged. "Only speculations."

"Where can I confirm these speculations?"

"You could go ask the Taker, he might tell you the truth," Malachi said, laughing softly.

"Or you could ask the light," Demetrius said. "A creature such as Selaphiel might know."

"But how?" Alexander said. "I suppose I could ask Chloe, but I doubt she would know. And even if I could confirm your theory, how would I convince Siduri to subject himself to that?"

"You said he was distraught over what had been done to his children," Balthazar said. "Perhaps he would view it as saving them from a fate worse than death."

"If he believed me," Alexander said, "but how could the light ever accept the shades' souls after what they've done?"

"The light *is* forgiveness," Demetrius said, looking at Malachi sadly, "provided that your repentance is real. If Siduri's account is correct, the shades were children when the Taker touched them. As such, they are innocent and worthy of redemption."

"That's a lot of ifs," Alexander said. "I'm not even sure how I would tell Siduri, if I could confirm everything you've suggested."

"I would start in the firmament," Constantine said. "If he truly resides there, he will be aware of your presence. Perhaps you can communicate with him."

"Or maybe he's just a projection sent by Phane to toy with you," Malachi said.

"Silence," Alexander shot back, even as doubt crept into his thoughts. He needed the potion to save Isabel. What if Siduri was an illusion, a deception wielded by Phane to prevent him from saving her?

The Sixth Sovereign sat back, looking smug.

Alexander stood, glaring at Malachi.

"Thank you, gentlemen," he said. "I'll pursue confirmation of your speculations and seek out Siduri."

Chapter 12

Alexander soared on the wind high over the ocean, shadowing Aedan as the big, dark green dragon coasted gracefully over his target. Alexander had been waiting for this. He'd been intent on watching this encounter from the moment Bragador sent her agent to retrieve the little black box and Princess Lacy.

They were up high ... so high Alexander could just barely make out the ship below. A ship that seemed to be sailing in a giant circle out of the way of normal shipping channels as if it was waiting for something.

The dragon banked and rolled into a dive, accelerating with terrifying quickness. Alexander stayed with him as he let gravity pull him toward his objective. With the sun at his back, the ship's crew was completely unaware of his sudden approach.

At the last possible moment, Aedan flared his wings, breaking his free-fall and sending a gust of wind into the sails sufficient to cause the entire ship to pitch to one side, causing many of the crew to lose their footing and go down.

He fluidly transformed into a human as he landed on the deck of the ship, striding to the first crewman still standing. "Where's the princess?" he demanded.

"I don't know," the crewman said.

Aedan grabbed him by the lapel and threw him overboard, locking eyes with the next nearest crewman.

"You there," he said, pointing at the man, "where's the princess?"

The man turned and ran.

Then Alexander saw him. He was poking his head up through a hatch from below decks. The possessed crewman smiled with gleeful malice as he came up to the main deck. In a crouch, he started toward Aedan.

Alexander could see the wrongness of his colors, he could see the darkness, but he couldn't warn Aedan.

Rankosi approached the shapeshifted dragon, smiling.

"I'll tell you where she is," he said. "All I ask is that you spare my life."

Alexander felt a sense of chilling helplessness penetrate his entire being. Rankosi took a step. Then another. One final step and he was close enough. He reached out and touched Aedan, clutching at his arm.

The dragon frowned with sudden anger, reaching for him, but it was too late. Rankosi flowed from the crewman into Aedan.

Alexander watched an epic struggle transpire in the colors of the two beings, but the shade won out, finally subjugating Aedan's free will and possessing the dragon completely.

He looked up at Alexander and smiled wickedly. "Oh, this is much better," he said, grabbing the frightened crewman by the throat, lifting him off the deck and leaping onto the railing before launching into the air over the ocean, transforming into a dragon in moments. Still holding the crewman by the throat, he flipped the man's legs into his mouth and bit them off at the waist before casting his screaming torso into the ocean.

Aedan, possessed by Rankosi, gained altitude and distance from the ship where Lacy Fellenden was being held captive.

Alexander slipped back into the firmament, then returned to the Wizard's Den.

"Little One, will you tell Bragador that I have grave news."

"Yes, My Love," Chloe said, floating up and kissing him on the cheek before spinning into a ball of light and vanishing.

Bragador arrived several minutes later.

"Thank you for coming," Alexander said.

"What news?"

"Aedan has been possessed by the shade Rankosi," he said.

"Impossible!" Bragador said.

"I just watched it happen," Alexander said.

"You are mistaken," Bragador said, "and I intend to prove it." She turned on her heel and left.

***

"I'm not sure if I can do this," Alexander said, more to himself than anyone.

"I believe in you, My Love," Chloe said.

"You said the sovereigns were only speculating about Mindbender's power transferring to you," Jack said, "and even then, they didn't know if you'd develop the same abilities the sword gave you. Maybe you're trying to do the wrong thing."

"Or maybe I just can't make it work because I'm stuck in this bed," Alexander said. "I just can't seem to make myself believe I'm in a fight enough to project an illusion."

"You've been trying for days, My Love," Chloe said. "Maybe you should just rest for a while."

"Maybe you're right. I'm not getting anywhere, anyway," he said, closing his eyes and relaxing into the bed that had become his home since his injury.

He relaxed his body and cleared his mind like he had so many times in the past prior to slipping into the firmament, but this time he simply let his mind wander, allowing the images to play across his mind's eye. He thought of Isabel, trying to remember exactly what she looked like, her chestnut-brown hair, her piercing green eyes and her perfect smile. He missed her terribly, but after seeing her nightmares, he'd come to terms with her decision. She was trying to protect him even though it hurt her as much as it hurt him.

He was looking at her in his mind's eye, seeing her in perfect detail, dressed in her riding armor, wearing her sword, the medallion of Glen Morillian around her neck, when he heard Jack gasp.

Alexander's eyes snapped open, and for just a moment, barely a blink, Isabel was standing in the room looking at him ... then she vanished. Alexander swallowed hard, his mind working furiously to comprehend what had just happened.

"Did you see her, too?" he asked.

Jack nodded.

"Lady Reishi appeared for just a moment, then vanished just as quickly," Hector said.

"But she didn't have any colors," Alexander said, realization flooding into him. "She was just an illusion."

"I don't understand, My Love," Chloe said.

"I've been going about this all wrong," Alexander said. "I've been trying to make illusions the same way I did when I had Mindbender, but the sword depended on my mindset—I had to believe I was in a fight for it to work. What if that mindset was only necessary because the power was bound to a sword, a weapon?"

"So you're saying you just projected that image of Isabel," Jack said.

Alexander nodded. "I was thinking about her, trying to see her in my mind, and then she was here."

"So you've just been doing it wrong," Jack said.

"Seems so," Alexander said. "I'm going to try again …" He looked to the door. "Anja's coming."

A moment later, the young dragon stuck her head inside and squeezed through the door into the Wizard's Den.

"You're almost too big to fit through the door, Anja," Alexander said, as she put her head on the bed, looking up at him with her big golden eyes. He rubbed her head affectionately.

"Have you fed today?"

She nodded.

"Does your mother know you're here?"

She shook her head.

"Anja, you shouldn't wander off without telling your mother where you're going," Alexander said. She whined slightly.

"That's good advice," Bragador said from the doorway. "I figured I'd find her here."

"Anja, go with your mother," Alexander said. "You have lessons to complete."

She whined again but reluctantly went to the door, squeezing through into the cave.

"If you keep coming in here, you're going to get stuck," Bragador said, as they left to attend to Anja's instruction.

"What are you going to do about her when we leave?" Jack asked.

"I don't know," Alexander said. "She can't come with us, but I'm afraid she's going to be sad when we go."

"She's resilient," Chloe said. "Her feelings will heal in time."

***

"That was much better," Jack said when Alexander opened his eyes.

"I still couldn't hold it for very long," Alexander said.

He'd been practicing with his illusions for days. Without the sword, he found that he could only cast an illusion when he was in a meditative state, and then only by carefully visualizing the illusion he desired in minute detail. It took a tremendous amount of concentration and focus to succeed, but he was getting better. At first he could only make projections of things or people he knew well. Isabel was the easiest for him because he could see her in his mind so clearly.

With some practice, he was able to conjure an image of himself, though it took a lot of work to get it right. Jack was his test subject. The bard carefully scrutinized each projection for detail, making notes and observations to help Alexander improve the authenticity.

At first, he was only able to create static images, still and lifeless, though with increasingly real detail, until Jack proclaimed that he couldn't tell Alexander's projection of himself from the real thing.

As days stretched into weeks, Alexander practiced with an almost single-mindedness determination to master his new talent. He was helpless to act until his wound was healed, so he was intent on using this time to some constructive end.

After he'd pushed his illusion practice as far as he could for the day, always a painful proposition, he practiced using his clairvoyance. At first, he explored the Seven Isles, paying particular attention to remote and unexplored areas. While fascinating in the extreme, Alexander didn't believe that such practice was helping to expand his clairvoyance, so he decided to take the sovereigns' suggestion and explore the nature of the world itself.

First he rose straight up through the mountain, floating over the volcano that was sputtering orange fire at the sky, then he rose through the clouds and higher. He kept going until he could see the entire world, outlines of several of the Seven Isles visible through the clouds. Alexander marveled at the calm of it—so peaceful, so tranquil. He turned his attention to the moon, traversing the distance in a blink, exploring the barren and lifeless rock for a few minutes before going to the sun. He spent the better part of a day exploring the space around the world before turning his attention to the very small.

He started by exploring his own body, examining bone and muscle and organs in detail before going smaller, drilling into the substance of the world and examining it at its most basic levels. Eventually, he reached the point where substance formed. He looked at the most basic building blocks of the world, substance so small it could only be viewed with magic, no human eye could see something so minute, yet Alexander was looking at these basic building blocks in detail, seeing how they were constructed in seemingly endless variation yet composed of only two opposing forces, coupled together to form all that is. Over the days that followed his discovery of the basic structure of substance, Alexander spent many hours wondering about the things he'd seen.

Over the weeks, Alexander watched Anja grow. She grew until she could no longer fit into the Wizard's Den. She started sleeping right outside the door, with her head and neck stretched out on the floor so she could still be close to Alexander. Each morning, Bragador would come to collect her and take her to her lessons, teaching her how to fly, hunt, fight, speak, and think like a dragon. Alexander encouraged her to spend time with her mother and the rest of the dragons whenever possible. He'd grown so fond of her, but he also understood with painful clarity that she would have to remain on the dragon isle when he left, for her own good as well as his.

Once Alexander had mastered a static projection of himself, he started working on a moving projection. That was much more difficult at first, there was so much to think about, so many parts to focus on, until he discovered the secret. It wasn't about seeing each part and coordinating them together, it was about visualizing the whole and seeing it clearly in his mind's eye. After that, he started to make progress much more quickly. Within a few weeks, he could create an image of himself that was indistinguishable from his real body, make it walk, talk, and behave as if it were really him.

He tried several other images, but found that each required such focus that it would take just as long to master them as it did to master an image of himself. While an illusion of a dragon or a revenant might be useful, he decided to start with something more simple for his next illusion—a ball of light. He reasoned that being able to produce light would be the most useful illusion he could learn, even if it wasn't terribly frightening.

On many occasions, he tried to project his illusions while in a normal frame of mind, but he simply couldn't envision the necessary detail to create a projection unless he was in a meditative state. His newfound power wouldn't be very useful in a fight, but he was sure it could be put to effective use, especially if he could learn how to project his illusions while using his clairvoyance.

He didn't speak of it openly, mostly out of a superstitious fear that voicing his hopes would prevent them from coming to fruition. He didn't even try for the longest time, until one day, he realized that he hadn't looked in on Isabel for days. She was nearly to Karth the last time he'd visited her, but that had been some time ago.

He'd gotten so caught up with his own work that he'd forgotten to check on her. With a feeling of terrible guilt, he slipped into the firmament and went to her. When he found her traveling through the jungle, unarmed and guarded by soldiers of Karth, it was such a shock that he slammed back into his body.

It took almost an hour to calm himself enough to reenter the firmament and go back to her. He followed her for an hour, periodically trying to manifest an illusion of himself and failing each time. She was talking with the leader of the unit of soldiers about the jungle, trying to learn everything she could about the new environment she found herself in.

The leader's tone was respectful, yet firm. Mostly, his colors reassured Alexander that his wife wasn't in any immediate danger, at least not from the soldiers she was traveling with. The jungle was another matter.

When he returned to his body, he lay staring at the ceiling for several minutes, trying to decide how to proceed.

"Isabel's been taken by the House of Karth," he said.

"What do they want with her?" Jack asked.

"I don't know, but I get the impression she's not in any immediate danger, although that could change once they get wherever it is they're going."

"Maybe she's trying to form an alliance," Jack said.

"Probably, but Karth has been ruled by tyranny for centuries on both sides. The man she's traveling with is honorable, but I doubt the people he answers to are."

"She's resourceful," Jack said. "Remember how she turned her capture by the Reishi Coven into a triumph. She could do the same here."

"I don't doubt her," Alexander said, "not for a minute, but she's all alone in hostile territory. She had Abigail at the fortress island."

"Did you try to project an illusion through your clairvoyance?"

"Yeah, but I failed," Alexander said. "Although, I think with some practice, I'll succeed. In the meantime, I'm going to send her some help. Hector, Horace, prepare to leave for Karth."

"But who will protect you, Lord Reishi?" Hector asked.

"I'll be safe enough here," Alexander said.

"Perhaps one of us could stay." Horace said.

"No, you're a team. You work better together."

"Commander P'Tal wouldn't approve," Hector said.

"No, I doubt he would," Alexander said, "but I'm sending you anyway. I'll be here for months, and Isabel needs help now. Go to Karth and find her, but remain in the background. Don't reveal your presence to her unless it's necessary to protect her. Phane's magic is still working within her, so you can't really trust her to be herself. I just need to know she has someone watching her back."

"If you command it, we will obey," Hector said, "but reluctantly."

"I understand," Alexander said. "Go to Karth and watch over Isabel. I'll talk to Bragador about transportation."

Chapter 13

Alexander continued to work on mastering his magic, alternately using his clairvoyance as the sovereigns had instructed, looking into the very nature of the substance around him and attempting to see the world and more as a whole. He came to understand the nature of things more intuitively, learning how substance held together and how the world revolved around the sun.

He meditated on the basic building blocks of substance, watching them interact with one another, trying to understand why they behaved as they did. It was a subject he found his mind returning to with maddening frequency. He had other things to attend to that were far more pressing than such an academic pursuit, yet he felt drawn to it, almost compelled to understand this infinitesimal new world he'd discovered.

Periodically, he would float in the firmament, calling out to Siduri, but he never heard even a hint of reply. At times he wondered if Malachi had been right, if Siduri had just been a projection, but then he thought about his conversation with the first adept and remembered his colors, vibrant and subtle, refined and complex, like nothing else Alexander had ever encountered. That fact, more than anything else, convinced him that Siduri was real. Given his eccentric nature, it was likely that he'd said everything he had to say and saw no value in making a second appearance to reiterate his warnings.

Besides, Alexander was in no position to use the blood of the earth anytime soon. The more he thought about it, the more he doubted the wisdom of proceeding with his plan to create the potion. If Siduri's warning had given him pause, the sovereigns' warning had unnerved him. As much as he wanted to save Isabel, he knew she would never countenance him risking the world of time and substance for her.

He came to believe as the sovereigns did, that such power was better left alone, yet he couldn't bring himself to even consider returning the tiny sample of the blood of the earth that he'd collected. To do so would be to cut off that option, that one precious chance to save Isabel. Even though reason told him he could never risk it, his heart told him to hold on to that hope in the event that all else failed.

Hector and Horace departed on a small boat rowed by Bragador herself. She took them to the coast of Lorraine and left them to their own devices to find passage to Karth, a task they both expressed supreme confidence in their ability to accomplish. Alexander felt much better knowing that help was on the way, that Isabel wouldn't be totally alone in enemy territory. It was small comfort, given her situation, but he would take what comfort he could.

Anja grew quickly, spending more time with her mother, feeding and flying until she was nearly her full size. When Alexander expressed his astonishment at how quickly she had grown, Bragador just smiled knowingly, taking pride in her daughter. Anja still came by to see him, though much less frequently as Bragador placed heavier demands on her time. Alexander was both relieved and saddened. He'd become very fond of the young dragon and enjoyed her company.

Alexander finally succeeded at projecting a still image of himself during clairvoyance. His illusion appeared inside his Wizard's Den and lasted for only an instant, but it was enough to confirm Alexander's hope that he could use his illusions at will through his clairvoyance. The possibilities left him breathless. He could act to help his friends and allies even while confined to his bed.

"I saw you appear for just an instant, then you flickered and disappeared," Jack said when Alexander opened his eyes.

"Really? I wasn't sure if you could see it," Alexander said.

"You appeared right over there," Jack said, pointing, "although, I think you might want to work on the details. Now that I think about it, you didn't look quite right—no Thinblade. The details matter."

"I'm just happy to have confirmation that I can use my illusions in conjunction with my clairvoyance," Alexander said. Then he froze, his blind eyes staring straight ahead, as he used his all around sight to scrutinize an area of the room that had begun to look unusual.

It started as a plane of color floating in the air near the ceiling, oval in shape. As it became clearer, Alexander could see a face through a window looking into his Wizard's Den. He could hardly breathe as realization filled him with trepidation and fear. What had he said in the preceding months? What secrets had he revealed?

Through a window in the fabric of the world itself, he saw Phane watching him like a bug in a jar. Jataan had said that Phane had powerful ways of gathering information, but Alexander had never questioned the Commander on the details, an oversight that he now sorely regretted.

Then it hit him. He was seeing Phane as the Reishi Prince looked at him through his magic mirror. The implications were staggering. How long had the prince been spying on him? On his companions and allies? No wonder Phane always seemed to be a step ahead.

Alexander wasn't the only one with the ability to see.

"My Love, the draft is making me cold. Could you close the door so I can get warm?" Chloe said out loud.

"Of course, Little One," Alexander said just before he willed the door to his Wizard's Den closed. The moment it shut, the window in the fabric of the world vanished, along with Phane.

"Phane was watching us," Alexander said. "It looked like he was peering through a window right over there."

Jack stood up, looking around uncomfortably. "Dear Maker, there's no telling what he's learned. Is this the first time you've seen him?"

"Yes, but I have no way of knowing if this is just a new ability or if this is the first time he's watched us," Alexander said.

"Let's assume it's a new ability," Jack said, sitting down again. "What have we told him?"

"He's got to know that Isabel's on Karth," Alexander said. "He probably also knows that Hector and Horace are on the way. They're in trouble."

"He also knows you can cast illusions through your clairvoyance," Jack said with a sigh, "so much for the element of surprise."

"But he doesn't know that I can see him," Alexander said. "We can use that."

"How, My Love?" Chloe asked.

"It's risky, but it might give us an option later," Alexander said.

"What do you have in mind?" Jack asked.

"When the Wizard's Den first opened, there were a number of magical books inside," Alexander said. "Two in particular might be used to lure Phane into a trap. Both are in that strongbox." Alexander pointed to the heavy steel box in the corner.

"Only a few people know about these books, and I'd like to keep it that way. If either fell into the wrong hands, the results could be disastrous."

"Well, you certainly have my attention," Jack said.

"The first book will draw the mind of anyone who reads even a single word of it into the netherworld, to be lost forever."

"A trap," Jack said.

"One set by Malachi for Phane should his wayward son murder him and claim the Stone," Alexander said.

"What a twisted way to live," Jack said, shaking his head sadly.

"The second book is even worse. It contains a spell that transfers one's soul into a specially prepared item, effectively killing the caster, yet animating his corpse at the same time. The result is an undead version of the caster that can't be killed without destroying the item containing his soul. Malachi was trying to become immortal."

"Dear Maker," Jack and Chloe whispered at the same time.

"So you want to let Phane know that this book exists and then trick him into reading the other one, the one that sucks his mind into the darkness," Jack said.

Alexander nodded.

"That's risky. If he ever got his hands on that undead book, there'd be no stopping him."

"I know, but it might be the best chance we have to kill him," Alexander said. "Let's face it, my magic will never be a match for his head-on."

"That's a terrible gamble," Jack said.

"You should destroy that book right now," Chloe said.

"I know, on both counts, but I just can't bring myself to do it," Alexander said. "I can't explain it, but for some reason I think it might become vitally important later."

"Hmm … I wouldn't bet against your insight," Jack said. "For all we know, your magic could be giving you that feeling. But the thought of an immortal and unkillable Phane running around the Seven Isles for all eternity is beyond insanity."

"I know," Alexander said, "but this is the first time I've been able to see a way to actually kill him. How can I pass up that chance?"

"Maybe you don't pass it up," Jack said, "maybe you put it off until you're healed. The moment Phane gets a whiff of that book, he'll send everything he can muster after it and you're not exactly in fighting form right now."

"You've got a point there," Alexander said, closing his eyes and considering his options. "I guess it wouldn't hurt to wait. I'm sure there'll be other opportunities to set the ruse in motion."

"I really think that's for the best," Jack said. "In the meantime, what should we do about Phane's snooping?"

"If you see me tap my finger three times, it means he's watching us," Alexander said. "For now, let's be careful what we say and have any important discussions inside the Wizard's Den with the door closed."

"Sounds like a plan," Jack said.

"Why don't you start a fire?" Alexander said. "I don't want Phane to know I can see him watching us ... and I closed the door because Chloe was cold."

Jack smiled and winked at Chloe before going to the hearth and stacking up logs over a bed of tinder and kindling. Once the fire was burning brightly, Alexander opened the door to the Wizard's Den.

He was surprised to see a young woman standing a few feet away, looking around with a mixture of curiosity and sadness. She was startled when the door opened, then she smiled broadly when she saw Alexander.

She was just over five feet tall, thin, not quite a woman yet. Her coppery red hair was cut short, flaring out just over her shoulders, and tiny freckles spread across her nose and cheeks. Her golden eyes reminded Alexander of his own.

"There you are, Alexander," she said.

He stared incredulously, focusing his all around sight on her intently. He'd never seen her before, yet her colors were unmistakable.

"Anja?"

"Do you like the way I look?" she asked, a bit self-consciously.

"You're beautiful ... but how?"

"She snuck into the Temple of Fire and used its power to cast a shapeshift spell ... without permission," Bragador said, striding purposefully into the cavern.

Anja looked down sheepishly, like she was trying to disappear.

"What have you to say for yourself?" Bragador asked her daughter.

After a moment, she looked up defiantly. "I wanted to be able to talk to Alexander," she said. "I can't make human words with my real mouth yet, and I have so many questions."

"Why didn't you come to me and ask for permission?" Bragador asked.

"Because I knew you'd say no," Anja said.

"You are but a child," Bragador said. "Your ability to wield magic is limited for a reason. In time, you will grow into your power. Until then, it is very dangerous to attempt to cast spells without guidance."

"But why? It didn't seem that hard."

"That's because the Temple of Fire was acting as a buffer between you and the firmament," Bragador said. "Without it, attempting such a spell would surely cost you your life."

"I still don't understand," Anja said. "When you cast a shapeshift spell, it doesn't hurt you."

"I am several centuries old," Bragador said, "you are a child."

Anja fixed her mother with a defiant scowl, still refusing to accept her answer.

Bragador continued in a more measured tone. "Dragons can access the firmament much like human wizards, but without the need to undergo the mana fast because we are innately magical creatures. Unfortunately, the firmament still tugs at our psyche as it does with humans, and we can become lost in the limitless potential just as easily, especially if we're careless." She fixed Anja with a stern glare before going on. "You must learn to master the passion that only a dragon can know and temper it with stillness of mind before you'll be ready to cast spells on your own. Until then, you risk your life each time you link with the firmament."

Anja swallowed, nodding a few times before looking down at the ground.

"Where did you even find a shapeshift spell, Child?" Bragador asked.

"There's a big pile of books in the treasure chamber," Anja said, suddenly excited. "Most of them are boring, but a few are really interesting."

"I'll have to have a closer look at those books," Bragador said.

Anja frowned, suddenly realizing that she'd given away too much.

"Come, Child, release the spell and return to your true form," Bragador said.

"No! Please let me stay like this for a while," Anja begged. "I have so many questions. I just want to talk with Alexander for a while. Please?"

Bragador let out an exasperated sigh, looking to Alexander for his approval.

"On one condition," Alexander said. "Promise me that you won't go behind your mother's back again."

"I promise," Anja said.

Bragador gave her a fond smile, before turning to Alexander. "Don't reveal too much to her, she's just a child, after all, and far too young to bear the weight of the world."

They spent the evening talking. Jack regaled them with stories of their adventures over the past year, told with mastery and more than a little exaggeration. Anja laughed and gasped in surprise and asked a thousand questions. Alexander answered her honestly in every instance, with Chloe adding detail as the opportunity presented itself. They deliberately shied away from some of the darker moments they'd experienced, sticking to their victories and focusing on the happy moments.

Anja wanted to know everything about Alexander's childhood, what it was like growing up on a ranch, how he met Isabel and if she was worthy of him, what his parents were like, even what he liked to eat. She was fond of large fish, preferably whole.

She cried when he told her of his brother's murder and cried again when he told her about his wedding. She cheered when he won the Thinblade and gasped in surprise when Jataan P'Tal abruptly switched sides because the Sovereign Stone bonded to Alexander. She sat on the edge of her seat with childlike wonder and limitless exuberance, hanging on every word of their stories.

And then she stopped, cocking her head to the side and looking at his wounded leg.

"How were you injured?" she asked, pointing at his leg.

"Perhaps another time," Alexander said, as a knowing came over him … Bragador was coming.

"But I want to know, Alexander," Anja said. "You haven't told me why you came here or how you got hurt." She frowned, dark and angry. "Someone did this to you, didn't they?"

"Indeed, Child," Bragador said, entering the Wizard's Den quietly. "Thieves stole into our home and took you, attempted to use you as a bargaining chip against me. They demanded that I kill Alexander or they would kill you. And I meant to meet their demand." She fixed her daughter with a look of dreadful purpose. "And though I hunted him, he found you before I found him and he protected you against those who took you from me, protected you from their blade with his own flesh. Alexander saved your life before you took your first breath, and that is why I have permitted him to remain among us. As a rule, humans are not permitted within the ring of the Spires, though we do make exceptions from time to time."

"You were hurt protecting me? But why? You didn't even know me. I wasn't even hatched yet."

Alexander smiled gently before answering. He realized in that moment that he had come to love this whelp of a dragon, masked in human form by a spell beyond her ability and so full of life that she was practically overflowing with it.

"I protected you because you're alive," Alexander said, "because you have a right to your life, because you are innocent and those who would have harmed you are not. I protected you because you were a child in harm's way and I had the power to do so."

She rushed to him, then stopped abruptly so that she could hug him gently. "Thank you, Alexander," she said.

"You're most welcome, Anja."

She stopped at the doorway as she was leaving with her mother and turned back to him.

"I love you," she whispered.

"I love you, too," Alexander said.

He saw Bragador close her eyes in pain for just a brief moment before she slipped past the edge of the doorway and into the dark of the cavern.

Chapter 14

As the days passed, Alexander worked on projecting an illusion through his clairvoyance until his head ached. He had limited success but nothing significant enough to be useful. He had just finished a particularly grueling meditation session and was resting his mind when Bragador stopped in the doorway. Again, he knew she was approaching moments before she appeared. He was starting to trust his newfound ability, even though it hadn't predicted much except her approach.

"May we speak?" she asked.

"Of course, please come in," Alexander said.

He closed the door to the Wizard's Den behind her. She stopped midstride, looking about warily.

"Don't be alarmed," he said. "I've closed the door as a precaution that I believe you'll understand and accept once I've explained."

"Then by all means, explain," she said, without taking another step.

Alexander told her of Phane and his ability to see them, and how he could now detect the Reishi Prince's surveillance.

"Very well, I accept your precaution, for now," Bragador said. "I have come to speak of Anja, but first I would like to apologize for questioning your report concerning Aedan. My agents confirm that Aedan is possessed by the shade and is holding station high over the ship carrying the princess, which is still sailing in circles."

Alexander nodded, motioning to a nearby chair.

"Thank you," he said. "I'm sorry I was right."

"Indeed. Aedan is, or perhaps was, a remarkable dragon," Bragador said. "He is very dangerous, resourceful and experienced. As for the shade, I don't understand his behavior. Why not just take the keystone?"

"I've given that question a lot of thought," Alexander said. "The shade was on that ship for some time, but he didn't take the keystone and he left Lacy alone as well. I believe he knows something about how the box is opened … and Lacy plays a necessary part. If I'm right, he won't harm her until the box is open. It could be that he intends to let Phane's ruse play out."

"So he would definitely move against us if we attempt to bring the princess and the box here," Bragador said. "I don't want to harm Aedan or the dragons I would have to send against him. For the time being, I believe that inaction is the best course. We are watching him and the ship, and we're prepared to move when the opportunity presents itself."

"Aedan is one of your own," Alexander said. "I wouldn't expect you to give up on him, but I should warn you, I was possessed by a shade once … they don't let go easily."

"How did you survive?" Bragador asked.

"Isabel," Alexander said. "Her magic saved me."

Bragador nodded thoughtfully.

"Another time I would like to speak with you about this magic your wife can wield," she said, "but right now, I've come to have a much more personal conversation with you.

"My daughter has bonded with you. That is something we dragons try very hard to prevent. A dragon that bonds with a human will have a difficult life.

"First, the child will wish to live in the world of humans in order to be near to the one they have bonded with, a world hostile to them, unwilling to understand, and afraid. Being a child, she ..." Bragador closed her eyes and took a deep breath, "the child bonded with a human will not have the wisdom to see the danger. Humans are violent and warlike, some are driven by an unquenchable thirst for power. Dragons are potent and fearsome, so those who lust for power will seek to control any dragon in their midst, usually through control of the human they are bonded with, while the rest of the humans will simply try to kill her out of fear.

"Second, humans are short-lived creatures. When you die, Anja will be devastated. She will survive, but as a shell of her former self, left to live the majority of her years brokenhearted and suffering.

"I'm grateful that you saved her life, Alexander, but I need you to understand the price. I don't blame you, but I wish you had never come to my home."

"I don't know what to say," Alexander said. "The last thing I want is to hurt her."

"I believe you, and I'm grateful for that as well," Bragador said. "She will want to accompany you when you leave. I would have her stay here."

"Me too," Alexander said. "As soon as I can walk, I'm going to Karth to find my wife. And quite honestly, I expect to have to cut a pretty bloody swath across that whole island to get to her. That's not going to be any place for a child, even a dragon. Anja should stay here with you."

Bragador let out a deep breath. "I'm glad we're in agreement on that point. Convincing her may prove more difficult."

"She doesn't have to agree with us, she just has to obey," Alexander said. "Where I'm going, what I'm planning, I can't have her with me. My feelings for her would just make her a liability and put her in even greater jeopardy than you've suggested."

"So you intend to take your war to Phane," Bragador said.

"He's taken my wife from me," Alexander said. "I'm going to find a way to make him bleed." He fixed her with his golden eyes and didn't flinch ... no easy feat holding the gaze of a dragon, even in human form.

"While your daughter must stay here, I would welcome your company," Alexander said.

Bragador chuckled softly. "My place is here. When your war is done and everyone who fought in it is long dead, I will still be here. We have watched humans war with themselves for as long as we can remember and the story is always the same—a deceiver convinces others to fight for his glory, that he may rule over others by force and lies, taking what he wishes for his own comfort and perceived greatness while the masses suffer and die.

"Yours is a sad tale, one that we've chosen to avoid."

"I can't fault your wisdom, even if I could really use your help," Alexander said.

Bragador stared into the fire for several minutes. Alexander was content to share the silence with her. Jack sat at the desk, furiously scribbling notes while they spoke, now stopping to wait patiently for the interchange to continue.

"Do you know the history of the Reishi War?" Bragador asked.

"Some of it."

"I suspect we see it very differently, given our part in it," Bragador said. "Malachi Reishi and the wizards under his command created a magical collar that had the power to bind a dragon to the will of the wearer of a matched ring. He captured hundreds of dragons, enslaved them to his will and fielded an army to battle the forces arrayed against him.

"The first attack of the dragon legion was devastating. The northernmost island of Tyr, now called Almeria, was burned to the ground, scorched black from coast to coast. Malachi's enemies were preparing a naval invasion of the Reishi Isle, using Almeria as a staging ground. He discovered their plan and used his newest weapon to terrible effect. There were no survivors.

"The free dragons of the Seven Isles became aware of his presumption. That he would enslave dragons was an affront worthy of death. That he would use them to murder the population of an entire island could only mean war.

"For a decade, one of the bloodiest periods in the history of the Seven Isles, dragon fought dragon. The enslaved dragon legion fought the dragons aligned with the Rebel Mage to a standstill ... until our kind was nearly extinct.

"Since then, we've kept to ourselves, preferring to keep our own company and live in peace, without the inevitable complications that humans bring."

"And here I am in your home, complications and all," Alexander said, leaning his head back and closing his eyes.

"Some humans are more tolerable than others," Bragador said, laying her hand atop his. "You give me hope for humanity, but for every man like you there is a man like Phane, and for every man like either of you, there are a thousand who will take the path of least resistance, flowing like water to whichever side will offer the greatest reward for the least effort without regard for principle."

"And yet, day in and day out, most people live honorable lives," Alexander said. "They raise their children, work to provide for their families, help their neighbors and try to do the right thing even when the choice is hard. Human beings are essentially good. We love our children, honor our elders, protect our vulnerable, and give charity to those in need."

"I don't question any of that," Bragador said, "but your history isn't written by those people, it's written by the ambitious and the power-hungry, those who crave rulership over others, those who will do anything for their own glory, those who would kill simply to prove that they are better than their victims.

"The saddest fact about humanity is that good, honest, honorable people fall prey to lies told by convincing deceivers and unwittingly work to undermine their own futures, all so that a handful of evil people can rule over them with an iron fist, and by the time the masses realize their folly, it's always too late. That is the story of human history, Alexander."

"History unfolds one day at a time," he said. "We always have a chance to do better. The Reishi guided the Seven Isles honorably for eighteen hundred years, protecting the people against the power lust of those who would rule and ensuring peace for countless generations. We *can* live up to their example. I know we can."

"Perhaps, but you fail to see the folly of the Reishi," Bragador said. "The concentration of power that allowed them to ensure peace for so long was the very thing that made them such a potent threat to peace when their power corrupted them, as power inevitably does."

"So what's the solution?" Alexander asked, a bit more defiantly than he would have liked.

"Simple … humans must learn to live without government," Bragador said. "Government, organized force, is the repository of evil. It is the source of corruption, the enemy of civilization and the problem with the world. As long as there is a place where concentrated power resides, it will attract evil people like dung attracts flies. The only solution is to remove the pile of dung."

"What about crime? What about other countries with powerful governments bent on war? How can there be peace without authority?" Alexander asked.

"Therein lies the human dilemma," Bragador said. "There will always be those who call for greater and greater control, out of fear or ignorance or greed. Until humanity learns restraint in governance, learns how to limit the power it grants to its leaders, learns that those who crave power over others are always deceivers, your kind will know only war and despair."

"If we haven't learned that lesson by now, I doubt we ever will," Alexander said.

"Some will, most won't," Bragador said. "Selfish interest is a powerful motivator. Governments can always be bought or manipulated or blackmailed to set rules that favor some at the expense of others. Evil people see government as a weapon to be used for their own purposes while spreading the lie that it exists to protect the innocent or ensure fairness or defend against some distant threat. The truth is, government has always existed for one single reason … the profit and power of those in government. Of course, there are always those working within government who are good and decent people. But those who vie for power, they can never be trusted."

"So where does that leave us?" Alexander asked.

"Right back where we started," Bragador said, "you are a guest in my home, my daughter is smitten with you, and it breaks my heart because it will surely break hers. I will not fight this war for you, Alexander. When you are well enough to travel, I will bid you farewell and hope that you and your complications never return."

Bragador got up and turned to the door that was not there. Alexander willed it to open with a thought and she started to leave.

"Bragador, I would like to be your friend," Alexander said.

She stopped, turning to face him again with a sad little smile.

"Alexander, you are my friend," she said. "If you weren't, I would have eaten you by now."

***

She was red with a hint of gold that glistened in the setting sun. Three rows of spikes ran the length of her back beginning with the crown of three horns that swept back from her brow. She banked hard, cutting into the evening breeze and turning impossibly sharp before losing her center of gravity and tumbling through the air out over the ocean.

Alexander held his breath as Anja rolled in the sky, falling out of control. Her wings flared out and started to right her but she tried to gain thrust too quickly and wasn't strong enough to pull out of the free-fall.

Bragador floated overhead, barking orders to her daughter in the guttural language of the dragons.

Anja spread her wings again, quickly folding them straight up, then gradually spreading them out, inducing a spiral that slowed her until she was able to turn into a dive, lock her wings and begin to ride the air currents back up to the level of the platform where Alexander stood, assisted by a cane, watching her flight practice.

Bragador was a stern taskmistress, running Anja through a grueling series of aerial maneuvers over and over again. Her exacting demands combined with Anja's hard work paid off with remarkable gains in her ability to fly safely, even while performing some very complicated aerial stunts.

Several days prior, Jack had presented Alexander with a beautiful cane, hand-carved from a piece of driftwood.

Alexander never realized how much he cherished the ability to walk. His leg hurt when he tried to put any weight on it, but he felt exhilarated at the same time. It took a few days of work before he felt confident enough to venture out of his Wizard's Den.

Once he had mastered using his new cane, he went to watch Anja fly every afternoon. When he wasn't watching her, he was practicing his clairvoyant illusions, using Jack as his observer, but try as Alexander might, Jack could always find something wrong with the illusion. On top of that, he was still unable to integrate movement, let alone speech.

He needed a way to act. The winter was just beginning, but it would be over all too soon and then the killing would start in earnest. Phane was poised to strike a terrible blow to Ruatha, while Zuhl would almost certainly reengage on Fellenden. These days of reprieve during the winter were vitally important for coordinating a strategy between his allies, and yet, his magic was failing him.

Alexander turned to the sovereigns for counsel.

"What's transpired since we last convened?" Balthazar Reishi asked.

Alexander gave the sovereigns a full report of his healing and his limited success with his illusion magic. He also told them of his conversation with Bragador, as well as his growing fondness for Anja.

"First and foremost," Balthazar said, "you must not take the dragon child with you when you depart. I cannot stress this enough. Bragador has forgiven you much, but if Anja accompanies you to war, she may well die. Dragons are not invincible, especially very young dragons. And they're very hard to hide."

Alexander cut him off with a raised hand.

"I agree, Anja will stay with her mother when I leave. What I need is help with my magic. I don't know what I'm doing wrong. I've visualized myself from every angle and I can even project a pretty good image, but I can't make it move without losing clarity."

Balthazar nodded to Constantine.

The Third Sovereign leaned forward.

"I recall a conversation I had with Benesh late one evening a very long time ago. He confided to me that his illusion magic was unworkable when he first discovered it within himself. Only after he learned to be the illusion rather than see the illusion was he able to create the visions he was so renowned for.

"In your practice, are you seeing the room from the perspective of your illusion or from elsewhere?"

"Always from a third point of view," Alexander said.

"Try it from the perspective of your illusion," Constantine said. "It's now clear that the magic of my brother lives on in you. That fact may be just simply helpful, or it may be of great significance."

"There have been so few adepts," Balthazar said, "for you to possess a link to the firmament from two such wizards is unique. Such a thing cannot be without risk. Be vigilant. Record your magical experiences with extra care over the coming weeks and consult your notes frequently."

"Thank you, gentlemen," Alexander said.

Chapter 15

"That was almost unsettling, Alexander," Jack said. "You were right there in front of me, carrying on a conversation, and at the same time you were right there in bed, lying still like a corpse."

"It'll work for now," Alexander said. "I'll be out for a while. There's a lot to do."

It took the better part of an afternoon to get used to seeing through the illusion. Then it just snapped into place and Alexander was there, seeing and hearing everything as if standing in the place his illusion occupied. He could move and talk and hear and be there in every way except the real way.

But it worked. He had the ability to act.

He methodically followed the well-worn path in his mind that led to the firmament and then he was in the endless ocean of creation—a moment later he was floating in a room half a world away, looking at his wife. He willed a perfect image of himself into place.

Isabel gasped, putting her hands over her mouth and looking at him with wide eyes as she stood frozen with a mixture of hope and surprise.

"How? Is it really you?" She reached out, taking a step forward.

Alexander shook his head. "Illusion."

"So you're still on Tyr, then," Isabel said, then flinched like she'd been slapped. "Wait! Don't answer that. In fact, don't tell me anything of any interest to Phane. I can't be trusted, Alexander." She stopped again and looked at him with longing. Approaching slowly, she reached for his face but found only emptiness. A tear slipped from each eye as she closed them in pain.

"I'm safe, well and healing," Alexander said. "Why did you leave?"

"I had to," Isabel said. "I was a threat to you. I couldn't live with myself if I killed you. I won't, no matter what. This is how it has to be for now."

"We could have found another way," Alexander said.

Isabel shook her head.

"This was the only sure way."

"And what if you get yourself killed?" Alexander asked.

"Better that than killing you," she said.

"You can't die," Alexander said. "I need you."

Isabel reached for him again, then stopped, turning around in frustration.

"I wish you were really here," she said. "I miss you terribly. I didn't want to leave, but I had to. You don't know what it's like, always second-guessing your own thoughts, questioning if it was really *your* thought. I can't trust myself with your life right now, so I can't be anywhere near you until I can." She turned back around, facing him sternly with tears running freely down her face. "Deal in what is, not what if. This is what is." She motioned to the locked room that had become her home in Karth's secret fortress.

"You're right," Alexander said, drawing himself up. "Report."

Isabel looked at him quizzically for a moment before smiling slightly and beginning a full accounting of her journey from Tyr to this place and time. She was thorough, yet concise, and delivered the entire summary without a hint of emotion.

"You've been through a lot," Alexander said. "Do you think you can trust Ayela?"

"My gut says yes, but I'm not entirely myself right now, so I don't know what to trust."

"Regardless, save that potion," Alexander said. "If she's telling the truth, it could make the difference. Reach out to her. See if you can get a better sense of her loyalties. That leaves us with questions. Who are the Sin'Rath? What's a Goiri? And what's a doppelganger spell?"

"What happens if it works?" Isabel asked. "I mean, what if the witch Clotus actually manages to kill Phane?"

Alexander frowned, shaking his head. "Phane will see right through her. Don't underestimate him. This witch Clotus will die badly."

"You're probably right," Isabel said, deflating somewhat, "but we can hope."

"I'm sorry," Alexander said, reminding himself how alone Isabel was right now. "If the witch kills Phane, I'll send forces for you immediately and then we'll sue for peace, courting the disparate factions within Phane's alliance and pitting one against the other until they're at war with themselves, while we withdraw and consolidate our forces before confronting them a piece at a time and bringing them under the Old Law."

Isabel laughed. "That does seem unlikely. If Phane kills Clotus, he'll know that I'm on Karth and that the Sin'Rath have me. He's almost sure to act."

"Agreed," Alexander said. "You need to escape. See if you can get Ayela to help you. She's defied her father already so she might again. Once you're out, then what?"

"I go kill Phane," Isabel said.

"No, you don't," Alexander said. "You find a way to come home to me, or at the very least somewhere safe while I get rid of Azugorath."

"Phane is expecting me," Isabel said. "I can get close. This may be the best shot we ever have. I have to take it."

"He'll see through you too," Alexander said. "He's a liar. You're not. How do you expect to deceive him?"

Isabel clenched her jaw and shrugged. "I haven't figured that out yet. I'll know more when I get closer."

"This is a very dangerous game you're playing," Alexander said.

"War is the most dangerous game there is," Isabel said.

"So I've heard," Alexander said. "I don't like this, but it is what it is, and you're obviously not open to reason at the moment, so all I have left to do is help you. I'm going to talk with Magda and Kelvin about your questions. I'll be back as soon as I have answers. I love you, Isabel."

"I love you, Alexander."

He faded away, back into the firmament. A moment later his awareness coalesced in a large room. Nearly the entire general staff of the army on Fellenden was assembled there, with Conner sitting in the seat to the right of an empty chair at the head of the table. Magda, the person Alexander had been looking for, was there as well.

Alexander seemingly materialized behind the empty chair. He gave everyone a moment to notice him before he spoke.

"Where's Abigail?" he asked Conner.

"Zuhl took her," Conner said, standing. "How? How can you be here?"

"I'm not," Alexander said. "I'm projecting an illusion of myself. I'm injured, but safe. How did Zuhl take my sister? And where's Anatoly?"

"With a dragon," Conner said to the first question. "Tore the roof off the room right in the middle of a war council, then a dozen of his minions, half-dragon, half-man, descended on us and took Abigail. Anatoly was severely injured in the attack and is currently recuperating."

"But he'll live?"

"Yes," Conner said.

"I'm going to find Abigail," Alexander said. "I'll be back as soon as I do. We'll consider our options when I return."

Alexander let his illusion vanish, then focused his mind's eye on Abigail … the world flashed by and he was in a circular room with his sister—she was pacing.

She stopped midstride when he appeared in front of her.

"Alex? How?" she said.

"Magic," he said with a shrug. "I'm not really here. Jack says hi."

Abigail smiled for just a moment.

"How do I know you're not a trick?"

"You don't, but I'm not," Alexander said.

"All right," Abigail said, "doesn't really matter since you can't tell me anything anyway. Zuhl claims to have a way of getting people to answer questions … some kind of ice slug or something. It's supposed to make you truthful and forthcoming, so don't tell me anything that Zuhl can use."

"Fair enough," Alexander said. "Tell me everything I need to know about how this happened." He motioned to her tower-room prison cell.

"Zuhl showed up at the shipyard riding a blue dragon and started killing our Sky Knights, so I flew up and cut him in half …"

"Wait, what?" Alexander said. "How did you get close enough?"

Abigail hesitated before answering. "I jumped off my wyvern."

"What?! Abigail, that was way too risky."

"It worked, and I made friends with the dragon. His name is Ixabrax. The problem is, it wasn't Zuhl riding the dragon—it was a simulacrum, a copy. The real Zuhl is still very much alive.

"He attacked Fellenden city a few days ago riding another blue dragon, an even bigger one than Ixabrax."

"How many dragons does Zuhl control?" Alexander asked.

"Six, now," Abigail said. "He has these collars that make the dragons obey him. I used the Thinblade to cut Ixabrax's collar. He told me that Zuhl has enslaved his whole family."

"Do you think Ixabrax might help us?" Alexander asked.

"He might," Abigail said with a shrug.

"What does Zuhl want with you anyway?" Alexander asked.

"He wants a book, he called it a lich book," Abigail said. "It's supposed to make you into an immortal undead. Zuhl says he'll trade me for the book, otherwise he's going to sacrifice me on the solstice to prolong his life for another year."

"That's two weeks from now," Alexander said.

"I know."

"You're not alone," Alexander said. "I'm going to get you out of this. I'll be back when I get the chance. I love you, Abigail. Oh ... and be more careful."

"Love you, Alex."

He faded into the firmament, then appeared behind Abigail's empty chair at the council table on Fellenden.

"Abigail is alive and well, but she's being held in Zuhl's fortress. Report," he said.

Conner stood and proceeded to provide a detailed report of the army's activity since they left the Gate, finishing with this very council meeting. Alexander listened patiently.

"Congratulations on your victory against Zuhl's forces," Alexander said. "Unfortunately, his counterattack could take a terrible toll. Abigail will be sacrificed on the solstice unless we can help her."

"I was just recommending an attack by a full flight of Sky Knights," Magda said.

"You'd lose far too many if Zuhl released his dragons against you," Alexander said.

"We're prepared to march through the Gate," Conner said.

"Zuhl outnumbers us by a factor of ten," Alexander said. "We have to do this unconventionally. I have an idea but I need to consult the Guild Mage first." He turned to Magda. "I had originally come to speak with you, Magda. May I have a few moments in private?"

Once they were alone, Alexander explained Isabel's situation. He told her how Isabel had traveled to Karth, how she had been captured and taken to the Sin'Rath, and finally how the witches had cast a doppelganger spell in an attempt to get close enough to Phane to kill him. Magda listened intently.

"Dear Maker," she said when he was finished. "The Sin'Rath are not entirely human. The Reishi Coven has had a long-standing agreement with them that we would not set foot on Karth if they didn't set foot outside of Karth. Isabel has broken that treaty. There's no telling how the Sin'Rath will react. They're completely mad.

"By far the most immediately dangerous development is the doppelganger spell. Such magic links the two subjects of the spell at a very basic level. If the Sin'Rath witch dies, Isabel will die as well.

"Alexander, I must call the coven to me at the fortress island. Only with all of our strength together do we have a chance of dispelling the doppelganger spell, and I assure you that Phane will see through it. We might not have much time."

"How long will it take you?"

"Several days to assemble all of the witches," Magda said. "Sooner if you deliver the messages with your newfound and quite impressive talent."

"Of course. I'll spread the word. Once you help Isabel, would you be willing to help get Abigail back?"

"Absolutely," Magda said. "Anything you need."

"It may involve travel," Alexander said.

"I'll pack warmly."

"Thank you, Magda," he said. "Oh, one more thing, do you know what a Goiri is?"

Magda frowned, shaking her head. "I've never heard the term before but I will consult the coven's library when I return to the fortress island. Perhaps I'll find something there."

"One of the Sin'Rath mentioned it to Isabel, then another silenced her like she was saying too much," Alexander said. "Might be nothing."

"Better to know for certain," Magda said.

"My thoughts exactly," Alexander said before he returned to the table and faced Prince Torin.

"We're not acquainted," Alexander said, "but I believe you are Prince Torin, brother of Princess Lacy."

"I am, and I swear Fellenden's allegiance to the Reishi," Torin said.

"No," Alexander said, "swear your allegiance to the Old Law, not the Reishi."

Torin blinked, then frowned quizzically.

"Tell me about your sister," Alexander said.

Torin thought for a moment, then described Lacy in look and manner.

"I have good but troubling news for you," Alexander said. "Lacy is alive, but she's being held prisoner aboard a ship manned by Phane's men disguised to look like Zuhl's men. I believe they're playing out an elaborate ruse to trick Lacy into opening the magical box she found in Carlyle Fellenden's tomb. I can't let that happen."

"Lady Abigail sent a hundred men after her, led by Captain Wyatt," Torin said. "They've clearly failed."

"It could be that they just haven't succeeded yet," Alexander said. "I know Wyatt, he's a good man in a fight and he doesn't quit."

"What do you propose then?" Torin asked.

"For the moment, we do nothing," Alexander said. "I'll gather more information and try to come up with a viable plan."

"That isn't very reassuring," Torin said. "She's all I have left. There must be something you can do."

"I can't project an illusion to speak with her because the man in the cell next to her works for Phane, although Lacy doesn't know that. I can talk to her in her dreams, but I'm not certain I should. Tell me, is she a good liar? If I reveal a plan to her, will she be able to keep it from Phane's agent?"

"No," Torin said, shaking his head. "She's a terrible liar. She's probably safer if she doesn't know what we're planning."

"Then we don't have a move right now," Alexander said. "We have to get our people closer first, then we'll start to have options. We'll get her back, Torin."

"I've always been there to protect her," Torin said. "It doesn't seem right that I'm not there for her now."

"I know exactly how you feel," Alexander said.

He vanished from behind the chair and reappeared at the foot of Anatoly's bed.

"Is that really you?" Anatoly asked, his voice weak.

"I'm not actually here, but it's me," Alexander said.

"I'm sorry," Anatoly whispered. "I couldn't stop them."

"As I heard it, you prevented her from being crushed by a falling ceiling," Alexander said. "You saved her life. How are you faring?"

"Healers say I should be on my feet in a few days," Anatoly said.

"If you're up to it, I want to send you after her," Alexander said.

"I'll be ready," Anatoly said.

"Don't push too hard, you don't want to reopen your wounds," Alexander said, "besides, my plan won't be ready for a few days."

"All right," Anatoly said. "How are things going with you?"

Alexander gave him a brief synopsis of his travels to the Spires and his current state.

"Things are going to get ugly come spring," Anatoly said. "Think you'll be in fighting form by then?"

"I'm hoping," Alexander said. "In the meantime, I'm going to make the most of this new magical talent I've developed and try to get us as ready as possible for spring thaw. Rest and heal. I'll be back in a few days. Oh, who has the Thinblade?"

"I do," Anatoly said, pulling the sheathed sword from under the covers. The hilt was tied to the scabbard to prevent it from being drawn. "I've got her bow, too. It's under the bed."

"Good man. Get well," Alexander said before vanishing.

He went to Cassandra next, materializing on the plateau of the fortress island and sending a gardener to retrieve the triumvir. She arrived, a bit perplexed and wary but willing to hear him out nonetheless. Once he explained the situation, she donned the mantle of leader and began preparing her coven for the spell casting.

Bianca had her people saddling wyverns for all of her witches before Alexander vanished into the firmament again.

Constance was in a command tent attending a war council with the senior staff of Alexander's Ruathan army in Buckwold. He appeared behind an empty chair at the table and waited for the room to fall silent.

"Hi, Dad," he said.

"Alexander? How?" Duncan asked.

"I just figured out how to do this today," Alexander said. "It's good to see you."

"You as well, Son," Duncan said. "I'm assuming you're not really here."

"No, I'm on Tyr," Alexander said. He spent several minutes explaining the situation they faced, Isabel's predicament and Abigail's abduction. Duncan took the news stoically, but Alexander could see the deep distress in his colors at the news that his only daughter was being held by the enemy.

"Do you have a plan to get your wife and sister back?" Duncan asked.

"I have a plan for Abigail," Alexander said. "It's risky, but it has a good chance of working, and it may deal a serious blow to Zuhl if it does. As for Isabel, Magda has called all of the witches back to the coven to dispel the doppelganger spell before Phane discovers the Sin'Rath's ruse and inadvertently kills Isabel."

"I'll gather the witches under my command and depart immediately," Constance said. "Unfortunately, I have a witch in Kai'Gorn and another in Southport."

"I'll go there next and deliver their orders," Alexander said. "How are things here?"

Duncan sighed. "We're in trouble. Come spring, the Lancers will breach our lines and pour into the northern plains. From there, once they're out in the open, they'll be able to attack anywhere north of the Great Forest."

"What do you need to stop them?" Alexander said.

"I don't think there's anything you can give me that will stop them," Duncan said. "Our line is just too long to hold. We'll probably stop their first attack and maybe even their second, but eventually, they will get through. Once that happens, I could really use a legion of Rangers."

"I'll see to it," Alexander said. "Would more infantry help?"

"Couldn't hurt," Duncan said. "Archers would be useful, too."

"I'll send you a legion of each," Alexander said. "Abigail cut Zuhl's numbers on Fellenden in half and Prince Torin has rallied about four legions from Fellenden to add to our strength. Most aren't soldiers but they're willing to learn so we're integrating them into our forces."

"At least there's that," Duncan said.

"I have to go, Dad," Alexander said. "I love you."

"I love you too, Son," Duncan said as Alexander faded into the firmament.

He went to Kai'Gorn next, then Southport relaying the message to the witches and briefing General Talia and Kevin on recent events.

He was floating on the firmament, considering his next move when he suddenly slammed back into his body. The pain was almost more than he could bear. His head felt like it was full of molten lead, searing agony throbbing with each beat of his heart. He nearly screamed, but couldn't draw a full enough breath past the torment.

Jack stopped shaking him and stood as Alexander sat up. Blood from his nose dripped onto the blanket. He felt a tickling on the sides of his cheeks and found blood leaking from his ears as well.

"When we saw you bleeding, we shook you out of your trance," Jack said.

"Are you all right, My Love?" Chloe asked, worry rippling through her voice.

He shook his head as he fumbled for a healing draught. After quickly quaffing the potion, he lay back, waiting for the welcome relief of unconsciousness.

He woke several hours later.

"How are you feeling?" Jack asked.

"Much better," Alexander said. "Apparently, I overdid it. After I went blind, I had similar headaches while my all around sight expanded, though none so intense. I'll have to be more careful in the future."

"I'll say," Jack said.

"I have bad news," Alexander said, closing his eyes. "Abigail's been taken by Zuhl."

"Dear Maker," Jack said, slumping back in his chair.

"I have a plan to get her back, but it's risky."

"I trust you'll do everything in your power," Jack said. "I just wish there was more I could do."

"I know," Alexander said, willing the door to his Wizard's Den closed. "Zuhl wants the book, the one that will make him into an immortal undead. He called it a lich book, says he'll trade it for Abigail."

"As much as I want her back, you can't give him that book," Jack said.

"I know, but maybe this is an opportunity," Alexander said.

"You want to give him the other book."

"I think the ruse has a better chance of working against Zuhl than Phane," Alexander said, "especially since he's already done the hard work for us."

"What do you mean?" Jack asked.

"Well, we'd have had to convince Phane that the book exists," Alexander said, "then entice him to come and steal it. Zuhl already knows it exists and he wants it badly enough to abduct Abigail to get it. The more I think about it, the more I like it."

"So how do we get it to him?" Jack asked.

"We'll have a Sky Knight come and get it," Alexander said. "Bragador might be reluctant but I think I can persuade her, especially once I tell her that Zuhl has collared half a dozen dragons."

"What?" Jack asked.

"Apparently, he's very interested in old books," Alexander said, "seems he's discovered the process for enchanting dragon collars. In fact, he was riding one during the battle, or so Abigail thought when she jumped off her wyvern in midflight and cut him in half."

"What?!" Jack said.

Alexander recounted the battle for the Fellenden shipyards to a stunned Jack and explained how Zuhl had cheated death. Jack sat listening, slack-jawed and shaking his head slightly until Alexander finished.

"And she tells you to be more careful," he said.

"My thoughts exactly," Alexander said. "I have to give it to her, though. It worked. If she hadn't taken that dragon out of the battle, there's no telling how things would have turned out for us."

Chapter 16

The following morning, Alexander slipped into the firmament again, mindful of his limitations and intent on taking care with his new ability. He wasn't sure what kind of damage it could do to him if he projected his illusion for too long but he didn't want to find out, especially in the wake of such a painful experience the day before.

He went to the fortress island where he requested that Cassandra send two Sky Knights to the Spires. She was reluctant but agreed after he explained his reasons and assured her that Bragador was willing to permit the intrusion.

He'd spoken to Bragador the night before about Zuhl's use of the collars to control dragons. She'd been incensed at the idea, nearly beside herself with rage. After she'd calmed down, Alexander explained his plan and the need for speedy couriers to take the book to Fellenden for the exchange. The fact that the Sky Knights were part of a plan to kill Zuhl was the thing that persuaded her to permit wyverns to encroach into her territory—an unthinkable breach of security under other circumstances.

Cassandra also reported that the coven was nearly fully assembled, and the Reishi witches were making preparations for the spell that would undo the link between Isabel and the Sin'Rath witch Clotus.

His message delivered, Alexander returned to his body.

"How do you feel?" Jack asked.

"My head hurts a little, but nothing serious," he said. "I'm going to talk to Zuhl next … tell him that I agree to his deal."

"Why don't you wait awhile? At least until your head stops hurting," Jack said.

"I agree with Jack, My Love," Chloe said. "It always worries me when you're away, but now more than ever. You should go slowly and be careful with this new power, at least until you understand it better and understand your limits better as well."

"There's just so much to do," Alexander said.

"I know, My Love, but you only have one healing draught left. What happens if you overdo it again? There's time to implement your plan. The most urgent part has been set in motion."

"Maybe you're right," he said, relaxing into his bed and closing his eyes.

After lunch, he took the next step, sending his consciousness into the enormous white marble fortress on the southern tip of the Isle of Zuhl.

He found Lord Zuhl in a room that would have made Lucky giddy. It was easily a hundred feet square with forty-foot ceilings supported by a row of polished white marble pillars. The entire room was filled with worktables, each occupied by a different project. The walls were lined with bookshelves filled to overflowing with all manner of written works.

Zuhl was talking with another man about some obscure point of magic that Alexander didn't understand. The man was old—judging from the magic swelling his colors, probably very old. He looked like the quintessential wizard, long white hair and beard, grey robes, and a staff leaning against the nearest bookshelf. The colors of the thin silver collar around his neck screamed of magic as well, dark and powerful.

As Alexander watched them from the firmament, Zuhl abruptly turned and looked right at him.

"Ah, hello," Zuhl said. "I was wondering when you might pay me a visit. Welcome to Whitehall, we have some business to discuss."

Alexander projected an illusion of himself in front of the two men.

"Quite impressive," the other man said, turning to Zuhl. "You say he is still on Tyr with the dragons, Lord Zuhl, yet he's capable of projecting all this way. Quite impressive, indeed."

"Ah, that is much better, Alexander. May I call you Alexander?" Zuhl said.

"Call me whatever you want," Alexander said.

"You and your sister certainly share one trait," Zuhl said, somewhat bemused, "a lack of respect for your elders."

"It isn't your age I don't respect," Alexander said.

"Quite," Zuhl said. "Allow me to introduce Mage Harkness. Aside from your Mage Gamaliel, I believe he is the only other enchanter mage in all of the Seven Isles."

"Mage Gamaliel doesn't belong to me or to anyone else," Alexander said. "From the looks of that collar, it doesn't seem that you can say the same, Mage Harkness."

"Indeed," Harkness said, absentmindedly touching the collar around his neck. "Lord Zuhl put this on me a very long time ago. The worst of it is the fact that I enchanted it myself. I was very bitter about it for many years, but in time I've come to see the value of my position within Lord Zuhl's court."

"You're a slave," Alexander said. "Whatever you get from Zuhl can't be worth your freedom."

"I have far more than most free people," Harkness said. "A workshop that any mage would envy, perfect security, and the liberty to pursue any line of enquiry that catches my fancy. I could do far worse."

"I suppose if you tell yourself that often enough, you might actually come to believe it," Alexander said. Then he looked at Zuhl. "You have my sister."

"Yes," Zuhl said, "have you received my terms?"

"You want an old book from Malachi Reishi's private collection," Alexander said. "I believe I have it."

"Your sister suggested that you would never part with it, not even for her."

"She underestimates her value to me."

"Huh, I was beginning to believe that both you and she were insane," Zuhl said. "Your decisions up to this point have been most perplexing, and yet speaking to you face to face, so to speak, you seem quite reasonable, rational even. Shall we make arrangements for the exchange?"

"Yes," Alexander said. "I propose that our representatives meet on the open plain south of the Iron Oak forest along the road to Irondale. No dragons, no wyverns."

"Agreed," Zuhl said. "I will escort your sister there myself so that I might verify the contents of the book."

"Regrettably, I'll be unable to make the exchange myself," Alexander said.

"Quite understandable," Zuhl said. "Your representatives will suffice. I must say, Alexander, I didn't expect you to be so … practical. Perhaps there's another matter we could discuss."

"I'm listening."

"Withdraw from Fellenden entirely, then open the Gate from Zuhl to Andalia, and I will wage war against your enemies, leaving Ruatha and Ithilian entirely unscathed."

"An interesting proposal, but what about the people of Fellenden?"

"What of them?" Zuhl said with a shrug.

"I'll consider your proposal," Alexander said, fading into the firmament.

A moment later he appeared in Abigail's quarters. "Hi, how're you doing?" he asked.

"I'm bored silly."

"All things considered, that's good," he said. "I'm working on a way to get you back."

"I know," Abigail said.

Alexander smiled at his sister as he faded back into the firmament and returned to his body and a splitting headache. He sat up and put his head in his hands.

"Oh Dear Maker, that hurts."

"I didn't see any bleeding," Jack said, sitting forward.

"It's not as bad as the first time, but it's not good either," Alexander said. "I think I'll rest for a while before I go find the dragon that Abigail befriended."

"Things didn't go well with Zuhl, I take it."

"No, he's a liar," Alexander said. "He has no intention of giving Abigail back, but I don't know what his game is yet."

"Well," Jack said, "if the objective is to get the book into his hands, then it doesn't really matter if he gives us Abigail, so long as you have another plan to rescue her."

Alexander nodded with his eyes closed. "I do, I think."

"That's not as reassuring as I'd like."

"No, but it's all I've got right now."

His headache persisted until he fell asleep that night. He was anxious to move his plan forward, but he was also determined to be cautious with his new power, at least until he knew if it could actually kill him or not.

The following morning, while he lay in bed wishing that his leg would heal faster, Bragador approached. He was starting to become familiar with the

sensation of danger that he felt when she was near. This time it was different …
there was another with her.

She stopped at the door to his Wizard's Den and shoved a man to the
floor, her eyes flashing with fury.

"A small boat entered our waters in the night," she said. "Twelve men
and one of Phane's abominations he calls wraithkin. All are dead save this one. I
have questioned him, but I do not believe the answers he has given me."

The man looked up at Alexander, a mixture of fear and determination in
his eyes as he fixed his gaze on the Sovereign Stone.

"What's your purpose here?" Alexander asked, knowing the answer
before the man spoke.

He hesitated the way a man does when searching for a plausible lie.

"Did you come for this?" Alexander asked, touching the Stone. The
man's colors flared with anxiety.

"Was this the only thing he sent you for?" Alexander asked. Again, the
man's colors shifted and rippled with fear and deceit, though he held his tongue.

"You will answer his questions or I will rip your arm off and eat it while
you watch," Bragador said.

He glanced back and flinched at the coiled rage boiling in her golden
eyes.

"Prince Phane sent us for the Sovereign Stone, your head, and any books
in your possession," the man said, his voice cracking. "He has my wife and son.
I'm just a sailor, nothing more."

Alexander sighed. "He speaks true."

"Very well," Bragador said. She fixed the sailor with an angry glare.
"You will carry a message to your master from me. If he or his agents invade my
home *one* more time, I will call forth every dragon in this mountain and we will
wage total war against him. You will tell him that my patience for his meddling is
at an end."

With that, Bragador grabbed the man by the throat, lifted him from the
floor and carried him outside the Wizard's Den where she transformed into her
true form, still holding the terrified sailor, and launched into the sky.

"I don't envy him," Jack said.

"No, I don't either," Alexander said. "But he did confirm that Phane is
aware of the lich book."

"That doesn't change anything, does it?"

"I don't think so," Alexander said. "The Sky Knights should be here
today. We'll proceed as planned."

"Can we destroy that terrible book now, My Love?" Chloe asked.

"No, Little One. I'm not sure why, but I feel like it might still be
important."

***

Alexander appeared before a startled Isabel.

"Hi," he said.

"I was beginning to wonder if you'd forgotten about me."

"Not a chance. There are some other things happening that required my attention, and I've discovered, rather painfully, that I can only project over such distances for a short period of time without hurting myself."

She closed her eyes and shook her head. "I'm sorry. I haven't spoken to anyone since you left and I'm starting to go a little crazy."

Isabel thought she was putting things mildly. She'd discovered that being alone was the most difficult. Azugorath seemed to sense her idle mind and choose those times to push against her will, sometimes hard, forcing Isabel to devote everything she had to resisting, other times slow and steady, forcing Isabel to be vigilant over long periods of time. Those attacks were the worst—she didn't dare try to sleep because the nightmares would be bad.

When she was on the move, with a goal in mind, something to focus on, she could keep the Wraith Queen out of her head much more easily, but here ... she had nothing to do and no one to talk to. It felt like Azugorath had been stalking her for months—she was exhausted.

"I wish I could stay and keep you company," he said.

"It's all right. Did you learn anything?"

"I'm afraid so," Alexander said, but before he could explain the danger, Isabel doubled over, collapsing to the floor. Then she screamed—a shriek of agony so piercing that he slammed back into his body from the sudden terror of it.

He sat bolt upright staring off into the distance, fear and helplessness threatening to overwhelm him.

"What is it, My Love?" Chloe asked.

"It's Isabel. I have to get back to her. I think Phane has the other witch."

He lay down and focused on his breathing, calming himself in spite of the turmoil roiling within his soul. The firmament came to him slower than he would have liked but he found his way there nonetheless. Then in a blink he was floating over his wife.

She lay doubled over, gasping for breath and writhing in pain.

A moment later he was at the fortress island, materializing next to Magda and Cassandra, surrounded by the entire Reishi Coven, save his wife. They were assembled in the scrying well atop the plateau.

"Isabel just collapsed," he said. "Cast your spell."

"We're nearly ready," Magda said. "You must withdraw before we can begin."

He vanished into the firmament, helplessness nearly overwhelming him. He couldn't lose her. After all of the threats she'd faced, to die like this was unthinkable. Worse, he doubted Phane was even trying to kill her ...

A moment later he was back on Karth, disembodied and unseen, in a large austere chamber with Phane and a woman that was so sublimely beautiful that he nearly lost his focus and returned to his body ... until he looked at her colors, dark and evil, filled with hate and malice, twisted and unnatural.

She was strapped to a torture table in the center of a magic circle and Phane was smiling as he sliced a deep gash along the outside of her arm. She screamed, rage mixed with agony reverberating off the bare stone walls.

Alexander appeared just outside the circle.

"Stop! You're killing Isabel!"

Phane looked up, droplets of blood splattered across his face, and smiled with such boyish delight that Alexander almost imagined that he could like this man ... but only for a moment.

"Ah, Dear Cousin, it's so good of you to visit me. I see that your command of magic is advancing quickly. Quite a feat in fact, projecting over such distances. I have it on good authority that you're still recuperating under the care and protection of the dragons. I must admit, I didn't see that one coming."

"Drop the small talk, Phane," Alexander said. "You're hurting Isabel."

Phane motioned toward the witch strapped to the table with his bloody knife and cocked his head.

"This isn't Isabel," he said. "Surely you can see that."

"No, but she's bound to this one by a doppelganger spell," Alexander said.

"Of course she is," Phane said. "I saw through her ruse the moment I laid eyes on her. Don't get me wrong, the Sin'Rath witches are dangerous, but they rarely think things through. Something to do with their lineage, I suspect."

"If you kill her, Isabel will die," Alexander said.

"Of course she will, you simpleton, that's how a doppelganger spell works," Phane said.

"I thought you had plans for Isabel," Alexander said.

"Oh, I do," Phane said. "Of course, I suppose I could just kill her now. Perhaps such a loss would crush you enough to make you give up. But then, it might just make you even more intractable. Decisions, decisions. I must say, seeing you like this, so distraught and helpless, is quite appealing to me. On balance, perhaps revealing more of my plans for your wife will cause you even greater distress.

"Yes, I think so. You see, Dear Cousin, pain leads one to feel anger and anger is one pathway to the darkness. Up until now, Isabel has resisted Azugorath's influence, but this," he plunged his knife through the outer shoulder of the Sin'Rath witch, eliciting a blood-curdling scream, "is bound to weaken Isabel's resolve and drive her toward the kind of action that will tarnish her soul forever and leave her nowhere to turn ... save to me."

"My sisters will feed on you, Phane," Clotus said through clenched teeth, "one way or another, we will take your link and finally free our mother. Then the Seven Isles will be ours for the taking."

"Hush, Witch," Phane said, twisting the knife in her shoulder. "Do you really think me such a fool? Do you really believe I would come here without taking precautions to protect myself against your charms? Here I stand, seeing you for the thing you are, not the impossibly beautiful woman you would have me see, immune to your magic.

"I will slaughter your entire coven and rid the world of your taint once and for all, and then kill the remaining rabble from the House of Karth in the bargain. Even better, you will deliver Isabel into my hands and give me the power to exact my vengeance against my dear cousin here. And the most delicious part of it all is that you have delivered the means to accomplish all of this simply by coming here."

Clotus looked alarmed, even through the pain of Phane's torture.

"Once again, you and your sisters have failed to fully think through the potential consequences of your actions, preferring to believe that your plans will unfold flawlessly. Even young Alexander here isn't so foolish."

"What are you talking about, Phane?" Alexander said.

He looked up, smiling warmly. "A doppelganger spell creates a link between two people, a link that I can use to locate Isabel, and a number of my enemies with her. So you see, the Sin'Rath have unwittingly played right into my hands. Soon, I will send a force of adequate strength, one uniquely suited to this very purpose, to eliminate the offspring of the Succubus Queen Sin'Rath, end the line of Karth, and collect my future bride.

"With Isabel at my side, you will fall and those you protect will have no choice but to kneel before me or be crushed. Come spring, my Lancers will break your father's defensive line and swarm into northern Ruatha leaving nothing but blood and fire in their wake. This war will soon be over and I will assume my rightful place as the Sovereign of the Seven Isles."

"You keep telling yourself that, Phane," Alexander said as he faded back into the firmament, reappearing next to Isabel. She was curled into a ball, struggling to breathe.

"Don't give in to it, Isabel," he said. "Phane is just trying to make you angry so Azugorath can exert greater influence over you. You have to fight it."

She nodded tightly.

"I wish I could stay with you."

"Go," she managed through clenched teeth.

"I love you," he said as he vanished.

He opened his eyes and sat up gasping from the pain, immediately feeling for blood dripping from his nose and ears. Finding none, he eased back into his bed and closed his eyes, willing the throbbing in his head to subside.

Chapter 17

Later that evening, Alexander went in search of Ixabrax and found him hiding in a cave accessible only through a deep fissure in the glacier north of Whitehall. The dragon was coiled up, sleeping fitfully. He was injured, deep gashes oozing blood along his side.

"Ixabrax," Alexander said, after his projection appeared.

The dragon opened one catlike eye and stared at Alexander.

"You have made a fatal mistake, Human," Ixabrax said. "I'm hungry and in no mood to hunt."

Faster than a blink, he snapped at Alexander, his fangs passing through the illusion and falling on empty air.

"What wizardry is this?" the dragon said, looking about warily.

"I'm Alexander Reishi. My sister freed you from your bondage and now she's in need of your help."

"And here you stand before me without standing before me," Ixabrax said. "While I am in her debt, I'm in no condition to help her."

"How were you injured?"

"I tried to free my sire," Ixabrax said. "I bit down on his collar with all my strength and yet it held. He did this to me, though he could have done far worse. Even as we fought, I knew he was resisting the power of his collar with all his might."

"If I can help you heal, will you help me free Abigail?"

Ixabrax's eyes narrowed. "How would you heal me?"

"In truth, I'm not sure yet," Alexander said.

Ixabrax chuckled, a deep rumbling coming from his belly.

"Another honest human," the dragon said, "you and your sister are indeed cut from the same cloth. If you help me heal, then I will help you free your sister but only if you give me your word that you will then help me free my family. Her sword can cut the collars that bind them. I know of nothing else that can."

"Bargain struck," Alexander said. "Look for my people within the week."

"How will I know them?"

"They'll call you by name," Alexander said, fading into the firmament.

His head hurt when he returned to his body, but less so. As he'd hoped, practice and experience were beginning to expand his ability to project an illusion over such vast distances.

By dark, his headache had subsided entirely. Not long after, a dragon in the form of a woman appeared at his door.

"I'm Tasia. Lady Bragador asked me to watch for your couriers. They have arrived."

Two Sky Knights entered, looking a little pale.

"Lord Reishi, we've come as quickly as our wyverns could carry us," the lead man said.

Alexander got up, leaning heavily on his cane, and hobbled to the strongbox. He removed a book, tied securely with a stout leather thong, and set it on the table before relocking the box.

"Take this book to Conner Ithilian in Fellenden City," Alexander said. "Do not open it for any reason."

As the man grasped the book, Alexander didn't let go, but instead fixed the man with his blind eyes.

"Give me your oath that you will not permit this book to be opened," he said.

"I swear on my life, Lord Reishi."

"That's good, because if you open this book you will surely die," Alexander said. "Make haste and deliver it into Prince Conner's hands and no other's."

"It will be done, Lord Reishi."

Tasia escorted the knights back to their wyverns, then transformed into her true form, a magnificent iridescent silver dragon nearly as large as Bragador, and flew with them until they passed over the Spires on their way north to Fellenden. Alexander watched with his clairvoyance until they were clear of the dragons' domain.

"Just one more piece to put into place," Alexander said. "I think I'll wait until tomorrow before I go to Blackstone. That conversation's liable to take some time and I'm not looking forward to the aftermath."

"So use your dream-whisper to set things in motion," Jack said. "Blackstone should still have some Rangers sleeping in shifts to receive your messages."

Alexander snorted, shaking his head. "I'd gotten so caught up in this new ability that I'd forgotten Blackstone is the one place where I can reliably send word without projecting an illusion. I'll be back soon."

He went to the message board first, disembodied awareness floating unnoticed in Kelvin's workshop as his people toiled on a variety of projects. There were a number of messages for him:

1. Blackstone's magic has failed. The heartstone is shattered.
2. Lucky has become a mage.
3. Wren has vanished, but we're certain that she didn't leave by crossing the bridge.
4. We're moving the Wizard's Guild to Glen Morillian.
5. Duane reports that the assassins assigned to kill Elred Rake have failed. Their heads were delivered to his sentries in a basket.

He floated there reading the messages over again, trying to make sense of all that had transpired. The news of the heartstone was grave and worrisome, yet expected.

Lucky's ascension to mage was a triumph that had the potential to turn the tide of the entire war. His security had quite suddenly become of paramount importance.

He was happy to see that Kelvin had decided to relocate his guild to the relative safety of Glen Morillian and sad to hear that four more good people had died by his order in the attempt to kill Elred Rake.

Wren's disappearance puzzled him. She was a beautiful and vibrant young woman, precious beyond measure for the simple fact that she was alive, but in the grand scheme of things, she was nothing more than a serving girl who'd befriended his wife and sister. Her disappearance troubled him, more for the inexplicability of it than anything else.

He faded into the firmament and thought of the waifish young woman. A moment later, his awareness coalesced over a small ship sailing south along the west coast of Ruatha near the Great Forest. He pushed into the ship, disembodied awareness floating among the crew. The men were pirates, but there were three among them that were more—two wizards and a wraithkin. Alexander avoided them and went into the hold of the ship.

He found Wren chained to a bulkhead. She was wrapped in a single thin blanket, shivering and crying softly.

Alexander materialized and knelt next to her, whispering her name softly. She looked up with a start, fear in her wide innocent eyes.

"Lord Reishi? Is that really you?"

"Yes and no," Alexander said. "You're seeing a projection of me. I'm not really here."

"So you didn't come to save me?" she sobbed.

"I just discovered you were missing," Alexander said. "You have to believe me, I'm going to help you and you're going to make it through this, but right now I need to know who took you and why."

"I don't know," Wren said. "I was in bed when they came. It was dark. They gagged me and put a bag over my head. A wagon took me for a while, then they put me on a boat. I've been here ever since. They don't talk to me, even when they bring me food. Why are they doing this to me?" she sobbed again, breaking down in tears.

"I don't know, but I'm going to find out and I'm going to send help," Alexander said. "I have to go now. I need you to be strong, Wren. Help is on the way."

She nodded, sniffing back her tears as he vanished.

He shifted his awareness to Blackstone's sleeping room in a blink. Three Rangers awaited his message. He slipped into the dreams of the nearest, manifesting on a battlefield as the Ranger fought to defend the walls of New Ruatha. The enemy was mounting a charge and Alexander could feel the fear and hopelessness of the Ranger as his nightmare threatened to overwhelm him.

Alexander imposed his will on the man's dream and cleared the field of everyone save himself and the Ranger. The man was confused at first but gathered his wits quickly once the unreality of the dream set in and he remembered that he was the vessel for Alexander's messages.

"Lord Reishi, I stand ready to deliver your orders."

"Tell Mage Gamaliel to send all of the explosive weapons he has to the Gate immediately. I'll have Lord Abel open it as soon as they arrive. Tell Mage

Alabrand to prepare to leave for Glen Morillian in the morning. Instruct Captain Alaric to send a thousand Rangers to escort him, then tell Mage Gamaliel to send as many wizards as he can spare and all of the Sky Knights still in the Keep as well. Lucky must arrive there safely as soon as possible.

"Tell Captain Alaric to send message riders to Southport immediately. Wren has been abducted and is aboard a ship sailing along the coastline toward the city. Have him instruct the Southport Navy to locate this ship and rescue the girl."

"I will deliver your messages immediately," the Ranger said.

Alexander slipped out of his dreams and back into the firmament. The source of all things had become a familiar place to him. He was comfortable floating on the ocean of potential that created each moment anew, listening to the song of creation as it unfolded.

Again, he wondered about Siduri. There was so much potential and so much danger bound up in his story. His mere existence was beyond reason, and yet Alexander had no doubt—Siduri was real. He'd accomplished feats of magic beyond anything that even the most accomplished arch mage had ever considered, and yet he'd withdrawn from the world, content to observe ... until Alexander's desperation had given him cause to act.

With a flick of his mind, Alexander was in the chamber where he'd found the blood of the earth. He floated above the crystal bowl filled with the potent liquid and pondered its purpose. It screamed of puissance, power beyond mortal comprehension, yet real enough to scoop up and put in a vial.

Not for the first time, he considered putting the small amount he'd taken back, but the thought of giving up even one chance of saving Isabel caused desperation to well up within him, driving out the idea and confirming his resolve.

If it came to it, he would use the blood of the earth to save his wife, come what may. Thoughts of Siduri evoked his worries about the shades. Even if Alexander managed to banish the last of them, they were eternal, existing in the netherworld, outside of time and substance and they were determined to unmake reality.

And now they knew how.

Even if he destroyed the Nether Gate, they now knew such a thing was possible—for that matter, the Taker knew it as well. Yet, if the Taker could manifest in this world, he would have, so it stood to reason that he needed agents to do his bidding in the world of time and substance. The shades were the real problem—the threat that could end all things.

As he floated there, pondering the nature of his most dangerous enemy, a thought occurred to him. The shades were nothing but disembodied souls, empowered by the Taker to exist unbound to flesh.

What if they could be bound to something else?

He had in his possession a book that detailed the process for placing one's soul within a specially prepared item so that the caster of the spell could become an immortal undead. What if he could use the principles within that book to create a device capable of capturing the soul of a shade and imprisoning it for all time?

One more item to discuss with the Guild Mage.

**

"Hello, Kelvin," Alexander said a moment after he seemingly materialized before the Guild Mage. "I've learned how to project illusions over great distances, but only for a short time. Summon Lucky and Jataan, I'll return when they arrive."

Kelvin smiled. "Hope was becoming very thin around here, Alexander. It's good to see you."

"You as well," Alexander said, fading out of sight but remaining present while awaiting his friends.

Lucky was the first to arrive. He'd regained the belly he'd lost from his travels and was flushed from his haste. Jataan entered the room several minutes later, moving stiffly and deliberately.

Alexander materialized in front of them.

"It's good to see you all," he said.

"Lord Reishi," Jataan said, "we received a report from Captain Kalderson of the Reishi Protectorate Navy that you'd been killed, yet the letter he carried from Lady Reishi claimed that you're alive but wounded on the central island of Tyr."

"Isabel told Captain Kalderson that I was dead to convince him to take her to Karth," Alexander said. "A wraithkin stabbed me through the leg. It'll be a while before I'm ready to travel, but I'm safe in the care of the dragons of Tyr."

"Bragador has accepted you into her home?" Kelvin asked, somewhat incredulously.

"I saved the life of her unborn daughter," Alexander said. "We've come to an agreement."

"Tread lightly, Alexander," Kelvin said.

"I'm doing my best. She's not happy with me being here, even less that I've befriended her daughter, but she's agreed to give me sanctuary until I heal. Ultimately, she wants nothing to do with our conflict, but Phane might just be foolish enough to force her hand."

"That may be his undoing," Lucky said.

"We can only hope," Alexander said. "She caught a ship full of assassins in her waters yesterday and sent the lone survivor back to Phane with a message to stay away. If he's dumb enough to keep messing with her, she might just solve our problem for us—permanently."

"Phane isn't stupid enough to risk the wrath of several hundred dragons," Jataan said.

"Pity," Alexander said. "Bragador and her family could end this war overnight."

"Don't be too eager to get the dragons involved," Kelvin said. "They fought in the Reishi War and it nearly wiped them out. This time they may choose to take the side of dragons against humans instead of fighting each other."

"I hadn't considered that," Alexander said.

"We've received your messages and have begun to implement your orders," Kelvin said. "Much has transpired since we last spoke."

"You have no idea," Alexander said. "I wish I had enough time to tell you everything that's happened, but I don't. For now, I need a way to heal a dragon."

Lucky looked perplexed for a moment before nodding. "I could combine a number of healing draughts into a very large dose. I've never tried to heal a dragon before, but I don't see why it shouldn't work."

"Good, send it to the Gate along with the explosive weapons," Alexander said. "Kelvin, do you think you could you use the principles contained in the undead book to create a container capable of trapping a shade?"

"Possibly, but I couldn't say for certain without extensive research," Kelvin said. "And, of course, I would need the book."

"That's what I was afraid of," Alexander said. "Both Zuhl and Phane want it, so I don't dare let it out of my sight. Think about it and do what research you can for now."

"Understood," Kelvin said.

"May I ask why you need to heal a dragon?" Lucky said.

"Abigail's been taken by Zuhl. I plan to send Anatoly and Magda to find the dragon Ixabrax, so he can help us get her back. I wish I had more time to explain, but I have to go. Say hi to my mom for me and make sure she knows I'm doing everything I can to get Abigail back."

He returned to his body and a pounding headache. All of the pieces were moving into place.

Chapter 18

Anatoly slipped the book into a satchel and looked to Magda. She nodded.

"I'm sending a hundred Rangers to ride escort," Conner said. "If there's any trouble, they'll cover your retreat."

"I know Alexander well enough to know he's not telling us everything," Anatoly said. "And he wouldn't do that without good reason, so I suspect there's going to be some kind of trouble."

Magda raised her eyebrow.

"Just make the trade and bring her back," Conner said.

Anatoly grunted. He was still a little stiff and the set of dragon-plate armor that Captain Sava had given him didn't fit quite as well as his ruined armor, but it was far lighter and more durable. Sava had lost several of his Strikers during Zuhl's attack, but their armor had survived unscathed.

Anatoly and Magda rode for the better part of the day, arriving at the location chosen for the exchange late in the afternoon. Zuhl and a hundred of his brutes were there waiting. Anatoly swallowed the sudden lump in his throat when he saw Abigail sitting atop the horse next to Zuhl. He clenched his jaw as he raised his hand, signaling the company of Rangers to halt.

He and Magda proceeded forward as Zuhl and Abigail trotted out from the protection of the men surrounding them, stopping ten feet away in the open space between both forces.

"Did he hurt you?" Anatoly asked.

"Just a few bruises but nothing that won't heal," she said.

"I've brought Lady Abigail, as promised," Zuhl said. "I would see the book."

Anatoly scowled as he withdrew the book from his satchel and held it up for the ancient mage.

Zuhl smiled ever so slightly. "May I?" he said, holding out his hand.

Anatoly rode forward cautiously, extending the book to Zuhl.

He took it and closed his eyes for a moment, muttering words in some long-dead language, and waited for some unseen response before smiling to himself.

"Excellent, our business is done," he said, turning away from them and leaving Abigail in their care.

She sighed with relief.

"Let's get out of here," she said, spurring her horse toward the Rangers.

Anatoly rode up next to Magda.

"Did that seem just a bit too easy to you?" he asked.

"Yes," she said, nodding.

Once they were well away from Zuhl and his brutes, they stopped to make camp for the night.

Anatoly was brushing his horse when Alexander appeared beside him.

"That's not Abigail," he said quietly. "I'm not even sure if it's human."

"What do you mean?" Anatoly asked, his mood visibly darkening.

"Zuhl sent an imposter."

"Are you sure?"

"Absolutely," Alexander said. "Her colors aren't right and it looks like she's under a powerful spell. But more to the point, I just looked in on Abigail in Whitehall. She's still being held by Zuhl."

"Then we gave him that book for nothing," Anatoly said.

Alexander smiled, shaking his head. "Not for nothing. Have Magda help you take the imposter alive. We might gain some valuable information."

Anatoly nodded, unslinging his war axe.

He approached the fire cautiously, catching Magda's eye and showing her the blade of his axe. She tensed slightly at his unspoken warning, made an excuse and left the fire where the Abigail double and a number of Rangers sat sipping hot tea.

"Abigail's an imposter," he whispered. "We need to take her alive."

She looked at him hard, searching his face for confirmation.

His unflinching gaze left no room for doubt.

She nodded before turning toward the campfire and beginning her spell.

Anatoly began to move quietly out of the way.

Magda released her spell, sending twin spheres streaking toward the imposter, one light blue, the other amber. The amber sphere hit first, striking a shell of magical energy surrounding the imposter and rebounding back at Magda. She tried to dodge her own spell but was struck on the shoulder. The amber light almost instantly encapsulated her, paralyzing her with her own magic and sending her toppling to the ground.

The blue sphere struck the imposter a fraction of a second later, spreading its light-blue magical energy across the surface of her body in an instant. A moment later the spell surrounding her broke, revealing a woman that didn't look quite human. Her skin had an almost imperceptible blue tinge to it and her eyes were catlike, similar to those of a dragon.

She sprang to her feet, muttering the words of a spell and extending her arm toward three nearby Rangers who were caught totally off guard by the sudden turn of events. A spray of frost leapt from her hand, coating the surprised men with ice and stunning them into near paralysis.

Anatoly didn't waste any time. He started rushing her the moment she stood, his axe raised high and ready. As she turned toward him, he brought the blade down, cleanly severing her forearm, her hand flopping to the ground. She screamed in pain as he continued into her, slamming his dragon-plate-armored shoulder into her chest and knocking her to the ground, stunned and wracked by the sudden pain of his assault.

Within seconds he had her bound and gagged.

"Check on Mistress Magda," he barked to a nearby Ranger as he secured the imposter's bindings.

Alexander appeared in their camp a few minutes after the imposter had been taken to a tent and tied to a post.

"Well done," he said.

"What about Abigail?" Anatoly asked, uncharacteristic worry seeping into his voice.

"You and Magda will ride for the Gate at first light," Alexander said. "I'll have Abel open it for you as soon as you arrive. From Ithilian, you'll go to Zuhl and find the dragon Ixabrax. He'll help you free Abigail."

"Why would a dragon help us?" Magda asked.

"I made a deal with him," Alexander said. "I believe he'll honor it."

"I hope you're right," Magda said. "Dragons are nothing to trifle with."

"Trust me when I tell you, I understand that better than most. Abel will fill in the details when you arrive."

"And what about that book?" Magda asked. "Ancient spellbooks can be exceedingly dangerous."

"You have no idea," Alexander said. "Fortunately, neither does Zuhl."

"I take it he didn't get what he was expecting either," Anatoly said.

"No, he did not," Alexander said. "With any luck, he'll be dead by the time you arrive."

"I'm starting to like this plan," Anatoly said.

"I thought you might," Alexander said, fading out of sight.

* * *

Dawn broke over clear skies on Ithilian. Anatoly and Magda stood before the Gate dressed in heavy furs as was the custom on the Isle of Zuhl. Twelve highly trained and skilled individuals handpicked by Jataan P'Tal stood behind them. Some were wizards, a few were Rangers, the rest soldiers, but all of these men had one characteristic in common: all of them were big, powerful-looking men.

Abel was there as well with General Kishor and Mage Lenox. Everything was in place.

Alexander appeared on the Gate platform and nodded his approval.

"The enemy is unaware of our plan," he said. "Our initial attack will take them entirely by surprise. Once you're through the Gate, I'll be able to communicate with you and coordinate your efforts, but other than that, you're on your own. This is your last chance to reconsider."

Anatoly grunted dismissively, Magda held her head high and stood her ground. All twelve members of the newly formed Reishi Elite Guard took a single step forward as one.

Alexander turned to Abel. "Proceed."

The King of Ithilian used his Thinblade to open the Gate to Zuhl. The moment the stone wall shimmered away and opened a passage to an island thousands of leagues away, the largest of Mage Gamaliel's explosive weapons rolled through. Shouts of alarm were heard from the soldiers of Zuhl as Abel closed the Gate. A moment later Mage Lenox crushed the activation stone, detonating the weapon.

Abel counted to ten before opening the Gate again to a scene of chaos and carnage. Thousands lay dead or dying, their broken bodies scattered haphazardly across the frozen tundra of southern Zuhl.

Fourteen souls stepped through into the disarray, separating into their assigned teams and heading in the direction of their respective objectives. Anatoly and Magda went north into the sea of soldiers surrounding the Gate. Their objective, the rescue of Abigail, was the most vital to Alexander, but the others had important work to do as well.

The members of the Elite Guard had been sent to collect information about Zuhl's army, his battle plans, and his ships. They were to blend into his army and look for vulnerabilities, striking where they could from the shadows, seeking opportunities to do the greatest harm with the minimum risk of capture or discovery. Each had volunteered. Many would never return. None could be taken alive. All of them had accepted the risks. All of them had suffered loss at Zuhl's hands. Once through the Gate they broke into teams of three and melted into the vast army that was working to understand the nature of the sudden threat that had disturbed their otherwise mundane morning.

Wearing clothes and furs taken from Zuhl's barbarian horde on Fellenden, Anatoly and Magda blended in without effort, just two more people in a sea of many. They wound their way through the tents and paddocks, avoiding contact as much as possible. Most of the soldiers were making ready for battle, donning armor and pulling on their boots. Few gave them a second look and most of them only to appraise Magda until they saw Anatoly with his axe resting on his shoulder.

It didn't take Anatoly long to notice that the men with emblems of rank also carried the finest weapons. Most of the soldiers were armed with mediocre blades and spears, but the officers all carried well-made weapons forged of quality steel. When he realized the significance of their weapons, that they served as an indication of rank, he made sure everyone passing by got a good look at his war axe.

It took most of the morning to reach the outskirts of the army encampment. A few sentries tried to question them but they were dissuaded by Anatoly's deliberate aggressiveness.

Rather than accept their challenge, he demanded to see their weapon or armor, inspecting it as a superior officer would, berating them for their lack of attention to detail and ordering them to repair whatever defects, imagined or real, that he happened to find.

He strode through the encampment like he was the commanding general and his demeanor was enough to cause most soldiers to look the other way or quickly attend to whatever task was at hand.

When they rounded a corner and caught their first glimpse of Whitehall, the enormous white marble fortress that stood in the center of the city, they came face to face with an officer dressed in polished white armor and armed with a spear of such craftsmanship that Anatoly was actually impressed.

To the officer's right was a woman who didn't look quite human. Her skin was tinged blue and almost looked scaled, her eyes were catlike and her fingernails had grown into talons.

To the officer's left was a man armed with a finely crafted sword and a shield formed from a dragon's scale.

"You there," the officer said, pointing his spear at Anatoly. "What's your name?"

Anatoly stepped forward, Magda began muttering under her breath. "Who are you to question me?" Anatoly barked, facing off with the man.

"I am General Kergen, commander of Lord Zuhl's army, and I know all of my senior officers by name. You are not among them, yet you carry a weapon of rank ... so I ask again, who are you?"

In a blink, Anatoly leveraged the axe off his shoulder and brought it down in a powerful stroke aimed at splitting Kergen's head in half, but the general shifted sideways just enough that Anatoly's axe came down on his shoulder plate instead, driving the man to the ground with the force of the blow but not even denting the armor protecting Zuhl's commanding general. Anatoly kicked him full in the face, sending him toppling over backward, blood spraying across the ground.

The second officer raised his shield and drew his sword in one fluid motion, rushing Anatoly, slamming him with his shield and knocking him off balance. He pressed his advantage with a powerful sword thrust, driving his blade into Anatoly's breastplate hard enough to penetrate even the most finely crafted steel armor, but the dragon-plate held.

Magda's shield spell encircled her with protective force and she began casting another.

"Flee, Priestess!" the second officer shouted as he squared off with Anatoly, who had regained his balance and had raised his axe into a high guard.

The woman with blue-tinged skin released her spell. The air grew cold and still, then a thick wall of ice grew rapidly from the ground, completely encircling both General Kergen and the woman.

Magda released her spell, a simple force-push that sent the man facing Anatoly flying to the ground.

A dozen or so nearby soldiers had noticed the fight and were coming to assist their commander.

"Time to go," Magda said.

Anatoly looked at the man sprawled on the ground, then at the onrushing soldiers and clenched his jaw as he nodded to Magda and turned toward the city.

They fled into the cover of the sprawling mass of poorly constructed homes and shops. The capital city of Zuhl was a study in contrasts. Most of the people lived in squalor, surviving just on the edge of desperation in the city's outer slums. Their homes were inadequate to the climate, cobbled together from stone or scraps of wood, animal pelts filling the gaps and serving as doors. Yet in the center of the city stood Whitehall, a magnificent fortress castle fashioned from polished white marble, its soaring towers capped in gold leaf, each flying Zuhl's banner, flapping in the wind.

Anatoly and Magda wove through the city evading their pursuers. Most of the people they encountered were women, children, or the elderly. Every man capable of wielding a weapon had been pressed into service, leaving the most vulnerable of their society to fend for themselves in the face of a harsh environment and a scarcity of food. The people of the city were cowed, dispirited, and afraid. They avoided eye contact and did their level best to ignore Anatoly and Magda.

Shouts of alarm filtered through the frigid morning air from their pursuers, but they were fading into the distance as Anatoly and Magda moved deeper into the city. Closer to Whitehall, the slums gave way to homes and shops constructed from stone with stout wooden doors, yet none were made from the white marble of Zuhl's fortress.

"We need a place to hole up until nightfall," Anatoly said.

"I agree," Magda said. "Perhaps that house would do."

"Judging from the smoke coming out of the chimney, I suspect someone's home," Anatoly said. "I'd rather not kill anyone who doesn't have it coming."

"Again, I agree," Magda said. "Give me a few moments to prepare and I can subdue them without bloodshed."

Anatoly nodded and she began casting another spell.

He knocked forcefully on the door. "By order of Lord Zuhl, you are commanded to open this door," he shouted.

A woman timidly opened the door, her eyes wide with fear. Before she could utter a word, Magda reached out and touched her on the forehead. The woman's eyes closed and she slumped to the floor. Anatoly entered quickly, followed by Magda. An elderly man sat by the fire eyeing them suspiciously, two children peeked around the corner of the doorframe leading out of the main room of the house. Magda closed and barred the front door.

"We won't harm you if you don't give us cause," Anatoly said, pointing his war axe at the old man.

"I'm old and frail," the man said, rocking in his chair, "you have nothing to fear from me, but my son will be home this evening. If you're still here when he returns, he'll gut you both while his sons watch."

"Come, children," Magda said to the two young boys in the other room. They stayed where they were.

"It's all right, boys," the old man said. "Our guests won't harm you." He fixed Anatoly with a look that was both a command and a desperate plea.

"Is there anyone else in your household?" Anatoly asked.

"No, just the four of us," the old man said, as the two boys went to their grandfather.

"I think I'll have a look around just to be sure," Anatoly said.

"I thought you might," the old man said, looking into his tea.

Anatoly returned a few moments later. "Three rooms and a cellar. Just the one door in the front and a window in back that's barred. I think we're good."

Magda nodded.

"What did you do to my mother?" demanded one of the boys.

"She will wake in a few minutes," Magda said.

Anatoly slung his axe, carefully picked the woman up and gently laid her on the couch.

"We have no quarrel with you," he said. "We just need a place to stay for a few hours."

"What did you do?" the old man asked. "Speak out against Lord Zuhl? Or are you just common criminals?"

"That doesn't concern you," Magda said.

"Fair enough," the old man said, "the less I know the less I can tell the soldiers when they question me."

"My thoughts exactly," Magda said.

The woman woke with a start, sitting up and looking around frantically. "Who are you? Why have you invaded our home?"

"We mean you no harm," Magda said. "All we need is a place to hide for a few hours, then we'll be on our way."

The woman looked at her boys, the beginning of panic spreading across her face. "And then what? Will you kill us? The soldiers will surely question us about your whereabouts. How can you afford to leave us unharmed knowing that we'll go to the authorities the moment we can?"

"Hush, Kayla," the old man said. "Why don't you make us another pot of tea? My cup has grown cold."

She looked from him to Anatoly, then back to the old man and nodded, getting up and going to a cabinet.

"You're not from the Isle of Zuhl, are you?" the old man said. "No, I thought not. You are clearly a seasoned warrior and you carry a weapon of rank, yet you treat this woman as an equal. That is not our way, so I can only surmise that you have come from another isle. That makes you an enemy of Lord Zuhl."

He fell silent and nodded to himself, smiling slightly. "There was a great explosion early this morning. Such a thing would make an excellent distraction, don't you think?"

"Stop speculating about us," Anatoly said. "You're an old soldier and you're trying to gather information."

"I'm an old man who was once a soldier. Quite honestly, my only interest here is that you don't harm my son's wife or my grandchildren. As for my speculation, well, let's just say I'm curious. I served Lord Zuhl for many years, my son serves him now. That service has provided this home for our family and guaranteed that we eat well while others go without, but I have no love for Lord Zuhl. He has kept the people of this island embroiled in war and petty disputes for centuries. I've often wondered at his motives ... until now."

"Go on," Anatoly said.

"Now that the Reishi scourge has returned, Lord Zuhl is prepared to defend us against it. All of those centuries of border wars between countless tribes have bred a people uniquely suited to making war. We are battle-hardened and prepared for the enemy we face. While I don't believe that Lord Zuhl is the god he claims to be, he is wise and prescient. I for one am glad that he's gone to such great lengths to preserve us against the Reishi threat."

Anatoly and Magda shared a look.

"As I suspected, you're infiltrators sent by the Reishi," the old man said. "You will fail. Lord Zuhl will find you and you will suffer greatly for your murderous ambitions."

Anatoly snorted and shook his head. "The truth is, you wouldn't believe the truth if I told you."

"Why not tell me?" the old man said. "We both know you're going to murder my family before this day is done. What do you have to lose by humoring an old man with your version of the truth?"

"I don't like where this is going," Magda said.

Kayla brought a tray of cups filled with steaming hot tea, timidly offering it to Anatoly first, the cups shaking from the trembling in her hands.

"I'll pass," he said.

"As will I," Magda said.

"Suit yourself," the old man said. "I want you boys to both drink your cups, all of it."

"Stop!" Anatoly said.

Kayla froze in midstride.

"Can you detect poison?" he asked Magda.

She looked at him sharply when the realization of what he was suggesting sank in, then nodded curtly, muttering the words of a spell. The tea began to glow a soft, menacing reddish color.

Anatoly swatted the tray out of the woman's hand, scattering cups of poisoned tea across the floor.

"You would kill your whole family?" he demanded.

"Better by my hand than by yours," the old man said, drawing a knife from the folds of his tunic and casting it at Anatoly with remarkable accuracy. It struck his breastplate just left of center and clattered to the floor.

Anatoly spun his war axe into his hands and stepped forward, shoving Kayla to the floor with the haft of it.

"Remain seated, old man," Anatoly said. Then turning to Magda, he said, "It's time to go."

Magda nodded, casting another spell. A pulse of soft white light shone from her outstretched hands, bathing the four in its power. A moment later they all slumped into a deep sleep.

"They'll be out for several hours and then they'll wake feeling refreshed and well," she said.

"That's quite a spell," Anatoly said.

"I actually devised it to help people through sickness," she said with a sad smile.

They banked the fire and left the family to their magically induced sleep.

"Do you think they'll believe any differently about us when they wake, alive and well?" Anatoly asked.

"I suspect they'll believe what they want to believe," Magda said.

"You're probably right."

Chapter 19

By midafternoon they were gaining altitude as they reached the base of the glacier that blanketed the mountain range to the north of Zuhl's capital city. The soldiers searching for them had fanned out throughout the city but it was such a large place that Anatoly and Magda had little difficulty evading them. Since there wasn't a wall surrounding the city itself, it had been relatively easy to escape, especially after darkness fell.

From their vantage point in the foothills overlooking the city, they could see the true size of Zuhl's army.

"I knew he had a lot of men, but I had no idea just how many," Anatoly said. "We have to come up with a way to eliminate those ships."

"Hopefully, the Elite Guard will have some luck on that front," Magda said. "And perhaps Alexander was successful against Zuhl himself. I don't know the contents of the book we gave him but I have my suspicions. If I'm right, Zuhl may well be dead already. If that's the case, it's only a matter of time before all those men down there start fighting amongst themselves."

"Wouldn't that be nice," Anatoly said.

"In the meantime, we should probably proceed as planned," Magda said, pointing to the base of the mountain range below them. "It looks like they've assembled a hunting party."

"It was only a matter of time," Anatoly said, "especially if that really was their commanding general."

"Given his weapons and armor, I would say it's highly likely," Magda said.

"Shame we didn't have more time with him," Anatoly said.

"Before this is over you may get your wish," Magda said. "It looks like his adjunct is leading the hunting party."

"How can you see him from here?" Anatoly said.

"Magic."

Anatoly grunted, turning toward the mountain slope leading up to the snowcapped peaks above.

Less than an hour later a shadow passed overhead. Anatoly spun his war axe into his hands as Magda began casting a spell. Flying overhead was one of the half-man, half-dragon creatures that had helped abduct Abigail from Fellenden. It roared but didn't attack, instead taking up a wide orbit high overhead, marking their position for the hunting party.

Anatoly slung his axe and withdrew Abigail's bow from its carrying case on his back. "I've never been very good with a bow, but I might be able to take that thing down with this."

"Perhaps we can lure the others into an ambush," Magda said.

"What did you have in mind?"

She pointed to a rocky outcropping overlooking the trail they were following. "From there I can eliminate most, if not all of the pursuing soldiers, provided I have a few minutes of uninterrupted time to cast my spell."

"You're sure?" Anatoly asked. "If your spell doesn't work, we'll be trapped."

"I'm sure, except for that one," she said, pointing to the creature flying overhead. "My spell will have no effect on it, so you may want to keep that bow handy."

"All right then, we'd better get into position."

They climbed to the top of the outcropping and cleared the area of debris so they could find firm footing, and then they waited, Magda watching the trail below, and Anatoly watching the creature floating above them, Abigail's bow in hand, an arrow nocked and ready.

An hour passed before they heard the sounds of men drifting through the crisp air. A few minutes later, the first of the hunting party rounded the corner, coming into view. Magda began her spell. The creature above called out again, alerting the hunters to their presence.

Twenty men fanned out in the narrow confines of the mountain pass. Magda continued to focus on her spell.

The nearest man raised his bow and sent an arrow at them but it fell short. They began to approach the base of the outcropping, looking for a way to climb to the top, while the leader, armed with his dragon-scale shield and finely crafted long sword, stood back, watching his men approach their quarry.

Anatoly looked over at Magda, who was lost in the concentration needed for her spell. He shrugged to himself as he raised Abigail's bow, taking aim at the creature floating overhead. The bow drew easily, he sighted down the length of the arrow, leading the creature as it glided on the cool mountain air ... then he released. The arrow flew true but the creature saw it coming and rolled away from it with just inches to spare. Anatoly frowned, looking down at the men approaching the outcropping. Then he drew another arrow.

Magda stretched out both hands and continued her spell. A minute had passed since she began, maybe two, and still she chanted under her breath. Anatoly could almost feel the coiled rage building within her as she projected her vision of the moments to come into the firmament, demanding that it bend the rules of reality to her will.

A man below shouted to his companions, pointing to the path leading to the top of the outcropping. The men began to move toward the path, clustering together as they did.

Magda paused, closing her eyes for a moment, then opening them as she spoke a single forceful word. A tattered bolt of unnatural grey energy shot forth from her outstretched hands and struck the ground in the center of the cluster of men. From the point of impact, the ground took on the same unnatural grey tinge in an expanding circle. It was forty feet across when it stopped a moment later. All of the men looked down expectantly, but none were close enough to the edge of the circle to act, even if they'd had the presence of mind to try.

Every hair on Anatoly's body stood on end as the laws of nature were violated in such extreme fashion that the ground itself seemed to cry out in distress.

Nineteen men and every loose stone and pebble within the unnatural grey circle fell up into the air as if gravity itself had been reversed. Thirty, forty, fifty feet they plummeted upward and then the spell's effects faded. The men reached their apex at about sixty feet before the natural order was restored and gravity claimed them once again. They screamed as one and then were silenced as one when their bodies crashed to the ground, bouncing once and then coming to rest, still and dead.

The leader backed away from the outcropping, shield raised, until he rounded the corner. The creature overhead roared once and fled as well.

"Huh," Anatoly said. "Not bad."

Magda smiled while some of the rage necessary for casting such a powerful spell still danced in her eyes.

They traveled the rest of the day, leaving the sure footing of mountain stone and setting out onto the glacier in the early afternoon. By evening they came to the chasm, right where Alexander said it should be.

Anatoly looked down the chasm and whistled. "That's going to take some doing."

"I can get us to the bottom safely," Magda said, "but if this isn't the right place, we'll be stuck."

As if on cue, Alexander appeared before them, smiling.

"I've been watching your progress," he said. "At the bottom of the chasm is a fissure that leads through the ice to a natural cave. Ixabrax is there."

"Are you sure this is a good idea?" Anatoly asked.

Alexander shrugged. "It's the only way. I've looked around Whitehall and it's a fortress in every sense of the word. Zuhl's guards are alert and suspicious of everything, calling for reinforcements at the first sign of anything out of the ordinary. I appeared in front of one just to see what would happen. Within a minute, there were twenty men sealing off the area, and three minutes after that one of his blue-skinned guys showed up. He cast spells for half an hour looking for me."

"What are those things anyway?" Anatoly asked.

"I did some more looking around to answer just that question," Alexander said. "The men address them as Priest or Priestess and they seem to have some of the characteristics of dragons. I can only guess that they're Zuhl's creations."

"The soldier with the dragon-scale shield called the one they were with Priestess," Anatoly said, "and she had magic."

"Perhaps Zuhl has devised a way to use his dragons to circumvent the need for the mana fast," Magda said.

"How do you mean?" Anatoly asked.

"Dragons are creatures of magic," Magda said. "Perhaps Zuhl is using their magic to imbue his minions with access to the firmament. Even if the magic they wield is limited and obviously produces side effects, it does give him an advantage in terms of numbers. He could have hundreds of these priests, maybe more."

"I don't like the sound of that," Anatoly said.

"Me neither," Alexander said, "but there's nothing we can do about it right now."

"It would be nice to know what we're up against," Anatoly said.

"I'll do some more looking around," Alexander said. "For now, I'll go let Ixabrax know you're coming so he won't be startled by your arrival."

"Good," Anatoly said, "wouldn't want to startle a wounded dragon that hasn't eaten for days."

"He wants to free his family more than he wants to eat you," Alexander said.

"Just the same, I wish I'd brought him a mountain goat or something," Anatoly said.

"Perhaps we could offer him a number of Zuhl's soldiers," Magda said.

Anatoly chuckled. "That's kind of gruesome, but I like it. So how are we going to get down there?"

"Take my hand," Magda said.

Anatoly frowned but did as he was told. She began casting her spell. A few moments later she looked at him and smiled mischievously.

"Now we jump," she said. "Just don't let go of my hand."

He looked from her to Alexander and back to her again. "You know I don't like heights and I like falling from high places even less."

"It'll be fine," Magda said. "My spell will slow our descent."

He took a deep breath and nodded to her.

"You don't have to break my hand, just hold onto it," she said, stepping from the edge of the chasm.

They fell quickly, but not as quickly as they would have left entirely to gravity's influence. At a hundred feet they began to slow until they landed easily at the bottom of the chasm two hundred feet below the surface of the glacier. The air was still and terribly cold, but Anatoly was sweating.

"I don't want to do that again," he said.

"I hate to bring this up right now," Magda said, "but I suspect that we're going to leave here on the back of a dragon."

"I was really trying not to think about that," he said.

"This way," Alexander said a moment after he appeared before them. "Ixabrax is expecting you."

They followed Alexander's illusion through a giant crack in the ice and finally into a cave that opened up into a wide-domed cavern. In the center, Ixabrax lay coiled tightly, one eye open, watching them as they entered.

"Ixabrax, these are my friends," Alexander said. "They've brought magic to heal you and they know where you can get an easy meal."

"Very well, Human," Ixabrax said. "I did not expect you to return, but I will honor our arrangement." He turned his eye toward Anatoly and Magda. "You may proceed."

"I'll be back when I'm needed," Alexander said, fading from sight.

Anatoly nodded, removing a jug from his pack. "This is a healing draught," he said, holding it up to the dragon. "Drink this and it will mend your wounds."

Ixabrax reached out with his taloned hand and took the jug, looking at it suspiciously for a moment before popping it into his mouth and crunching it with a single bite, swallowing the broken clay jug along with its contents.

"How long?" he asked.

"A few hours," Magda said. "You'll probably go to sleep while it does its work."

"Very well," he said, curling up and closing his eyes.

"We might as well get some rest, too," Anatoly said.

"Given the frigid temperature down here I suggest we share our warmth," Magda said.

Anatoly grunted agreement.

Chapter 20

Anatoly smoothly rolled out of the furs wrapped around Magda and himself, bringing his war axe up, then freezing in place, listening for a threat. Magda woke and looked at him questioningly. He motioned to the entrance of the cave with his chin. She quietly stood up, muttering the words of a spell under her breath.

The sound of whooshing air followed by three distinct thuds filtered through the cave entrance. Magda's shield formed around her and she began casting another spell. Anatoly slowly made his way to the cave wall on one side of the entrance. Magda moved to the other side of the entrance, still whispering the words of a spell.

As the first of the half-man, half-dragon creatures entered, Magda released her spell. A blade the length of a sword appeared in her hand, except this blade was formed of light-blue magical force, almost transparent yet substantial enough to be deadly.

The creature noticed the sudden appearance of Magda's weapon and turned toward her, giving Anatoly the opportunity to attack from behind with his axe, cleaving its head free of its body with a single stroke.

The second and third creatures roared in anger at the sudden attack. One breathed a gout of frigid air at Anatoly, completely engulfing him. Ice formed on his armor and he toppled over, paralyzed with the chill.

The other breathed at Magda, coating her shield with frost that sloughed off a moment later. Its companion charged her from the side, crashing into her shield and knocking her off balance. As she struggled to regain her footing, the creature hit her from the front, knocking her flat on her back. It leapt up, assisted by its wings and landed in the middle of her shield, weakening the magical bubble of protection as it flailed and thrashed against the nearly invisible barrier.

The other, seeing Magda struggling to defend against its companion, turned its attention to Anatoly, leaping into the air, gaining altitude with a single downward thrust of its wings before descending toward the helpless man-at-arms.

Magda swung her magical sword, severing the creature's foot just above the ankle. It shrieked in pain, thrusting with its wings, lifting it well out of Magda's sword range. She stumbled to her feet, turning toward Anatoly, helpless to defend him against the beast as it plummeted toward him, one taloned foot aiming for his unprotected head.

Then Ixabrax stirred, opening one eye and taking in the situation unfurling around him in a blink. His tail shot out, striking the descending creature in the chest, impaling it and driving his bone blade two feet into the stone wall with the force of the strike. The half-man, half-dragon slumped forward, pinned to the wall.

The last of the creatures, wounded and alone, turned and fled toward the cave entrance. Magda dropped her sword, the blue force fading before it reached the ground, and started casting another spell. Her rage was complete and her determination resolute. She raised her hand and released a light-lance. Brilliant light flooded the cave, dancing on the ice in dazzling fashion before striking the creature full in the back and burning a hole the size of a man's head through its chest. It crashed to the ground.

Ixabrax casually brought the intruder impaled on his tail to his mouth and slowly chewed it before swallowing.

Magda went to Anatoly and began casting another spell, this one creating a number of glowing orbs bobbling about him, each radiating gentle warmth. His teeth began to chatter and he started to shiver violently.

Magda retrieved their blankets and laid them out beside him, then helped him roll onto the hasty bedroll to protect him from the cold of the frozen ground while the warmth of her spell soaked into him.

"Seems Zuhl has found us," Ixabrax said, as he stood and stretched, inspecting the now healed gashes along his flank. "At least your magic worked. I believe I'm fit for flight."

"We'll leave as soon as Master Grace has recovered," Magda said.

"As you wish," Ixabrax said, casually picking up the first of the creatures to fall and eating it.

"What are those things, anyway?" Magda asked.

"They're an abomination," Ixabrax said. "Zuhl has crossed a man with a dragon to create a creature that should not be. He calls them drakini. They're sterile, completely devoted to him, and none-too-bright. Even worse, they don't taste very good, but they will sustain me until I can find a more suitable meal." His tail darted out into the cave, stabbing the last of the three and bringing it to his mouth where it quickly disappeared.

"I haven't eaten in over a week," Ixabrax said. "I hope my ... table manners don't offend you."

"Not in the least, Dragon," Magda said. "Can you tell me how many of these drakini Zuhl has in his service?"

"Probably hundreds. He's been breeding them for centuries. As I understand it, they don't always survive the birthing process and then they're slow to mature, many developing abnormalities that ultimately result in death, but some are successful. Once mature, they age as slowly as a dragon and only grow stronger with each passing year."

"Do they have any vulnerabilities that we can exploit?" Magda asked.

"Fire and heat," Ixabrax said. "They are immune to cold, even my breath would have no effect on them, but they fear fire. Their scales act as armor, protecting them against most attacks unless the weapon is wielded with great force or imbued with magic."

"Delightful," Magda said. "Has Zuhl created any other abominations we should be aware of?"

"His clergy," Ixabrax said.

Magda frowned.

"After he captured my sire and dam, he began to circulate the story that he is the dragon god, worshipped by dragons and therefore surely worthy of human devotion. As a reward for his most devout adherents, he provides our blood to drink in ceremonial rites of passage. He calls these servants his priests and priestesses. They begin to take on some of the characteristics of the dragons whose blood they've consumed, a blue tinge to their skin, sharper features, talons, and catlike eyes.

"Most noteworthy is the access to the firmament they gain as a result. His clergy are capable of wielding potent magic but of a limited scope. They can create a wide variety of cold-based effects and many are capable of causing their skin to scale over for a limited time, rendering them virtually immune to normal weapons. Some few of the more advanced can actually transform themselves into the form of a dragon, though smaller and weaker than any true dragon."

"Well, he's just full of surprises, isn't he?" Anatoly said.

"How are you feeling?" Magda asked.

"Cold and irritated," he said, sitting up and scrutinizing one of the glowing orbs bobbling around him.

"For warmth," Magda said.

"Huh," he said, struggling to his feet. "When do we leave?"

"Once you've fully recovered," Magda said.

"I'm well enough."

"I suspect the journey will be a cold one," Magda said. "Perhaps you should take more time to warm yourself."

Anatoly frowned but nodded as he began unbuckling his breastplate. "I'll never get warm with this thing on."

"Your armor is made from the scales of a dragon," Ixabrax said, his eyes narrowing.

"Yep, one that died during the Reishi War," Anatoly said, ignoring the suspicious look. "We found quite a few scales in Blackstone Keep. Mage Gamaliel used them to fashion several suits of armor such as this one."

Ixabrax sniffed him. "Scales from a bronze dragon. Those that remain alive can be found in the high mountains on the east coast of Ruatha."

Anatoly nodded. "Right again. I met Lady Tanis last summer. She's magnificent and terrifying all at once. Unfortunately, she wanted no part of our fight with Phane or Zuhl."

"No, I don't imagine she did," Ixabrax said.

"I'm not sure our enemies will be as understanding as we are," Anatoly said.

"Challenging Tanis in her domain would be … unwise," Ixabrax said.

"Yeah, I got that too," Anatoly said. "But I'm not convinced wisdom is the driving force behind either Zuhl or Phane."

Ixabrax chuckled, a deep rumble emanating from his enormous chest. "I suppose you're right about that. Hopefully, Zuhl will learn the folly of his lack of wisdom, and soon."

After drinking a cup of hot tea prepared over an oil lamp, Anatoly strapped his armor on and hoisted his pack.

"I'm as ready as I'm going to be," he said.

"Very well," Ixabrax said, lowering his neck to the ground. "Climb up and sit between my spikes. Hold on tight, I wouldn't want to lose you before I've freed my family."

"Your concern is touching," Anatoly said, offering his hand to help Magda onto the dragon's neck.

Ixabrax was unable to unfurl his wings in the narrow chasm, so he climbed the side of the ice cliff to the surface, a harrowing experience for Anatoly and Magda. Once he reached the glacier, he spread his wings and tested them with a few flaps.

"You spoke of an easy meal nearby," he said, looking back at his two riders.

"I'll guide you from the air," Magda said.

"Very well." Ixabrax crouched down and launched, springing scores of feet over the glacier before thrusting down with his wings and propelling them higher still.

Magda laughed with glee. Anatoly held on for his life, trying not to look down while the dragon gained altitude. Within minutes they landed in the field of dead that had been left in the wake of Magda's reverse-gravity spell.

Ixabrax sniffed at his meal and frowned.

"Perhaps you could remove their armor, it tends to unsettle my stomach," he said.

Anatoly looked at Magda incredulously. She shrugged with a wry smile and they went to work, stripping the men of their belongings before Ixabrax ate them one by one.

"I don't actually prefer humans," he said, chewing, "but you'll do in a pinch."

"I suppose that's good to know," Anatoly said, dumping the contents of one man's pouch onto the frozen ground. "Hey, what's this?" he asked, holding up a vial of slightly blue liquid.

Magda frowned, shrugging and looking to Ixabrax.

"Dragon draught," he said. "It's made from the filings of dragon scales. When consumed, it will render you virtually immune from the effects of the cold for several hours."

"I like the sound of that," Anatoly said, working the stopper loose and drinking half of it before handing the vial to Magda. She quaffed the rest.

"Perhaps others are carrying more," she said.

Anatoly nodded and went to work searching the men more thoroughly as he removed their armor and weapons, piling them to one side. He found five more vials of dragon draught.

Once they'd finished searching the dead, and Ixabrax had eaten his fill, Magda cast a spell over the pile of equipment. A dagger began to glow softly.

"Ah, this might be useful," she said, retrieving the well-made blade and attaching it to her belt.

"What's it do?" Anatoly asked.

She shrugged. "I'd have to cast many more spells to determine the effect of its enchantment ... or I could simply stab someone with it."

"Fair enough," he said, chuckling. "Are we ready?"

Ixabrax belched, the noise reverberating down the narrow canyon.

"It's nearly nightfall," the dragon said. "We should attack soon."

Alexander appeared in their midst.

Ixabrax reared back, slightly startled.

"Sounds like you're ready to go," he said.

"Indeed, Human," Ixabrax said. "You have a habit of appearing from nowhere."

"I've been watching and gathering information," Alexander said.

"I don't pretend to understand the scope of your wizardry, but I'll accept your guidance ... for now," Ixabrax said.

"Good," Alexander said, motioning to a small patch of empty ground. An image of Whitehall appeared. "I've been working on this all day. At first I couldn't even make a ball of light appear but I find the more I use my illusion magic the more capable I become, though I'm still fairly limited in duration so I'll make this quick."

He pointed to a tower near the middle of the sprawling marble fortress. "Abigail is in the topmost room of this tower," he said. "Breach the wall here on the north side. Make sure you hit it from this side only. If you strike from a different angle you could hurt her. She'll be hiding behind some furniture and ready to go when you get there."

"Understood," Anatoly said. "Once we have her, then what?"

"Retreat into the wilds and hide while we formulate a plan to free Ixabrax's family," Alexander said. "I haven't had time yet to scout their aerie or the surrounding defenses. Besides, Abigail's going to need some time to get her bearings."

Ixabrax eyed him suspiciously.

"Do not consider reneging on your word, Human," he said.

"Not a chance, Dragon," Alexander said. "Freeing your family will hurt Zuhl's military capability more than anything else ... and it also happens to be the right thing to do. Your enslavement is a profound violation of the Old Law and I intend to set it right."

"We shall see," Ixabrax said.

"Given your experience with Zuhl, your suspicions are understandable but unnecessary," Alexander said. "It's nearly dark ... you should begin your attack soon. Once you have Abigail, I'll lead you to an empty cave farther north where you can rest and prepare for the next strike."

He faded from view as Anatoly and Magda climbed onto the dragon's back.

Chapter 21

Abigail was pacing. The sun had just slipped past the horizon on the last day before the winter solstice. Tomorrow was the day Zuhl would perform his yearly sacrifice, giving over her life to the darkness in exchange for another year of life without aging.

She knew Alexander was working on her rescue. She trusted her brother to do everything within his power. What she wasn't sure about was whether he would be able to help her. He was so far away with only his newly discovered and untested magic at his disposal.

"Hi, Abby."

She spun around at hearing the familiar voice.

"Cutting it a little close, aren't you?" she said.

Alexander shrugged. "I had to make some preparations."

"Not to sound ungrateful, but Zuhl's going to sacrifice me tomorrow," Abigail said. "Any chance you have a plan to get me out of here before then?"

"They're coming right now," Alexander said. "Push your bed over to the south side of the room, then tip it over and hide behind it. Hurry, you don't have much time."

"Now you tell me," Abigail said, going to work on moving the bed. As she shoved it into place, she heard the muffled roar of a drakini from outside her tower. Moments later the temperature of the room fell precipitously, ice forming on the northern wall. She glanced back before turning her bed over and scurrying around behind it.

Seconds later the frozen wall shattered, sending stones flying across the room in every direction and opening the tower to the sky. A horn sounded in the distance and was immediately answered by another. The alarm had been raised.

Ixabrax landed on the breach, extending his head into the room as the door was thrown open and guards started to enter. The first man to cross the threshold stopped in his tracks and stared at Ixabrax eyeing him from a distance of only a few feet. He backed away slowly.

"Abigail!" Anatoly shouted from his perch on the dragon's neck. "Hurry!"

She was up and running in a blink. Anatoly caught her outstretched hand and hoisted her onto the dragon. Two drakini flew behind them, both breathing frost that fell harmlessly on Magda's shield.

"Go!" Anatoly shouted as soon as Abigail was seated between two of Ixabrax's back spikes.

When the dragon launched into the sky, two drakini attacked, attempting to tear his wing membranes. Ixabrax tucked his wings in and fell into a steep dive toward the battlements, freeing himself of the drakini and forcing them to break off or risk plummeting to the ground. At the last moment, Ixabrax pulled up hard and turned north.

Abigail felt the crushing pull of gravity as Ixabrax thrust against the air to gain altitude. Behind them, a number of drakini were taking flight in pursuit. Farther behind, the roar of a dragon echoed from the battlements.

"My sire," Ixabrax said.

Abigail would never have believed that she might hear a hint of fear in a dragon's voice.

"Fly north," Anatoly said. "Head for the cave where we found you."

Ixabrax adjusted course without a word.

While Magda was focused on casting a spell, Anatoly handed Abigail the Thinblade. She looked at him with a fierce smile, then slipped her hand through the thong on the hilt and strapped the belt around her waist.

A dozen or more drakini were in pursuit, but they couldn't keep up with Ixabrax. The other dragon could, however. Abigail looked back and saw a blue dragon almost half again as big as Ixabrax flying higher and faster, gaining on them with every stroke of its enormous wings. Riding atop the terrifying beast was Zuhl, although Abigail was certain it wasn't the real Zuhl but another simulacrum. She suspected that the reclusive mage hadn't actually set foot outside of Whitehall in centuries.

Zuhl released a spell, sending a shard of ice six feet long and a foot thick toward them with frightening speed. It struck Magda's shield with such force that it exploded, sending splinters of ice in every direction and collapsing her shield in the process but harming no one.

She finished her spell a moment later. Dozens of blue orbs appeared nearby, floating around Ixabrax in a dizzying array of erratic orbits.

Zuhl sent another shard of ice at them but one of Magda's orbs broke off from its orbit, streaking toward Zuhl's spell and meeting it in the open sky, shattering it into powder.

Ixabrax narrowly dodged a jagged mountain ridge before diving sharply to evade the onslaught from above. Zuhl unleashed another spell, or possibly expended some enchanted item, tossing a stone into the air and pointing toward Ixabrax. When the stone reached its apex, it burst into dozens of crystalline splinters, exploding in all directions before arcing toward Ixabrax, each trailing a streamer of unnatural black smoke.

Magda's protective orbs rose to the defense, streaking toward the incoming barrage of missiles, each orb targeting a stone splinter with unerring precision and shattering it into powder … but there weren't enough orbs.

The rain of missiles crashed into Ixabrax, several punching through his wings, leaving tattered holes in the flesh membrane stretching between the bone struts, several more glancing off his scales. Two struck Anatoly in the back, shattering against his dragon-plate armor as he hunched over Abigail to protect her from the sudden attack. One pierced Magda's shoulder, driving cleanly through her body and ricocheting off Ixabrax's scales, trailing a streamer of blood in its wake. She gasped in startled agony, losing the focus necessary to finish the spell she'd begun casting.

Ixabrax dove for the chasm, narrowly escaping the unnaturally cold breath of his own sire as he crashed into the opposite wall of the rift in the glacier and fell, slowing his descent with a combination of his unfurled wings and claws against the frozen wall, creating a spray of powdered ice that served to both obscure their position and lower the temperature even further.

Abigail held on for dear life, the cold penetrating into her bones, her lips and knuckles turning blue while her mind raced, formulating a strategy to defend against the coming assault.

They hit hard, jarring them all and eliciting a gasp of pain from Magda. Ixabrax wasted no time carrying them into the cave, away from the threat of falling ice or an attack from above.

Abigail quickly dismounted while Anatoly helped Magda to the ground. She muttered a few words and a pair of glowing orbs appeared above them, softly illuminating the cave. She was bleeding seriously and looked to be nearly at the end of her strength.

"What now, Human?" Ixabrax growled.

"Now we're in a confined space where we might have a chance against whatever Zuhl sends against us," Anatoly said, wrapping a bandage around Magda's shoulder.

"I cannot best my sire in single combat," Ixabrax said.

"You don't have to," Abigail said, drawing the Thinblade. "All you have to do is give me a chance to cut that collar off."

Anatoly finished bandaging Magda and helped her to a place behind a large rock before he spun his axe up into his hands and faced the cave entrance with Abigail and Ixabrax.

The air grew cold and still, tension rising as they waited for the assault, but it didn't come.

"I don't understand," Abigail said. "He was right behind us, why isn't he attacking?"

"Might have something to do with that sword of yours," Anatoly said.

A moment later they heard drakini coming down the chasm.

"Dragon draught," Magda said. "Drink it, quickly."

Anatoly tossed a vial of the magical liquid to Abigail and trotted back to Magda with another, drinking a third as he took up a position at the side of the cave entrance opposite Abigail.

The drakini came quickly, several rushing into the cave and breathing frost in all directions at once. The temperature fell dramatically but the dragon draught tempered the numbing chill of the unnatural beasts' breath.

Abigail cut the first drakini in half. Anatoly cleaved the wing from another. Ixabrax lunged into the fight, snapping at the next and crushing it with his powerful jaws while simultaneously whipping his tail over his head and stabbing another through the chest.

The next crashed into Anatoly, driving him to the ground and pinning him with its weight. Anatoly gained leverage a moment later and heaved the beast off of his chest, rolling over on top of the drakini and taking its head in his hands. The creature clawed at him frantically as Anatoly repeatedly beat the back of its head into the frozen ground.

Another rose into the air in an arc that would bring it down on Anatoly's back, but just as it reached the apex, Magda's light-lance burned a hole through its chest. It died in midair, falling on Anatoly and pinning him atop the dead drakini, brains oozing from its shattered skull.

Abigail charged the next drakini. It swiped at her with a taloned hand but she ducked under the attack, slashing back and up with the Thinblade, taking the drakini's arm at the elbow, then bringing her sword back across the beast's body diagonally and cutting it in half from shoulder to hip.

Ixabrax lunged past her, crushing the next two underfoot as he clamped his jaws down on the final drakini.

Anatoly regained his feet and surveyed the scene.

"Well fought," Alexander said, appearing in the middle of the room. "Zuhl has retreated. He sent the drakini instead, and there are more forces on the way, probably half an hour out. Can you move?"

Magda staggered to her feet, her face ashen white from loss of blood. "If we are to leave this place, then we need to move now, before the dragon draught wears off."

"I don't understand," Abigail said. "Why didn't Zuhl come after us himself?"

"Cowardice and evil are character traits that are invariably bound together," Ixabrax said.

"I think Ixabrax is right," Alexander said. "He didn't want to risk a fight in such tight quarters. Besides, he has a sacrifice to prepare for."

"Whatever the reason, let's take advantage of it," Anatoly said.

"Agreed," Ixabrax said.

"Several dozen miles to the north is a cave with a warm spring nearby and a grove of trees," Alexander said. "It's the best place I've been able to find for you to hide while we plan our attack."

**

Alexander opened his eyes, ignoring the slight pain behind his forehead, and turned to Jack who was nodding off in the chair next to his bed. "You awake?"

"Sort of," Jack said. "Anything new?"

"Anatoly and Magda managed to get Abigail out of Zuhl's fortress."

"So she's safe," Jack said, breathing a sigh of relief.

"I wouldn't go that far," Alexander said. "Magda's hurt and they don't have much support, especially considering what they're planning."

"What do you mean?" Jack asked, sitting forward, completely awake now.

"It was part of the deal," Alexander said. "Now that Abigail's been rescued, they're going to try to free the rest of the dragons that Zuhl has enslaved."

"Are you kidding me?" Jack asked, surging to his feet. "Hasn't she been through enough?"

"It was the only way I could get her out, Jack. I needed Ixabrax, and he wouldn't help us unless we agreed to help his family."

"So now that she's free, you expect her to waltz back into Zuhl's stronghold and cut a bunch of dragons loose?"

"Pretty much," Alexander said.

"When does this get to be too much for you, Alexander?" Jack asked, walking out of the Wizard's Den before Alexander could answer.

Chloe buzzed into sight. "He'll come around, My Love."

"I know. Honestly, I'm surprised he's held it together for as long as he has. I know how hard it is to be away from the ones you love, especially knowing that they're in danger when you're safe."

Anja stuck her snout into the Wizard's Den. "I don't understand why he's mad at you. Isn't he your friend?" In recent days she had discovered how to make human words while in her true form and was ever eager to make use of her new talent.

"Yes, one of the best friends I've ever had," Alexander said. "But he's in love with my sister and she's in great danger right now and there's nothing he can do to help her. It's hard for him."

"Is it not hard for you?" Anja asked.

"Yes, but I can go to her and talk with her and help her," Alexander said. "Jack can't. He's stuck here with me, knowing that Abigail's life is at risk, and it eats at him."

"I can see how he would feel that way," Anja said. "If you were elsewhere and in harm's way, I would be distraught."

Alexander closed his eyes but didn't respond.

"I still don't understand how you do that," Anja said. "Be somewhere other than here, that is."

"Honestly, neither do I," Alexander said. "The best I can do is to call it magic."

Anja snorted. "I guess I can understand that, sort of. I don't really know how the shapeshift spell made me into a young woman, but it did."

"Magic is like that," Alexander said. "Some wizards understand the principles they're using while others, like me, just wield the power at our disposal."

Anja was silent for several moments before she spoke again, this time much softer, almost timidly.

"Where will we go when you're healed?" she asked.

Chloe buzzed into a ball of light and vanished.

Alexander took a deep breath and let it out slowly before looking Anja in the eye. "Your mother and I have spoken of this and we agree. You will stay here when I leave."

"No!" Anja said.

"Yes. Where I'm going you wouldn't be safe."

"I don't care. If you're in danger, then I want to be there with you."

"Anja, you can't. You're just a child."

"I'm a dragon! I can go where I choose."

"Yes, but you won't be safe," Alexander said. "More than that, you sort of attract attention. Where I'm going, I'll need to be able to hide. I can't do that with you."

"But I love you," Anja said.

"I know, and I love you, too," Alexander said. "That's why I want you to stay here where you'll be safe. I can't protect you out there."

"I don't need protecting … I'm a dragon. But I could protect you."

"I know you think that," Alexander said, "but danger isn't always something you can confront directly. I have a lot of very powerful enemies and they wouldn't hesitate to hurt you to get to me."

"Not if I hurt them first," Anja said.

"Anja, you're so young," Alexander said. "And for all your youth, you have great power, but you don't yet possess the wisdom to wield that power well."

"What if I shapeshift into a woman again?"

"You'd be even more vulnerable," Alexander said. "Anja, I'm going to war. The moment I can walk without a cane, I'm going into enemy territory. As a human woman, you would be far too vulnerable, and I would be far too worried about your safety to do what I need to do."

"Alexander, I can't stand the idea of you being in harm's way while I'm safe," Anja said. "Please don't put me through that."

"I'm sorry, Anja, but I'd rather put you through that than see you get hurt," Alexander said.

"I'm a dragon, I can take care of myself," she said, withdrawing from the Wizard's Den and launching into the evening sky.

Jack returned a few moments later, looking rather sheepish. "I'm sorry, he said.

"You have nothing to apologize for," Alexander said.

"But I do," Jack said. "After all we've been through together, I have no cause to doubt you. I know you'd move the world to save Abigail. I just feel so helpless here."

"I know," Alexander said, "but I'm really glad you're here."

Jack smiled and sat down, nodding. "Me too. So what's next?"

"Isabel. It's about time I got back to helping her," Alexander said.

Chapter 22

"Hi, Isabel," Alexander said.

She opened her eyes and rolled out of bed.

"How're you holding up?"

"I've been better ... but I've been worse, too," she said, not wanting to tell him how bad it was getting. All of this time spent alone was making her doubt her sanity. She spent far too much time scrutinizing her thoughts, always wondering if any given thought was planted by Azugorath.

The Wraith Queen was becoming more cunning, taking the circuitous route into Isabel's psyche by inserting ideas that led to very dark places. All too often, Isabel would be well down the path Azugorath had laid out for her before she realized she was chasing a ghost within her own mind. That's when the real attack would come, swift and powerful, Azugorath would bring her full strength to bear, attempting to subvert Isabel's free will and gain control, even if just for a moment.

"What's happening? They won't tell me anything."

"Quite a lot actually," Alexander said. "Phane used the link between you and the witch Clotus to locate this place. He has a sizable force headed here as we speak."

"I'm not sure what good that'll do him," Isabel said. "All of the men here are completely charmed by the Sin'Rath. I don't see why Phane's men won't succumb just as easily."

"Because he's sending women," Alexander said. "Except for three wraithkin, the entire force, five hundred strong, is all women, very well trained and very well equipped women."

"Oh ... that changes things," Isabel said.

"They'll be here in a week or so, and when they get here, the Sin'Rath are going to have their hands full. I also spoke with the sovereigns about them. They're a lot more dangerous than I thought. Turns out they're descended from the union of a demon called a succubus and the last Wizard King of Karth, a man named Siavrax. He led the Isle of Karth during the Reishi War, but it doesn't sound like he was much better than Malachi.

"Apparently, Siavrax turned to the netherworld in an attempt to even the odds against the Reishi. Malachi called him the second most powerful necromancer in the Seven Isles, after himself, of course."

"Of course," Isabel said.

"Siavrax specialized in creating hybrid creatures to use as weapons against the Reishi. He's actually the one who created the gorledons.

"In one of his more desperate moments, he summoned Sin'Rath, the Succubus Queen, to use against Malachi, but Siavrax succumbed to her seductive charms instead. Sin'Rath bore him a half-breed daughter, then vanished into the swamp for decades. Once his half-breed daughter matured, mother and daughter returned to kill him.

"This is where it gets interesting. When his daughter killed him, she consumed his link to the firmament and became the first witch of the Sin'Rath Coven. Worse, she inherited her mother's ability to charm men. Malachi immediately saw the threat they posed and sent none other than Prince Phane to banish Sin'Rath."

"But why didn't she just charm him, too?" Isabel asked.

"Azugorath," Alexander said. "Malachi summoned the Wraith Queen and used her in much the same way that Phane is using her, but instead of giving Phane unnatural abilities, she simply protected him from the influence of other demons."

"That explains how Phane got the idea for his wraithkin," Isabel said.

"Yeah, and it worked then, too. Phane banished Sin'Rath, but her daughter got away," Alexander said. "Her descendants are the Sin'Rath witches of today. After a bit of prodding, I got Malachi to offer some speculation on the matter. He thinks the Sin'Rath want to kill Phane and consume his link to the firmament, so they can summon their mother."

"As much as I like the killing Phane part, I don't want these crazy witches to have his power," Isabel said.

"No," Alexander said. "So here's where Siavrax might have saved us. After his failure with Sin'Rath, he supposedly created a creature he called a Goiri."

"The thing the witches were talking about," Isabel said.

Alexander nodded. "Malachi says the creature was rumored to nullify magic anywhere in close proximity. Unfortunately, it also proved to be completely insane and uncontrollable. So much so that Siavrax sealed it up in the hidden facility where he created it, and left it to die."

"So how does that help us?" Isabel asked.

"Apparently, Malachi believes that the power to nullify magic was bound up in its bones. I found the fortress, but when I got close to the chamber where I think it died, I was suddenly back in my body on Tyr. I believe the Goiri's bones are still there."

"We could kill Phane," Isabel said, suddenly excited.

"More importantly, we could destroy the Nether Gate," Alexander said.

"That too. So what's the catch?"

"That mountain is crawling with all sorts of unnatural creatures," Alexander said. "The people of Karth say the swamp surrounding it is haunted, but it's really just full of things that Siavrax created and abandoned when the Goiri didn't work out."

"So it's dangerous," Isabel said. "This is our chance, we have to take it."

"Even if you can escape this place, you can't go alone," Alexander said. "I want you to find a place to hide until I can come for you. We'll go together."

"I don't think there's time," Isabel said. "Phane knows where I am. I won't get a better chance to escape than when he attacks. After that, I'll be on the run. I'm not sure I'd be able to hide until spring. Also, Azugorath is eating away at me. It's getting harder and harder to hold out against her, especially after the torture."

Alexander nodded, sighing with resignation. "Hector and Horace are on Karth. I spoke to them a few days ago and told them where you are. They'll be here within the week. They know Karth. With their help, you can find a place to hide."

"Alexander, if I told you how to kill Phane and destroy the Nether Gate, would you sit on your hands for the next two months? All the while worrying that you might be possessed by a demon and turn on your friends?"

He said nothing.

"Me neither," she said.

"I almost withheld this information from you because I knew exactly what you'd want to do."

"But you didn't because you also know exactly how important this is," Isabel said, smiling. "I told you things would become clearer as I got closer to my target."

"So you did. I don't want to risk you, but if we're going to do this, we need a plan."

"All right, what do you have in mind?"

"Ayela knows the secret passages running through this place," Alexander said. "If we can get her help, you'll have a far better chance of escaping while the Sin'Rath fight Phane's forces."

"I agree, but I haven't seen her since she came to me with the potion."

"I'll find her and make her an offer," he said.

"What kind of offer?" she asked.

"She helps us get the Goiri's bones and we help her eliminate the Sin'Rath," Alexander said.

"She might actually go for that," Isabel said, "but you should probably wait until Phane's people are closer. If she doesn't agree, I don't want her to have time to get in the way."

"Fair enough," Alexander said. "I'll keep an eye on you and make the offer a few hours before Phane's people are ready to attack. Once you're out of this place, I'll have Hector and Horace meet up with you. Hopefully, with a little clairvoyant guidance, the four of you can get to the fortress with a minimum of difficulty."

"I'll be ready," Isabel said.

***

After more than a week of pushing his new illusion magic to its limits, often with painful consequences, he found himself with time to address other concerns. It would be a while before Abigail was ready to free Zuhl's dragons and at least a week before the conditions on Karth would be right for Isabel to make her escape.

Alexander stretched his leg. The wound had finally closed up but it hurt, especially when he tried to walk. It would still be a month or more before he was fit to travel and even then he feared his leg wouldn't be as strong as he'd like.

Fortunately, he didn't need to leave his bed to work against his enemies. With Abigail and Isabel out of immediate danger, he could focus on other, less urgent but still vitally important matters.

He slipped easily into the firmament, spending a few moments listening to the song of creation before focusing his attention on the Reishi Keep. After he appeared before Commander Perry, it took several minutes of convincing to assure the suspicious commander of his legitimacy.

"Very well, Lord Reishi, I accept that this illusion is indeed being projected by you."

"Thank you, Commander," Alexander said. "I'd like a report."

"We've completed the wall and begun the process of clearing the Keep," Commander Perry said. "It's difficult and dangerous, both because of the creatures living within and the magical defenses that are still active. The wall is holding, though there are still attempts by some of the more aggressive predators to penetrate our defenses. Supplies are beginning to become a concern, so I've been sending out hunting parties to augment our food stores.

"The Keep itself is quite large, nothing like Blackstone of course, but it has proven difficult to navigate for some of my men. The lack of lighting is an issue, forcing us to rely on torches and lanterns which sometimes alert the creatures we're hunting to our presence."

"What of the mission to the hidden fortress?" Alexander asked.

"They arrived several weeks ago and departed the safety of our position within the hour," Perry said. "I haven't heard from them since."

"Very good, Commander," Alexander said. "You've done well with a difficult situation. I'm going to spend some time scouting the Keep. When I finish, I'd like to speak with your officers."

Alexander spent an hour or more doing a thorough search of the entire Keep. Much of it was abandoned and empty of everything save debris but there were still several areas occupied by a variety of dangerous creatures, of most concern being the tentacle demon which had taken up residence in the throne room. From the remains scattered around the cavernous chamber it had clearly been hunting some of the lesser creatures living in the Keep.

He came to lament the fact that he hadn't taken the time to enter the Keep himself and claim control of the ancient fortress. Had he done so, he suspected that many of the magical capabilities of the Keep would be available to him, even at such a distance.

After an exhaustive search, he returned to Commander Perry and spent a few minutes telling him where each of the creatures within the Keep had chosen to make its lair. There were several families of gorledons, a fact Commander Perry and his men were painfully aware of, but Alexander was able to pinpoint the location where each family slept, giving his soldiers a powerful tactical advantage.

In one of the lower chambers lived a snake that was easily fifty feet long, though it seemed content to hunt the catacombs beneath the Keep as none of the soldiers had even seen it.

By far the greatest concern, aside from the tentacle demon, was the pack of five nether wolves living in one of the lower chambers. Perry had reported that something was hunting his men in the night, taking a man every few days or so. Alexander explained how they fought, their aversion to light and their immunity to most forms of attack save decapitation.

Wizard Dinh suggested that he could provide light for the men to corral the nether wolves into an ambush and Commander Perry began formulating an attack plan to eliminate the nether wolves immediately. Alexander bid them good luck and faded out of sight.

Next, he went to Abel on Ithilian and requested a resupply be sent to the expedition at the Reishi Keep. Then he sought out the men tasked with placing one of Kelvin's explosive weapons in the chamber that held the Nether Gate.

What he found was a scene from a nightmare. The entire force had been killed to a man. They'd reached the fortress, but they'd fought a retreating action for nearly a league while something picked them apart, one man at a time. Broken bodies, some half eaten, lay in a trail leading to the fortress entrance and into the entry chamber. The wizard leading the mission was dead, fallen beside the wagon carrying the weapon. The only consolation Alexander took from the massacre was that whatever had killed these men hadn't been interested in the weapon at all.

He considered detonating it right now, he had the activation stone with him on Tyr, all he had to do was crush it and the weapon would detonate, even at this distance, sealing off the fortress under tons of stone, but he knew that would only be enough to slow Phane down once the arch mage got around to coming for the Nether Gate.

Alexander faded back into the firmament, saddened by the loss of yet more good men by his order, and returned to his body to consider his options.

***

"Hello, Captain Wyatt," Alexander said, his projection standing on the deck of an Ithilian warship.

"Lord Reishi, is that really you?" a startled Wyatt asked.

"It is," Alexander said, then proceeded to name all eleven men that Wyatt had lost in the first battle with the wraithkin at Northport.

"Very well, I believe you, though I don't comprehend how you've come to be here," Wyatt said.

"Report," Alexander said, as another man approached with two sailors in tow.

"I've commandeered these four warships from the Ithilian Navy in pursuit of Princess Lacy. And although Captain Riggs here," Wyatt said, motioning to the man who'd just approached, "isn't entirely convinced of my authority, he has accepted my command for now, mostly because of Knight Kinley." Wyatt looked up at the wyvern circling overhead.

"Captain Riggs, I'm Alexander Reishi. Consider Captain Wyatt to be the commander of your flotilla. You will assist him in every way possible. Is that understood?"

"Yes, but I'm confused? How did you get aboard?" Captain Riggs asked, looking around for any ships other than his four vessels.

"I'm a projection, Captain," Alexander said, waving his hand through the foredeck railing, "an illusion."

"I don't pretend to understand such wizardry," Captain Riggs said, "but Lord Abel spoke to every captain in the fleet and told us that if you were to come to us in our dreams, we were to obey your orders as if they'd come from him. I suppose this is enough like a dream to count. I accept Captain Wyatt's command, my ships are at his disposal."

"Thank you, Captain," Alexander said, turning back to Wyatt. "You're about a day and a half away from the ship carrying Lacy. It's manned by men dressed like Zuhl's soldiers but they're really Regency soldiers."

Wyatt frowned in puzzlement. "What's their game?"

"Phane wants the contents of a magical box that Lacy has in her possession and she's the only one who can open it," Alexander said. "And I think he's trying to trick her into doing just that. There are two warships flying the Regency flag a few days out and they're headed right for Lacy's ship."

"Sounds like this ocean is about to get very crowded," Wyatt said.

"It gets worse," Alexander said, holding Wyatt's eyes for a moment. "A dragon named Aedan was sent by Lady Bragador to retrieve Lacy from the ship, but the shade possessed him and then retreated."

Wyatt blinked a few times and shook his head. "I don't know what we can do against a dragon," he said. "There isn't a single wizard aboard any of these ships and I doubt our weapons will have much effect."

"Trust me, they won't," Alexander said. "If the shade wants to sink you, you're sunk."

"Why doesn't he just take Princess Lacy and the box?" Wyatt asked.

"He can't open it or he would," Alexander said. "I think he's waiting for Phane's ruse to play out. Besides, Phane already has the other two keystones, so the shade will have to get them from him for his plan to succeed. For now, the shade is playing a waiting game."

"Very well, what are my orders?" Wyatt asked.

"Use Knight Kinley to scout for the dragon," Alexander said. "If you have clear skies, I want you to attack, board the ship and retrieve Princess Lacy with all of her personal effects. She's traveling with one of Phane's agents, a man named Drogan, but she isn't aware of his true purpose. Do not trust him no matter how much the princess vouches for him."

"Once we have her, then what?" Wyatt asked.

"Ensure she has the box and make haste for Ithilian," Alexander said. "Abel and the Ithilian wizards will be ready to protect her the moment she makes landfall."

"And if the dragon is present?" Wyatt asked.

"Hold back and follow at a safe distance," Alexander said. "In any event, I'll be keeping an eye on the situation, so I'll be here to provide further guidance when you need it."

"Thank you, Lord Reishi," Wyatt said, saluting, fist to heart.

Alexander returned the salute as he faded out of sight.

Chapter 23

Lacy woke shivering. The single thin blanket wasn't enough to ward against the chill of the early morning ocean air. The ache of her broken hand had become a constant part of her day, throbbing, sometimes stabbing and sharp, but always hurting ... and the cold didn't help. Drogan was standing at his cell door listening intently. A moment later a crashing noise was followed by shouts and screams.

"Get ready to move," Drogan said, retrieving a piece of wire from the hem of his blanket.

"Where did you get that?"

He ignored her, going to work on the lock to his cell door. A moment later he was out and picking the lock to her door.

"Why didn't you do that before?" Lacy asked.

"Where would we have gone?" he asked, not waiting for an answer before he went to the footlocker containing their belongings. Within minutes, they had their weapons and equipment and were moving toward the stairs leading above decks.

Shouts of fighting and the ring of steel filtered through the deck boards. Drogan stuck his head above, then retreated quickly, cursing under his breath.

"What is it?" Lacy asked. "What's wrong?"

He ignored her, motioning for her to follow quietly. As they hurried through the hatch, Lacy looked around almost frantically at the battle taking place on the main deck. Zuhl's soldiers were fighting with almost reckless desperation against the well-organized unit of men that had boarded from an adjacent warship. Three more ships surrounded them, preventing escape while the boarding party worked to seize the ship.

Drogan led her to the aft deck, avoiding Zuhl's men who were surging toward the foredeck and the boarding party. Lacy recognized their uniforms—the boarding party was from the Reishi Protectorate, the soldiers that had been chasing her on Fellenden before she and Drogan escaped aboard the refugee ship.

"There," Drogan said, pointing off into the distance.

Two more ships were coming toward them.

"Who's that?" Lacy asked, trying to overcome the tremor of fear rippling in her voice.

"Regency Navy," Drogan said.

In the back of her mind, Lacy wondered at the timing. How could Drogan know to look for friendly vessels amid such chaos?

Then she saw the dragon. It flew over the ship, the man riding the beast looking down intensely, locking eyes with her for only a moment before banking hard and circling back over the attacking ship, shouting something that she couldn't make out over the wind.

A man standing on the foredeck of the nearest attacking ship signaled to the dragon and it started to gain altitude, wheeling at the apex of its climb and diving toward her ship, clearly intent on an attack.

What happened next defied reason. A man aboard her ship ran for the railing toward the inbound dragon and leapt off the side of the boat. She stared in disbelief as he transformed into a dragon ... a real dragon.

In that moment she knew that the thing headed toward her ship, the creature that she believed was a dragon—was not, could not be a true dragon because the terrible and magnificent creature rising to meet it was easily twice its size and seemed to radiate power.

The man riding the smaller creature pulled hard on his reins, trying to avoid the dragon coming for him, but he was too late—already committed to his attack, he was unable to change course quickly enough. The true dragon flared its wings, bringing its hind legs up and raking the belly of the other creature, flipping it over and casting it into the ocean with a roar that seemed to still the air and freeze in place the men fighting for their lives—alerting everyone that the situation had just changed in a very fundamental way.

The dragon banked hard, breathing fire onto the ship holding anchor at the port side, setting man and timber alike aflame in a whoosh.

The ships holding aft and starboard raised anchors and turned away from the engagement while the boarding ship sounded horns, signaling a retreat ... but it was too late. The green dragon circled, calmly and gracefully breathing fire on the aft ship, setting it ablaze in an instant. Men leapt into the ocean to avoid the conflagration, but too few and some too late, dousing their flaming clothes in the ocean.

As Lacy stood mesmerized by the unimaginable battle taking place, two men from the Reishi Protectorate approached with weapons drawn.

"Princess Lacy, please ... come with us," the first said.

"There isn't much time," the other said.

Drogan threw a knife, burying it to the hilt in the throat of the first man.

The second man raised his sword and engaged, stabbing into Drogan quickly, but not quickly enough. Drogan shifted his weight, turning his body sideways, just barely avoiding the blade, then grabbed the man by the back of the neck and threw him overboard with one powerful heave.

The dragon set the third of the retreating ships alight as the boarding party scrambled to return to their ship.

Lacy was thrown to the deck when the entire ship rocked violently and then righted itself again. She scrambled to her feet and saw that one of the two Regency Navy ships had rammed them, crushing in the side of Zuhl's ship and allowing soldiers to pour aboard.

The dragon roared again, drawing her attention away from the new flood of soldiers. She looked up to see another dragon, this one silver and regal, crash into the green dragon and drive him underwater before he could attack the last remaining vessel of the four that had first initiated the attack against Zuhl's ship.

The barbarians that had strutted about with such overstated confidence were now fighting with desperation against men from the Regency. Drogan guided

Lacy toward the soldiers as he shouted at them. A man with the insignia of an officer saw them and directed his troops toward them. A few moments later they were being escorted aboard the ramming ship and then from there to the other vessel that had drawn up alongside.

Lacy watched the entangled ships still fighting while the Regency ship she'd boarded turned away. In the distance, she almost thought she saw the Ithilian flag flying over the ship that had started the fight.

"I'm Commander Arnd of the Regency Navy. Welcome aboard, Princess Lacy."

"I don't understand what just happened."

"We rescued you from Zuhl," Commander Arnd said.

"But who were those other ships?" Lacy asked.

"Reishi Protectorate," Drogan said, before Commander Arnd could answer.

"And what about the dragons?" Lacy asked.

Drogan shrugged.

"We have no knowledge of them." Commander Arnd said. "Might I suggest a meal and a hot bath while we put some distance between us and our enemies?"

"I am hungry, but I still don't understand what's going on." Lacy said.

"I could eat," Drogan said.

"It's settled then," Commander Arnd said. "These men will show you to your quarters."

"But ..." Lacy said.

"Princess," Drogan said. "Please just let it go for now. We'll have plenty of time to wonder about the events of this morning after we eat. I would also like the ship's healer to look at your hand."

Lacy nodded reluctantly.

***

"There's another," shouted a deckhand.

Wyatt and his crew had been fishing men out of the ocean for the better part of an hour. Most were dead, but there were a few survivors. Three of the four ships he'd commandeered were burned and already claimed by the ocean. The other two enemy ships had abruptly stopped fighting and fled once the princess had boarded the Regency ship. Wyatt had the sinking feeling that he'd just made matters worse.

He'd lost most of his company of Rangers, as well as most of Captain Riggs's sailors. Knight Kinley had reported clear skies, but now he was dead too, along with his wyvern. Wyatt had always been impressed by the capabilities of the Sky Knights, but the dragon that had come out of nowhere had bested Knight Kinley with virtually no effort.

Alexander appeared on the deck of the ship and sighed. "I'm sorry, Captain Wyatt," he said. "I should have seen this coming."

"You can't see everything, Lord Reishi," Wyatt said. "I just don't understand where the dragon came from."

"He was aboard the ship in human form," Alexander said. "If I had just looked closer, I would have seen it."

"Captain," called out a deckhand, "this one's a woman."

Alexander flickered out of sight, appearing next to the woman they'd just pulled from the water. She was wounded and unconscious.

"Her name is Tasia and she's a dragon," he said, as Wyatt approached.

The deckhand backed away, his colors flaring with fear.

"She won't hurt you," Alexander said. "Do everything in your power to care for her. I'll let Bragador know."

"But she just burned my flotilla," Captain Riggs said, his face smeared with soot and grime.

"No, she didn't," Alexander said. "She's the silver dragon who stopped the green dragon from finishing you off."

Riggs frowned skeptically. "I didn't see that happen, what with so much going on at the time, but I did wonder where that fiery beast went all of a sudden."

"I saw her, Captain," a deckhand said, "bright and silver, shining in the sun she was, just before she crashed into that terrible green dragon and drove it under the waves. They was both gone after that."

"Care for her," Alexander said.

"What about the princess?" Wyatt asked.

"Follow at a safe distance," Alexander said. "I'll scout the enemy ships and determine if you have any chance against them."

"Where are they headed?" Captain Riggs asked.

"Karth."

Chapter 24

Isabel stopped pacing and listened. She thought she heard the sounds of battle, muffled by stone and distance. Then she heard footsteps coming toward her cell door. As the footsteps grew near, the secret passage opened behind her.

Ayela peered through from the shadows.

"We have to go, right now," she said, motioning for Isabel to hurry.

She hoisted her pack and headed for the passage without a word. Though they'd removed all of her weapons, she'd been permitted to keep the rest of her belongings and she was glad for that. Simple things like a bedroll and a cloak might make all the difference on the run in the jungle.

She slipped into the passage, and Ayela quickly closed the hidden panel just before the soldiers reached the cell door. Isabel and Ayela froze, barely daring to breathe when Trajan and one of the Sin'Rath entered—he had a sword in hand and she was sniffing about suspiciously.

"I don't understand, where could she have gone?" Trajan asked.

The witch began casting a spell. Isabel drank the potion Ayela had given her, the one that would nullify the effects of the malaise weed she'd been forced to consume every day since Trajan had captured her.

The witch released her spell, a cloud of darkness forming before her, then taking the shape of a disembodied dog's head, it began sniffing around the edge of the room.

"Your sister has betrayed you," the witch said in a raspy voice. "But we will find her."

Isabel motioned for Ayela to lead the way down the hidden passage. It was narrow, only four feet wide and barely six feet tall. Roots hung from the ceiling at uneven intervals, dripping with cold water.

Ayela held up a small jar of greenish glowing lichen to light the way. Isabel followed without a word, silently testing her feelings for the intensity she would need to cast a spell.

Behind them they heard a thud, then another and another followed by the sound of splintering wood.

"Ayela!" Trajan shouted.

They quickened their pace. The passage branched and Ayela went to the right without hesitation. It branched again … this time Ayela took the passage to the left that led down a flight of stairs into another passage that looked more like a natural tunnel than a constructed corridor.

Then Ayela started running. "We haven't much time before the enemy arrives," she said.

The passage ran in a meandering course for several hundred feet until it came to an abrupt stop. A rope ladder dangled against the wall to one side, leading up into the darkness.

Isabel saw light in the distance behind them.

"Quickly, your brother is coming."

Ayela nodded and started climbing. Once they reached the top of the ladder, they scrambled through a hole that had been broken into the stone floor of a small room and Isabel pulled the ladder up.

"Ayela!" Trajan shouted from below.

"Where to now?" Isabel asked.

"This way," Ayela said, leading her through a door into another hidden passage. Several minutes and many turns later, Ayela stopped and motioned for silence as she peered through a tiny hole in the wall. Satisfied, she pulled a lever and a secret panel popped open.

"This is my room," Ayela said. "I just need to get my things before we leave." She started loading her pack.

"Why were they coming for me?" Isabel asked.

"I warned them about the attack," Ayela said. "Your husband appeared before me and told me your plan. At first I thought I was losing my mind, but he knew things he couldn't have known, things that only you could have told him, so I listened, though I don't pretend to understand how he could do such a thing.

"He told me of your plan. I know the legend of the Goiri but never truly believed it existed, much less that it can help us now. When he told me of the coming attack, I went straight to Trajan to warn him. I begged him not to tell the Sin'Rath, but that was the very first thing he did.

"I came for you as quickly as I could. They'll kill you for revealing their location to Phane."

"Let's not give them the chance," Isabel said, motioning for Ayela to hurry.

She buckled her belt and cinched down the straps of her pack, then hoisted it over her shoulders. She handed Isabel a dagger and said, "The hidden passages can take us to one of the entry halls, but none leads out of the fortress. We'll have to escape from one of the guarded entrances."

"That could be complicated," Isabel said.

"I have a few things that might help," Ayela said, patting her belt pouch. "Once we're out, then what?"

"I have friends waiting for me," Isabel said. "We'll meet up with them and head for the Goiri's crypt."

Ayela followed a confusing maze of passages until they reached a small room where she motioned for silence, pointing to a peephole in the wall. Isabel looked through into a large entry hall filled with soldiers of Karth. Among them was one of the witches, a hideous creature with clawed hands, pale white skin, and thin black hair that barely covered her scalp. She stood amid the soldiers facing the door as the first thud of a battering ram slammed home.

Phane's forces had arrived.

Alexander appeared and motioned for Isabel to follow him back into the passage, far enough away from the soldiers so they could talk without fear of being discovered.

"Hector and Horace are in the jungle waiting for you," he said. "Once Phane's people breach the defenses and enter the fortress, you should face minimal resistance."

"What about my father and brother?" Ayela asked.

"As long as they're under the influence of the Sin'Rath, I can't help them," Alexander said.

"Phane's people will kill them," Ayela said. "They're all that's left of my family."

"The Sin'Rath have a secret way out of this fortress," Alexander said. "They've already begun retreating and your father's with them."

"How can you know this? How can I trust you?" Ayela said.

"It's a little late now, Ayela," Isabel said. "If the witches catch you now, they'll kill you. Besides, your family will always be at their mercy unless we destroy them."

"And you think the legend of the Goiri is true?" Ayela said. "What if you're wrong? What if we go into the gloaming swamp and find nothing but death?"

"We don't have much choice, do we? Remember, you came to me," Isabel said. "And the truth is, we need each other. You know this jungle better than I ever will. Help me and I promise I will help you."

Ayela seemed torn, struggling to reconcile her decision to help Isabel with her loyalty to her family, flinching with each rhythmic thud of the battering ram pounding on the heavy fortress door.

"Once we go, there'll be no turning back," Isabel said. "I need to know if you'll see this through."

Ayela nodded tightly, a tear slipping down her cheek.

"I'll help you free your family of the Sin'Rath," Isabel said, putting her hand on Ayela's arm and looking her in the eye, "but this isn't going to be easy."

"I know," Ayela said.

A terrible splitting sound followed by battle cries and the ring of steel signaled the breach of the doors.

"It'll be time soon," Alexander said. "I'll be back when I have information you need." He smiled at Isabel as he vanished from sight.

"How does he do that?" Ayela asked.

Isabel shrugged. "I'm not sure he even really understands it. I know I don't, but the how doesn't matter. He's watching over us, he'll guide us and protect us any way he can."

"Wait, why would you have left him?" Ayela asked.

Isabel smiled sadly and shook her head. "That's a story for another time." She didn't give Ayela a chance to ask another question, instead quietly heading back up the passage into the room with the peephole.

She carefully peered through just in time to see the witch unleash a terrible spell. A jet of thick green gas erupted from her outstretched hands, shooting forth in a billowing cloud into the breached door, pouring through into the space beyond. Screams of agony followed. One of Phane's female warriors stumbled out of the side of the cloud of green gas, her face and one arm almost melted away. She took a few aimless steps until the flesh of her shoulder dissolved and her arm thudded to the ground in a sickening mass. A look of realization ghosted across what was left of her face as she fell to the ground, dead.

The attack faltered in the face of such a horrific display of power, but the Regency retreated for only a few minutes, allowing the corrosive gas to dissipate, revealing a gaping hole in the door where before there had only been a splintered crack wide enough for a single person to pass through at a time. While frighteningly effective, the witch's spell allowed the regrouped soldiers of Phane's female brigade to form a front line and attack with renewed energy and organization.

They came through in a wedge, shields raised against the crossbow bolts and blow darts assailing them. On command, as one, the front line went to a knee and the second line loosed a volley of arrows from short bows. Several defenders fell. An arrow grazed the shoulder of the witch. She snarled in rage before she began chanting in guttural, almost animalistic tones.

Another volley of arrows took a few more of the defenders before the witch's next spell was unleashed. A wave of darkness, a smudge in the air, radiated from her hand toward the wedge of attackers, widening as it moved toward them with inescapable speed. It passed through them and into the tunnel beyond for several feet. For a moment nothing happened, almost as if the spell had no effect, but then the metal weapons and armor carried by Phane's soldiers simply dissolved into rust and fell to the floor in reddish powder, leaving their front line completely defenseless against the onslaught of blow darts and crossbow bolts that followed. Dozens died in moments.

Then a man appeared in the midst of Karth's defending soldiers, black wisps of smoke swirling around him as he casually stabbed a surprised solider in the throat, vanishing again an instant later.

Isabel stopped breathing, willing her heart to beat more quietly, lest the wraithkin hear her.

He appeared in front of the witch, smiling cruelly, casually slashing her throat, spilling a gout of black blood onto the floor, then vanishing again. The soldiers of Karth were stunned by the sudden turn of events, but even more unnerved at the sudden realization of the Sin'Rath witch's true form, her charms losing their hold in death.

They broke and ran and the wraithkin gleefully picked them apart a man at a time. Soldiers, all of them women, entered a few moments later, carefully surveying the scene, moving quickly through the room and making sure that any survivors died quickly before regrouping and pushing farther into the fortress.

Four soldiers remained behind to secure the entry hall. Isabel looked at Ayela and held up four fingers as she drew her dagger and started building her rage. It came easily, almost too easily, boiling into nearly uncontrollable fury in just a few seconds. Recognizing the influence of Azugorath, she reined it in … but not too much.

Seeing the glittering anger dancing in her eyes, Ayela almost looked afraid of her as Isabel began muttering the words of her shield spell. Once the bubble of protective magical energy formed, she motioned for Ayela to open the door and began her next spell.

When the door opened, Isabel stepped out and burned a hole through the chest of the nearest soldier, charging the next without hesitation and catching her by surprise. The woman flailed with her sword, attempting to ward against Isabel's reckless attack with her blade but it bounced harmlessly off Isabel's shield. A moment later, Isabel sliced the woman's throat and moved past her.

The other two spread out, raising their shields and facing the sudden threat. Isabel sheathed her dagger as she knelt down to retrieve a sword. Still kneeling, she unleashed a force-push at her farthest remaining adversary, then lunged toward the nearest.

The woman raised her shield and thrust into Isabel, stabbing hard against the magical barrier protecting her, but Isabel was already spinning, lending the inertia of her motion to the force of the blow that fell against the side of her opponent's neck, taking her head in a single stroke.

She stalked toward the final soldier, the woman staggering to her feet, facing Isabel in a crouch, looking around like a cornered rat. Isabel surged forward suddenly, catching the top of her opponent's shield in her off hand and pushing it down across her body, pinning her sword arm in the process as she crashed into it with her shoulder, knocking her off balance and slamming her against the wall, exposing her left side. Isabel brought the tip of her sword up against the thin section of armor under the woman's armpit and thrust the point through her ribs and into her heart.

The entire battle lasted about twelve seconds. Ayela stood, wide-eyed and frozen in place, watching Isabel survey the room, looking for more enemies. Finding none, Isabel retrieved a sheath for her new sword, collected another dagger, two waterskins and some food before peering up the tunnel leading to the surface.

"We should go," she said, willing the rage out of her voice as much as possible. The tunnel was cut through the ground at a shallow angle leading to a natural cave. When they reached the top, Alexander appeared before them, motioning for them to stop and wait. Isabel knelt down, linking her mind with Slyder and calling him to her.

A moment later they heard a shout from outside.

"Hey, you there, stop!"

"Follow him!" another voice said.

A few moments later, Alexander appeared again.

"Go out and to the left," he said. "Follow the base of the ridge for a league or so and you'll come to Hector and Horace. I'll make sure they know you're coming. Hurry."

Isabel nodded, already moving as he faded out of sight. Ayela followed close behind her into the thick jungle.

Several hundred feet from the cave entrance, Isabel stopped and linked her mind with Slyder again, looking at the terrain through his eyes, locating the four soldiers at the cave entrance who had followed Alexander's projection and given up the chase in favor of returning to their post. It didn't look like they'd noticed Isabel and Ayela's escape. Good enough. She called Shadowfang to her and then they pressed on, traveling quickly but quietly through the dense brush until Ayela stopped her with a hand on her arm.

Isabel squatted down.

"What is it?" she whispered.

"We can't go that way," Ayela said, pointing to the course Isabel was taking. "We have to go around."

"Why?"

"Grapple vine," Ayela said. "See those bright red flowers on that patch of ground cover? That's grapple vine. If we try to go through there it will entangle us and we may not be able to cut ourselves free."

Isabel frowned questioningly.

Ayela picked up a stout branch and tossed it into the flowers. Within a few seconds, several thick vines coiled around it and pulled it to the ground, holding it in place tightly before once again taking on the appearance of a harmless patch of flowers.

"I see what you mean," Isabel said. "What happens to its victims?"

"The vines are covered with tiny barbs that secrete a potent poison. First it paralyzes, then it causes rapid decomposition. A person caught by the grapple vine dies within a day and their body is often completely gone within a few weeks. It dissolves into the soil and feeds the plant," Ayela said.

"That's terrifying," Isabel said, appraising the bright red flowers. They were beautiful and alluring, the kind of thing she might put in her hair on a warm spring day … in another life, anyway.

"I'm glad you're with me, Ayela," Isabel said. "I would have walked right into them."

Ayela smiled, motioning to a safe route around the deadly jungle flora.

Isabel spotted Hector and Horace through Slyder's eyes and adjusted course to rendezvous with them. Within the hour they approached the well-hidden brothers.

"Hector, Horace, it's Isabel," she said softly.

They both seemed to materialize out of the jungle.

"Lady Reishi, you're a welcome sight," Hector said.

"Lord Reishi was most distraught when he discovered your absence," Horace said.

"I imagine," Isabel said. "This is Ayela Karth. She helped me escape—protect her as you would me."

Both Hector and Horace bowed formally to Ayela. She flushed slightly and seemed a bit flustered at their deference.

Shadowfang slipped between the brush and into the little clearing. Ayela nearly screamed, slapping a hand over her mouth. Hector and Horace drew swords as one, positioning themselves between the cat and their charges.

"Stop," Isabel said, moving between them and scratching the jaguar affectionately under the jaw.

"This is Shadowfang ... he's my friend," she said. "He won't hurt any of you and he should keep some of the other predators away from us while we travel."

"The jaguar is my house crest," Ayela said. "They're revered as well as feared. How can this be?"

Isabel shrugged. "Magic."

"Forgive me," Ayela said. "For so long, magic has been forbidden to the people of Karth. We've always believed it to be evil, so this is difficult for me. I saw how the Sin'Rath witch killed so many so horribly with her spells and then watched you dispatch four soldiers with almost casual ease. I was coming to think that witchcraft is only good for killing, and then you presented Shadowfang. He's so beautiful and regal, I'm finding it hard to reconcile everything I've been taught all my life with the things I'm seeing."

"The things you've been taught about magic are mostly lies," Isabel said. "The Sin'Rath have controlled this entire isle, both your family and the Regency, for centuries. They're the ones who forbade magic, and they did it to protect their power over your family and the Regency leadership."

"But we've been at war with the Regency for so long," Ayela said. "Why would the Sin'Rath want to perpetuate such suffering?"

"You saw the one that died in the entry chamber," Isabel said. "They're not human ... they're monsters. As for their motives, I couldn't tell you, except to say they're totally insane."

Ayela was silent for several moments, staring at Shadowfang through teary eyes. "Do you really think the Goiri's bones can help us kill them?" she asked.

"I do," Isabel said, "and maybe much, much more. What we do here might be the most important thing anyone does for a very long time."

Ayela nodded, sniffing back her tears. "Will you teach me how to fight?"

"I will," Isabel said, "but not here. We need distance from the enemy."

"Lord Reishi said we should head due east for several days," Hector said. "The jungle is thick, but it will keep us out of the swamp for as long as possible."

"That's wise," Ayela said. "The gloaming swamp is feared by all on Karth, and for good reason. Few who venture into its waters ever return."

Alexander appeared again.

"You better get moving," he said. "It looks like Phane has some means of communicating with his people, because they suddenly sent out a search party looking for you."

"How many?" Isabel asked.

"Twenty soldiers and a wraithkin," Alexander said.

"What's a wraithkin?" Ayela asked.

"Remember the man who vanished and then reappeared right in front of the witch?" Isabel asked. "The one who killed her?"

Ayela nodded.

"He was a wraithkin," Isabel said. "He can teleport short distances and heal every time he does. They're very hard to kill."

"How far behind us, Lord Reishi?" Hector asked.

"Not far enough," Alexander said. "Maybe an hour. Get moving. I'll be watching." Then he vanished into the firmament.

Chapter 25

Isabel nodded to Hector to take the lead and they moved into the jungle. It was slow-going through the dense brush. While the air was cool and damp, Isabel found herself sweating before long.

They tried to leave as little sign of their passage as possible but it was a difficult, if not impossible, task. Often, they had to double back to circumvent some obstacle or other.

First it was a patch of quagmire sands. Hector stopped short as his leading foot started to sink into the innocent-looking jungle floor. He'd lived on the Isle of Karth for long enough that he was aware of the danger and easily backed out before it was too late.

"I wonder how far this goes?" he asked.

"That's hard to say," Ayela said. "Quagmire sands can stretch for miles or just cover a small patch of ground."

Isabel tipped her head back and linked with Slyder who was perched in a tree above. "It looks like there are a fair number of clear patches of dirt around here," she said.

"To be safe, we should stick to areas covered in vegetation," Ayela said. "Plants almost never grow in sands."

Hector plotted a new path through the jungle, avoiding open ground, which slowed their progress even further. Isabel only hoped that the soldiers following them might lose some of their number to the perils of the jungle.

She sent Slyder back to scout the enemy's location and found them almost a league behind but tracking steadily. It seemed that the denseness of the brush was both making it easier for Phane's forces to follow their trail and causing them to follow more slowly because they followed every dead-end path that Isabel and her friends had taken and been forced to backtrack out of.

Late in the day they heard the bark of a wild dog, then a yelp as it died. Isabel linked with Slyder and found Shadowfang, surrounded by six more dogs, standing over his kill. He didn't look too worried about the opponents he faced as he snarled at them.

Seeing the dogs gave Isabel an idea. She forced her mind into the psyches of all six and imposed her will on them. It was more difficult controlling several animals than just one but well within her capability, for a short time anyway. After she reined in Shadowfang, she sent the dogs to hunt the Regency soldiers. Isabel felt a little guilty using the animals in such a way, knowing that some would probably die as a result, but she consoled herself with the knowledge that they would have attacked her party instead, had she not intervened.

As darkness fell, the jungle became far too treacherous for them to press on. Isabel felt anxious about calling a halt, knowing that the enemy might decide to make up time by moving through the darkness, but she knew better than to risk running into some unseen danger in the night, especially given how hostile the jungle had proven to be.

They found a small clearing in a depression surrounded by heavy foliage and carefully tested the ground for firmness before stopping for the night.

In the last of the day's light, Isabel found Phane's forces through Slyder's eyes and was relieved to see that they had stopped as well.

No one slept well that night. The noises of the jungle created an eerie song that was far too often punctuated by the death cry of some hapless animal as it gave its life to provide a predator with a meal. Isabel found herself lying awake waiting for the dawn as the dark of night began to ebb. She was grateful to be on the move again, eating a cold breakfast while she walked.

Alexander appeared next to her, smiling at her when she jumped slightly.

"You need to warn me before you do that," she said without breaking stride.

He walked by her side, passing through the foliage. "You've picked up another hunting party," he said. "Looks like two of the witches and about thirty soldiers of Karth."

"How far back?" Isabel asked.

"A day," Alexander said, "but they seem to know their way around the jungle better than Phane's people."

"They do," Ayela said. "Our soldiers have been using our superior knowledge of the jungle to exact vengeance against the Regency since Phane sent the demons against us. Rather than fight a battle we knew we couldn't win, we've chosen to fight only when we have the advantage."

"A wise strategy," Alexander said. "Unfortunately, it means that this new hunting party is probably going to gain on you pretty steadily."

"We could play them off against Phane's people," Hector suggested.

"Please don't," Ayela said. "These are my people, my brother is probably leading them. Were it not for the influence of the Sin'Rath, they would be pursuing Phane's soldiers rather than us."

"Maybe I can lead them away," Alexander said. "I've been working on other illusions, and I can project a pretty good image of you, Isabel."

"If they fall for it, it might buy us some time," she said. "At this point I'll take what I can get. This jungle is thick and I think it wants to kill us; I can only imagine how hospitable the gloaming swamp is going to be."

"You don't have to do this alone, Isabel," Alexander said. "You could always find a place to hide until I can come help you."

"Nice try, but we're not stopping. With your help we should be able to avoid some of the more dangerous parts of the swamp and make our way to Siavrax's laboratory well before any of our pursuers get close. And who knows, maybe the swamp will make them change their mind, or at least thin them out."

"You really think they want to go back to Phane empty-handed?" Alexander asked.

"I guess there's that," Isabel said.

"The edge of the swamp is still a few days away," Alexander said. "Once you get there you'll need to make a raft. The swamp looks pretty deep in places and there's no telling what's beneath the surface."

"I was trying not to think about that," Isabel said. "Are you sure there isn't another way?"

"Not unless you can fly," Alexander said. "Siavrax's hidden laboratory is built inside the top of a stone mountain that rises from the middle of the swamp. I'm pretty sure he picked the location for just that reason."

"I wonder if Asteroth can hear me from here," Isabel said.

"Even if he could and even if he could get past Andalia, where would he land?" Alexander asked, motioning to the jungle around them.

"Yeah, I guess you're right," Isabel said. "The swamp it is."

"Try to get there as soon as possible," Alexander said. "You'll need time to make a raft, and it doesn't really matter if you leave a trail because you'll be able to lose them easily enough once you're on the water."

Isabel nodded and looked over at his projection, smiling sadly. "I wish you were here," she said.

"Me too," he said, fading out of sight.

They pushed through the day, moving as quickly as possible through the dense brush. Isabel periodically checked on the progress of the Regency soldiers through Slyder's eyes and was relieved to see that they were falling farther behind.

Midway through the afternoon she heard an odd chittering coming from above. When she looked up into the thick canopy she thought she saw movement. Stopping to look more closely, she was sure of it.

"Tree rats," Ayela said. "We must keep moving."

"Tree rats?" Isabel said.

"Large rodents, maybe twenty pounds, with very sharp teeth and claws," Ayela said. "They hunt in packs and have been known to take down creatures much larger than themselves."

"Hector, Horace, keep your eyes open," Isabel said.

As they continued through the jungle, the tree rats followed in the canopy above. Isabel thought there must be about twenty. A few times she got a good enough look at one to know that she didn't want to see them any closer.

She tried to link her mind with them but failed, a fact that made her even more nervous. These little beasts weren't natural creatures. She presumed that they were yet another of Siavrax Karth's creations. What purpose he'd intended them for was beyond speculation.

When they reached a clearing, Isabel stopped, smiling at the patch of odd flowers near one side of the open space—deathwalker root. "We'll stop here for a few minutes," she said, as she started pulling flowers from the ground, one by one.

"Be careful," Ayela said. "The powder in those flowers will make you sleepy."

Isabel smiled up at her. "You know about the deathwalker root?"

Ayela nodded. "Healers often use the roots to make a poultice, and the powder in the flower sacs is a potent sleeping agent that can be prepared in a variety of ways. Some tribes use it to create a poison for their darts, others use it to help sick people rest through the night."

"We're going to use it to make a healing salve," Isabel said. "Your brother took my potions, so this might come in handy."

"We still have one healing potion each and a jar of Master Alabrand's salve between us," Horace said.

"Good," Isabel said, continuing to work. "I fear we're going to need everything we can get before this is over."

Ayela knelt down to help Isabel. She seemed familiar with the process, pulling the root out of the ground and carefully breaking it from the stem.

The noise of the tree rats started to grow as more arrived.

"Any chance we can lure those little monsters down here?" Hector asked. "I'm tired of constantly looking over my shoulder."

"Doubtful," Ayela said. "They're skittish, preferring to attack only by surprise and in large numbers."

"Looks like they have the numbers," Isabel said, surveying the trees surrounding the clearing.

There were well over twenty now, all looking down at them through their beady little eyes and chittering angrily, as if scolding Isabel and her friends for trespassing.

Shadowfang strolled into the clearing and rubbed up against Isabel's leg. The tree rats grew more animated at his sudden appearance. Isabel was debating whether she should try to scare them off with a light-lance when she felt a sudden stabbing pain on the back of her neck. It was so sharp and unexpected that she yelped, slapping at the source.

She killed a bug that looked almost like a horsefly, only twice as big or more.

Ayela looked closely at it and worry creased her brow. "This could be very bad," she said.

"What is it?" Horace asked.

"A lightning fly," Ayela said. "They create the shocking power of lightning itself and use it to overpower their prey. Usually, they only attack small animals and birds, but a swarm of lightning flies has been known to overpower a horse."

"Then what?" Hector said. "A horse is more than a meal for a swarm of bugs."

"They're parasites," Ayela said. "They lay their eggs inside their victims, usually in early winter. Come spring, the eggs hatch and the larvae eat their way out of the body, then feed until they're ready to cocoon for several weeks and emerge in their adult form."

Isabel looked around at the tree rats. "Maybe these bugs will go after them instead of us," she said.

"Perhaps, but the tree rats will return to their nests at night," Ayela said, "which is when the lightning flies come out to hunt."

"So how do we defend against them?" Hector asked.

"Either find some form of shelter or build a fire," Ayela said.

"All right, let's keep moving," Isabel said. "Everyone keep an eye out for a cave to hide in for the night."

When they started moving, the tree rats started following again, always staying well above them and out of reach but making an unsettling racket with their incessant chittering.

A dark mood started to come over Isabel. The threat of the little rodents coupled with all of the other threats surrounding her in this unfamiliar place started to wear on her nerves. Before she knew what she was doing, she unleashed a light-lance at the nearest tree rat, burning a hole through the predatory rodent and sending its companions scattering into the jungle.

She stopped and looked at her hand in near surprise. "I'm sorry, I'm not sure what came over me," she said.

But she knew. Azugorath was pushing her to act against her will again. It seemed that the Wraith Queen worked on her sporadically, pushing with great effort to gain a foothold within her psyche and then leaving her alone for long periods of time. She didn't understand why, but she did know that she couldn't afford to let her gain control. She resolved to redouble her vigilance within her own mind.

At nightfall, she took one last look at the Regency soldiers following in the distance. They were half a day behind and they'd come upon the tree rats. It seemed that the little rodents were just as unsettling to them as they were to Isabel. She smiled, calling Slyder back to her.

"There," Ayela said, pointing into the growing darkness.

Isabel thought she saw a flickering, electric-blue spark in the distance.

"We need a fire," Ayela said. "Where there's one, there are more."

"A fire will give away our position," Hector said.

"Yes, but without fire we won't survive the night," Ayela said.

He and Horace looked to Isabel. She nodded reluctantly and the two men went to work rounding up wood while Ayela and Isabel prepared a fire pit and collected kindling.

"We'll need a supply of firewood sufficient to last the night," Ayela said.

Hector muttered something under his breath on his way back into the jungle, looking for more wood. By dark, they had a roaring fire burning hot and bright.

Shadowfang was reluctant to venture into the light of the flames, but the increasing number of crackling blue-white sparks Isabel saw in the darkness prompted her to impose her will on her pet and soothe his anxiety at being near the flame, lest he be killed by the lightning flies in the night.

The darkness surrounding them was alight with the terrifying little insects—there must have been hundreds, lightning arcing between their wings as they buzzed around their would-be prey.

"Will they follow us tomorrow?" Isabel asked.

"Doubtful," Ayela said. "They're somewhat territorial, rarely venturing too far from the area where they were born."

After the first hot meal in days, Isabel went to work cooking the deathwalker root down into a rudimentary healing salve. Ayela watched with interest while she carefully cut each flower sac and emptied the contents into a small jar she'd produced from the bag she carried over her shoulder.

"I have a friend you'd like," Isabel said. "He's very knowledgeable about the uses of plants. He taught me how to do this."

"Knowledge of the jungle is valuable to my people," Ayela said. "It's a source of many poisons but also many medicines. The most respected person in any tribe is almost always the person with the greatest knowledge of the jungle, even more than the warriors."

"Lucky would love to see this place. He'd have a thousand questions for you. In fact, I suspect the only way you'd get him to stop asking you questions would be to hand him something to eat."

"You must miss your friends and your family," Ayela said.

"I do," Isabel said, "very much."

"Then why come here, so far away from them, and all alone?" Ayela asked.

"It's complicated," Isabel said, shaking her head.

"Perhaps, when you trust me more, you will tell me the truth of your situation," Ayela said.

"I do trust you, Ayela," Isabel said. "I wouldn't be out here with you if I didn't."

"Then tell me your reasons for coming to my country when reason itself argues against you being here," Ayela said.

Hector and Horace remained silent but shared a look.

Isabel sighed. "I guess you have a right to know. Phane summoned a very powerful demon named Azugorath. She's touched me and is trying to subvert my free will, trying to turn me away from the light and to the darkness so that I will serve Phane. Because of this demon's influence, I nearly killed my husband. I left him that very night because that was the only way I knew to protect him."

"Should I fear you?" Ayela asked, a slight tremor running through her voice.

"I don't know," Isabel whispered. "So far I've been able to control what Azugorath is doing to me, but she keeps pushing against my will, trying to find a way in. I fear that one day, I won't be able to stop her."

Ayela stared into the fire for several minutes without saying a word.

"That must be a horrible burden to bear," she said, finally.

Isabel nodded.

"It seems we have something in common," Ayela said. "Our loved ones are being held hostage by evil and the only way to get them back is to destroy the evil."

"Exactly," Isabel said.

Chapter 26

Hector woke Isabel quietly just before dawn. The darkness surrounding them was still crackling with lightning flies, but Hector was far more concerned about something else. He pointed silently into the jungle.

Isabel had to look carefully before she saw it—the light of a torch, then another. She motioned for Hector to wake Ayela, then she roused Shadowfang with her mind while she strapped on her boots and sword.

"We're going to have to fight," she said. "We can't risk the jungle with all of these lightning flies."

"So how did they manage to travel through the night without being eaten alive?" Horace asked.

"Their torches would have kept the lightning flies at bay ... mostly, anyway," Ayela said. "I'm sure they've been bitten more than a few times."

She drew her dagger and fished a vial of thick black liquid from her pouch. Carefully, she drizzled her blade with the liquid, then held her dagger over the fire until it dried, forming a coating on her blade.

"What's that?" Horace asked.

"Poison," Ayela said.

"Oh," Horace said, inching away from her.

The jungle started to lighten and the torches grew closer.

"Spread out and hide," Isabel said. "We don't want to let them take us with crossbows. Attack when you see my light-lance."

Hector and Horace nodded, disappearing into the jungle just outside the clearing. The lightning flies seemed to sense the coming dawn and had almost completely disappeared by the time the soldiers approached the camp.

Isabel waited until they were close before she cast her shield spell, but then held her place, waiting for just the right moment to strike. Six women slipped into the camp, warily looking around as they approached the fire, inspecting the ground for any sign of where their quarry had gone. Isabel started to whisper the words of her light-lance spell, allowing her anger to boil into tightly controlled rage.

The wraithkin appeared in the midst of the women. Isabel smiled fiercely as she unleashed her spell, burning a hole through the side of his head the size of an apple. Hector and Horace swept into the six women a moment later, dual short swords drawn and flashing in the firelight.

Four of the women immediately formed a battle line, raising shields and swords to face the attack, while the other two faced away from the line, searching the jungle for any sign of additional enemy.

Hector and Horace split, each targeting a soldier on the outside of the line. Hector raced toward the soldiers recklessly as if he was going to crash into the shields and expose himself to their blades, but at the last moment he transformed into vapor and slipped through the line, solidifying a moment later behind them and stabbing the surprised woman in the back before rolling around the outside of her dying body and facing the next soldier in the line.

Horace skirted around the edge of the line, forcing his opponent to turn to face him before lunging toward her with his leading blade. When she stepped back to brace herself, she tripped over Horace's invisible servant, falling into her companion and knocking her over as well. Horace darted in and stabbed her in the lower leg, then backed off, circling around toward the front of the now broken line, looking for his next opportunity to strike.

The woman screamed in pain from the leg wound. At the same time, one of the two soldiers guarding the rear of their hasty formation screamed in fear. Shadowfang lunged at her, swatting her shield aside and going for her throat. With three of their number wounded or dead in seconds, the remaining three women of the Regency Army chose to flee. The first ran straight into Ayela, who stepped into view too late for the woman to stop, crouched down low to avoid a shield smash and stabbed her in the leg before rolling to the side. The woman stumbled, whipping her sword around in a clumsy strike that was several feet too high before stopping suddenly, realization slowly spreading across her face.

"You poisoned me," she said, falling to the ground.

The soldier that had fallen under Horace's opponent scrambled to her feet and looked at Hector and Horace wildly, trying to watch them both as they positioned themselves to split her focus. She lunged at Horace, exposing her back to Hector. When Horace blocked, Hector struck, stabbing her in the base of the skull just under her helmet and killing her almost instantly.

The last remaining soldier was nearly to the edge of the clearing when Isabel burned a hole through her, leaving only the wounded soldier left, her leg bleeding profusely, her face already pasty white.

"Hector, Horace, search the fallen for anything of use," Isabel said, linking her mind with Slyder. A quick survey of the area told her that the bulk of the Regency force was still a half a day behind.

"What about her?" Ayela asked, pointing to the wounded woman.

"What are your orders?" Isabel asked the woman.

She just scowled at her.

"Fair enough," Isabel said. "Let me guess. You were sent to kill the Sin'Rath and the House of Karth."

The woman clenched her jaw and almost flinched.

"I'll leave it up to you, Ayela," Isabel said. "She came to kill your family. Do we kill her quickly or leave her for the jungle?"

Ayela frowned as the weight of the decision settled on her but she didn't hesitate for long.

"I would like to leave her to the jungle," Ayela said, "but we can't afford the risk that she might survive and make a report to the other soldiers."

Isabel nodded approvingly, then looked at Horace. In a blink, he stabbed the woman in the side of the neck.

After an hour on the move, Ayela stepped up beside Isabel. "Is it always so easy?" she asked.

"What exactly?" Isabel asked.

"Fighting and killing," Ayela said. "I've seen you in a fight twice and both times your enemies didn't have a chance. Both times they died so quickly."

"The killing is never easy," Isabel said. "It stays with you, even when it needs to be done, even when the only choice is to kill or die, it stays with you, puts a mark on your soul. As for the fighting being easy, it isn't. Both times you've seen me fight, I had the benefit of surprise and that makes all the difference."

"So then a fair fight would be harder," Ayela said.

Isabel stopped and fixed Ayela with her piercing green eyes.

"Hear me well," she said, "there's no such thing as a fair fight. You asked me to teach you how to fight ... well, consider this your first lesson. Don't ever fight for glory or honor or pride. Only fight to protect life and liberty. If you do that, then any tactic is acceptable. Give your enemy no mercy and no quarter. Kill them quickly, by whatever means you can, and don't ever let the notion of fairness enter your mind."

Isabel started walking again. Ayela was silent for the rest of the morning while they trudged through the jungle. It had started raining gently, a kind of heavy mist that penetrated everything. By midday, the jungle was dripping wet and they were soaked to the bone. Hector found a rock outcropping with a patch of dry ground large enough for them to stop and rest.

"I've never killed anyone before," Ayela whispered.

Isabel put her hand on her shoulder. "I know it's hard, but you did well," she said.

"If I may ask," Hector said.

Ayela nodded.

"If you've never killed before, then why are you carrying such a virulent poison?"

She shrugged. "I learned how to make blackwort many years ago and sometimes my brother will ask me for tinctures and even poisons when he doesn't want to bother making them himself, so I try to keep such things in my workroom. When I knew I would be leaving with you, I thought it might be useful to bring it along."

"I was impressed with how quickly it took effect," Horace said.

"Me too," Isabel said. "Is it difficult to make?"

"Not really," Ayela said. "Many tribes use it on their darts, so it's a well-known recipe. It's a mixture of three different ingredients: two types of mushrooms and a kind of lichen. All three are poisonous if eaten, but when mixed correctly, they make blackwort, one of the most fast-acting and deadly poisons known in the jungles of Karth."

"If we have the time and you can find the ingredients, I'd like you to show me how it's made," Isabel said.

"I'd be happy to, but wouldn't it just be easier to use your magic if you want to kill someone?"

"When you're at war, you can never have too many weapons," Isabel said, hoisting her pack. "We'd better get moving."

"At least we don't have to worry about lightning flies anymore," Ayela said. "They hate the rain."

"Good to know," Hector said, taking the lead.

They walked steadily for the rest of the day, stopping shortly before dark when they found a large fallen tree that created a natural shelter and offered a patch of dry ground to sleep on. After a few minutes of work, they'd built a cozy space just big enough for the four of them to sleep and enclosed enough that they felt safe building a fire to warm themselves and dry their clothes.

The rain had stopped late in the afternoon, but the jungle was still dripping wet and the brush they'd been traveling through had kept them soaked. Isabel was grateful for the simple luxury of warmth and a hot cup of tea.

Alexander appeared while they were breaking camp the next morning.

"I was starting to wonder if you'd forgotten about me," Isabel said.

"You know better than that," he said. "I've been attending to a few other matters of pressing importance."

"Is everything all right?" Isabel asked, suddenly worried.

"Not really," Alexander said, "but when has it ever been?"

"Anything you want to talk about?" she asked.

"Nothing I can tell you right now," he said. "I've done some scouting. The two Regency forces are still coming, the first is less than half a day away and the second, larger force is two days back. The hunting party from Karth is gaining on you. The witches with them seem to know where you are, so they aren't bothering with your trail. Instead, they're coming straight for you, as much as the jungle will allow, anyway."

"Any chance you could distract them again?" Isabel asked.

"I tried already," Alexander said. "The witches have figured out that I'm just a projection, so they're not falling for that anymore."

"How far is the swamp?" she asked.

"At least a day, maybe more," he said. "The jungle looks pretty thick between here and there."

"Will we make it before they reach us?"

"You won't have much time to work on a raft before the first Regency hunting party gets to you," Alexander said. "Fortunately, there are only ten left."

"We killed six plus the wraithkin," Isabel said. "The jungle must have gotten another four."

"I'm glad you got the wraithkin," Alexander said. "I've been worrying about him."

"Me too," Isabel said. "If we can ambush the rest of them, maybe we can buy some time to build that raft before the Karth hunters arrive."

"Is my brother with them?" Ayela asked.

"I don't know," Alexander said. "Can you describe him?"

"Black hair and dark eyes, tall, but thin and wiry. If he's with them, he'd be leading the men."

"He's there," Alexander said. "The two witches only talk to him, completely ignoring the rest of the men, and he seems totally charmed by them."

"Isabel, promise me you won't kill my brother," Ayela said.

"Ayela, if we have to fight them, I'm going to focus all my efforts on killing those two witches. With them gone, I'm hoping the men will come to their senses."

Ayela nodded. "He and my father are all that's left of my family. I can't lose them."

"I understand how you feel, Ayela," Alexander said. "Let's focus on avoiding them, all right?"

She nodded.

"I'll be back when I have more information," he said, fading out of sight.

Despite their fatigue, they pushed hard for most of the day, trying to widen their lead over the Regency soldiers, hoping to avoid a confrontation or to at least buy the time they needed to prepare an ambush if it came to that. As they neared the edge of the swamp, the jungle seemed to grow denser, the trees larger, ancient and wild. Isabel started to feel like each footstep was a trespass, an affront to a place that wanted to be untamed.

When the jungle gave way to a clearing occupied by a giant tree, she started to get the feeling that they were being watched. Then she saw Shadowfang perched atop a stout trunk that rose twelve to fifteen feet and split into five giant branches, each radiating away from the base and extending toward the sky. The jaguar's tail was flicking about and his yellow eyes were fixed on a spot in the jungle.

Isabel looked where he was looking but saw nothing.

"What is it?" Hector asked.

"I'm not sure," Isabel said, "but I don't like it."

As one, Hector and Horace drew swords and fanned out, searching for any sign of threat. The jungle was deathly silent, all of the birdsong, buzzing of insects, and chattering of small mammals silent.

Isabel started casting her shield spell.

"We're being stalked," Ayela said, drawing her dagger, black with poison.

"By what?" Hector asked.

Before anyone could answer, a shimmer raced toward them from out of the jungle, more like a blur in the air than a distinct shape. It hit Hector, knocking him to the ground, the raptor becoming almost visible. It was large, easily seven feet tall, with razor-sharp talons and a long snout opening in a powerful mouth filled with rows of needlelike teeth. It snapped at Hector but he became a cloud of vapor, and the beast roared in frustration.

Then the spot in the jungle where Shadowfang had been watching started to move toward them—it looked almost like a mirage, but fast and deadly.

Horace stabbed the chameleon lizard twice in the side, once with each short sword. It flinched and roared in pain and fury before racing away into the jungle, vanishing from sight before it reached the cover of the dense foliage.

Then Isabel was hit from behind. The attack came without warning, knocking her to the ground and pinning her beneath the beast as it snapped at her head, its teeth landing on her shield instead. It leapt back in frustration, turning its attention to Ayela. Isabel called out to Shadowfang.

Isabel and Hector regained their feet at the same time. The beast leapt on Ayela, shoving her to the ground, her struggling impotent against its weight and strength. Isabel released a force-push spell, knocking the beast off Ayela, but not before it raked her with its talons, leaving six deep gashes across her chest and shoulders.

Hector faced the beast charging toward them with swords at the ready, but Shadowfang reached it first, hitting it broadside and tumbling to the ground in a furious whirl of claws and fangs. They separated, both bleeding but both still focused on the other as they circled.

"Hector, Horace, get Ayela into the tree," Isabel shouted.

She cast a light-lance at the chameleon lizard, but instead of burning through it, the focused beam of intensely hot light hit the creature and refracted in every direction, creating a brilliant display that lit up the surrounding jungle. The chameleon lizard turned and bolted away. Before Shadowfang could follow, Isabel ordered him back to the tree.

Hector transformed into vapor and gently floated up to the crook in the giant tree. A moment after he retook solid form, Horace tossed a rope up to him, then looped the trailing end around Ayela's waist. He quickly climbed the tree and he and Hector pulled Ayela up to safety while Isabel watched the jungle for any sign of the chameleon lizards.

She didn't have to wait long. Two of the creatures came at her from different angles. She could hear their rhythmic footfalls more than she could see them. Bracing herself against the trunk of the tree, trusting her shield to hold, she drew her sword and waited. A moment later she was knocked sideways by the first, landing hard and trying to roll out of the way when the second pounced, landing on top of her and pinning her to the ground, trying to crush her skull with its powerful jaws.

Her shield held, but only just. She could feel it failing under the force of the attack. Looking into the mouth of the beast, she stabbed wildly with her sword, hitting the lizard in the leg, not deeply, not seriously, but enough to get its attention.

It leapt back in pain and surprise, opening the way for the second to attack. It landed on top of her, one foot to the side and the other on her chest. When her shield failed, its talons gouged holes into her armor, piercing her flesh. Then Hector was there, stabbing the creature in the side, driving his blade deeply into its chest and pushing it off Isabel.

She struggled to her feet. The lizard roared in frustration at Hector, who was now facing it, swords drawn.

"Get to the tree," Hector said.

Isabel didn't hesitate. She reached the rope and expended the last of her strength scrambling to the relative safety of the tree just as the first of the three chameleon lizards reemerged from the jungle, racing toward her. It leapt for her, missing her by inches, snapping at the air and clawing at the side of the tree.

Horace took her hand and shouted to his brother, "I have her!"

Hector transformed into vapor and floated into the tree, leaving the two chameleon lizards below, wounded and circling, hissing in fury at the narrow escape of their prey.

Ayela had lost consciousness, her face was pasty and uncharacteristically white.

"You said you still have healing potions," Isabel said.

Horace nodded, digging into his pouch for his last of the magical draughts.

"Help her sit up," Isabel said, gently slapping her face. "Wake up, Ayela, you have to swallow this."

Ayela blinked and murmured something.

"Tip her head back and hold her nose," Isabel said, carefully pouring the potion into her mouth. Ayela coughed and sputtered but managed to swallow most of it before slipping back into unconsciousness.

"Take the other," Hector said, holding the last of the healing potions out to Isabel.

"No. Save it," Isabel said, stiffly unbuckling her armor. "I'll just use some of the salve you brought."

Hector handed her a jar barely a quarter full of Lucky's salve. She carefully spread it into her wounds under her tunic and lay back against one of the giant limbs.

"Keep watch while we're out," she muttered, already succumbing to the effects of the magical salve.

Chapter 27

Alexander appeared moments after she woke, groggy and disoriented.

"Are you all right?" he asked.

"I think so," she said. "How's Ayela?"

"Still asleep," Hector said, "but it looks like her wounds are healing well."

"What about the lizards?" Isabel asked.

"They're lying in wait," Alexander said, pointing out two different spots in the jungle. "One's right over there and the other is there."

"And the Regency?" Isabel asked.

"About an hour away," Alexander said.

"Then they'll be here before nightfall," Isabel said. "This isn't exactly the kind of ambush I had in mind."

"The lizards might take care of them for us," Hector said. "If we're quiet and stay low, they may not see us."

"I guess that's all we really can do for now," Isabel said. "Ayela won't be able to move until tomorrow at the earliest. How far out are the Sin'Rath?"

"Still a day behind," Alexander said.

"At least there's that," Isabel said.

"I'll be watching until the Regency soldiers arrive," Alexander said. "If the lizards kill them all, good enough, if not I'll try and draw off those that remain. Try and get some rest while you wait. I'll warn you just before they arrive."

She smiled at him as he faded out of sight.

***

Isabel waited quietly, her shield firmly in place, while Ayela slept. Hector and Horace had concealed themselves as well as possible, lying on the broad branches of the banyan tree, trying to blend in with the growing shadows. Alexander had come a few minutes before to warn them of the approaching enemy soldiers, and was now unseen but watching.

Isabel held her breath when she heard the rustling coming through the brush in the early evening gloom. The first soldier entered the clearing cautiously, stopping and scanning the area a step from the brush line. When the woman saw the dead lizard, she froze in place, looking for any hint of a threat. After a moment, she signaled those following as she quietly, slowly drew her sword.

Several more women slipped into the clearing and spread out, looking for sign of their quarry. Two soldiers carefully examined the tracks and markings from the fight while the rest fanned out and formed a perimeter.

One soldier screamed, then vanished into the brush. Followed by another. The remaining soldiers fell back into a tight group, their shields and swords pointing out toward the jungle, haunted looks ghosting across their faces as they listened to their companions screaming in agony and terror. Then there was silence.

They waited, their tension palpable in the way they flinched at the slightest noise, their fear barely held in check.

"What was that?" one said.

"One of those," another answered, motioning to the dead lizard.

"Do you think they got Lady Reishi?" yet another asked.

"There aren't any bodies."

"Maybe they dragged her off into the jungle."

"What difference does it make?" another said. "We won't make it through the night out in the open."

"Over there!" one shouted, pointing toward the far edge of the clearing. Isabel looked down and saw herself crouching in the brush. Her image got up and raced off into the jungle.

"Stay together," one of the soldiers said, motioning for the remains of the Regency platoon to give chase. Within a few moments, sounds of their movement through the jungle faded into the distance.

Isabel started breathing a little easier until a scream shattered the calm evening air, followed by another. Several minutes later, three women crashed through the jungle, stumbling back into the clearing.

"I don't understand."

"She just vanished."

"At least we got one of those blasted lizards."

"Yeah, and they got seven of us."

Isabel almost felt sorry for them. She started casting her light-lance spell, but stopped when a blurry patch of air pounced on one of the women, pinning her to the ground, taking her head in its mouth and quickly snapping her neck. The other two attacked, stabbing the chameleon lizard in the side, fatally wounding it, then pressing their advantage, they stabbed it repeatedly until it lay lifeless and mutilated.

Bloody and alone, the two soldiers looked around frantically. Night was falling.

"What do we do now?"

"What else can we do? We go back and try to find the rest of our battalion."

"Shouldn't we wait until morning?"

"I'm not staying here," she said, looking around the clearing at their dead companion and the two dead lizards. "This carrion is bound to draw scavengers."

The first soldier nodded and they started for the brush line. Hector looked to Isabel; she shook her head slowly. A few moments after the soldiers slipped into the darkening jungle, Shadowfang leapt to the ground.

Ayela woke not long after. "Did I hear screaming?"

"It was nothing," Isabel said. "Try to rest."

***

Isabel stretched, trying to work the stiffness out of her back from sleeping in a tree. Dawn broke over an overcast sky, but it didn't look like rain, a small thing that she reminded herself to be grateful for.

Ayela was nearly healed but still stiff and tender from her wounds, yet she was determined to press on. Then she saw the dead soldier. "What happened last night?" she asked, looking around warily.

"The soldiers arrived and the lizards killed them," Isabel said.

"Most of them, anyway," Hector said, looking at Shadowfang who was busy cleaning his face by licking his paw and rubbing it along his snout.

"They didn't even notice us?" Ayela asked.

Isabel shook her head and said, "We had Alexander's help."

"I can't believe I slept through the whole thing," Ayela said.

"The healing potion we gave you has that effect on people," Isabel said. Then she turned and looked at the dead chameleon lizards. "I wish we had time to skin them."

"What for?" Horace asked.

"Remember Jack and his cloak?" Isabel said. "What do you think it was made out of?"

"Really?" Horace said, appraising the two dead lizards, then looking at his brother. "With a pair of cloaks like that, we'd be dangerous."

"You're already dangerous," Isabel said. "Besides, we'd have to get the skins to Mage Gamaliel and he'd have to take the time to enchant them. We have more important things to do right now and I suspect he does too."

"Pity," Hector said. Horace nodded.

"I just hope we don't run into any more of those things," Ayela said, tenderly touching her nearly healed wound and grimacing.

"On that count, I agree," Hector said.

"The swamp shouldn't be far," Horace said.

Isabel tipped her head back for a moment. "It's a few hours that way. I see why they call it the gloaming swamp, the place is completely shrouded in mist. It won't be easy to navigate in there."

"Hopefully, Lord Reishi will provide us with guidance," Horace said.

"I'm sure he'll be there when we need him," Isabel said, cinching down the straps on her pack.

They set out cautiously. The chameleon lizards had them all a little spooked. Isabel used her link with Slyder to guide their course and watch for any sign of danger while keeping Shadowfang out in front several dozen feet to meet any threat they might encounter. He had proven to be an invaluable ally in the jungle.

Ayela stepped up next to her while they walked.

"I think I understand what you said about surprise better now," she said.

"Tell me," Isabel said, taking on the mantle of teacher.

"When you were able to surprise the enemy, they fell quickly," Ayela said. "When the chameleon lizards surprised us, we barely survived, or at least I barely survived. I always thought that battle was supposed to be like the stories I heard as a child around the campfire ... until now."

"And now?"

"It's terrifying and it all happens so fast ... then it's just sad and ugly once it's over."

Isabel nodded. "Good, you're starting to understand."

They walked on for a time while Ayela thought about Isabel's words. "Not all battles can be won by surprise," she said.

"No, but surprise is just a small part of the lesson. Surprise is simply your enemy's belief that they aren't about to be attacked, thus they aren't prepared and thus they're at a sudden and often decisive disadvantage. The greater lesson is about belief."

"Belief about what?" Ayela said, frowning.

"First, about your circumstances," Isabel said. "Believing that your enemy is wounded when they're actually feigning an injury, believing that you outnumber the enemy when they in fact have soldiers hidden from view, believing that an enemy is really an ally, believing that your enemy is more powerful or less powerful than they really are ... these are all factors that can decide the day. The most important thing in any fight is knowledge, knowledge of yourself and knowledge of your enemy. If you accurately understand both your own capabilities and those of your enemy, you'll carry the day because you'll know how to use your strengths to exploit your enemy's weaknesses.

"Second, and far more importantly, believing in the rightness of your cause will give you the strength to persevere even when it seems that all is lost. This is the greatest power of those who fight for the light—we're on the right side and we know it.

"Those who ally themselves with the darkness are selfish and greedy, seeking power and dominion over others for their own glory, but those qualities are inextricably linked with cowardice and an inability to trust others. Evil people can only lead through fear, intimidation, and deception, so their allies will inevitably betray them, either because they're selfish and greedy themselves or because they're secretly good and can't stomach the wrong they're being asked to do.

"Belief is the key to everything."

"That's a lot to think about," Ayela said, falling back behind Isabel as they trudged through the jungle.

They reached the edge of the swamp about midday, solid ground abruptly giving way to algae-covered stagnant water. A pall of fog hung over the water, stretching out under the branches of sparsely spaced, ancient cypress trees, their trunks flaring just before they reached the water, looking like a hundred roots clustered together, all wrapped tightly with a single outer skin of bark.

Hector found a branch and reached out into the water, searching for solid ground under the thick, bright green algae.

"It's only about two feet deep."

"Right here at the edge," Horace said. "There's no telling how deep it gets farther in."

"Or what's in the water," Ayela said. "It's said that the black waters of the gloaming swamp are deadly."

"We'd better get to work," Isabel said.

It took the better part of the afternoon to build a small raft capable of supporting their weight. They found three relatively large limbs that had broken from nearby trees and used them for the base, lashing smaller branches in the eight-foot span between them, forming a platform. It wasn't pretty and it was far too heavy to carry over much distance, but it floated even with the four of them aboard.

When it came time to push off, Shadowfang simply sat down at the edge of the water. Isabel smiled at her friend. She knew she could force him with her magic, but she also knew that it would take greater effort to control him and he would be far less useful within the confines of the swamp than he was in the jungle.

"Goodbye, Shadowfang," she said, releasing him from her will as they shoved off into the murkiness. He roared once and disappeared into the jungle.

Hector and Horace used stout poles to propel the unwieldy raft through the water, leaving a trail of disturbed algae on the surface, marking their passage.

"That's unfortunate," Isabel said. "I was hoping we would vanish without a trace, as far as the enemy was concerned anyway."

"Hopefully, the Regency won't arrive until the algae has had a chance to cover our passage," Hector said. "But I don't think it matters much to the Sin'Rath."

They poled their way through the mist until darkness started to fall.

"I haven't seen a scrap of dirt big enough for a camp," Horace said.

"Me neither," Hector said.

"I guess we're sleeping on the raft," Isabel said. "How deep is the water?"

"Three to five feet," said Hector.

"We should tie off to a tree for the night," Isabel said.

"What was that?" Ayela asked, pointing off the side of the raft into the water.

"I didn't see it," Horace said.

"Looked like a snake to me," Hector said. "And it was big."

Isabel reached out with her mind and found it, imposing her will on the reptile and finding it to have a distinctly different, and quite distasteful, mind. At her command, it rose up out of the water, displaying itself to them.

It was glistening black, easily a foot thick in the body and probably twenty-five feet long. Its fangs looked long enough to pierce completely through a man's forearm.

"Well, what shall we call you?" Isabel said.

"Ugly?" Ayela said under her breath.

"More like terrifying," Hector said.

"How about Scales?" Isabel said. "Yes, I think I like that. Scales it is."

"You aren't really going to keep that thing around, are you?" Ayela asked.

"Of course," Isabel said. "What better guard dog could we ask for in this place?"

The snake slipped back into the water, leaving only disturbed algae to prove it was ever there.

"Scales will stand guard, but we'll all take our turn at watch as well," Isabel said.

"I don't like this place," Ayela said. "I'm starting to understand why nobody returns from here. Without your magic, that snake could have easily taken one of us underwater and disappeared."

"Probably," Isabel said. "Unfortunately, this is the only way to get where we need to go. Hopefully, we won't encounter anything more dangerous than a giant snake."

Hector and Horace nodded, looking at each other.

Night fell, shrouding them in darkness so void of light, Isabel might have imagined that this was what the netherworld looked like … if she didn't know better.

Ayela left her jar of glowing lichen with Horace, who drew first watch. The lichen didn't provide much light, but it was enough to prevent them from accidentally stumbling off the raft into the murky water.

No one slept well. The swamp was eerie and foreboding, occasional sounds of small animals moving about were muted by the heavy mist hanging over everything like a burial shroud, only serving to make the sounds more haunting and forcing one to strain to hear what might be coming through the dark waters.

Isabel woke tired and irritable. It was impossible to tell what the weather looked like above the swamp. Within, it was a dull grey in every direction, limiting visibility to less than a hundred feet, the world beyond fading into the unknown.

"Well, at least we know the algae will cover our tracks," Hector said, motioning to the uniformly green water as if presenting an act on a stage.

"Unfortunately, we also have no idea which way we came from or where we're going," Horace said.

Isabel tipped her head back and closed her eyes. Slyder was perched in the high branches at the top of the cypress tree they were tied to. She could see that the day was clear and bright above the swamp, the winter sun climbing gradually into the southern sky. Off in the distance, a craggy stone mountain jutted abruptly from the swamp, a lone high point in a sea of level green.

"We have to go that way," Isabel pointed, her eyes still closed.

"That way it is," Hector said, unlashing the raft from the tree trunk. As he and Horace shoved off, Scales broke the surface and started out ahead of them. Ayela shivered, but held her tongue.

It was cold under the cover of the fog and the air was so still, they left a wake of swirling eddies in the mist, momentarily marking their passage. Isabel guided them with Slyder's help, keeping them moving in the general direction of the mountain. The algae covering every inch of the swamp gave way about midmorning, revealing inky black water that stank of rot and decay, but the thick mist persisted.

The water grew shallower, revealing patches of land covered in thick vegetation that obstructed their path. Isabel found herself relying on Slyder more and more to get her bearings as they wound through the confusing maze of passable waterways. By midafternoon the water grew so shallow and the vegetation so dense that they were spending more time working to free the raft from entanglements than they were moving forward ... until they came to a place where they ran aground, the raft sinking into the thick mud and becoming stuck.

"Looks like we're on foot for a while," Isabel said.

Scales slithered out of the water, his tongue flicking the air.

"We should probably disassemble the raft and take the rope with us," Hector said.

"I agree," Isabel said. "There's no telling how far this patch of high ground goes."

It wasn't long before they were trudging through the muck. The ground was coated with a thick layer of mud and the vegetation was dripping from the heavy blanket of fog. Isabel found her feet growing heavier by the step, mud caking to her boots. Within a few hundred feet, they all needed to stop to scrape their boots clean.

"We haven't seen much life," Horace said. "I'm starting to wonder if the biggest danger in this place is just disorientation."

"I wouldn't bet on it," Hector said.

"Nor I," Ayela said. "I've heard stories of terrible monsters living within the gloaming swamp. Things that occasionally wander into the jungle to hunt before disappearing back into the mist with their prey."

Their progress was slower on land than it had been by raft. The ground was riddled with pools of stagnant water, all of it black and cold. Late in the day, they came to a place where their path was blocked by a channel of water about twenty feet across.

"We could backtrack and see if there's another way," Horace suggested.

Isabel shook her head. "We're still being pursued. I doubt the Regency soldiers have our trail anymore, but the Sin'Rath probably do and I'd rather avoid them if at all possible."

"That looks pretty deep," Hector said.

Scales slipped into the water and vanished, reemerging on the far side after a minute or so.

"Any predators down there would have probably taken issue with the snake," Horace said.

"Maybe," Ayela said. "Predators come in many sizes."

"I can get across without getting wet," Hector said. "Once I'm on the other side, toss me a rope and then tie it around your waists so I can help you cross."

He transformed into vapor, floating gently and slowly across the surface of the water.

Horace tossed him a coil of rope and he tied it off to a nearby tree. Isabel, Ayela, and Horace then tied the rope around themselves, leaving a space of five or six feet between them. Isabel took a long branch and cleaned off the smaller branches to make a measuring pole.

A few feet into the water, it was almost three feet deep. Several more feet and it was almost five feet deep. She discarded the pole, shaking her head.

"Looks like we're going to get soaked," she said, carefully stepping into the water and inhaling sharply at the cold.

A few steps from the bank, she was up to her chest in the chill water. A few feet more and she was swimming, aided by Hector who kept tension on the rope. After all three of them were in the water, and Isabel was about halfway across, she felt a sharp pain on her leg, then another on her arm and another on her back. She started to flounder, fear gripping her as something unseen attacked her from under the murky water.

Hector saw her begin to panic and started pulling them toward the bank with all his strength. Each in turn started trying to ward off some unknown menace, adding to the difficulty of pulling them across the channel.

Isabel reached the shore first, scrambling out of the water in a frenzy to escape. Ayela was next, just as panicked, followed by Horace. Each in turn collapsed into the mud within a few steps.

Chapter 28

Isabel woke, sitting bolt upright and nearly screaming, looking about frantically and finding herself on top of a little patch of high ground just a few dozen feet from the water. She was wrapped in her blanket and shivering. Hector was sitting nearby, looking totally exhausted. Scales was wound around the limb of a nearby tree.

"What happened?" Isabel asked.

"Leeches," Hector said, holding up a jar with one of the vile little creatures floating in swamp water. "I pulled several off each of you after I got you on solid ground. I'm pretty sure they knocked you out."

Horace and Ayela were still unconscious but breathing steadily.

"How long?" Isabel asked, hunger suddenly rumbling in her belly.

"At least a day," Hector said. "The only thing I know for sure is that at least one night has passed."

"Dear Maker," Isabel said. "No wonder nothing makes it out of this place alive."

"I was thinking the same thing," Hector said. "Fortunately, it's been quiet as a tomb since you lost consciousness."

Isabel tipped her head back and closed her eyes for a few moments.

"Looks like late afternoon," she said. "Get some rest, you look exhausted."

Hector nodded. "I haven't slept since I pulled you out."

"I'll keep watch," Isabel said, getting to her feet and shivering anew. Her clothes were soaked and stuck to her skin, sapping her warmth.

She spent a few minutes walking around the camp in circles to get her blood flowing. When the penetrating cold didn't subside, she decided that, while a fire was probably out of the question, she could still make some warmth. After gathering a pile of rocks, she cast her light-lance spell but deliberately reduced its power so she could heat the stones without burning them into vapor. It took a few castings, but she succeeded in heating the stones to a dull glowing red, producing much-needed heat.

Horace and Ayela both woke some time later, each shivering uncontrollably, each waking in a state of near panic.

"Come, get warm," Isabel said to them. They didn't hesitate to huddle around the glowing stones, soaking in the heat and trying to calm their chattering teeth.

"What did this?" Ayela asked, inspecting a welt on her forearm.

Isabel handed her the jar with the leech.

"What a terrible little creature," she said. "But its venom may prove useful, if I can figure out how to extract it."

"I thought you might find it interesting," Isabel said. "Needless to say, we'll be avoiding the water from now on. I don't know how much of this swamp is infested with those things and I don't want to find out."

"That's going to slow us down even more," Horace said.

"I know, but those things will stop us permanently," Isabel said. "Besides, our pursuers are bound to have the same problem, and there are a lot more of them to move across the water, so I'm hoping it'll take them that much longer."

They camped there for the night, drying their clothes and resting. Again, the swamp was nearly silent, save for the ubiquitous dripping of condensed fog on tree leaves. The place was cold and eerie, lifeless and desolate as if the light and the dark had fought a great battle here long ago and the darkness had won, slowly sapping the will to live from everything shrouded by the oppressive fog.

Isabel woke irritable and agitated. She nursed her anger for a moment before getting up, when Azugorath slammed into her. Isabel gasped, clenching her teeth and focusing her will in opposition to the invader, railing against her with all of the fury she could muster ... and that was her mistake.

As Isabel loosed her rage, Azugorath slipped into her mind and seized control. Isabel saw herself get up and quietly draw her sword, eyeing Hector while he slept. Ayela was sitting watch. She cocked her head and frowned at Isabel's odd behavior.

"Isabel, what's wrong?"

At that moment, she broke Azugorath's hold over her and regained control, deliriously happy to be sovereign over her own body again, but terrified at the implications of what just happened. Ayela was looking at her curiously and Isabel realized her sword was still drawn. She sheathed it quietly.

"I thought I heard something," she said, sitting next to Ayela and yawning, worry racing around in her mind.

"I've been hearing things since we got here," Ayela said. "Worse, I keep having this dream about an old hag in the swamp, beckoning to me, and then I wake up but I can never get back to sleep."

"I imagine this swamp plays tricks on anybody who's fool enough, or desperate enough, to trespass here," Isabel said.

The light of dawn was just beginning to filter through the mist, gradually lifting the total darkness of night in the gloaming swamp and transforming it into a uniform grey. Slyder showed her that they were still a fair distance from their destination. Given the difficulty of the terrain, probably several days away.

Even though they'd managed to completely dry their clothes during the prior evening, the chill of the fog seemed to cling to Isabel like a damp blanket. She was eager to get moving, more for the warmth of exertion than anything else.

They carefully picked their way through the swamp, a new respect for the deadliness of the water fortifying their patience on the many occasions when they encountered water and had to double back to find another way around. Fortunately, there was enough ground above water for them to make good progress during the morning.

About midday, Alexander appeared in their midst.

"How're you holding up?" he asked Isabel. "This place looks pretty bad."

"We're still alive," Isabel said, more irritably than she would have liked.

Alexander nodded. "The Regency stopped at the edge of the swamp and sent one soldier into the water. She waded out over her knees, then screamed and tried to get back to solid ground before she fell into the water and went under. The rest decided that you couldn't be stupid enough to go into the gloaming swamp, so they split their force in two. They're busy searching for you along the banks to the north and south.

"The Sin'Rath and Trajan's soldiers are about a day behind and making good time on six rafts they cobbled together. Have you had any trouble?"

"Show him," Isabel said to Ayela. She dutifully held up the jar containing the leech.

"These things almost killed us all," Isabel said. "We went into the water and barely made it out alive. Cost us the better part of a day."

"It looks like a common leech," Alexander said, inspecting the slimy little creature.

"Trust me, it's not," Isabel said. "I've had leeches latch on to me before, these are different. I had four stick to me and was unconscious in under a minute—didn't wake for almost a full day."

Alexander looked around. "No wonder this place seems so devoid of life."

"I was thinking the same thing."

"I scouted ahead," Alexander said. "It looks like you should be able to stay on land for about half the distance to the mountain, then the water gets deeper again."

"Thanks," Isabel said with an apologetic smile.

"I'll look in on you whenever I get a chance," Alexander said, vanishing into the mist.

They traveled a confusing path, avoiding water at every turn. A few times they were forced to cross small sections of standing water. In each case they felled trees to use as bridges rather than risk the water itself.

Late in the afternoon, Hector stopped and signaled for silence, pointing at a form in the mist. Isabel stepped up beside him, trying to figure out what she was looking at. Deciding that the intervening mist was playing with her eyes, she started forward again, as cautiously and as quietly as possible.

Atop a little knoll almost a hundred feet away, surrounded by water and cypress trees standing like sentinels around it, was the remnants of a tree like nothing she'd ever seen before. It must have been huge in its time with a trunk easily thirty feet in diameter, but now it was just a husk of its former glory. Several stout limbs grew out of it at odd angles, ending in splayed-out branches that almost resembled fingers. Five wide roots raised the stump off the ground by about six feet, creating a space underneath that might have made for an excellent camping spot.

Then an eye opened on the side of the trunk ... then another and another.

"I don't like this," Ayela said.

One of the stout root limbs pulled free of the earth as the thing came alive. The bark split along one side, opening a giant maw four feet wide that ran vertically up the side of the tree. Another root came free, revealing a base of splayed-out roots that served as a foot.

"We should leave," Hector said.

"Yeah, I think you're right," Isabel said.

With two legs free, the tree thrust up and toward them, pulling its other three legs from the ground. The creature stood, turning in the mist, stretching its limbs like it had been sleeping for a very long time. Isabel counted five eyes, seven arms, and three giant mouths. Then it roared. A kind of gibbering, gurgling cackle that shattered the calm of the swamp, filling the deathly still air with madness.

"Run!" Isabel yelled.

And run they did. The swamp creature shambled behind them, splashing through the water, closing the distance with alarming quickness. Isabel looked over her shoulder, trying to reconcile the thing chasing her with everything she understood about reality. It was as if nature herself had gone mad … and the insanity was gaining on Isabel.

With a thought, she sent Scales to entangle the creature's legs. The giant snake obediently attacked, winding itself around several of the thing's stout root limbs, hobbling it and slowing its pursuit.

The swamp thing stopped, grabbing the snake with several of its branch-like arms and jerking it away from its legs, then unceremoniously thrusting a section of the snake into one of its giant vertical maws, clamping down so hard that Scales was torn in half, both ends writhing about in pain and panic. Isabel felt the link to her pet sever as he died.

The creature stopped its chase and started eating the snake with all three mouths, stuffing huge sections of the dead reptile into each maw with almost frantic hunger, barely bothering to chew before taking another bite.

Isabel and her companions stopped, staring with macabre fascination as the thing devoured the giant snake in less than a minute. When it was finished, it looked around with its five eyes, each moving independently of the others, but sensing nothing in the immediate vicinity, it started digging into the muddy soil with its roots as, one by one, its eyes began to close.

Isabel motioned to move away quietly. They traveled in silence for over an hour before Hector stopped, shaking his head.

"What in the name of the Maker was that thing?"

"I don't know," Isabel said, "and I don't really want to."

"I'm with Isabel," Ayela said. "That was literally something out of a nightmare."

"I kind of feel bad for Scales," Horace said.

"Me too," Isabel said, "but I think he saved us."

"I had the same thought," Hector said. "I wouldn't even know where to start in a fight with something like that."

"Can we just get farther away from it, please?" Ayela said.

Horace pointed at her and nodded.

The ground got firmer and higher as they traveled through the afternoon. There were still plenty of pools of standing water but they became much easier to avoid. Near nightfall, they found a shelf of exposed stone that was big enough for them to make camp. Isabel used her light-lance to ignite a damp log and give them some much-needed warmth and light for the night.

She was sitting her watch in the middle of the night when Ayela came awake with a start. She looked around wildly before taking a deep breath and calming herself.

"Nightmare?" Isabel asked quietly.

"Sort of," Ayela whispered. "An old woman came to me, here at this exact spot, and told me the path we must follow. She showed me the soldiers coming through the night and said we would only survive if we did as she instructed."

"That sounds pretty specific," Isabel said, sitting up a little straighter.

"I've seen this woman in my dreams before," Ayela said, shivering.

"What else did she say?"

"Nothing, she was just standing at the edge of the swamp, beckoning for me to come to her."

Isabel leaned forward. "Have you had this dream more than once?"

"Yes, several times since Phane came and killed my family. I try not to think about it."

"Magic can be used to speak to people in their dreams," Isabel said. "Maybe someone is calling to you."

"But why?"

Isabel shrugged and shook her head.

Alexander appeared a moment later. "They're coming," he said, urgently. "I'm sorry I wasn't here earlier, I could have given you more warning."

Isabel came instantly alert, not from what he said but from how desperate he seemed.

"How close?"

"Seven or eight hundred feet," Alexander said. "You have to go ... now."

She and Ayela woke Hector and Horace and they were up and moving within a few minutes. Ayela gave Hector her jar filled with lichen to light the way, but it wasn't nearly enough. Then Alexander transformed into a bobbling sphere of pure white light floating above them, providing just enough illumination to guide their steps but not enough to penetrate the mist more than a few dozen feet.

Ayela stopped dead in her tracks. "I know this place ... from my dreams."

They heard a muffled shout in the distance. The Sin'Rath and Trajan's soldiers had found their campsite.

"Lead the way," Isabel said, hoping she was making the right decision.

Alexander re-formed a few minutes later, the glowing sphere floating over his head.

"Where are you taking them, Ayela?" he asked.

"I'm not sure, I'm following instructions I received in a dream."

He turned to Isabel. "We have no way of knowing who cast the dream-whisper. You could be walking right into a trap laid by the Sin'Rath."

"I considered that," Isabel said, "but they're so close to catching us that I don't think they'd bother."

"I hope you know what you're doing," he said, transforming back into a bobbling light.

"Me too," Isabel said, motioning for Ayela to continue.

The Princess of Karth wound through the swamp with unsettling confidence, seeming to know the path as if she'd walked it a hundred times, avoiding water at every turn, even to the point of guiding them across a rope bridge strung between two trees. They would never have found it on their own—it was hung above the mist and accessible only by climbing a tree that had notches in the side, forming the rungs of a ladder.

The bridge was sturdy and well kept, spanning fifty feet between two stout cypress trees at a height of twenty feet from the ground and two or three feet over the mist. Isabel smiled up at the stars when she broke free of the mist and sighed with resignation when she had to descend back into the murky air.

Not long after, Ayela led them to the concealed mouth of a cave, which turned out to be a tunnel leading through solid stone. They followed it for several minutes, winding through the earth until it stopped abruptly at a stone wall. Ayela stopped, placing her hand on the wall in confusion … then the wall vanished, opening into a little clearing. Alexander's light disappeared when they crossed the threshold, and the mist shrouding the swamp was completely gone, revealing a clear sky above.

An old woman approached, smiling thinly. She wore a tattered robe over her thin and frail frame. Her hair was long and grey, her nose resembled a beak, several strands of jet black hair grew from the prominent mole on her cheek, but her slate grey eyes were clear and filled with intelligence and purpose.

"Hello, Child," she said. "I've been waiting for you, though I did not expect you to bring friends."

She stopped a few feet from Ayela and her crooked smiled warmed, then she turned to Isabel and the coldness in her eyes gave the lie to her smile. Isabel felt every hair stand on end as the woman casually blew a handful of powder into her face and blackness engulfed her.

Chapter 29

"How's she doing?" Abigail asked, quietly sitting down next to Anatoly. He stared into the fire for several moments before answering.

"Not well. Her fever is only getting worse and I don't know what to do for her."

Abigail nodded, looking over at Magda sleeping fitfully under most of their blankets. They had arrived at this cave several days ago, guided by Alexander. It was a large round cavern that looked like it had been formed by an enormous air bubble trapped inside hardening lava. The entrance was narrow, almost too narrow for Ixabrax to squeeze through, but the interior was spacious and dry. It was located in a stand of evergreen trees on the side of a mountain just a few hundred feet below the timberline. Most importantly, there was a hot spring a dozen feet from the cave entrance that melted the snow as it filled the little mountain pool and ran off down the mountain in a steaming rivulet bordered on both sides by intricate and delicate ice formations and bright green foliage. The forest surrounding them provided an ample supply of firewood, but little in the way of food.

There were paintings on the walls of the cave, scenes of hunts and predators from ages long past. Abigail spent hours looking at the primitive art, wondering about the people who had stood in this very place so long ago … but that had been in the first few days before Magda had come down with a fever and become delirious. Now she was worried for her friend's survival. She and Anatoly took turns watching over her as she struggled to overcome the infection plaguing her shoulder wound.

They didn't have any healing potions or salve, so they'd done the best they could to clean and bandage her wound. Beyond that, all they could do was keep her warm and provide her with food and water when she was strong enough to take it.

Ixabrax was curled up on the far side of the cave as far away from the fire as he could get. For the most part he was patient, content to sleep while they fretted over Magda. Only occasionally did one of his big, catlike eyes open and assess the situation before closing again.

When Alexander appeared, standing near the fire, both Anatoly and Abigail stood quickly, urgently.

"Where have you been?" Abigail said, almost accusingly.

"Isabel's been in trouble. I've been helping her for the past several days and it's taken most of my strength."

Anatoly nodded, looking over at Magda with worry in his eyes.

"Magda's in trouble, too," Abigail said. "We don't know how to help her."

Alexander scrutinized Magda's colors, and seeing the ugly base colors of infection, fixed Abigail with a resolute look.

"I don't either, but Lucky will. I'll be back as soon as I can," he said, fading from sight.

He found Lucky in a workroom next door to Mason Kallentera's expansive laboratory in Glen Morillian. Lucky was busy spooning biscuit batter onto a sheet pan when Alexander appeared nearby.

"Hi, Lucky."

The rotund mage alchemist looked startled but then smiled broadly.

"Ah, there you are, my boy. It's so good to see you. I trust all is well. Your leg is healing properly, yes?"

"My leg is healing well enough, but slowly. I've come because Magda is injured. She has an infection in her shoulder and it's spreading. I'm hoping you can help me."

Lucky set the bowl of batter aside and wiped his hands on his apron. "Of course, of course. Does she have a fever? Is she conscious?"

"She's sleeping fitfully and burning up."

"How serious is the wound?"

"Zuhl put a spike clean through her shoulder."

Lucky nodded thoughtfully. "I assume she was injured rescuing Abigail."

"Yes. I'm sorry, Lucky. You must have been worried sick about her. She and Anatoly are with Magda, along with a dragon named Ixabrax. They're safe and well hidden but they don't know what to do for her."

"Is there any foliage around?"

Alexander nodded. "They're in an evergreen forest just below the timberline."

"Old Man's Beard should be growing on some of the nearby trees," Lucky said, looking around at the disorder of his workroom. "I'm afraid I don't have a sample but perhaps Mason does. He'd like to see you, anyway."

Lucky led him next door to Mason's workroom. The wizard was sitting in front of the fire reading an ancient book.

He stood with a smile when Alexander and Lucky entered.

"Hello Alexander, or should I call you Lord Reishi?"

"Alexander, please. It's good to see you, Mason."

"You, as well. How can I be of service?"

"Do you happen to have a sample of Old Man's Beard?" Lucky asked.

Mason nodded thoughtfully, looking this way and that for a moment before smiling and winding his way through the tables scattered haphazardly around his workroom and selecting a jar from one of his many shelves.

Alexander examined the strange-looking lichen. It was light green and stringy, almost like thick strands of hair.

"What do you do with it?"

"Crush it slightly, preserving the strands, then place it directly on the wound," Lucky said. "Wrap a loose bandage around it and change the dressing morning and night, replacing the Old Man's Beard with each changing."

"How long before she starts to show signs of improvement?"

"That depends on the degree of infection, but probably just a few days," Lucky said.

"Good, how're you settling in here?"

"Well enough. Mason has provided me with ample space to work and the rest of the wizards are converting a nearby manor house for use as the guild house. Kelvin is there now."

"I feel better knowing you're both safely out of Phane's reach."

"I wish I could say the same about you and your sister," Lucky said.

"We'll manage. Is this place secure from prying eyes?"

"Quite," Mason said. "In addition to the magic circles surrounding the valley and castle, this level is spelled to prevent scrying."

"Yet I'm able to enter."

"Yes, but you bear the Mark of Cedric," Mason said. "This place exists to assist you, so you're always welcome here."

"I hope you're right, Mason. Phane can see just as far as I can."

"I assure you, he can't see anywhere within this valley."

"I was hoping that would be the case," Alexander said. "It's been good to see you both." Alexander vanished from sight but followed Lucky back to his workshop, reappearing once his old mentor was alone.

"It's time you started on your next project, Lucky."

"Yes, of course," Lucky said, closing the door and dropping the bar in place.

"Start by procuring the necessary ingredients to make a quart of aqua regia."

"Aqua regia is a very potent acid and difficult to make," Lucky said. "It will take some time to produce such a quantity."

"I know, but it's a necessary first step," Alexander said. "I'll check back when you're ready to make it and let you know the next step."

"Give my love to Abigail and Isabel."

"I will," Alexander said, fading from sight.

***

Abigail was pacing when Alexander reappeared.

"Any luck?"

"There's a type of lichen growing near here that will help with the infection," he said. "It's not far … I can guide you to it."

Abigail tossed her heavy, fur-lined cloak over her shoulders and picked up her bow.

"Don't you think I should go instead?" Anatoly said.

"I'll be fine," Abigail said. "Besides, I need to get out of this cave or I'm going to go crazy and one of us should say with Magda."

"Suit yourself, but don't be too long."

Abigail trudged through the deep snow in the general direction Alexander had shown her. The air was crisp and clean. The sun fell through the trees, creating a dazzling display of light and shadow on the forest floor. Alexander appeared again after a few minutes of walking.

"It's up in that tree," he said pointing, then fading from sight once again.

The snow was deep enough that reaching the ladder-like branches of the fir tree was easy, and climbing to the place where the stringy green lichen grew took only a minute or so. After gathering all she could find, Abigail straddled two branches and took in the scene through the fir boughs. The sparse forest stretched out below her like a patchwork quilt, small groves of trees interrupting the untrammeled snow for as far as she could see.

Movement in the distance caught her eye. Five, maybe six men were headed straight for the cave. Glancing back to the cave mouth, she saw a thin streamer of smoke escaping from the entrance and rising like a beacon into the sky.

"Are you still here, Alex?"

When he didn't appear, Abigail climbed out of the tree and headed back to the cave as quickly as she could through the deep snow. Alexander reappeared a moment after she entered the cave.

"We have company," she said.

"Six men, scouts from a larger force farther away," Alexander said.

"How much larger?" Anatoly asked.

"Company-sized, but I didn't see anything except soldiers … no drakini, no priests."

"At least there's that," Abigail said, going to the fire and starting to prepare the Old Man's Beard.

"How soon will they get here?" Anatoly asked.

"Probably an hour. The smoke from your fire gave you away," Alexander said.

"We can take the six, especially if they don't know what they're up against," Anatoly said, "but a company is something else altogether. Magda is still delirious. Even if this stuff works, it'll be days before she can travel."

Ixabrax sleepily opened one eye. "Let them come, I was starting to get hungry anyway."

"I thought you didn't want to help fight this war," Alexander said.

"I don't, but your sister and her sword remain the only way I know of to free my family. I'm not about to let a few hundred of Zuhl's soldiers come between me and their freedom."

"That evens the odds," Anatoly said.

Ixabrax snorted. "More than even I would say. Dispatch the scouts and wake me when the rest of the enemy forces draw near." With that he closed his eye and went back to sleep.

Abigail finished dressing Magda's wound and then strapped on her quiver. "How do you want to do this?"

"Let them get close enough so none can escape," Anatoly said.

"All right, let's go find a good spot for an ambush."

"They're following the draw created by the hot spring's runoff," Alexander said.

"Good, more vegetation to hide behind," Anatoly said.

They moved down the draw several hundred feet until they found a place with a boulder just to the side of the tiny little stream.

"I'll wait behind the rock," Anatoly said. "The draw is narrow enough right here to prevent them from surrounding me. You take a position on the far side, behind those bushes and target the last man in the squad. Attack when they reach the boulder."

Abigail nodded and doubled back along the draw so she could circle around to her position on the high ground without leaving any footprints in the snow that might give her away.

The soldiers approached with less caution than was wise, given their quarry. They walked as if they felt no fear, as if the world was their hunting ground and no enemy or predator was their match. Abigail shook her head with disdain. Zuhl's men were as arrogant as they were brutish, placing more stock in strength and size than prowess and strategy. She nocked an arrow and waited until the point man in the single file of soldiers was a step from the boulder where Anatoly waited, axe held high.

Her arrow penetrated to the feathers through the last man's head, spraying the clean snow with blood and brain. He fell with a thud. When the other five turned at the noise, Anatoly stepped out of his hiding place and swung his axe, taking the point man's head with a stroke.

The remaining four men drew weapons as one, shattering the calm mountain air with a collective battle cry. An arrow silenced the next to the last man in line, driving into one side of his neck and out the other, blood dripping from its fletching as it came to rest in the snow along the bank of the rivulet, the soldier slumping to the ground a moment later.

The second man in line attacked Anatoly without hesitation, but without forethought either, his broadsword sweeping from his scabbard and arcing toward Anatoly's midsection. The big man-at-arms stepped into the blow, allowing the blade to fall harmlessly on his dragon-plate armor as he stabbed the man in the heart with the top spike of his war axe. The next man in line lunged forward into his dying companion, pushing him into Anatoly and sending them both crashing into the foot-wide stream of warm water.

The last man standing took an arrow in the side of the chest, staggering forward a step before going to his knees, blood sputtering from his lips. He toppled into the snow with a groan of pain and resignation.

Abigail was up and running through the snow toward Anatoly. He lay pinned under the combined weight of a dead soldier and the last living enemy. Zuhl's man dropped his sword and drew a dagger, angling to stab Anatoly in the face. When he raised his hand to bring the dagger down, Anatoly heaved against the weight of them both, tossing them aside into the snow bank next to the stream with the corpse now on top of the last remaining soldier.

Abigail reached the opposite bank a moment after Anatoly regained his feet, water flowing from his armor. Both faced the soldier, Anatoly with his axe, Abigail with her bow. Seeing that he was beaten, the soldier tossed his dagger aside and spread his hands without making any move to free himself from the corpse still splayed out across his chest.

"I surrender," he said without any emotion.

"Why should I accept your surrender?" Abigail said

"I can't think of a reason," he said, slowly pushing his dead companion off his chest and coming to his knees. "If I am to die here, I would ask that he kill me."

"What difference does that make?" Abigail asked, incredulously. "Dead is dead."

"Women are not suited for battle. To be killed by a woman, especially with a bow, is a dishonor, but a clean death at the hands of a man wearing armor and wielding a battle axe, there's honor in that."

"These people are all crazy," Abigail said to Anatoly.

"They definitely have a different perspective on war."

"Look around you," Abigail said. "I don't see honor or valor or glory, all I see is blood and death."

"You ambushed us, killed us without facing us, attacked us by surprise. You fight like cowards, not warriors. In a face-to-face battle, you wouldn't stand a chance against me or any of my brothers."

"Want to try me?" Abigail said.

"You would face me, sword to sword?"

Abigail stuck the end of her bow in the snow and drew the Thinblade, pointing the ancient badge of the Island Kings at his heart. "I'd be happy to. I saw what others like you did to the people of Fellenden. As far as I'm concerned, you all deserve to die."

The soldier looked at the Thinblade for several moments, confusion transforming into understanding and finally into fear.

"Maybe he could be useful," Anatoly said.

"How so?"

"Ixabrax mentioned that he's getting hungry and I don't want to carry these corpses up to the cave, do you?"

"And after that?"

"After that, I suspect he'll be much more inclined to provide us with some useful information about his unit and their mission."

Abigail chuckled, nodding her approval and sheathing the Thinblade. "Pick up your friend there and start walking."

When they entered the cave, the man looked around, assessing his situation, then staggered back, dropping the corpse of his companion and backing away until he was pressed up against the wall. Ixabrax opened his eye, then raised his head and sniffed at the corpse.

"I see you've brought me a snack. Any chance you could unwrap it for me?"

"Take off your friend's armor," Anatoly said to his prisoner.

The soldier hesitated, still staring in disbelief at Ixabrax.

"I don't understand," he said. "Lord Zuhl is the dragon god, how can you betray him?"

Ixabrax extended his giant head until his snout was inches from the soldier's breastplate, regarding him steadily until the man started trembling and wet himself.

"I worship no human. Zuhl is a dark and evil wizard who has enslaved my family by means of his magic, nothing more. Once the enchanted collar binding me to his will was cut from my neck, I was free of his influence, and given the chance, I will eat him just as I'm going to eat your friend here. Now take off his armor."

Ixabrax withdrew his head, still eyeing the man like a cat eyes a mouse, but the soldier didn't move, standing transfixed, frozen by fear.

"I suggest you do as he says," Anatoly said.

Still trembling, the soldier slowly started to unbuckle his dead companion's breastplate. When he was finished and backed away, Ixabrax's tail rose over the dead man and suddenly skewered him through the chest, then casually lifted the man to the dragon's mouth where he took his time chewing, all the while looking intently at the captured soldier.

"Are there more where this came from?" he said, stifling a belch.

"Come on, let's go get the next one," Abigail said, motioning to the cave entrance.

The soldier swallowed hard, his eyes wide, sweat beading on his brow despite the chill air, but he obeyed. An hour later, they had a pile of armor and weapons stacked up in one corner of the cave and Ixabrax was snoring contentedly. All five of the enemy soldiers were gone and the remaining man was standing against the wall, looking at Ixabrax with a mixture of fear and awe.

"Everything I've been taught for my whole life is a lie," he whispered, a look of horror on his blood-stained face.

"Yes," Abigail said. Anatoly nodded. Both were sitting next to the fire. The soldier had been disarmed and his armor removed, though given his fear of Ixabrax, Abigail suspected that both precautions were unnecessary.

"But why?"

"Because Zuhl wants to rule the world," Abigail said. "And you can't do that if you tell people that that's what you're trying to do. Tyrants have to lie, they have to fabricate fear within the hearts of their people and then promise to protect them from the imagined threat they've created.

"Zuhl has been working toward this for centuries. He's kept your tribes stirred up and at war for generations so he would have just the kind of men he needed to fight in his army. He's used every sort of propaganda known to humanity to fabricate the myth of Zuhl as savior when he is the perpetrator of war, the cause of your suffering, the reason for the plight of the people on this island. And the worst part is, your people believe the lie so completely that most will never be persuaded to believe otherwise."

"But the Reishi have returned, as he said they would," he said, trying to hold on to his crumbling beliefs.

"Yes, but Zuhl only told you half the story," Abigail said. "Phane Reishi is an evil bastard who needs to die … yesterday. But he's not the real Reishi Sovereign. My brother is and he sent his army to Fellenden to protect the people there against Zuhl's army even when our home of Ruatha is under attack by Phane's forces."

"Why would he do that?"

"Because it was the right thing to do. Because there was horrible suffering being inflicted on innocent people and he had the power to make it stop ... so he did."

The soldier slumped down against the wall and put his head in his hands. "Why don't you just kill me?"

"I'm not going to kill you," Abigail said. "I'm going to let you go."

Anatoly looked at her with a questioning frown.

"Why would you do that?" the soldier asked, looking up at her.

"So you can tell your brothers-in-arms the truth," Abigail said. "Once you do that, I'm quite sure they'll kill you for treason. Just make sure to deliver this message for me before they do: If they come near this cave, my dragon friend here will feast."

The soldier looked from her to Ixabrax and back again.

"They'll never believe me, but you're right about one thing, they will kill me."

Abigail shrugged. "So run away instead. Find a village where you can make a life for yourself. Leave your companions ignorant of the threat they face if they come to attack us. It's up to you. Take the honorable path and give your fellow soldiers a chance to survive or run away like a coward, your choice. Just be certain of one thing, if you return here, you will die. Now take your cloak and your sword, but leave your armor and go."

Haltingly, the soldier strapped on his sword from the pile of gear they'd collected and pulled a cloak over his shoulders. He stopped at the mouth of the cave and turned back, shaking his head slightly.

"I don't understand you."

"What's your name?" Abigail asked.

"Haldir."

"I wouldn't expect you to understand, Haldir. Now get out of here and don't come back."

Chapter 30

Several minutes passed without a word, both of them content to stare into the fire crackling in the growing darkness of late evening.

"I'm not sure if that was mercy or vengeance," Anatoly said.

"Maybe a little of both. Or maybe I just wanted to give Haldir the chance to exercise his free will informed by all of the facts."

"He'll probably lead them right to us," Anatoly said.

"Maybe, but I doubt it. Zuhl's soldiers have come to revere and fear the dragons, even if under false pretenses. I doubt Haldir wants to meet Ixabrax ever again."

"Either way, we should be vigilant tonight," Anatoly said.

Abigail nodded. "Why should tonight be any different?"

They kept the fire low and built up a screen to diminish the soft glow it cast from the mouth of the cave, but the soldiers didn't come. The next morning, Abigail watched the sun rise over the sparsely wooded slope of the mountain, expecting to see troops marching toward her, but there was no sign of them.

Magda's fever broke that morning and the infection in her wound started to diminish with each successive application of Old Man's Beard. While the infection was no longer a danger, the wound was still serious and debilitating.

"You should go without me," she said after listening to them recount the events that had transpired since she'd become delirious with fever.

"Not a chance," Abigail said.

"I won't be fit to fight for weeks. You can't afford to wait that long. Zuhl's already sent soldiers after us. When they fail to produce results, he'll send something else, or he'll come himself."

"We're not leaving you here alone," Abigail said flatly.

"She's right," Anatoly said. "You're not strong enough to feed the fire, let alone hunt and we don't have enough food to last you until you heal. We're staying."

"Then we need to figure out how to help me heal faster," Magda said. "Has Alexander visited lately?"

"A few days ago," Abigail said.

"Apparently, Isabel is still in a bit of trouble, so I suspect he's trying to help her," Anatoly said.

It was several days before Alexander returned. Abigail was starting to get restless, but Magda's wound was still too serious for her to travel, let alone fight. Abigail was pacing outside the entrance to the cave when Alexander appeared.

She stopped and glared at him. "You really should check in more often."

"Sorry. Isabel was captured and I couldn't find her. I've been spending every moment trying to get past the magical defenses surrounding the place where she's being held."

"Is she all right?" Abigail asked, suddenly worried.

"I'm not sure. I don't know who has her or why."

"I'm sorry, Alex. Sometimes I forget how much you're tying to manage all at once."

Magda smiled from her bedroll as Alexander and Abigail entered the cave.

"How're you feeling?"

"Much better, though not well enough," Magda said. "I fear that Zuhl will find us before I've healed sufficiently to travel."

"What can I do?"

"Consult with Master Alabrand," Magda said. "Perhaps he's aware of some medicinal herbs native to this part of the world that would speed my healing."

"I was just going to pay him a visit. I'll see what he knows."

"How's everything else going?" Anatoly asked.

"Aside from Isabel, mostly the same. Dad's building up his line in Buckwold. Blackstone's magic has failed, so the wizards have relocated to Glen Morillian. Mom and Emma have gone with them. All that's left in the Keep are Rangers and a few Sky Knights. Phane is working day and night to build ships, both in Karth and Andalia, but he seems content to wait out the winter before making his move. Bianca has secured the northern fortress island and is running patrols into Fellenden. Cassandra is busy with her wyvern-breeding program and training new Sky Knights; she's already increased her ranks by fifty. My leg is stiff and sore but healing, and Jack is going stir-crazy."

Abigail smiled. "I know how he feels."

"He misses you, by the way."

"Me too."

"I'll be back with Lucky's advice in a few minutes."

He faded into the firmament, reappearing in Lucky's workshop in a blink. Lucky was sipping a cup of tea, reading and listening to the sputtering and bubbling from several tables filled with glassware.

"Ah, Alexander, there you are. I've acquired the ingredients to make a quart of aqua regia. I've been eagerly awaiting the next step in the process."

"Excellent, but I need some more advice for Magda first. The Old Man's Beard eliminated her infection, but her wound is still pretty serious. Any suggestions?"

"There are a number of healing herbs that grow in colder climates but most are rare." He got up and went to a bookshelf, searching briefly before selecting a tome and flipping through the pages until he found what he was looking for. He laid the book open on the nearest table.

"This is called snowbell ... it's similar to deathwalker root in its healing properties, but it's hard to find, growing almost exclusively on rocky outcroppings high in the mountains."

It looked like a creeper vine that covered the rock it lived on without actually putting down roots. The leaves were small and very dark green, and tiny white, bell-shaped flowers grew in clusters on the end of long stems.

"What part of it do I need?"

"The vine itself," Lucky said. "The flowers are useless except for decoration, but the vine can be prepared just like deathwalker root to make a healing salve."

"How quickly does it work?"

"Depending on the severity of the wound, days or weeks, but generally much more quickly than the natural healing process."

"If I can't find any, is there anything else that might work?"

"Not this time of year," Lucky said. "If they can find an apothecary, they may be able to purchase it."

Alexander nodded thoughtfully. "I have no idea how the people on Zuhl might react to their presence."

Lucky shrugged with a smile. "Why not go and ask for yourself?"

Alexander chuckled softly. "The simplest solutions are usually the best."

"Indeed they are. Now, I'm eager to proceed with my project."

"All right, the sovereigns tell me that one of the ingredients of aqua regia is muriatic acid."

"Yes, essentially a concentrate of stomach acid."

"Good, so mix the aqua regia, but keep a quantity of muriatic acid aside for use later. Dissolve an ounce of gold into the aqua regia and boil it down to one-tenth of its initial volume, being cautious of the fumes."

"Wait, am I to understand that *gold* is the secret of Wizard's Dust?"

Alexander nodded, smiling. "Essentially, yes, but it's more than that. Gold *is* Wizard's Dust, or more to the point, Wizard's Dust *is* gold, only in a much different state than it's normally found."

"Miraculous. I've often wondered why men are so obsessed with gold. It isn't very useful as a metal, except for jewelry, of course, yet it's been used by every society in history as money. Now I think I understand that better. Gold is the link between consciousness and the firmament, the source of life and magic. No wonder we're drawn to it, no wonder men crave it, even if we don't fully understand why."

Lucky sat down chuckling softly with a mixture of awe and revelation ghosting across his face.

"The sovereigns have outdone themselves with this. Keeping such a thing secret for so long is almost beyond imagining. Consider how many people are carrying gold in their pouch as we speak."

"I know, and that's exactly why it must remain secret," Alexander said. "Tell no one … ever."

"I understand, of course," Lucky said, nodding solemnly. "So, I've dissolved an ounce of gold in a quart of aqua regia and boiled it down to one-tenth of its original volume."

"Add an equal quantity of muriatic acid and boil it down again. Repeat this step until no more fumes are produced, then gently boil it down until the solids are just dry. Be careful not to burn it. Take the resulting material and repeat the steps from the beginning until the product is a rich orange-red in color."

"This is very exciting, Alexander. I'm quite sure that every wizard who's ever lived since the fall of the Reishi has dreamed of learning the secret of

Wizard's Dust, the secret of magic itself. Thank you for entrusting me with this task."

"You're welcome, Lucky, but it's important for you to understand that you are literally one of only two people in the world capable of producing Wizard's Dust. It's more than just gold manipulated by a complicated process … it requires magic to create, powerful magic."

"In a way that's reassuring," Lucky said. "If just anyone could learn the process and make it work, we'd have people attempting the mana fast left and right; most would fail and die horribly, but those who succeeded would lack the guidance and wisdom of other, more experienced wizards. There's no telling what they might do, even if by accident or mistake."

"I couldn't agree more. The power to manipulate the fabric of reality itself must be guarded and protected. To do any less would be to unleash a thousand Phanes or Zuhls on the people of the Seven Isles.

"When Balthazar Reishi told me of the crushing burden he felt after he first discovered the process for creating Wizard's Dust, I didn't fully understand. It seemed to me that he'd just unlocked the secret of life. I imagined that I would be jubilant in his place, but now I understand the weight he felt.

"Honestly, if we weren't at war with such dangerous enemies, I'd give serious thought to letting this secret die with me."

"You can't mean that, Alexander."

"Consider the consequences for the world if we fail to control this. If this secret falls into the wrong hands, it'll be our fault. We will bear some of the blame for the evil they do, the suffering they cause."

"Magic is power. Like a hammer, it can be used to pound a nail or beat someone's brains in," Lucky said, donning the hat of the tutor. "We don't deprive the world of hammers because they can be misused."

"No, but a hammer can't be used to destroy tens of thousands of lives or enslave whole countries … magic can. While I agree that it *is* a tool, it's far too powerful a tool to be left lying around like a hammer."

"Fair enough, just don't forget that magic is also used for good, enriching and improving countless lives, assisting with food production, building construction, and healing, just to name a few of the limitless uses of magic that benefit not just those entrusted with wielding it but society in general."

Alexander nodded, smiling at his old teacher. "I miss these conversations."

"Me too, my boy, me too."

"I should be going. The process will take you a few days to complete, but the end result will be stable. Just keep it someplace dry until I can return with the next steps."

"Take care," Lucky said as Alexander faded out of sight.

Chapter 31

After returning to the cave and clairvoyantly searching the surrounding area for any hint of snowbell, Alexander finally decided that seeking out an apothecary was probably the best chance they had for procuring the rare root. He floated high over the cave and found the telltale streamers of smoke rising over a village in the distance. It was several leagues away over rough terrain but it was also fairly large, more of a small town than a mountain village.

It was perched on the high ground of a bluff overlooking a winding stretch of fast-moving mountain stream. A single road led into the town from the south, crossing the stream over a well-made stone bridge that arced gently across the steep ravine. Several smaller roads led from the town into the less tame parts of the island farther north.

Alexander discreetly materialized between two buildings near the market square and strolled out into the flow of people coming and going, taking care to avoid being near enough to anyone for them to brush up against him and wonder about his lack of substance.

The marketplace was busy, filled with stalls and carts offering goods for sale. There was no sign of war except for the absence of men. There were adolescent boys and old men aplenty; women comprised the majority of the people in the square. Men of fighting age were nowhere to be seen.

One woman took notice of him standing in the middle of the throng of people looking this way and that. She strode up to him with her jaw set and her eyes alight with passion. "What's your excuse?" she demanded, looking him up and down.

"I beg your pardon?"

"Why aren't you with the army like my husband and brothers? You look fit enough, even if you are a bit scrawny."

Alexander hesitated, unsure of how to answer her question. That only seemed to enflame her more.

"What, are you a coward? Don't have the spine to face the enemy?" She reached for him as a crowd of other women started to converge on him. He backed away.

"Why, you little weasel. Here you are, all safe and cozy while every other man of age in the entire country is risking his life for us, standing against the Reishi scourge. What makes you special?"

The crowd started to jeer and taunt him as they closed in. They weren't overtly violent but he knew it was only a matter of seconds before one of them tried to lay hands on him and he didn't want to arouse suspicion, knowing full well that Abigail and Anatoly might have to come here to procure the medicine Magda needed.

"I've had enough of your mouth, woman," Alexander said, stepping closer but not too close. He spoke loud enough for the crowd to hear and with enough arrogant anger to give them pause. "I'm a courier in service to Lord Zuhl. He's sent me to collect inventory reports from all of the apothecaries along this road. The soldiers will have need of their medicines come spring and Lord Zuhl wants updated reports on any additions made to their stores over the past month."

The woman stepped back as if he'd slapped her, clenching her jaw and bowing her head. The crowd that had been encircling him melted away within seconds. Though her colors still flared with anger, she schooled her voice, speaking in measured and overly deferential tones. "Apologies, My Lord."

"Where is your apothecary?"

She pointed toward a shop at the corner of the square. Alexander turned away without another word, weaving carefully through the crowd. Rather than attempt to enter the little stone building, he slipped between it and the next building over and vanished from sight before floating through the wall into the shop, nothing but disembodied awareness.

The apothecary was well stocked with such a wide variety of different herbs, plants, and concoctions that it took him several minutes of searching the shelves behind the counter before he found a jar labeled *snowbell*, stuffed tightly with a ball of wound-up vines, stoppered with a cork and sealed with wax. Satisfied with his reconnaissance, he returned to the cave with a flick of his mind and reappeared next to the fire.

"Hello, Alexander," Magda said, being the first to notice his appearance. "Any luck?"

"Sort of. Lucky told me about a plant called snowbell that grows in the mountains around here. It works like deathwalker root. When I couldn't find any nearby, I went to a town a few leagues to the east and found it on the shelves of their apothecary."

"That sounds more promising than waiting here for my shoulder to heal over the next several weeks," Magda said.

"The terrain is pretty rough between here and there," Alexander said. "It would probably take a full day each way."

"I can survive for a couple of days by myself," Magda said. "If Abigail and Anatoly just leave me some firewood and some food."

"You won't be entirely alone," Ixabrax said from behind them.

"Quite right," Magda said with a smile. "I couldn't hope for a more formidable guardian, and honestly, I want out of this bed more than you can imagine."

"You might be surprised," Alexander said.

"Sorry, I forget you're injured as well."

"One other thing," Alexander said to Anatoly. "All of the men are away with the army and the women are pretty put out about it. I nearly got mobbed when I strolled through their market. I suggest you wear some of that armor," he gestured toward the pile of armor and weapons they'd collected, "and come up with a story that involves Lord Zuhl's official business."

"Right," Anatoly said. "With the size of his army, I imagine he's got every able-bodied man on the entire island under his banner."

"I'm sure of it," Alexander said. "I'll be back in a few days."

Alexander opened his eyes as he lay in his bed on Tyr. He was greeted by throbbing pain behind his eyes and Anja's snout shoved into the doorway of his Wizard's Den.

"Are you back?" she asked.

He nodded, closing his eyes and sitting up. He swung his legs off the bed, knowing it would hurt and welcoming the distraction of the pain in his leg over the pounding in his head.

"I'm sorry I got mad at you," Anja said, "but I just can't stand the idea of you leaving me. It makes my stomach hurt."

"I know, but it's for the best. Once this war is over, I promise I'll visit, provided your mother permits it."

"That's not enough. I want to be with you. I could help you."

"I'm sorry, Anja. I know you believe that, but you're wrong. You would only put me in greater danger and risk your life in the bargain."

"Put yourself in my place. If I was going off to war and you were being made to stay here, wouldn't you want to come with me? Wouldn't you want to protect me?"

"Of course I would. Believe it or not, I understand how you feel more than you know. My wife and sister are both in danger, and my father is leading my army against a force he can't withstand. I want to be there with all of them, but I can't and it hurts."

A big tear welled up in Anja's catlike eye and rolled down her snout onto the floor. "Please don't leave me."

"Anja ..." he stopped when he felt Bragador approach. His precognitive awareness of her or any other dragon, save Anja, still puzzled him.

"Child, stop torturing the man," Bragador said, stepping up next to her daughter. "Can't you see that leaving you will hurt him as well? He's made the right decision for both of you."

"But I hate it," Anja said. "I want to go with him. I can't stand the idea of losing him."

"I know, Child," Bragador whispered. "You never should have had to suffer this."

"What do you mean?"

"You were never meant to bond with a human. Young dragons are supposed to bond with their mothers. You were supposed to bond with me." Bragador's voice was steady, stoic even, but Alexander could see the turmoil in her colors.

"I'm sorry that I love Alexander, Mother, but I can't help it."

"I know. You have nothing to apologize for. The fault is mine. I allowed Phane's people to steal you away from me and it breaks my heart that you will suffer for my failure."

"It's not your fault, Mother. Just like it's not Alexander's fault. The blame rests squarely with Phane and he deserves to pay for everything he's done."

"Perhaps you're right, but we are not meant to exact that price."

"Maybe not, but that's what Alexander is going to do, and I want to help him."

"Anja, hear me well, Phane would kill you, or worse," Bragador said. "Child, in single combat, he would kill me. You're rushing into something you do not understand, something quite beyond you."

"Then we should all go," Anja said. "He can't kill all of us, and when we're done, he'll be dead."

"At what cost? Who among us would you sacrifice to kill this one human? He will die of age before you are old enough to bear children of your own. How many dragons would you see die to kill Phane?"

Anja frowned but didn't respond, instead withdrawing her snout from the Wizard's Den and taking flight.

"May I come in?" Bragador said.

"Please," Alexander said.

Bragador sat in the chair next to his bed and sighed. "She's stubborn and headstrong. I fear we will not be able to persuade her to stay."

"I'm starting to get that sense as well. What can we do?"

"Perhaps if she were allowed to spend more time with you prior to your departure, it would ease the pain of your leaving."

"It could just make things worse, too," Alexander said. "Don't get me wrong, I'd love to spend more time with her, but I don't want to do anything that's going to hurt her."

"Thank you for that, but I fear she's going to suffer no matter what we do. I had hoped that keeping her busy during your stay would distract her enough for her feelings toward you to diminish. Clearly, that hasn't worked, so I would give her this time with you."

"She's your daughter, I'll do whatever you think best."

Bragador nodded sadly and fell silent. Alexander left her to her thoughts, waiting patiently for her to continue. After a few moments, Bragador shook off her feelings and with a deep breath, composed herself.

"There are other matters we should discuss."

Alexander nodded for her to continue.

"Tasia has returned from the ship that fished her out of the water after her battle with Aedan. Her account is much the same as yours." She paused, holding Alexander with her gaze very deliberately for several moments. "Perhaps it's time to consider more drastic measures."

"What did you have in mind?"

"Tasia can return and sink the ship carrying the box you fear contains the final keystone."

"Princess Lacy is aboard that ship," Alexander said, shaking his head.

"If your fears are realized, Phane will have the means to enslave the entire Seven Isles. Worse, the shade is still in possession of Aedan. He will no doubt make his move the moment Phane is able to open the box. Either way, we lose."

"I'm well aware of that, but I can't sentence Lacy to death, I won't. She's innocent."

"Forgive me Alexander, but there is more to my plan, and I know you will not accept it, but I fear it is the only way to protect the future."

"What are you suggesting?"

"Sinking the ship will accomplish two important tasks. First, it will cast the final keystone into the depths of the ocean where it will never be found, and second it will kill Princess Lacy, forever preventing her from opening the box. Once the ship is destroyed, Tasia will go to Fellenden and kill Prince Torin, her brother. With the appointed bloodline extinguished, the keystone will remain forever out of reach and the world will be safe from the threat of the Nether Gate."

Alexander schooled his breathing, his blood running like ice through his veins. He willed the look of horror from his face and slowly shook his head, steadily holding Bragador's gaze.

"Your plan is sound, as far as it goes, but I beg you not to go through with it. Such action is a violation of everything I hold dear. Both Lacy and Torin are victims in all of this. We can't kill them for an accident of their birth."

"Your view of history is short and limited," Bragador said. "I suppose that's to be expected, given your age and probable lifespan, but the threat you've described, and that I've come to believe is very real, is so great that it literally threatens the *entire* future. Countless generations going forward will suffer or simply never exist if we fail. How can we not consider every option available to us? What are two lives when weighed against every single life that will ever come after this moment?"

"They're exactly that, two lives, each precious beyond measure in their own right, but there's more to this than just their lives. The Old Law is the key to creating a future worth having and it must have a champion. How can I stand for the Old Law if I'm willing to violate it in the most heinous way possible when circumstances become difficult?"

"What good will the Old Law do the future if there isn't one? I realize this is a hard choice, Alexander, but sometimes leaders must make hard choices."

Alexander looked down, slowly shaking his head, almost in denial, as a tear slipped down his cheek. "Please don't do this, Bragador. Please, let me find another way," he whispered.

"And if you fail?"

He looked up at her, his face set in a mask of misery and anguish as he swallowed the lump in his throat. "I've set other plans in motion, plans to destroy the complex where the Nether Gate is housed. Captain Wyatt is still in pursuit of the enemy ship—he won't give up until he succeeds ..."

"Or dies trying," Bragador said. "Tasia spoke highly of him. You've surrounded yourself with good people, but they may not be enough and my plan can only work until the box is opened. After that, we're all lost."

"Perhaps, but have you considered the shade? You can be sure he's watching that ship; he's probably on board. If you send Tasia to sink it, he'll try to stop her. Can she best Aedan? Also, Phane will have to persuade Lacy to open the box of her own free will. Before that happens, I'll make sure she understands the stakes. I trust she'll do the right thing when the time comes."

"You would place the fate of the world in the hands of one young woman?"

"I would. I've seen the goodness in her."

"Your faith is touching, though not terribly persuasive. As for the shade, I can always send several dragons."

"And what if he could retrieve the box from the depths of the ocean?"

"Hence my plan to end the line of Fellenden as well. Their blood is the key, and they're far more vulnerable than the box itself."

"Bragador, I'm asking you not to do this, begging you not to do this. Please."

"The plan is sound."

"Yes, and it's also *wrong*!"

She regarded Alexander silently, frowning and shaking her head as he held her gaze.

"You would risk so much for your principles?"

"Yes!" he whispered.

"I wonder how many other humans would place such value on the lives of two people they don't even know."

Chloe appeared between them in a ball of light.

"Lady Bragador, that is precisely why Alexander is the right person to bear the Sovereign Stone. I know his heart, he cannot sanction what you suggest."

"Which is why I'm offering to do it for him and for the world."

"Don't you see, if you do this, My Love will have to stop you, he will have to become your enemy. Please don't put him in that position. He loves your daughter as surely as he loves me and he counts you as his friend, but he has sworn to protect the Old Law and I know that oath to be true."

"I count you as a friend as well, Alexander. Would you really oppose me in this?"

"What choice would I have?"

"You are wounded and surrounded by dragons, what hope would you have against me?"

Alexander shook his head sadly. "None," he whispered.

"And yet you would still oppose me?"

"Yes."

"You value your principles more than even your own life?"

"Yes."

Bragador stood and started pacing, shaking her head and muttering curses under her breath. She stopped and faced Alexander, shaking her head in frustration. "I will never understand you, but I will respect your wishes in this matter. I only hope you aren't dooming the world."

Chapter 32

"They're still following us," Anatoly said, squinting through the brightness of sunlight on snow.

They were half a day away from the town where they hoped to procure snowbell for Magda and they were being followed by a pack of snow wolves, beautiful creatures in thick white fur coats that both protected them from the frigid temperatures and helped them blend into their surroundings. The wolves had picked up their trail a few hours after they'd left the cave and were pursuing, but not as quickly as they could have. Abigail wondered if they were holding back until nightfall and hoped that she and Anatoly would reach the relative safety of the town before then.

"Not much we can do about it except press on," Abigail said.

"Agreed."

The snow was deep and difficult to travel through. The rough, rugged terrain forced them to backtrack occasionally to find a navigable path over or around a number of crevasses and ridges. By the time they caught their first glimpse of the smoke from cook fires in town, they were nearing exhaustion. Fortunately, the wolves were still distant enough to pose no immediate threat.

The sun was just setting when they came to one of the northern trading roads leading to the town and stepped onto the hard-packed snow. As late in the day as it was, they encountered no traffic until they entered the town itself. The town wasn't walled, but there was a high berm of snow surrounding it, probably more the result of removing the snow from the streets than from an attempt to build a defensive perimeter.

Anatoly had taken Alexander's advice and donned a breastplate emblazoned with Zuhl's crest and marked with emblems of rank. He strode into the village with Abigail a step behind and to the left, his battle axe resting on his shoulder and an expression of disdain on his face. The market was nearly deserted when they arrived, all of the shops were closed and the vendor carts tarped over for the night, their owners cooking dinner and preparing for bed as the light rapidly faded and the temperature fell.

"There's the apothecary," Anatoly said, motioning to the building in the corner of the marketplace with his chin. "Either we wait 'til dark and break in, or we find an inn and hope we don't arouse enough suspicion to attract the city guard, then come back tomorrow and buy what we need."

"We'll wait until tomorrow," Abigail said. "I can't justify stealing from the apothecary ... she's not our enemy, she's just a shopkeeper trying to make a living. Besides, we need some rest before we head back."

"Fair enough, looks like the inn is down there."

All eyes turned toward them when they entered the ale hall that served as the main room for the inn. The building was constructed of stone, as were most buildings on the Isle of Zuhl. The stone tables and benches of the ale hall were coarsely chiseled without any artistry, but functional nonetheless.

Most of the people in the room were old men, too frail to stand in battle, yet still possessed of the experience from many battles past. They regarded Anatoly with a mixture of scrutiny as if weighing his mettle were they to face him at their prime and respect for a man who still had battles left to fight.

Anatoly ignored them, striding purposefully up to the innkeeper. "One room, two beds for the night and a hot meal for us both."

"Two silver crowns," the innkeeper said, picking up a mug that was already clean and starting to wipe it down with the towel thrown over his shoulder.

Anatoly slapped two coins onto the counter. The innkeeper raised an eyebrow at him and nodded almost skeptically before collecting the coins and calling to his errand boy to fetch a key.

"So what's your business here?"

"My business is Lord Zuhl's business and none of yours," Anatoly said.

"Don't mean nothing by it, just curious is all. Most of the men are with the army. We don't see many soldiers up here now days, let alone an officer."

Abigail noticed several of the men seated around the room perk up with interest. She started casually looking around, locating the exits and finding the choke points in the room where she could fight without being flanked or surrounded.

"Who should I tell Lord Zuhl is inquiring into his business?" Anatoly asked pointedly. Before the man could stammer out an answer he continued. "What is your name?"

"Forgive me, sir," the innkeeper said as the errand boy approached with a key. "Please, your room is ready. I'll have a meal sent up right away."

Anatoly regarded him calmly until the man started to fidget, then snatched the key from the startled boy, motioning for him to lead the way. Most of the men in the bar went back to their drinks as if the encounter had played out about like they expected it would. Abigail was relieved for that.

The room was simple, the food was bland but plentiful, no doubt a result of Anatoly's gruff handling of the innkeeper, and the door was stout with a heavy bar. Even though the bed was lumpy, Abigail was asleep within minutes of lying down.

Sometime in the night she woke to the sound of pounding on the door.

"Open up!" a muffled voice demanded.

She schooled her breathing and tried to calm her racing heart as she slipped her feet into her boots and started lacing them up. Anatoly looked to her while lacing his own boots. She nodded for him to answer.

"Who's asking?" Anatoly said with an undercurrent of menace.

"Captain Voss of Lord Zuhl's home guard. We're hunting a fugitive, a woman with silvery blond hair. I have a report that just such a woman is sharing your bed, so I say again, open up."

"Fight or flee?" Anatoly whispered.

"Flee," Abigail said, drawing the Thinblade and cutting open the heavy shutters covering the window.

"Just a minute," Anatoly growled, "let me get my pants on." Abigail was already on the ground and Anatoly was hanging from the windowsill when he spoke. They landed in a dark alley and moved quietly into the night, sticking to the shadows skirting around the edge of the market square, heading toward the apothecary.

"Looks like we're going to have to steal it after all," Anatoly said.

"We'll leave her some coin for the snowbell and the damage I'm going to do to her door."

They slipped up to the back door and Abigail slid the Thinblade along the doorjamb, cutting the bolt effortlessly. They entered quietly and cautiously, assuming that the shopkeeper was probably sleeping within the building. Anatoly motioned to the bed on the far side of the room where a woman covered in furs was lying, breathing deeply and evenly.

Abigail motioned for him to watch her while she went in search of the snowbell. She moved slowly, with deliberate care, stopping for several moments to let her eyes adjust to the low light before continuing into the room lined with shelves behind the counter. It took several minutes before she found what she was looking for, but she managed to get the jar of snowbell without making a sound. She left five gold coins in its place, easily triple its value, and returned to Anatoly.

The woman was still sleeping but rolled over, muttering in her sleep when Abigail stepped back into the room. She froze, waiting for the woman's deep, even breathing to resume. When she and Anatoly thought it was safe, they slipped out into the alley and closed the door without a sound before melting into the shadows.

"That went well," Abigail whispered.

"A little too well," Anatoly said. "Makes me nervous."

They moved to the edge of town and made their way along the inside of the berm wall toward the road leading to the northwest but stopped when they saw a squad of soldiers waiting quietly in the shadows on either side of the road. Abigail motioned to Anatoly to backtrack. Once out of sight of the road, they climbed up the berm wall and down the other side, setting out across the snow toward the relative safety of the cave.

"They're going to pick up our trail," Anatoly said.

"I know, but there's not much we can do about that. Besides, they probably won't notice it until daylight. At least we'll have time to prepare for their attack."

"If they come with the whole company, the dragon's our only hope."

"I know," Abigail said.

Dawn broke over an overcast sky, heavy grey clouds floating so low that the mountain peaks in the distance were shrouded in gloom. In the rising light of dawn, the sky started spitting snow in fits and starts as if it couldn't make up its mind. As unpleasant as it would be to travel in such weather, Abigail hoped it would snow heavily enough to cover their trail.

By midday Abigail was entirely disappointed with the weather. The snow came in flurries driven by gusts of wind coming off the mountain, not enough to erase their tracks, but plenty enough to make their journey miserable.

Trudging across a snow-covered plain, skirting a copse of trees, she caught motion from the corner of her eye, but a moment too late. In the next second a wolf had her by the leg, biting hard enough to draw blood, shaking his head back and forth, trying to drive her to the ground. He'd been nearly buried in the snow, all but invisible—and there were more, all coming to their feet now that the ambush had been sprung.

Abigail stumbled back, crying out in pain and surprise at the sudden and unexpected attack, her heart pounding in her chest as she toppled into the snow. The wolf released his grip on her leg and sprang on top of her, snapping at her face and throat. She jammed her forearm into his mouth. He clamped down on her bracer, crushing it into her arm.

Anatoly unleashed a battle cry that rivaled the howling of the wind, startling the rest of the wolves and giving them pause. He charged, driving the top spike of his war axe into the side of the wolf atop Abigail and lifted him clear, tossing his mewling body into the snow.

Abigail scrambled to her feet, unbalanced from the wound she'd sustained but steady enough to draw the Thinblade. Five wolves were circling them, looking for an opportunity to strike. Abigail and Anatoly stood back to back, watching the predators as closely as they were being watched by them. One darted close to them, snapping at Abigail's good leg, but she met his snout with the Thinblade, stabbing down through the top of his head and dropping him in an instant, sweeping the blade up his spine, spilling blood and entrails across the snow.

The rest were suddenly more skittish about this prey, dancing farther away but snarling and growling just the same. Abigail sheathed the Thinblade and drew her bow, killing the nearest wolf with a single arrow through the skull. The rest turned and fled.

She sat down heavily in the snow, blood oozing from the puncture wounds in her leg. She grimaced in pain while she gingerly pulled her pant leg up and inspected the wound. "This is going to slow me down," she muttered.

Anatoly went to work wrapping her leg. "I should have guessed those wolves hadn't given up on us," he said.

"Didn't occur to me either." She sucked in a quick breath, clenching her eyes in pain when Anatoly secured the bandage. "Like to make a coat out of 'em."

He chuckled, getting to his feet and offering her his hand. She stood, testing the strength of her leg and wincing. "We'll be lucky if we make it back before dark."

"Put your arm around my shoulder, I'll help you."

They set out, leaving the wolves where they lay, walking into the wind and finally arriving at the cave several hours after dark. Abigail was numb from the cold, except for her leg which burned with pain, every step a jolt of agony. She carefully sat next to the fire and began unwrapping her wound while Anatoly went to work adding wood to the fire and putting water on to boil.

Magda came awake at the commotion, as did Ixabrax, but he only opened his eye, took in the situation and closed it again.

"What happened?"

"Wolves," Abigail said, pouring some water from her waterskin onto a strip of cloth and gently cleaning the area around the wound. After she rewrapped her bandage and had a cup of hot tea and something to eat, she went to work on the snowbell vine, stripping the flowers and crushing it slightly before cooking it down into a pulp. After removing the fibers, she set it aside to let it cool and thicken.

She applied a generous quantity to Magda's wound first and then dabbed a smaller amount onto her leg. There was enough of the salve left for a few more applications, but she suspected Magda would need it all before her wound was fully healed. It wasn't long before a deep tiredness came over her and she slipped into a dreamless sleep. Anatoly was still awake the following morning. He looked exhausted.

"Did you stay up all night?"

He nodded wearily. "I was afraid the wolves might have followed us, and we have no way of knowing if the soldiers found our trail. How's your leg?"

"Much better but still a bit tender. Snowbell definitely works, but nowhere near as well as Lucky's salve. Get some sleep, I'll keep watch."

He nodded, going to his bedroll without a word. Before long he was breathing as deeply and evenly as Magda. Abigail got to her feet, carefully testing her leg and, satisfied with her strength, limped over to the cave mouth. She smiled at the sight of a foot of new-fallen snow blanketing the mountainside. The sky was overcast and the air was cold, but more importantly, their trail was completely gone.

Alexander appeared next to her without a word.

"I was wondering when you'd show up again. Is everything all right?"

"I wouldn't go that far, but it could easily be worse. What happened to your leg?"

"Had a disagreement with a wolf," she said, shaking her head. "It's nothing that won't heal. The snowbell seems to work. Magda should be ready to travel in a few days, a week at the outside."

"Good, I'll do some looking around Zuhl's fortress and see if I can come up with a viable plan of attack."

Abigail nodded. "Some soldiers were snooping around town looking for me. Any chance you could see if they're headed this way?"

"I'll be back in a couple of minutes," he said, vanishing.

Abigail went back to the fire and started heating water for tea. Before it came to a boil, Alexander was back.

"Looks like they're searching closer to town. They've divided up into squads and seem to be looking for any sign of your trail."

"I doubt they'll find it after last night's snowstorm.

"Probably not. I think you're safe for now. I'll be back in a few days."

She smiled at him as he vanished.

Chapter 33

The first thing Isabel felt when she woke was throbbing pain in her head. It took several seconds for her to regain enough sense to be alarmed, then she sat bolt upright, looking around in near panic, pain exploding behind her eyes from the sudden movement.

She was lying on a blanket spread out in one corner of a cozy little cottage. A fire burned in the crudely constructed hearth with a black cauldron warming over the flames. Ayela sat across from the old woman, listening to her every word with rapt attention. Hector and Horace were nowhere to be seen.

Isabel's weapons were gone. She rose quietly, unleashing her rage to protect herself from the pull of the firmament, but the rage didn't come. Instead, she felt the all-too-familiar emotional numbness caused by malaise weed. She cast about, looking for anything she could use as a weapon, when the old woman turned and appraised her coolly.

"How's your head, dear?" she asked, knowingly.

"Who are you? What did you do to me?"

"My name is Hazel Karth, aunt of Severine Karth, though he doesn't know of my existence. As for what I've done to you," she patted a little pouch at her belt, "I dosed you with henbane."

"What's henbane? Have you poisoned me?"

"No … well, not in the traditional sense of the word," Hazel said. "Henbane is a potent herb. When properly prepared, it renders a person completely obedient for a period of several hours. One under the influence of henbane will comply with almost any instruction during that period of time, then fall into a deep sleep for about an hour as the effects wear off, waking with no memory of the experience … and a powerful headache."

"Why?" Isabel demanded.

"I needed to question you and I needed the truth," Hazel said.

"What about Hector and Horace? What have you done with them?"

"Ah … the boys are outside chopping firewood," Hazel said. "Aside from some sore muscles, they'll be just fine."

"What did she ask me about?" Isabel said, turning to Ayela.

"Everything," Ayela said. "Where you came from, who your allies are, your purpose here on Karth, and where we were going. You told her everything."

"So what now?" Isabel asked, pointedly. "You've abducted us, disarmed me, and rendered my magic useless. What do you plan to do with us?"

"First, I thought I would offer you lunch," Hazel said, ladling stew from the cauldron into a wooden bowl and offering it to Isabel. "Sit and eat. I will explain."

Isabel took the bowl, still somewhat suspicious of her host, and sat down, trying to shake the fog of pain from her head and focus on the situation at hand. She reminded herself that battlefields come in all shapes and sizes.

"By all means, explain," Isabel said, making no move to eat the stew.

"The House of Karth has been at the mercy of the Sin'Rath for centuries. Since the men are hopelessly charmed by the demon-spawn witches, the women of our house set out long ago to break the stranglehold they have on our family. That has proven a more difficult task than we imagined.

"I am the last of the true witches of Karth and now my family line is perilously close to its end. I can't allow that to happen, so I've called Ayela to me to become my apprentice. I didn't expect her to bring you as well, but perhaps that's for the best. We have common enemies, after all."

"Then why disarm me?" Isabel asked.

"Caution," Hazel said. "I'm old and frail. You are young and vibrant. In a fair fight, I wouldn't stand a chance, so I needed to ensure that any contest between us would be decidedly unfair."

"So what happens next?" Isabel asked.

"We wait until the demon-spawn and the soldiers who serve them give up looking for you and move on, then you leave and Ayela stays here."

"Is this what you want?" Isabel asked Ayela.

"I don't know," she said. "I think I could learn a lot from Aunt Hazel, but I also think the House of Karth is running out of time. Your plan may be the only hope we have for eliminating the Sin'Rath for good."

"Don't be foolish, Child," Hazel said, dismissively. "If you go to the mountain, you will die with your friends and all hope for your family line will die with you."

"What makes you so sure we'll die?" Isabel said.

"Because no one ever returns from that cursed place," Hazel said. "Few venture into the swamp, even fewer return, but in all my years of living in this place, I have never known anyone to return from that mountain."

"So others have come," Isabel said.

"Of course," Hazel said. "The mountain was known to be a stronghold of Siavrax Karth, the last Wizard King. Legends have grown over the years, telling of fabulous treasures to be found there. I suspect those legends are the product of wishful thinking more than anything else."

"If you've questioned me as thoroughly as Ayela says, then you know what I'm after," Isabel said.

"Yes, you're after a myth ... a legend that may or may not have ever existed. And even if it did, it has long since decayed to dust. You will find only death on that mountain, and I will not permit you to lead Ayela to her untimely end."

"Isn't that her choice?" Isabel asked.

Hazel's eyes narrowed and she sat forward. "No! She is the last woman of the Karth line, the last who could serve as my apprentice, the last hope for our family to end the influence of the Sin'Rath. She must stay here."

"But what if Isabel's right?" Ayela said. "What if we could destroy the Sin'Rath? And Phane with them? Wouldn't that be worth the risk?"

"This one has poisoned your mind, Child," Hazel said, gesturing toward Isabel. "Oh, don't get me wrong, she believes what she says, believes it desperately, because she wants to believe it, needs to believe it. But reality is a funny thing, it doesn't require your belief to be what it is. And the truth is, there's nothing but death waiting for you on that mountain."

"You're wrong," Isabel said. "The Goiri was real, its bones are waiting for me up there."

"I hate to see you throw your life away, dear," Hazel said, shaking her head sadly. "But it's clear to me that you can't be reasoned with, so I won't try to stop you. You and your friends are free to leave anytime you wish, although I suggest you stay here until the Sin'Rath give up their search."

"Where are they?"

"Close," Hazel said. "They lost your trail nearby so they're circling in an effort to find it once again."

"What if they find this place?" Ayela asked.

"They won't," Hazel said. "This isn't the first time the demon-spawn have hunted me. We are very well protected here."

"How so?" Isabel asked.

"Magic," Hazel said. "You are a Reishi witch. Your coven has always favored magic of a very direct nature, probably because of your use of wyverns as steeds. While direct magic can be useful in some situations, it pales in comparison to the magic of belief. My magic focuses on creating belief in the minds of my enemies. As we speak, my warding spells are influencing the soldiers searching for us, redirecting their attention away from clues to our whereabouts and planting suggestions that will lead them astray."

"If your magic is so powerful, then why haven't you succeeded against the Sin'Rath after all these years?" Isabel asked.

"I'm very close," Hazel said, leaning forward excitedly. "I've nearly perfected a spell that will prevent the Sin'Rath's charms from influencing the men. Once they see the true nature of the demon-spawn witches, they'll turn against them and the Sin'Rath will be hunted to extinction."

"So what's stopping you from figuring it out?" Isabel asked.

Hazel clenched her teeth, scowling with sudden frustration. "It's complicated. The Sin'Rath's charms are unnatural, beyond the scope of any charm spell I've ever heard of."

Isabel nodded, feeling a surge of anger well up within her, only to be dampened by the malaise weed. She directed her focus within and found the telltale touch of Azugorath. The Wraith Queen was trying to exert her influence again, trying to provoke a blind and uncontrollable rage within Isabel, but this time the malaise weed hindered her efforts with ease. With a deep breath, she dismissed Azugorath's attempt at control and smiled at Hazel. "You're no closer to creating your spell than you were when you first conceived of the idea, are you?"

"What do you know of it?" Hazel shot back. "You're just a child, an infant without any real understanding of the craft."

"So teach me," Isabel said. "Show me why your kind of magic is so much better than mine."

"I think not," Hazel said. "You already have a coven, let them teach you. Besides, I have Ayela to instruct."

Isabel smiled humorlessly. "I want to talk to Hector and Horace. Where are they?"

"I told you," Hazel said, motioning to the door. "They're outside."

Isabel left the cottage without another word, stepping out into a secluded valley surrounded entirely by granite cliffs rising fifty feet into the air. The ubiquitous fog enshrouding the swamp was completely absent, revealing a sunny winter afternoon. The valley was lush with a wide variety of plants that looked like natural growth at first glance, but upon consideration must have been cultivated by Hazel for the sheer variety on display.

Isabel tipped her head back and closed her eyes. Slyder was perched on top of a cypress tree. She sent him into the air, circling higher and higher, trying to get a view of the valley but all she could see was swamp stretching away in every direction to the horizon. It made no sense. Slyder was close, she could feel it. He should have been able to see the valley, yet it didn't appear to exist.

She followed a well-worn path through the artificial jungle toward the sound of men chopping wood. Not far from the cottage, Hector and Horace were cheerfully working away, splitting rounds of wood and stacking the wedges neatly along one side of the little clearing.

"Oh, hello Isabel," Hector said. "Mistress Hazel said you'd wake soon. Isn't this a wonderful place?" He went back to work stacking a round of wood atop his chopping block without waiting for an answer.

"I really like it here," Horace said. "Do you think Mistress Hazel will let us stay?"

"What's gotten into you?" Isabel demanded. "We have work to do."

"I'll say," Hector said, motioning to the stack of rounds still awaiting the axe.

Isabel looked at him incredulously for a moment before turning on her heel and marching back to the cottage.

"What have you done to them?" she demanded, stalking toward Hazel.

"Just a simple charm spell," Hazel said. "They'll be fine."

"Dispel it," Isabel said. "Right now!"

"No," Hazel said. "I'll need that firewood for the winter."

"They're not your servants," Isabel said. "Remove your charm or I'll …"

"What will you do?" Hazel asked, pointedly. "Mind your tongue or I'll send you back into the swamp alone. If the death leeches don't get you, the Sin'Rath surely will."

Isabel fixed her with a glare, her eyes flashing, but said nothing. Ayela looked from one to the other and then down into the fire. Isabel left the cottage, nursing her growing anger in the hopes that she could overcome the effects of the malaise weed, but her anger just didn't quite rise to the level necessary to shield her from the pull of the firmament.

She started walking without any real destination, mostly just trying to put distance between herself and Hazel. She didn't trust the old witch and she wasn't about to let her take Ayela. She hadn't known the Princess of Karth for long, but she felt she owed Ayela for helping her escape the Sin'Rath and she admired her for her strength in the face of powers that were so clearly beyond her. But more than any of that, Ayela had become her friend.

Isabel turned the facts of her situation over in her head while she walked around the little valley, an island of growth and life in a sea of desolation that was the gloaming swamp. The valley was lush and green with literally thousands of different types of plants, some still producing fruit, even this late in the year, others flowering as if it were spring.

She was essentially alone against Hazel, without access to her magic, stripped of her weapons and worse, she had very little understanding of the foe she faced. She wished Alexander would come to her. At the thought she stopped, frowning in thought.

He had been traveling with them when they entered the valley, providing light with his illusions until they crossed the threshold of the valley entrance and then he'd vanished. It wasn't like him. He would have been there for her the moment she woke from the henbane. Worry slammed into her followed by helplessness. What if he was hurt? A thousand possibilities cascaded through her mind, each worse than the last. With an act of will and a deep breath she imposed a sense of relative calm on her mind. He would come to her when he could. There were more things happening in the Seven Isles than her predicament.

She started walking again, this time with a renewed sense of purpose. She explored the valley, looking for a way out, anything she could use as a weapon, and anything out of the ordinary. During her first trip around she didn't find the entrance. Even though she did find the clearing where they'd entered, there was nothing but a smooth stone wall of natural granite where the entrance had been. The walls were too high and too sheer for her to have any hope of climbing out, so she decided that Hazel had at least been telling the truth about the place being guarded by magic.

As for a weapon, she found a few garden tools and several stout branches that she could use as clubs, but she finally settled on a piece of broken stick with one end splintered at an angle. It wasn't exactly a knife but it was good for one thrust, maybe two. If it came to that, Isabel hoped that would be all she needed.

She found herself back at the cottage near dusk. Hearing Ayela, Hector, and Horace within, she stuck her head through the door.

"Ah, there you are," Hazel said, amiably. "Come, have some stew." She dished a bowl and set it on the table before an empty chair as if nothing had happened. "You must be hungry."

Isabel sat down without a word and ate her dinner while listening to Horace tell stories of adventures from his past. Hector interjected periodically, adding detail or perspective to the tale. Hazel listened intently, but Isabel got the impression that she wasn't as interested in the stories themselves as she was in what those stories revealed about the brothers. She seemed especially curious about their magical talents.

While Hazel observed the brothers, Isabel observed Hazel. The old witch seemed anxious but Isabel couldn't tell if it was just a natural reaction to having sudden houseguests or something else. Her wish to take Ayela as an apprentice was plausible enough, but Isabel couldn't help feeling like Hazel had other motives. She wished Alexander was here. He would know the truth of her. The fact that he hadn't reappeared since they entered the protective confines of Hazel's valley worried her. After working through the myriad possibilities for his absence, she decided to believe that the magical protections surrounding the place were preventing him from entering.

Chapter 34

When Isabel woke early the next morning, she saw Hazel sitting in front of the fire sipping tea and took the chair opposite her without a word. Hazel smiled thinly as she prepared a cup of tea for Isabel, but her eyes didn't smile at all. Isabel nodded her thanks, taking a few sips, thinking through her list of questions.

"What do you want from us?"

"I've told you, dear," Hazel said. "I want Ayela. Beyond her, I have no interest in you except that we both have a common enemy. I would think that offering you sanctuary when those hunting you are so close would count for something."

"It would count for more if you hadn't drugged me the moment I set foot in your valley," Isabel said.

Hazel nodded with a shrug. "I can understand your feelings, but I would hope you can understand my reasoning. You are a witch from a different coven. It's only natural for me to be suspicious, even threatened, by your presence. If you were a man, even a wizard, you wouldn't pose such a danger because my charms would protect me, but they are useless against one such as you. So, when you entered my home, I was caught by surprise. Perhaps I acted rashly, but I am an old woman, frail and vulnerable. You are young and strong. I needed to know the truth of your purpose here. While henbane leaves one with a terrible headache, it's otherwise harmless and it gave me the answers I needed."

Isabel thought it over for a few moments. The story was plausible, believable even, and yet, Isabel didn't believe it, at least not entirely. She just couldn't shake the feeling that Hazel had some other agenda, but she also knew that revealing her suspicions wouldn't serve her.

"I hadn't thought it through from your perspective," she said, looking into her tea. "You must not have guests very often."

"No, I can't say I do," Hazel said.

"I can imagine how unsettling it must have been to have several armed people show up on your doorstep, and a witch to boot," Isabel said. "I hope we can put this unpleasantness behind us."

"Me too, dear," Hazel said. "After all, it looks like you're going to have to stay here for a while."

"What do you mean?" Isabel asked, a thrill of fear racing through her. She had the feeling that Hazel was springing a trap.

The old witch eyed her sagely, nodding to herself ever so slightly. "I scried the surrounding area early this morning. It seems that the Sin'Rath and their puppet soldiers haven't given up on you yet."

"Do you think they'll find your valley?" Isabel asked.

"Doubtful," Hazel said. "This place is very well protected. They've searched for the doorway along the stone face where you entered several times already and failed to see it. While powerful and dangerous in the extreme, the

Sin'Rath are rash, and subtlety is often lost on them. I suspect they'll move on in a day or so."

"And if they don't?" Isabel asked.

"We wait," Hazel said, indifferently. "Eventually, they'll tire of the hunt."

Isabel nodded, calmly sipping her tea while thoughts raced through her mind. She felt a sense of urgency building in the pit of her stomach, the need to be on her way, to find the bones of the Goiri and use them to wage a very personal war against Phane. Every day he was allowed to draw breath was another day that innocent people would meet their untimely demise. Yet, she had to be smart about it if she was to succeed. No realistic plan of attack against the Sin'Rath had any chance of success. Two witches and nearly thirty soldiers were simply beyond her and she knew it.

"Ayela asked me to teach her to fight," Isabel said. "Can I have my weapons back so I can teach her how to use them?"

Hazel frowned, staring into the fire for several moments before slowly shaking her head. "While you are a guest in my home, I would prefer that you remain unarmed. You're still a witch of another coven and I don't know you well enough to trust my life to you. You are, however, welcome to use sticks or branches to simulate weapons, like the one you have concealed in your sleeve." She looked at Isabel pointedly.

Isabel froze for a moment before smiling with a shrug. "I'm a woman at war. I feel naked without a weapon."

"Understandable," Hazel said. "I'm sure you can teach Ayela the basics without your weapons and I assure you that all of your possessions will be returned to you when you leave."

The others woke a few minutes later. Hector and Horace prepared breakfast for everyone at Hazel's direction. They seemed eager to please her and worked cheerfully. Isabel noted that both men were also without their weapons. After breakfast, Hazel sent them out to work on more firewood. She caught Isabel's frown.

"You disapprove," Hazel said.

"Yes," Isabel said without elaborating.

"It isn't often that I have two strong young men at my disposal," Hazel said. "There are so many chores that need to be done around here, it only makes sense to put them to work. After all, I've opened my home to you, fed you, and sheltered you from your enemies. Their labor seems a fair price for all I've done for you."

Isabel found it difficult to formulate a counterargument so she changed the subject. "How does that work, anyway?" she asked. "They're clearly charmed by you, why not just use your charm on me as well?"

"Very well," Hazel said. "Ayela, you should pay close attention here. A charm spell works best on one of the opposite gender, but there's more to it than that. A charm creates a strong emotional bond to the caster of the spell within the subject, and while this bond is artificial and temporary, it is nonetheless quite powerful while it lasts. Since women are prone to more intense emotions than men, we tend to be better able to manage such emotions. Add to that the natural need of a witch to manufacture powerful emotion for spell casting and the fact that other witches are usually all but immune to such magic."

"Huh," Isabel said. "That's very interesting."

"So why not just charm my father or brother and tell them the truth about the Sin'Rath?" Ayela asked.

"They're already under the influence of a charm," Hazel said, "a much darker and more powerful charm than I can cast. The Sin'Rath are descended from the Succubus Queen, Sin'Rath, and as such have inherited a number of powerful natural abilities. One of those is their venom. A single bite from a Sin'Rath witch will permanently charm any man, rendering them completely obedient to the witch who bit them. No simple charm spell can overcome something so insidious."

"Then how can we save them?" Ayela asked, new worry quavering in her voice.

"Kill the witch who bit them," Hazel said. "Or … as I've said, I'm working on a spell that will render their venom impotent. Once I've succeeded, I'll be able to free the men of Karth from the grip of the Sin'Rath once and for all."

"I say we just kill the witches," Isabel said. "We could start with the two wandering around the swamp looking for us."

Ayela nodded.

"And how do you propose we do that?" Hazel asked.

"I was hoping you had some magic to help us," Isabel said. "If we could separate one of the witches from the soldiers and catch her by surprise, I think we'd have a good chance of killing her." Isabel didn't really expect Hazel to agree, but she was hoping to draw out more information about her capabilities without questioning her directly.

"Your plan is based on speculation and an expectation of good fortune," Hazel said. "More than that, it's far too dangerous. Even if we succeeded in killing one, her death would ensure that the remaining soldiers would continue their search indefinitely. Eventually they might find this place."

"I'm not worried about the soldiers," Isabel said. "If we kill the witches, the soldiers will come around. Surely you have something else we could use against them. Would henbane work on the Sin'Rath?"

"Possibly, but it's hard to say for certain," Hazel said. "Their lineage gives me pause. Besides, henbane can only be administered from a very short distance. If it failed, you would be at their mercy."

"There has to be something we can do," Isabel said.

"There is," Hazel said. "We can wait until they leave. Any other course is suicide."

"I'm not good at waiting," Isabel said, disappointed that she hadn't gained more insight into Hazel's magic.

"Then I suggest you look at this as an opportunity to improve your proficiency in that regard," Hazel said. "Now if you'll excuse me, I have to see how the boys are coming along with the firewood."

Once Hazel left, Isabel reached across the table and took Ayela's hand. "Are you really going to stay with her?"

"I think so," Ayela said. "I could do so much more for my family if I had magic like you."

"I understand how you feel," Isabel said, "but I just can't shake the feeling that something is wrong. I don't trust her."

"I know and I even understand why," Ayela said. "She hasn't been exactly hospitable, but she's willing to teach me how to fight the Sin'Rath. How can I pass that up?"

"But we already have a plan," Isabel said. "With the Goiri bone, we can hunt the witches down and kill them without having to worry about their magic. Without it, they're nearly helpless."

"But what if Hazel's right?" Ayela said. "What if the Goiri is just a myth? What if the mountain is as dangerous as she says? We could be throwing our lives away for nothing. At least here, I have a real chance to make a difference."

"I hope you're right, Ayela," Isabel said.

"Me too."

"While we have the time, do you want to learn a few things about fighting?" Isabel asked.

"I'd love to," Ayela said.

Isabel spent the day alternately lecturing and drilling Ayela in the use of a knife. She started there because it was the weapon Ayela was already most familiar with and because it was the easiest for her to wield.

"Fighting with a knife is about speed and accuracy," Isabel said while Ayela practiced thrusting with the blade. "Strength is secondary. Let the sharpness of the blade do the work for you. Your task is just to deliver it to the right spot as quickly as possible, then to withdraw to a safe distance in anticipation of your enemy's counterattack.

"Remember, striking some points on the body are deadly with a single cut, but it's often more effective to weaken your opponent with a less deadly strike first. Cut their arm or their hand to weaken their ability to hold their weapon. Draw blood to unnerve them. Put them on the defensive and pick your moment to deliver the killing blow. Be patient if you have the time, especially if you've already cut them. Let their blood drain away until their head becomes light and their judgment falters before going for the kill.

"Your kill strike can fall on many different parts of the body. With a knife, accuracy is all-important. With a sword, you can simply stab a person in the midsection. Such a strike is harder to accomplish with a shorter blade, especially if your opponent is armored. Target the eyes and the throat if you have a shot. Both spots are almost always unprotected and a strike to either can be deadly in the extreme."

Ayela worked on her technique, carefully following Isabel's instructions for handling the knife—how to hold it, when to choose a thrust over a slice, how to conceal a drawn blade to gain the element of surprise.

"Remember, regardless of how damaging a point of attack is, it's better to draw blood than wait for the perfect opening. Wounding your enemy weakens them. If you're down and the only shot you have is to stab them in the side of the leg, then do it. If you're on the defensive and all you can manage is a slash along the outer arm, then do it. Cut your enemy when and where you can.

"Once you've committed to the fight, give them no mercy, no quarter, and feel no remorse. Press any advantage you have with single-minded determination and don't let up until you're certain the enemy is finished. Even when they look defeated, strike again just to be sure."

After Ayela had learned the basics of a number of thrusting and slicing attacks, Isabel started working those techniques into combinations, targeting first the arm, then moving in for more ruinous parts of the body. She worked on several multiple-strike combinations at low speed, focusing on accuracy until Ayela was comfortable with the series of movements, then began increasing the speed of the movements until Ayela was dripping with sweat.

As evening fell, she stopped her relentless drilling and smiled at the young Princess of Karth. "You've done well today."

"Thank you, Isabel. I learned so much. I'm already starting to see how to string one technique after the other to create different combinations and how it all depends on the enemy, what they're armed with, if they have armor, how they move, where they're standing in relation to me ... there are just so many factors."

"That's why the basics are important," Isabel said. "Master those and you'll be able to apply them to any situation you face."

Ayela nodded. "I'm so tired, but I can't imagine I'll sleep a wink tonight with all of these new ideas floating around in my head."

"You might be surprised," Isabel said. "Honestly, the best way to really absorb everything you've learned today is to put it out of your mind. Stop thinking about it and let your mind absorb it. You'll be surprised how much clearer these lessons will be tomorrow."

They found Hector and Horace in the cottage cooking dinner under Hazel's close supervision. Isabel suddenly thought it odd that Hazel seemed to want to be close to the brothers, almost as if her charm spell required proximity. She made a mental note on her way to the table.

Chapter 35

The next three days passed slowly for Isabel. She was becoming increasingly anxious to be on her way, but Hazel steadfastly maintained that the soldiers were still camped in the vicinity, apparently believing that Isabel and her friends were hiding in the swamp and choosing to wait them out. Hazel didn't seem concerned about the matter, going about the business of directing Hector and Horace in nearly a dozen projects around her little sanctuary, from mending the roof of her cottage to tilling compost into several garden plots.

Isabel used the time to teach Ayela everything she could about fighting. Ayela was a quick learner but there was only so much a person could learn in such a short period of time. Isabel focused on drilling a number of basic attacks with a knife, knowing full well that learning how to fight was as much about teaching the mind as it was about teaching the muscles and tendons of the body to perform complex movements in a blink. That took time and practice—a fact that Ayela accepted with resignation after discovering how grueling knife-fighting drills were.

She kept at it though. Isabel admired her dedication and drive. Ayela wanted these skills enough to do the work. Isabel had no doubt she would succeed in becoming quite effective with a blade, just not anytime soon. Mastery took years of work. Isabel had started drilling with the Rangers when she was fourteen and remembered all too well how difficult the exercises could be.

The morning of the next day, Isabel could tell that Ayela wanted to say something but was reluctant. Once Hector and Horace had gone to work under the watchful eye of Hazel, Isabel smiled at Ayela.

"Out with it," she said.

"I'm so sore," Ayela said. "Could we take the day off? My body needs to rest."

"Of course," Isabel said, chuckling. "I was wondering when all your hard work would catch up with you."

"Yesterday," Ayela said, stretching her arms. "I asked Hazel if I could pick some of her plants today and she said yes. You said you wanted to learn how to make blackwort, so why don't I teach you?"

"All right," Isabel said. "I'll be the student today."

They left the cottage and Ayela led her to the valley wall. "The first ingredient we'll look for is bluecap," she said. "It's a type of mushroom that likes to grow under fallen logs." She knelt down, peering under a rotting tree trunk and looking at the ground carefully. There were a number of different mushrooms of various shapes and sizes, but all growing in little patches of their own as if they were being cultivated.

"Ah, here we are," Ayela said, pointing to a small group of mushrooms with long stems and dark bell-shaped caps tinged with an iridescent blue.

"When harvesting bluecaps, it's important that you don't touch the cap itself," Ayela said, carefully cutting the long stem with her knife and pinching the stem against the blade so she could drop the mushroom into a jar without handling the top.

"What happens if you touch the cap?" Isabel asked.

"Most people spend many hours vomiting," Ayela said. "Some get sick enough to die, but that's rare."

"Good to know," Isabel said.

After picking three bluecaps, Ayela put the lid on the jar and stood up. "Next we need Fly Agaric," she said. "They tend to grow in the shade of trees." She pointed to a small grove across the little valley. It suddenly struck Isabel how out of place some of the trees were, given their location. Hazel must have transplanted them and carefully cultivated them since most weren't native to the jungle.

"Fly Agaric is another type of mushroom. It has a broad red cap with lots of white spots, and the stem and gills are white," Ayela said. "They tend to grow in small clumps of eight to twelve."

After a few minutes of searching and discovering several different varieties of fungus, all growing in segregated patches, they found what they were looking for. Ayela unceremoniously plucked the cap from the largest in the bunch and put it into her jar with the bluecaps.

"These are harmless … unless you eat them," she said. "Now all we need is wolf lichen. It's a bright green, loose-hanging lichen that grows on the shady side of trees."

While they were searching through the grove of trees, Isabel thought she saw a cave along one wall of the valley. It was covered in dense bushes with shiny green leaves. When she started toward them, Ayela stopped her with a hand on her arm.

"You don't want to touch those," she said. "You'll be scratching for a week and the more you scratch, the more your skin will welt."

"Oh! Thanks for warning me," Isabel said, making a mental note of the location for future investigation.

"I think we'll have better luck over there," Ayela said, pointing to the north side of the grove. A few minutes later she stopped, pointing several feet up the side of a fir tree … yet another species of tree very out of place in the swamp.

Ayela used a stick to scrape off a chunk of the lichen, which she stuffed into her jar.

"That's all we need, except for some water and a fire."

They returned to an empty cottage. Isabel suspected Hazel had Hector and Horace hard at work mending a fence or something equally as mundane.

Ayela started filling a pan with some water to make blackwort. "First, we bring the water to a boil," she said. "Then we add the bluecaps." She'd removed the other ingredients from the jar, leaving only the bluecaps to dump into the boiling water.

"Let them cook for a few minutes until they get soft, then smash them into mush against the side of the pan. Let the mixture boil for another few minutes, then add the Fly Agaric and the wolf lichen. Set the pan off to the side of the fire and let it sit for about an hour, then remove the Fly Agaric and the wolf lichen. Reduce the liquid that remains until it turns black and starts to thicken, stirring frequently."

Ayela worked carefully and attentively, explaining each step until she held up a vial of blackwort and handed it to Isabel.

"Cook some onto your blade and your enemy won't survive," Ayela said.

"Blackwort is dangerous, Child," Hazel said from behind them. "Where did you learn to make such a thing?"

Ayela shrugged innocently. "My mother taught me. She taught me about most of the medicines and poisons I know how to make."

"Ah, well, who am I to question a mother's wisdom," Hazel said. "Make sure you scrub that pot with sand before you use it for your dinner." Hazel left quickly, almost too quickly.

"Thank you, Ayela," Isabel said. "I'm always amazed at the wonders nature has to offer."

"I know exactly what you mean," Ayela said, looking down into the fire and falling silent.

Isabel waited for her to continue.

"I'm going to miss you, Isabel. I've never had many friends. It's nice to have someone to talk to who treats me like a person, like an equal."

"It's not too late to change your mind," Isabel said. "You can still come with us."

"I know, but the more I think about it, the more certain I am that my place is here, for now anyway."

"I hope you're right," Isabel said.

The following morning, Isabel woke suddenly. She'd been dreaming of Alexander, except the dream seemed more real than most and he'd been desperate to find her, to warn her.

Hazel was sitting by the fire. She turned and looked at Isabel as if she knew.

"Release your hold over Hector and Horace," Isabel said. "Return our weapons and let us go, today."

"You're hardly in a position to be making demands," Hazel said.

"I know you've been lying to us," Isabel said. "I know the Sin'Rath have moved on, yet you continue with your lies. What's your game?"

"I give you shelter in my home and this is how you repay me?" Hazel said. "With baseless accusations and suspicion?"

"My husband came to my dreams last night and warned me about you."

"Impossible," Hazel said, though Isabel could sense growing alarm from the old witch. "This place is protected from such magic."

"Alexander is very persistent and more powerful than you might imagine," Isabel said. "What's more, he knows where you live. I'd be very careful if I were you."

"Don't threaten me," Hazel snapped. "Even if I believed you, your husband is a world away. You left him, remember? He can hardly help you and I doubt very much he would long mourn your loss."

"Don't count on that," Alexander said, materializing beside Isabel. "It took me quite a while to figure out your defenses. I have to admit, even I was surprised by what I learned in the process, but that's beside the point. If you harm Isabel, I will wage total war against you until I have your head. I will set aside my battle with Phane and postpone my war with Zuhl and I will focus all of my efforts on finding you and killing you."

"How can this be?" Hazel said, standing with a look of shock and dismay. "My defenses have never been breached. They're impenetrable."

"Are they now?" Alexander said.

Hazel's eyes narrowed and a bit of the color drained from her face. "It can't be … yet how can it be otherwise? You're like the one who watches."

Alexander smiled ever so slightly, just to communicate understanding to the old witch without revealing the existence of Siduri to Isabel. He wasn't ready for her to have that information, not as long as Phane had his hooks in her.

Hazel looked around like a trapped rat.

"There's nowhere to run, nowhere to hide," Alexander said. "But I'll make you a deal—release Isabel and her companions, all of them, and I'll leave you alone."

Something within Hazel seemed to snap, as if years of planning and effort was about to be washed away and it was more than she could take.

"Never," she snarled savagely, tossing a pinch of powder into Isabel's face. "You can have your wife, she's more trouble than she's worth, but the rest are mine."

Isabel slumped to her knees and fell over. A glance at her colors told Alexander that she was alive but unconscious.

"If you know what I am, then you know there's nowhere you can hide," Alexander said. "Especially now that I've figured out how to penetrate your warding spells. Release them and I will leave you in peace."

"I can't," Hazel said. "I need them. I'm so close. You don't understand. I've been working for over a century to defeat the Sin'Rath, and now I finally have the means, but I can't do it without them." She pointed to Hector, Horace, and Ayela who were standing over their bedrolls, watching the exchange.

"Had you simply asked, I'm sure Isabel would have been willing to help you," Alexander said.

"I doubt that very much," Hazel said.

"What have you done to Isabel?" Ayela asked.

"She's just sleeping, Child," Hazel said, dismissively. "Pack your things. We'll be leaving today."

"I'm not going anywhere with you until I'm sure Isabel is all right," Ayela said.

"Don't be a fool," Hazel snapped. "Do as you're told."

"No," Ayela said, drawing her dagger. "Isabel is my friend."

"Hector, be a dear and take her weapon," Hazel said.

Hector grabbed Ayela by the wrist and calmly pried the blade from her hand.

"This is your doing," Hazel said to Alexander before she stepped up to Ayela and blew a pinch of powder into her face. The Princess of Karth blinked a few times, then her eyes went glassy and her face went slack.

"Pack your things," Hazel said.

Ayela slowly started gathering her belongings, moving in a methodical, almost shambling sort of way.

"For what it's worth, I won't harm Isabel. She may yet prove useful, provided she survives the swamp."

Alexander faded from sight but remained to watch. He wanted to shout, to rage against the witch, to threaten her, but he was afraid of what she might do to Isabel.

So he simply watched.

Chapter 36

Isabel woke, lying in the mud, shrouded in fog. She sat up sleepily at first before she realized where she was and then she scrambled to her feet, looking around in near panic. She was in the swamp, alone, without her weapons or pack. She focused on breathing, calming her racing heart while she thought about her situation, trying to find a scrap of hope she might leverage into survival.

Alexander appeared a few feet away.

"What happened?" Isabel asked.

"Hazel left you in the swamp without even a knife and took everyone else with her," Alexander said. "It looks like they're headed for the mountain."

"What would she want there?" Isabel asked. "She made the place out to be a death trap."

"Maybe there's something there she doesn't want anyone to know about," Alexander said. "Her plan seems to hinge on your traveling companions."

"I really thought Ayela was coming around," Isabel said, getting to her feet and wiping the mud from her pants.

"Hazel cast some kind of spell over her involving a charm that Ayela is now wearing around her neck," Alexander said. "She's just as obedient as Hector and Horace."

Isabel surveyed the swamp, still and quiet as a tomb. "I'm in trouble here," she said.

"I know. Let's start by getting your weapons and equipment back. Maybe we'll find some answers along the way."

"I don't even know which way to go," Isabel said, feeling helpless.

"I do," Alexander said, transforming into a ball of light and bobbling away into the mist.

Isabel followed, more afraid of the swamp than ever before. He led her along a path that became familiar when she reached the tree with notches cut into the side like the rungs of a ladder. Once across the rope bridge and down again, she found the place in the stone wall that was a cave entrance when last she came this way.

"It's right here," Alexander said, transforming back into an image of himself and pointing. "The wall is about a foot thick. She controls it with a few words in a language I don't understand, so you'll have to burn your way through."

Isabel nodded, reaching for her rage but finding only the numbing sensation of the malaise weed in its place.

"She's been drugging my food. I'll have to wait for the effects to wear off before I can cast a spell."

"How long?"

"Could be hours, could be tomorrow."

"I want to stay with you but I can't hold an illusion for that long," Alexander said.

"I know, just check on me now and then," Isabel said. "I'll need your help once I get into her valley."

"Be strong, we'll get through this," he said, fading from sight.

Isabel waited, attempting every hour or so to build her anger into a rage sufficient to cast her light-lance spell. As night fell, her fear grew. It was so dark. She listened to the deathly quiet of the swamp, expecting some horrible monster to come for her in the darkness, but nothing did. She woke the next morning shivering and hungry … but more importantly, she was angry. Her rage bloomed into fury easily, almost too easily, but she fed it as she spoke the words of her spell.

The hole she burned clean through the stone wall revealed the passage beyond. It took her dozens of castings to cut an opening large enough for her to crawl through. By the time she was done, her rage was spent and she was exhausted from the effort.

Alexander appeared not long after, finding her facing the darkness of the cave with no way to make light. "I see your magic is back," he said with a smile.

She nodded wearily.

"Fortunately, I think the wall on the inside of the valley is just an illusion," he said, transforming into a ball of light to guide her way.

A few minutes later, she reached the wall on the other end of the tunnel only to discover that it felt solid. Emotionally spent, she sat down with her back against the side of the tunnel and closed her eyes.

"I don't have the strength to burn my way through right now."

"Try pushing against it," Alexander said. "It doesn't look entirely solid to me."

More to humor him than anything else, she reached out and put a hand against the wall, leaning into it with halfhearted effort. To her amazement, her hand sank into the stone. There was still resistance, but the farther she passed through, the more it gave. Getting to her feet, she pushed through the wall to the other side, stepping into the little clearing on the edge of Hazel's valley and a clear winter morning.

"I would never have guessed," she said, feeling the wall on the other side. It felt solid until she made an effort to pass through. "Well, that's a pretty effective secret door."

After placing a few stones in front of the door to mark its location, she headed for the cottage under a bright sunny sky. "I don't get this place. I couldn't find it with Slyder, yet it's obviously open to the sky."

"I'm not so sure," Alexander said. "I couldn't find it either and I searched pretty extensively."

"So … what, then? A variation on a Wizard's Den?" Isabel asked.

"No, I think it's really a cavern with an elaborate illusion that looks like a sky."

Isabel stopped in her tracks, looking up. "Is that really possible?"

Alexander spread out his hands and shrugged. "I'm lying in a bed on Tyr."

"Good point," she said, continuing on toward the cottage.

Before searching for her things, she found some food and ate a quick breakfast. Once her gnawing hunger was sated, she started looking for her equipment. After more than an hour, she found a hidden panel in the back of Hazel's armoire that opened to a staircase leading below the cottage into a small stone room that looked like it had been magically carved into the bedrock.

Isabel's pack and weapons sat atop a trunk at the bottom of the stairs. The room appeared to be Hazel's workspace. Dozens of jars of green glowing lichen hung from the ceiling, casting an eerie glow over the room. There were many shelves of books and a table covered with glassware. A large cauldron sat over a cold fire pit in one corner and several shelves contained a plethora of ingredients, some Isabel recognized, but most were unfamiliar. One shelf held a number of powder-filled jars with labels that read: *sleep, henbane, poison, smoke,* and *concealment*. Below that were several vials filled with liquids of various colors and consistencies. They were labeled as well: *healing draught, blackwort* and *invisibility*.

"Do you think these are potions?" Isabel asked.

"I'm sure of it," Alexander said. "The healing draught has the same colors as the ones Lucky gave us. The others all contain magic, except the blackwort and it's the only one with dangerous-looking colors."

"Should I take them?" Isabel asked.

"Absolutely," Alexander said. "Hazel drugged you and left you for dead in the swamp without any of your equipment, then abducted Hector, Horace, and Ayela. Take everything of use that you can carry, then light this place on fire. We're at war with that old witch."

"When you put it that way," Isabel said, going to a bookshelf and looking at the titles on the spines. "Most of these are in languages I don't understand, but these two I can read." She carefully opened the first book. It was small and bound in leather and written in the common tongue. The next was similar in size and binding except it contained many more pages.

"These might be useful," Isabel said. "This one is a charm spell and this one is a shapeshift spell."

"Take them both," Alexander said. "Do you see any others you can read?"

Isabel shook her head, scanning the remaining titles on the shelf before turning her attention to the book resting on the desk and flipping it open to a random page toward the end. It was blank. She flipped forward until she found writing.

"I think this is her journal," Isabel said, scanning the latest entry. "It seems we rushed her plans." She flipped forward to the next page. "Doesn't say why, but she's pretty excited to have Hector and Horace. Wait. Oh Dear Maker … she plans to sacrifice them! We have to catch up to her before she reaches the mountain!"

"What's she going to sacrifice them to?" Alexander asked.

"She calls it a ghidora," Isabel said, flipping forward several pages. "Listen to this. 'With the transference complete, I will have both my youth and my rightful place in the House of Karth once again.' What do you think that means?"

"I don't know, but I doubt it's good," Alexander said. "Take that, too …
it might offer some useful insight."

Isabel went to work packing the books and potions before carefully
storing the jars of powder in her pouch. Except for the poison, since she didn't
understand how it was administered and didn't want to accidentally poison herself.

"Anything else look useful?" she asked, scanning the room.

"One of those glowing jars of lichen," Alexander said.

Once back in the cottage, she took what food she could carry and a length
of sturdy rope, then filled her waterskin. Finally, she built a fire in the hearth and
prepared a hot meal which she ate while cooking blackwort onto the blade of her
dagger and boot knife. Finally, she tossed several burning logs into the corners of
the cottage, then waited until the place was fully ablaze before heading for the exit
to the hidden valley. The more she thought about it, the more she knew that
Alexander was right. Hazel's actions were those of an enemy … so war it was. She
resolved to kill the old witch on sight lest she gain the upper hand yet again.

Isabel wasn't anxious to be back in the swamp, especially alone, but she
was in a hurry. It didn't take long to pick up Hazel's trail, in spite of the multitude
of tracks left by the soldiers. The mud made for easy tracking and since the
soldiers had left days ago, her friends' tracks were fresh by comparison, which
allowed her to make good time while still being alert to potential dangers and
avoiding the water.

Alexander appeared at random intervals, sometimes just to keep her
company, other times to warn her of some potential danger ahead. Even when he
wasn't visible, Isabel knew he was watching over her, a fact that was no small
comfort in the dreariness and desolation of the swamp.

By the time she'd left the hidden valley, Hazel and her friends had several
hours lead on her, but Isabel was fit and strong, driven by purpose and anger,
while Hazel was old and frail. Isabel could make out the witch's footprints
amongst her friends, her stride was short and her gait was uneven, she could only
be slowing them down.

"You're gaining on them," Alexander said, appearing next to her.
"Unfortunately, they're headed for a boathouse on the edge of deeper water. I
doubt you can reach them before they get there."

"And, of course, there's only one boat," Isabel said.

"I'm afraid so, but the boathouse is made of evenly cut timbers you can
use to build a raft."

"How far across the water?" Isabel asked.

"Couple of days," Alexander said. "The foothills of the mountain are on
the other side."

"That's going to put me at least a day behind them, and that's without any
unforeseen delays. I just hope I can catch up before Hazel gets where she's going."

"Me too," Alexander said, fading from sight with a helpless shrug.

Isabel pressed on. The water became deeper, claiming more area, but she
was able to stay on solid ground by following the trail Hazel and her friends had
made. The old witch seemed to know exactly where she was going, a fact that
made Isabel wonder even more about the mountain that once housed Siavrax

Karth's most secret laboratory. Clearly, Hazel knew much more about the place than she'd let on. Isabel only hoped her assertions about the Goiri were either wrong or just lies. The more she thought about it, the more she reasoned that Hazel would have felt threatened by the bones. After all, she was an old woman. Without her magic, she was helpless. If the stories were true, the Goiri's bones were nothing but a threat to her.

This part of the swamp was nearly as dead as the parts covered by deeper water, except for the birds living in the treetops. From the sound of it, the trees were teeming with them, probably all of the variety that ate insects, which were becoming quite abundant.

When Isabel came across a different set of footprints, she stopped to examine them. A closer look told her that it was two men, walking in each other's prints. Soldiers from Karth had found her friends' trail and were following them. She wondered at the meaning of it. Were they lost or were they scouts? Did they have some means of communicating with the bulk of their forces? And how close were the Sin'Rath witches? Isabel was far more concerned about running into them than she was about the soldiers. Her shield spell made her all but invulnerable to normal weapons, but the witches were something else altogether.

She slowed her pace, taking more time to stop and listen for the enemy in the mist, but the fog had a dampening effect, muffling sound and limiting visibility. After some time, she decided the dampening effect worked both ways and started moving more quickly again, still stopping to examine the trail from time to time, but not as often.

Before long, she thought she heard a voice up ahead. She froze, listening intently, caution mixing with trepidation. She heard it again and started moving, swiftly but quietly closing with the soldiers.

"We're lost," one man said.

"All we have to do is follow these tracks and they'll lead us right to the rest of the men," another said.

Isabel could just make out their forms in the fog ahead. She stopped, crouching down behind a stump, and considered her options. They were soldiers of Karth, either controlled by the Sin'Rath or acting on orders from someone who was. Ultimately, they were innocent, undeserving of the swift death that Isabel could have easily delivered. But that inconvenient fact presented a dilemma. While they were innocent, they were still after her. What's more, they were going to wind up at the boathouse just ahead of her and discover that they were following the wrong set of footprints. Lost and alone in the swamp, it was hard to say how they would react to her arrival.

She had to subdue them or lead them astray … but how? She decided to follow at a distance, even though they were traveling slower than she would have liked, while she waited for Alexander to check in on her. She didn't have to wait long.

"How long have you been following them?" he asked quietly, appearing next to her.

"Half an hour," she whispered. "I don't want to kill them, but I need them out of my way."

He smiled at her and winked before vanishing. She crouched in the mist, waiting. A few moments later she heard them shouting.

"Stop!"

"You're our prisoner!"

Then she heard running, muffled by distance and fog. She waited until Alexander returned.

"They should be off chasing ghosts for a while," he said. "You can get ahead of them for now."

"Keep an eye on them for me?"

"Of course," Alexander said and then he was gone and Isabel was again moving through the swamp, remaining vigilant but focusing on covering ground as quickly as possible. She knew they would probably double back when they lost Alexander in the mist. If they got back on the trail, they might reach the boathouse before she could build any kind of decent raft, and given the death leeches in the water, Isabel wasn't willing to cut corners.

Then she stopped dead in her tracks, blinking in wonderment, remembering that one of the jars of powder in Hazel's workshop was labeled *concealment*. She wasn't sure what that meant, but it was certainly worth a try. She found the jar of dust and carefully sprinkled a pinch on the ground behind her. The trail left by her friends' passage as well as her own vanished for twenty feet. Smiling fiercely, she raced forward another twenty feet and sprinkled more powder, erasing any evidence of her passage for forty feet. Satisfied with the effect of her vial of magical powder, she forged ahead. Even experienced trackers would be thrown by the sudden disappearance of tracks that were so clearly evident before. At a minimum, they'd have to circle to reacquire her trail and that would take time.

It was late in the day when she reached the boathouse, which was really no more than a shack with a little dock jutting into the black and murky water of the swamp. The trail had become more circuitous as she neared the deeper water, winding around pools and bogs to stay on solid ground.

Alexander appeared when she arrived.

"They're half a day ahead of you and moving steadily toward the mountain. The water stays pretty deep between here and there, so once you're floating, you probably won't set foot on solid ground until you get there. Those two men have picked up your trail again but I don't think they'll get here before dark."

"Good," Isabel said. "If I'm quick, I can have a raft in the water with an hour to spare."

Isabel worked steadily, tearing down support beams and wall struts from the boathouse to use as the foundation of her raft and wall boards to use as the floor, tying them all together with rope until she had a simple raft about eight feet long and five feet wide. She cut a board into a paddle and then found two long, straight branches to serve as poles. It was nearly dark when she shoved off. As the mist and coming night swallowed the silhouette of the skeletal boathouse, she heard two men complaining that they'd followed the wrong trail. Then their voices were swallowed by the gloaming swamp as well.

She poled her way through the cypress trees until it was too dark to continue, then tied off to a tree and lay down for the night, calling Slyder to her for company and comfort. It was a fitful night. Isabel wasn't afraid of the dark, but she was wary of what might be lurking in the swamp. While the dangers she'd faced since entering the mist weren't what she'd expected at all, they were deadly in the extreme. Anything that upset her raft and tossed her into the water would be the end of her, so every little ripple brought her fully awake and alert. By morning she was exhausted and sore from trying to sleep on bare boards.

She sent Slyder into the treetops, above the mist, to get her bearings and then set out, pushing herself through the water with one of the long poles. The water was nearly four feet deep in most places, but occasionally much deeper. She worked steadily through the morning until her shoulders burned from exertion. Over ground, Hazel was much slower, but on the water in a boat, with Hector and Horace to row, they would be moving much faster than she could. Isabel had no expectation of gaining on them, but she was determined not to fall too far behind.

From the absence of waterfowl, she assumed that this part of the swamp was also infested with death leeches. It was a frightening thought: nothing but murky water in every direction and all of it hiding death. She shuddered, trying to focus on her goal, on what she intended to do once she arrived. That was much simpler. She was going to burn a hole through Hazel.

Alexander appeared near midday.

"This part of the swamp looks as devoid of life as the rest of it," he said.

"This whole place is like a tomb," she said. "I wonder where those leeches came from."

"Probably Siavrax—what better way to keep unwanted guests away from your secret laboratory?"

"Do you think he would really kill a whole swamp just to keep people away?"

"He summoned the Succubus Queen," Alexander said. "There's no telling what he was capable of."

"I wonder what I'm going to find on that mountain," Isabel said.

"I had a look around and I'm afraid it's not so empty of life," Alexander said. "It's mostly a jungle until you get up toward the top where the vegetation thins out."

"Any predators I should know about?"

"A few animals: jaguars, snakes, boar, monkeys, and some type of wild dog that hunts in packs," Alexander said. "But there's also something else. I consulted the sovereigns about them before I came to you. They're called vorash ... another one of Siavrax's creations."

"I don't like the sound of that," Isabel said.

"No, they're built almost like a man, two arms and two legs, except they have two broad, powerful, clawed fingers forward and one back on both their hands and their feet. The head is elongated like a dog's, only bigger, and they have tentacles sprouting from each shoulder ending in clawed hands as well. They're supposed to be terribly strong, very aggressive, and completely territorial. They can climb better than a monkey and prefer to attack from above, sometimes carrying prey into the trees and dropping them to their death."

"Great," Isabel said. "I think I'll try to avoid them altogether."

"Probably wise if you can," Alexander said. "Malachi said Siavrax created them to use as soldiers in the jungle but they were less than obedient and not terribly smart."

"Anything else?" Isabel asked.

"The fortress is mostly inside the mountain except for the ruins of the keep on the very top," Alexander said. "It looks like there are a number of ways into the lower levels that are accessible from smaller structures in the jungle."

"That sounds promising," Isabel said. "The less time I can spend in the trees, the less time the vorash will have to hunt me."

"From the course Hazel's taking, it looks like she's heading for one of these side entrances."

"Almost like she knows where she's going," Isabel said.

Alexander nodded.

"She was playing us all along," Isabel said. "I wish I had time to read more of her journal."

"Maybe when you stop for the night," Alexander said. "I'll be back when I know more."

Isabel moved through the swamp, damp from mist and sweat, her arms and shoulders burning, but she pushed, determined to cover the distance quickly. At dark she tied off to a tree and tried to read some of Hazel's journal, but it was like reading one side of a conversation. Isabel wondered how much of that conversation had taken place in Hazel's mind and how much actually made it onto the page.

From what she could gather, Hazel needed a woman of her lineage to complete the transference, whatever that was, and she was very excited to have finally brought Ayela to her. Apparently, she'd been trying to influence the Princess of Karth for some time, using a dream-whisper spell and had all but given up. When Ayela arrived, Hazel began making preparations for the transference spell but could only complete it in the mountain.

She didn't say why.

Chapter 37

Despite her desire to study the rest of the journal and the uneasiness caused by the eerie noises in the darkness, Isabel's exhaustion caught up with her. She woke the following morning, stiff and sore from sitting up against her pack all night. She rubbed her neck as she stood up and looked around. The swamp was as quiet and dreary as ever.

She moved slower due to her sore muscles but still managed to reach solid ground just before nightfall. Rather than going ashore and risking the predators that lived there, she tied off a hundred feet from the swamp's edge and slept on her raft. Alexander appeared when she woke.

"Were you watching me sleep?" she asked groggily as she stretched.

He just smiled with a shrug.

"Their boat is tied off a few hundred feet to the north," he said. "They went straight to an overgrown structure on the side of the mountain and made camp just inside. Hazel has them up and moving like she knows where she's going and that's saying something because that place is like a maze."

"How will I find them?"

"I'll guide you," Alexander said, "but you should probably get moving."

"First, I'm going to move their boat," Isabel said with a devious smile.

After finding their boat and rowing it to a thicket just south of where she'd hidden her raft, she headed along the edge of the swamp, reasoning that the vorash would probably do most of their hunting deeper in the jungle that covered the foothills surrounding the mountain.

Near where Hazel and her friends had come ashore, she picked up their trail and cautiously made her way into the jungle, keeping a watchful eye for any sign of danger, using Slyder to scout for her as well. Several hundred feet from a small stone structure built into the side of the mountain, now completely overgrown and barely discernable, Isabel stopped again to survey her surroundings through Slyder's eyes.

Four creatures were sniffing around the entrance—vorash. They were even more frightening than Alexander's description. They seemed to be searching the area but were unwilling to enter the structure itself. Isabel waited, watching them until they used their tentacles to pull themselves up into nearby trees where they concealed themselves in the foliage, lying in wait over the entrance.

Isabel weighed her options. She could try to fight her way through, but she doubted she could kill all four before they were on her, and even if she could make it to the structure and get inside, there was no guarantee that they wouldn't pursue her. She settled on using the potion of invisibility she'd discovered in Hazel's workshop, hoping it would work as expected.

After drinking the syrupy sweet liquid, she was pleased to see herself vanish from view. Carefully, quietly, she made her way toward the structure. The vorash were watching the area intently and were starting to become restless as if they sensed something nearby. She drew closer to the partially obstructed entrance; a large support stone had fallen across the doorway leaving just a small gap at the base.

Twenty feet from her objective, the vorash roared as one and she realized that the potion had run its course. She was visible again. The vorash were coming, all four of them swinging from their perches high in the trees overhead and reaching the ground far more quickly than she would have imagined.

She raced for the entrance, relying on speed driven by fear to help her reach the relative safety of the structure before the vorash reached her. A tentacle snapped out from the brush, hitting her across the shins, sending her sprawling on her face just feet from the entrance. She scrambled toward the opening, willing the pain shooting up her legs to the back of her mind when a viselike grip caught her by the ankle.

Rolling onto her back and swinging her sword wildly, she caught the tentacle of the creature just above the three-fingered hand, severing it and drawing a scream of rage and pain. Another tentacle struck her in the chest, knocking her breath out as she crawled backward, struggling desperately to reach the structure before the vorash reached her. The other three were nearly within reach when the first leapt into the air, coming down on top of her. She rolled to the side, slashing frantically with her sword, her blade cutting to the bone in the back of the monster's leg. The vorash shrieked in pain and leapt away with Isabel's sword still stuck in its leg.

She scrambled through the hole into the darkness but another tentacle grabbed her by the ankle, sending pain shooting anew up her leg, trying to drag her back into the daylight. She turned and plunged her dagger into the tentacle and it released her, the vorash howling in pain. Isabel scrambled backward into the relative shelter of the ruined building.

She found herself in a simple stone room that was once nothing but a secure entry hall with one door leading to the jungle and another leading into the fortress. Two tentacles pursued her into the darkness, flailing around near the entrance as she backed up to the opposite wall, muttering the words of her shield spell. As much as they wanted her, they didn't seem willing to enter the structure to come and get her, a fact she was grateful for ... the pain throbbing in her legs was threatening to overwhelm her. She was bleeding from the ankle and her shins were so bruised, she doubted she could stand.

Holding up her jar of glowing lichen, she peered down the corridor leading into the darkness for as far as she could see. When she heard the vorash making noise outside like they were feasting on something, she lay on her side to get a view through what was left of the door. Two of the vorash were savagely eating the other two, the one she'd seriously wounded with her sword and the one she'd stabbed with her poisoned dagger. The beasts were tearing their former companions apart and devouring them in chunks.

Isabel stifled an urge to vomit as she started pulling herself down the corridor into the darkness. Once she was several dozen feet away from the entry chamber, she stopped to rest, listening intently for any hint that the vorash would follow her. When the sounds of their cannibalistic meal subsided, she decided she was safe for the moment and drank the healing potion, knowing full well that she would be unconscious and vulnerable while it did its work, but also knowing that she didn't have any time to waste. Her legs were too badly injured to carry her and she needed speed if she was to prevent Hazel from sacrificing Hector and Horace.

When she awoke, Alexander was standing over her.

"That was a terrible risk," he said.

"Which part? Trying to get past the vorash or drinking the healing potion?"

"Both, but I guess I understand," he said. "Two of them are still out there waiting up in the trees."

"I used the invisibility potion and it worked," Isabel said, "for about a minute, then I became visible again right under them. They almost got me. I'm just glad they don't like the indoors."

"Small favors," Alexander said. "Looks like they're using your sword as bait. I wouldn't recommend going back for it."

"Wasn't planning on it," Isabel said, removing her scabbard from her belt and setting it against the wall. "In fact, I might look for another way out of this place just in case they're patient enough to wait for me here."

"Probably not a bad idea," Alexander said. "I asked the sovereigns about the ghidora. Malachi said it's a stalker-demon sort of like a scourgling."

"Dear Maker," Isabel whispered.

"Once summoned, it requires a sacrifice for each target it's given," Alexander said, "and the one sacrificed has to have a link with the firmament, even a limited link like that of a sorcerer."

"What's it do in the meantime?" Isabel asked.

"Apparently, it goes to the place where it was originally summoned and turns to stone."

"Can it be killed?"

"With sufficient damage," Alexander said. "Its skin isn't impenetrable like a scourgling but its hide is like armor."

"What's it look like?"

"Malachi didn't know since he's never summoned one," Alexander said.

"All right, so where do I go from here?"

"I'll guide you," Alexander said, transforming into a ball of light and floating slowly down the corridor, which ran straight into the mountain for several hundred feet before coming to a spiral staircase leading up. By the time Isabel reached the top, her legs burned from the exertion and she was breathing heavily. The stairs ended on a landing facing a bare stone wall with a lever beside it. She pulled the lever and watched the wall slide toward her, then swing open on a hinge.

She peered into the room beyond. It looked like it had once been a reading room but now the walls were lined with moldering mounds of decaying books. After she stepped inside, the door closed behind her, forming a nondescript wall.

"This must have been one of his escape routes," she said.

"That's what I figured too," Alexander said, though he didn't change from his form as a ball of light.

"Huh, I didn't know you could do that."

"I'm getting better with practice."

Isabel headed for the only door and stepped through into a larger room that looked like it was once the central room in an elaborate suite of living quarters. The furniture was all decayed beyond recognition and the place felt as cold and dead as the reading room, except for the freshly killed creature splayed out on the floor and the signs of a recent struggle.

Isabel couldn't even begin to guess what the creature was. It looked like a cross between a giant rat and an armadillo, heavily scaled along the sides and back with an elongated snout ending in fangs. It must have weighed a hundred pounds.

"Looks like Hector and Horace were here," Isabel said. "I'd feel a lot better if I had a sword."

"I can imagine. We should keep moving."

Alexander led the way, bobbling through the air and illuminating the path as he navigated through the living quarters of the underground facility. Passing an intersection, Isabel heard a squeal and a scuffling coming toward her from the darkness. She immediately started casting a spell.

Another creature like the one killed in the living quarters charged toward her out of the darkness of the side passage. She released her force-push, sending the ugly-looking beast sprawling backward. It scrambled to its feet and raced away back into the darkness.

"At least it's a coward," Isabel said. "What do you think we should call those things?"

"Ugly. Come on, let's get out of here before it comes back with its friends."

A few minutes and a number of twists and turns through the sprawling complex later, they came to a large room with a line of support pillars running down the middle. In the corners near the door stood a pair of grotesquely ugly statues; the carved stone creatures were squatting down on top of short round pedestals with their clawed hands grasping the edge between their feet. Their faces were almost like a dog's, except their snouts were shorter; their mouths were open wide, revealing rows of needlelike teeth. Horns swept back and out from their brows, and batlike wings sprouted from their shoulders.

When Isabel stepped into the room, she heard a muffled click and felt the stone beneath her feet shift ever so slightly. She froze in place, waiting for the trap to spring, her heart hammering in her chest.

One of the statues began to move. Its eyes took on a dull reddish glow and it slowly turned to look at her as it started to stand. Isabel didn't waste another second, racing deeper into the room as she muttered the words of her shield spell.

Alexander separated into six glowing orbs, increasing the illumination enough to fill the entire room with light. Both statues were up and stretching as if they'd been standing in place for a very long time. Even though they moved like flesh and bone, they looked like they were still made of stone.

The moment her shield formed, Isabel started casting a light-lance. The first statue to wake leapt from the pedestal, gliding toward her on outstretched wings. Her spell fired, burning its right wing off at the shoulder and sending it crashing into the ground in a jumble.

"Get through the door," Alexander said as the second took to wing.

Isabel raced for the far end of the large room and the heavy circular stone door that looked like it was designed to roll into place from a slot in the wall. It had long since broken and rolled slightly back into its recess, opening the way to the room beyond but just barely.

Just as she reached the door, the creature crashed into her, clawing and snapping with single-minded malevolence, yet failing to penetrate her shield. Isabel turned to face the thing. It had her pinned to the door, flailing against her shield with mindless determination and almost desperate viciousness. She reached out, placing her hand on its chest as she cast her force-push, blasting the creature up and back. It struck the nearest pillar squarely, cracking the ancient stone and causing it to buckle.

Seeing the first creature charging toward her, she scrambled through the narrow gap just as the support pillar buckled and the heavy stone ceiling collapsed, crushing the two creatures, sealing the entrance, and filling the room she now occupied with a cloud of dust.

Isabel got to her feet and looked around. She was in a large workroom. Once, long ago, the place might have housed a forge and a variety of other tools and machines designed to work stone, steel, and wood into works of art or utility. Now it was empty and cold.

Alexander bobbled over to the far side of the room and stopped at the top of another spiral staircase leading back down into the heart of the mountain. Isabel headed toward him while quickly looking around for anything she could use as a weapon. Unfortunately, time had rendered everything in the room worthless.

The staircase spiraled down into the mountain. When they reached a level with a door leading into a dark hallway, Alexander continued downward.

"What's in there?"

"I'm not sure, but Hazel is farther down."

Finally, the staircase stopped at a point perhaps even deeper than where she'd entered the vast underground fortress and laboratory. It opened into a large circular room with a dozen passages leading away like spokes on the hub of a wheel. The floor was laid out with black and white tiles in a checkerboard pattern, each about two feet square. Several corpses, long-dead, littered the room. The only thing they all had in common was that each appeared to have been standing on a black square when he died.

Isabel cautiously worked her way to the first man, taking his sword and testing it, but finding that it had rusted to the point of uselessness. Deciding that none of the dead explorers' equipment was still useful, she looked closer at the dust covering the floor and saw several sets of footprints, all stepping on white squares, leading to one passage. She made her way there, relieved to be out of the deadly chamber.

"This passage leads to where they were when I last checked on them," Alexander said, floating into the darkness of the corridor.

It ran for hundreds of feet until Isabel could just make out a faint glow coming from the far end of the passage. Alexander vanished, leaving her in the darkness, so she could approach without alerting Hazel. She cast her shield spell while she walked, mentally preparing for the battle to come, knowing that she might have to fight Hector and Horace in the bargain.

The passage opened into a circular room. Two veins of softly glowing crystal rose from the floor to the ceiling. Within each was carved a chamber. A conduit of crystal running between both chambers held a panel with a single emerald set into it. Isabel heard whimpering before she saw the figure slumped to the floor in one of the chambers. She approached cautiously, her anger hot and ready. Seeing the form of Hazel in the chamber, she began speaking the words of her light-lance, forcefully and deliberately.

She raised her hand toward Hazel and the old witch looked up, tears streaming down her face, confusion and fear in her eyes.

"Isabel, please help me," she said.

Isabel frowned in momentary confusion until she remembered that the focus of Hazel's magic was belief.

Seeing Isabel's resolve harden, Hazel sobbed and put her hands up in front of her face to ward against a spell that would kill her in a flash.

"Stop!" Alexander said, materializing before Hazel.

Isabel reined in her spell, letting go of the thought-form she was about to release into the firmament but holding on to her anger.

"Why? You said it yourself; we're at war with her."

"I don't think this is Hazel," Alexander said. "Her colors are all wrong."

"Please help me, Isabel. It's me … Ayela. Hazel stole my body."

Isabel gasped, her eyes going wide. "Dear Maker, is such a thing even possible?"

"I think that's what these chambers do," Alexander said. "Also, her colors say she's telling the truth."

"How do we reverse it?" Isabel asked.

"I'm not sure, but if I had to guess, I'd say you would have to put them both back into these chambers again. I'll go consult with the sovereigns and then find Hector, Horace, and Hazel. Take care of Ayela and make your way back to the black-and-white room. Wait for me there."

Isabel nodded, going to Ayela. "I'm so sorry, Ayela. I didn't know."

"How could you? This kind of thing isn't supposed to be possible. I'm the one who should apologize. I took you right to her and she left you in the swamp to die. I can't believe I trusted her."

"You believed what you wanted to believe," Isabel said. "It happens to the best of us."

"What am I going to do? I feel like my life is suddenly over."

"I'm going to help you. I promise."

"Thank you, Isabel," Ayela said, wiping tears from her old and wrinkled face and looking up sheepishly. "Do you have anything to eat? Hazel took all of my things when she left me here."

Isabel gave her a bag of dried apples and they started toward the black-and-white room.

Alexander appeared just before they arrived.

Chapter 38

"Isabel, you have to hurry," Alexander said. "They're down that passage. I think Hazel is about to sacrifice Horace to the ghidora. She's preparing a spell, and he's laid out on a table in front of a hideous-looking statue."

Isabel raced across the black-and-white room, calling out to Ayela behind her, "Stick to the white squares only!"

The passage was a hundred feet long, opening into a giant cavern filled with cages and lined with doorways leading out of the room in every direction. She caught glimpses of the remains of unspeakable and indescribable creatures as she raced past the cages, following Alexander's bobbling light.

Some of the cages contained magic circles cut into the stone just inside the bars, while others were ordinary iron cages that had long since rusted to the point of crumbling. Most contained long-dead corpses of unidentifiable creatures but a few were empty. Two still held live creatures, but fortunately both of those cages were still intact and the magic circles within were holding the unnatural creations of Siavrax Karth at bay. That didn't stop those creatures from snapping and snarling at Isabel when she raced by.

She reached the threshold of a large doorway that used to hold double doors, but was now open to the cavern. She stopped in horror at the scene playing out before her under the flickering light of two torches.

Horace lay on a platform before the statue of a creature from out of a nightmare. Eight feet tall at the back with six-foot-wide shoulders, it stood on six powerful legs, each ending in seven clawed toes. It had four eyes, the lower two set closer together than the upper two, all of which looked like they moved independently, allowing for a very wide field of vision. Its mouth was almost two feet across and lined with razor-sharp teeth. Its long tail split into three, each ending in a blade a foot long.

Hazel, in Ayela's body, stood before the platform, chanting the words to an ancient invocation while streamers of light flowed from Horace to the statue. Hector lay unconscious on the floor, oblivious to his brother's plight.

"Stop!" Isabel cried, but she was too late. As the light stopped flowing from Horace, the creature came to life, its eyes glowing ember-red and each of the blades on its tail taking on the hue of flowing lava.

Hazel looked back and smiled as the demon bounded down a long hall that ended with a point of daylight from an opening in the side of the mountain.

"What have you done?!" Isabel demanded, drawing her dagger and advancing toward Hazel.

"I've just killed the leader of the Sin'Rath Coven," Hazel said.

"By killing Horace?" Isabel glanced over at his withered and desiccated husk. His face was blackened, lips pulled away from his teeth, his eyes hollow and empty.

"A necessary sacrifice," Hazel said. "The Sin'Rath must be destroyed, no matter the cost."

The words hit Isabel like a slap in the face. She had uttered very similar words about Phane. And she'd meant them, yet looking at the cost Hazel had been willing to pay in order to deal a blow to the Sin'Rath, Isabel realized that some costs were too great, no matter the gain.

Hazel began whispering words under her breath. Sensing the threat, Isabel fled the chamber, taking a position behind a nearby pillar and casting a shield spell. She wasn't sure what magic Hazel could wield and didn't want to find out the hard way. If Hazel was able to charm her or even blow a pinch of henbane into her face, Isabel might be the next one sacrificed to the ghidora.

"You can't hide from me," Hazel said from inside the room. "And I fear you haven't fully considered your tactical disadvantage. Do you really want to kill Ayela's body? I'm sure you have plans to undo what I've done." Her tone was taunting, filled with mirth.

Alexander appeared next to Isabel. "Slip up next to the doorway and be ready with your force-push. I'll distract her."

Isabel nodded and started to make her way around several cages so she could come up along the wall in the dark. Once in position, she saw herself step out from behind a pillar and advance toward the door as if she meant to murder Hazel ... and Ayela with her.

"Come, Child, be reasonable," Hazel said, a thinly veiled attempt to stall for time while the illusion of Isabel drew closer, becoming more vulnerable to Hazel's magic with each step.

"There," Hazel said with a triumphant smile as the illusion of Isabel entered the room. She clapped her hands once and the dust covering the section of the floor where the illusion stood rose up in a cloud surrounding her. When the illusion didn't react, Hazel became alarmed. Isabel rolled around the edge of the door and unleashed her force-push. Hazel flew backward, tumbling to the floor and shaking her head before struggling to her feet.

Isabel was moving the moment she cast her spell, but Hazel regained her feet and quaffed a potion before she could reach her, vanishing with derisive laughter.

Ayela came into the room. Hearing her own laughter but not seeing her body, she backed up against the wall next to the door and shouted, "Give me my body back!" Laughter was the only response.

"Duck!" Alexander's disembodied voice said.

Isabel saw a puff of powder appear before her; she immediately stopped breathing, closed her eyes, and rolled backward away from the threat, coming up with another force-push that fell on empty air.

"Your invisibility won't last forever," Isabel said, watching the dust on the ground for any hint of Hazel's passage, straining to hear her footsteps or breathing.

Alexander appeared as a ball of light. "Target me," he said.

Isabel didn't hesitate, firing off a force-push that sent Hazel sprawling near the door, becoming visible a few moments after she hit the ground. Ayela lunged toward her, falling on top of her and trying to pin her to the ground, but her new body was no match for the youth and strength of her real body. Hazel easily overpowered her, tossing a pinch of powder into her face once she'd rolled to her feet.

Isabel raised her hand to cast another force-push, but Hazel fled into the menagerie. Ayela tried to regain her feet but collapsed, falling into a deep sleep.

"I'll keep watch," Alexander said. "See if you can wake Hector."

"What about Hazel?"

"She can't hide from me. Besides, you can't leave them here like this. There's no telling what's lurking in the shadows just waiting for an easy meal."

Isabel looked from Hector to Ayela and nodded reluctantly, her anger draining away, only to be replaced with sorrow. She went to Horace, shaking her head and wiping a tear from her face. He looked like he'd been dead for years, his body drained of every vestige of life.

Hector woke more easily than she'd expected, his eyes snapping open when she shook him by the shoulder. He looked up, confusion turning to alarm at the look on her face.

"I'm so sorry, Hector."

He sat up, looking around, the haze of confusion fading slowly until he saw the form of his dead brother. He took a sharp breath and looked away, as if his unwillingness to believe the horrible reality of the situation could change it.

"I don't understand," he said. "Who did this?"

"Hazel," Isabel whispered.

"But … Hazel loves us."

"No, she doesn't. She was using you."

"I don't understand," Hector said, stumbling to his feet and shambling over to his brother, staring at the desiccated corpse with disbelief, then breaking down and sobbing with his head resting on Horace's breastplate.

Isabel sat down and cried quietly while Hector mourned the loss of his brother. He sobbed for several minutes before he tipped his head back and howled, shattering the silence with his anguish, his death knell reverberating off the ancient stone walls.

"Where is she?" he said, turning away from Horace.

"She fled," Isabel said, regaining her feet.

"That's not her?" Hector asked, pointing toward Ayela.

Isabel shook her head sadly. "That's Ayela … Hazel switched bodies with her."

He sniffed back his tears and looked at the ground. "Well then, it seems we both have a score to settle."

"We all do," Isabel said, taking Hector by the shoulders, "but we have to give Ayela her body back first. Do you understand, Hector?"

He looked at Ayela for a moment and nodded slowly. "Promise me one thing."

Isabel nodded, knowing what he wanted without him voicing his request.

"Let me be the one to kill her," Hector said.

She nodded again. "You have my word."

Ayela didn't wake quickly. After shaking her, gently slapping her face, and even splashing her with water, they decided they'd just have to wait, knowing full well that every minute widened the gap between them and Hazel.

Hector stood stock-still before the platform where his dead brother lay, a mask of desolation and resolve contorting his face. Isabel left him to his grief.

"You don't have a sword," he said, without looking away from his dead brother. "You should take Horace's blades. They've served him well and I know he would want you to have them."

"Are you sure?"

Hector nodded. "Did you see how she did this?"

"I was just a few minutes too late," Isabel said, new tears filling her eyes. "Hazel was chanting a series of words over and over again, but I don't remember what they were."

"I think I know, I just don't know how to read them," he said, pointing to some writing engraved into the side of the platform. "Do you think Lord Reishi is watching?"

Alexander appeared beside him. "I've been here the whole time. I'm sorry for your loss, Hector. Your brother was a good man."

"He was," Hector said, running his hand along the words on the platform. "Can you read this?"

"No, but I can ask the sovereigns."

"I would consider it a favor, Lord Reishi."

"What are you thinking?"

"I'm thinking that I know exactly how I intend to kill that old witch."

"That's dangerous business, Hector. I don't know what it might do to you."

"I don't care so long as it kills her."

"I do care, Hector."

"Will you tell me what these words say or not, Lord Reishi?"

Alexander held his gaze for a moment, and, seeing the resolution in his eyes, nodded solemnly before vanishing.

Ayela woke an hour later, groggy and disoriented. It took her a few more minutes before she was steady enough to walk.

Hector gave her a knife that Horace had carried for years, then took a necklace and ring that his brother was never without before bidding him a last farewell and turning away.

"I wish we had time to bury him," Isabel said sadly.

Hector shook his head. "He never liked enclosed spaces anyway."

They headed out into the cavern filled with cages, this time cautiously exploring, looking for any sign of Hazel. Her footsteps led from the room where she'd sacrificed Horace but stopped abruptly, vanishing without a trace.

"She's using concealment powder," Isabel said. "Let's head for the entrance and see if we can pick up her trail in the hallway."

As they rounded a large pillar, Hazel stepped out and blew a handful of dust into Isabel's face, catching her by surprise. Isabel stumbled and went to her

knees, struggling against the effects of the powder. Alexander appeared next to her
and Hector drew his swords, anger flashing in his eyes.

"I'll have my vengeance, Witch."

"Not today," Hazel said. The air blurred and five exact duplicates
appeared around her. Then all six Hazels ran off in different directions.

Hector started to give chase.

"Stop," Alexander said. "She wants you to go after her. She's counting on
it. She can't face all of you at once, but she can pick you off one at a time."

"Horace deserves to be avenged!"

"Yes, but not right now. Stay with Isabel. Protect her."

Hector looked at Alexander, then off into the darkness, then back at
Isabel who lay unconscious with Ayela kneeling next to her. His inner turmoil was
palpable but he reined it in, releasing the surge of anger that was demanding
action.

"By your command, Lord Reishi."

"She's not going to get away, Hector," Alexander said, lowering his voice
to a whisper. "The way you came in is blocked by a cave-in. When she reaches
that point, she'll have to turn back. Then we'll have her."

Hector clenched his jaw and nodded, accepting Alexander's plan.

Isabel was out for almost an hour. Ayela rested Isabel's head on her lap
and tried to wake her periodically while Hector paced.

Chapter 39

Alexander vanished from sight and found Hazel. As predicted, she was trying to flee the keep rather than face Isabel and Hector again. When she reached the cave-in and started cursing, Alexander projected just his voice, just his laughter into the room, moving it past her as if he were walking behind her.

She spun, looking around frantically. "Show yourself!"

"There's no way out," he whispered tauntingly, almost imperceptibly.

She turned toward the voice and found nothing. Clearly agitated, she hastily returned to the staircase and started down, moving cautiously as if she expected the walls themselves to reach out and grab her.

Satisfied with the fear in her colors, Alexander returned to Isabel, reappearing when she woke. She was groggy at first, taking a few minutes to fully recover from the sleeping powder.

"Hazel's coming back down the spiral staircase."

"We should set a trap in the black-and-white room," Isabel said.

"I can distract her when she enters, so you and Hector can subdue her," Alexander said, "but you don't have much time to get into position."

They moved quickly, carefully taking positions on either side of the door to the staircase in the black-and-white room. Isabel prepared a pinch of sleeping powder and they waited ... and waited.

"It's been too long," Isabel said.

Alexander appeared, nodding. "I'll go find her," he said, vanishing again.

Several moments later, he returned. "She went into the level above. Maybe she knows another way out."

"All right, let's go find her," Isabel said, heading up the staircase.

She stopped at the threshold. They had bypassed this level on their way down into the heart of Siavrax Karth's laboratory, but now there was a single set of footprints moving off into the dark hallway. Isabel motioned for Hector to take the lead. Alexander provided light, revealing a long straight passage almost twenty feet wide with ten foot ceilings. Thirty feet into the hallway, they came to two doorways, one on each side, both open with the remains of their doors long since rotted away.

Isabel motioned to the one on the right and they slipped inside, Hector in the lead.

"Looks like living quarters," he said.

"Alexander, can you tell us where Hazel went?"

The ball of light bobbled and vanished, returning several moments later.

"The corridor leads to a big room that was probably a dining hall," Alexander's disembodied voice said. "Past that is another corridor just like this one. She's about halfway down that hall, heading for the stairs on the other end."

They raced toward the dining hall, stopping briefly at the entrance to let Ayela catch up. When they reached the far side of the large room, Isabel heard voices coming from the hallway ahead. She motioned for silence and Alexander vanished, plunging them into darkness.

Each peering around a side of the doorframe, Isabel and Hector saw Hazel stopped near the end of the hallway, frozen in place, the sound of footsteps coming down the staircase on the far end. She acted just a moment too late, running for one of the rooms lining the hall but not before one of Trajan's men reached the landing and saw her.

"Stop!"

She was trapped. Almost a dozen soldiers poured into the hallway, followed by Trajan and the two Sin'Rath witches.

"Princess Ayela fled into that room," the soldier reported.

"Take her alive," one of the witches said.

"Thank you, Mistress," Trajan said, motioning for his men to approach the door. Four men entered. Sounds of a struggle filtered down the hallway and then two men dragged Hazel back into the hallway, unconscious and limp as a rag doll.

"Change of plans," Isabel whispered, slipping away from the door and motioning for them to follow.

Once through the dining hall, Hector and Ayela stopped.

In the darkness, Isabel couldn't see their expressions but she could almost feel the intensity of their emotions.

"I will have my vengeance," Hector whispered intently.

"And I need my body back," Ayela said.

"I agree on both counts, but we can't take them. If we try, they'll kill us."

"So ... what then?" Hector said.

"We go after the bones. Once we have them, the witches will be powerless and the soldiers will see them for what they really are. Trajan's men will probably kill them for us."

"Very well," Hector said, emotion draining from his voice.

They retraced their steps through the dark, feeling their way along the wall and trying to remain silent. Dim light flickered in the distance and the sounds of soldiers' boots reverberated softly off the walls of the corridor. Reaching the staircase, Isabel looked back to see an orb of unnatural green light streaking toward her. She didn't hesitate, racing into the staircase, urging Ayela to move faster into the darkness. Echoes of boots running on stone chased them back down into the heart of the mountain.

Alexander returned as an orb of light, providing illumination. Reaching the black-and-white room, Isabel stopped, looking around at the ten remaining doorways leading from the room.

"Which way?"

Alexander appeared and pointed to the wall just to the left of the staircase entrance. "There's a corridor behind that wall. I think it's down there, but I can't be sure. When I get close to the door at the other end of that corridor, I suddenly find myself back in my body on Tyr."

"That complicates things," Isabel said. "What's down the rest of these passages?"

"Mostly old workrooms."

"Any of them have tools?"

"That one," Alexander said, pointing to a passage across from the staircase entrance. "It looks like it used to be a smithy."

"Good enough," Isabel said, heading for the passage and sprinkling a pinch of concealment dust after they'd passed the threshold. They moved cautiously by the soft, eerie glow cast by the jar of luminescent lichen Isabel had taken from Hazel's workroom. The corridor ran for a hundred feet before reaching several flights of stairs leading deeper under the mountain. It opened into a large room, cold and dark. Alexander appeared again as a ball of light, revealing dozens of workstations lining the walls of the room. Each included a forge, anvil, and an assortment of tools, many of which were rusted to the point of uselessness.

Isabel was beginning to think they wouldn't find anything they could use until she came to the workstation at the far end of the room. It was larger and more elaborate than the rest, flanked by two heavy stone tables, each cluttered with an assortment of old tools. Resting on the large anvil were two hammers, both rust-free and sturdy. One was a single-handed tool while the other was a heavy sledge hammer.

"Those are enchanted," Alexander's disembodied voice said.

"Good, maybe they'll be enough to break through the wall," Isabel said. "Any idea what they do?"

"No clue."

Isabel picked up the smaller of the two. It was lighter than she expected, far lighter than it should have been. Frowning, she brought it down on the corner of one of the stone tables. As the blow fell, the weight of the hammer increased markedly, striking the table with tremendous force, breaking a chunk off the corner and sending it bouncing across the floor.

"These will do nicely," she said, handing the larger of the two to Hector.

"Now we just have to break through the wall without the Sin'Rath hearing us," Hector said.

"Not much chance of that," Isabel said. "I'm hoping they followed our tracks into the menagerie, but I suspect they left a man or two behind in the black-and-white room so we'll have to be careful."

Ayela was sitting on the floor, leaning against the forge nearest the door. "This body is so weak," she said, struggling to stand. "I've never felt so tired in my whole life."

"Ayela, I need you to be strong right now," Isabel said. "It won't be much longer but we have to move. Can you move?"

She nodded wearily. Isabel smiled, putting a hand on her shoulder before heading back up the stairs. They stopped at the top for a moment so Ayela could catch her breath, then headed back toward the black-and-white room in the dark, feeling along the walls for guidance. Near the entrance, the flickering light of torches warned them of the soldiers standing guard.

"Two men, one in the staircase landing, the other just inside the corridor leading to the menagerie," Alexander said.

"Please don't kill them if you don't have to," Ayela said.

"We won't," Isabel said. "We'll target the one in the corridor first. I'll hit him with a force-push, then finish him with sleeping powder. Hector, you keep the other one off me, then we'll do the same to him. Ayela, you wait in the corridor until they're both down."

Isabel cast her shield spell, then they crept up to the threshold silently, remaining in the shadows to assess the situation. One of the first soldiers to enter the room had stepped on a black square and now lay dead on the floor with dozens of darts stuck in him from all different directions. The other two were exactly where Alexander said they would be.

Isabel prepared a pinch of sleeping powder and started muttering the words of her spell, then sprang into a dead run across the room being careful to stay on the white squares. She caught the man in the corridor by surprise with her force-push, sending him sprawling. She was on him a moment later, holding her breath as she flicked the dust into his nose and mouth. His struggling subsided a few moments later and she rolled to her feet.

Hector had the other man down, one arm wrapped around his neck from behind; the man struggled against the choke hold but succumbed moments later. Isabel sprinkled sleeping dust over his face just to make sure he remained unconscious.

"Good work," she said to Hector. "Once we take this wall down, we won't have much time. They'll probably hear us and come running."

"They're in the chamber with the ghidora," Alexander said, appearing beside Isabel. "If you're going to do this, now's the time."

She nodded to Hector. His first blow against the wall cracked it from floor to ceiling. He looked at his hammer with renewed respect before landing his second blow. Each strike weakened the integrity of the stone wall until a large chunk fell through into the darkness beyond. Each strike also reverberated through the stone of the keep, no doubt alerting the Sin'Rath to their presence.

A few blows later and there was a hole large enough for them to climb through. Isabel went first, Alexander lighting her way. Ayela was next, followed by Hector. The passage was easily twenty feet wide and almost as tall. They moved quickly but cautiously for several hundred feet down the gently sloping passage before Alexander stopped a few dozen feet in front of a huge circular stone door. It looked almost like a giant gear with teeth along the edge fitting into a recessed track that ran off into the wall to the left. In the recesses of several of the teeth were heavy steel locking pins that fit into slots in the wall surrounding the door, holding it in place.

"I can't go any farther," Alexander said, appearing next to Isabel with a ball of light hovering over his head, "but I'll stay here to provide light. Once you get the bones, I won't be able to get near you."

"I hadn't thought of that," Isabel said.

"I'll still keep an eye on you," he said as his body vanished, leaving only the orb of light.

Isabel approached the door, then stopped, staggered by the effects of the Goiri bones as their power enveloped her. Azugorath's tendril that had been gripping her soul for so long released and withdrew like smoke blowing away on a breeze. Feelings of relief washed over her. The constant effort of resisting the Wraith Queen's influence coupled with the vigilance necessary to prevent her occasional pushes to gain control had been taking its toll.

Then she realized that she could no longer touch the firmament, she could no longer feel her link to the light or the dark … or link her mind with Slyder. Sudden fear gripped her. She could deal with losing her magic, but Slyder was her oldest friend. She couldn't stand the thought of losing him. Then she thought about what she'd said … that killing Phane was worth any cost. With a lump in her throat and renewed resolve, she stepped farther into the null magic field and examined the door.

The locking pins were all that was keeping it from rolling aside into the wall. She tried to pry one free but it was wedged, so she went to work on it with her hammer, which had become heavier when she entered the area and lost its ability to change weight in midswing.

Hector started working on another pin. It was difficult and slow-going but before long they had all of the locking pins removed. At first the door wouldn't budge when they pushed against it, trying to roll it sideways along its track. Only after Hector used his hammer like a crowbar against the teeth at the base of the door did it break free and start to slowly roll aside.

Beyond was a large circular room with a domed ceiling covered in gently glowing green lichen. In a heap before the door was a pile of bones. The creature had been large, maybe nine feet tall during its brief lifespan. It had died trying to escape the place of its unnatural birth.

Isabel knelt before the remains of the Goiri, looking into the empty eye sockets of the unnatural skull half-buried in debris, wondering about its brief existence. The sound of boots came reverberating down the hallway, followed by the flickering of torchlight that played across the fine dust swirling over the Goiri's bones.

"Here they come," Hector said. "My magic is gone."

"Mine too," Isabel said. "Hold your ground and don't leave the area. If our magic doesn't work, then neither does theirs."

Hector drew his twin short swords and took his position to the right of Isabel. She drew a sword and a dagger coated with blackwort. Ayela stiffly moved off to the side and sat down against the wall, crying softly. "I was really hoping that these bones would reverse what Hazel did to me," she said.

The soldiers approached, fanning out with the two Sin'Rath witches behind them. Isabel backed up like she was afraid, trying to draw the witches into the room. They stopped before the edge of the field, smiling fiendishly. The one on the right looked almost human, except her skin was an unnatural grey, her canines were long and sharp, protruding past her lips and her eyes were completely black without any pupils or irises. One sharp horn jutted from her forehead, curving over her jet black hair, her spiked tail flicking about behind her.

The other wasn't nearly so attractive. She was hunchbacked, her right shoulder large and powerful, her right arm longer and stronger than the left, which looked like a child's arm except that it ended in black claws as did the right. Her eyes were red, the color of glowing embers, and her teeth were all black and needle-sharp. Grey, tangled hair grew in patches on her mottled scalp and her face was misshapen, almost like it was made of wax that had melted slightly out of form and then hardened.

"Well, well … will you look at this, Agneza," said the first witch to her sister in a very reasonable voice. "The Reishi witch has finally run out of places to hide."

"Yes, Peti," Agneza said in a mewling voice. "We should eats her."

"Seize them," Peti said.

The soldiers started moving forward, entering the null magic field and moving to surround Isabel and Hector, not seeming to notice Ayela sitting off to the side. Isabel made no move to resist.

Trajan approached her and stopped ten feet in front of her.

"Throw down your weapons and surrender. You have nowhere left to run."

"Trajan," Ayela said weakly.

He looked at her sharply, noticing her for the first time.

"Who are you?"

"I'm your sister, but that isn't important right now."

When he turned to look at the unconscious body that one of his soldiers had placed in the hallway, the true form of the witches caught his attention. He spun to face them, frozen in place and staring in disbelief as the effects of the magic broke.

"That's what they really look like, Trajan," Isabel said.

His men were all turning to look at the two hideous witches, muttering and gasping in dismay, conferring with each other to see if their companions were seeing what they were seeing.

"You've been under their spell, Trajan," Ayela said. "Just like our father is, just like his father before him. Our house has been at the mercy of the Sin'Rath for centuries."

He looked at Ayela again, frowning in confusion.

"You're not my sister."

"Stop this!" Peti commanded. "Kill them! Kill them now!"

Trajan turned to face the witches, anger starting to build on his face.

"How is it that you look so hideous when only moments ago you were the most beautiful women I've ever seen? More importantly, how is it that I no longer feel compelled to obey you?"

Agneza snarled, raising her hands and unleashing a spell toward him. Blackness, the color of the netherworld itself, erupted from her fingertips and streaked toward Trajan. He raised his hands to ward against the attack … but it simply vanished when it passed into the null magic field created by the Goiri's bones.

"It's the bones, Trajan," Ayela said. "They cancel out magic."

"They don't cancel out steel," Peti said, turning to the unconscious form of Hazel in the hall. "Kill them or I'll kill your sister."

Isabel quickly scooped up a handful of rib bones and tossed them into the hallway all around Hazel. Peti tried to cast her spell but nothing happened.

"You've lost, Witch," Isabel said. "These men can finally see you for what you really are."

Trajan looked back at Isabel, their eyes met and she smiled.

"On behalf of Lord Reishi, I offer the House of Karth an alliance against the Sin'Rath and Phane," she said, sheathing her sword and offering her hand.

Trajan looked at the witches for a moment, then turned back to Isabel and took her hand. Both of the witches shrieked in fear and rage before they fled.

Trajan picked up a femur lying near his feet and struck it against the floor, testing its strength, before smiling fiercely and sprinting up the hallway after the witches, followed by most of his men.

Before they could close the distance, both witches escaped the null magic field and turned their magic on the corridor ceiling, dark arcs of unnatural energy leaping from their hands, unmaking the very stone itself.

Trajan stopped and scrambled back toward the room, dragging Hazel's unconscious form with him, as the ceiling in the corridor collapsed under several tons of stone and dirt, burying them alive in the Goiri's tomb.

Chapter 40

"I'm worried about Alexander," Abigail said.

"He's got a lot more than just us to deal with," Anatoly said. "He'll be back when the time is right."

It had been a week since his last visit. Magda was almost completely healed, though she still favored her shoulder, occasionally wincing in pain when she forgot about her injury and moved too quickly. Their food was starting to run low and Ixabrax was beginning to grumble.

"We could assault Whitehall on our own," Abigail said.

Anatoly looked at her reprovingly. "You know better than that. Good information about your enemy is half the battle. Alexander can provide us with near perfect information. Patience is the wise course."

"Patience has never been my strong suit," Abigail muttered, getting up and wandering over to the cave entrance. The sky was bright and cold, and there was just enough breeze to add a biting edge to the day. She scanned the snow-covered slope of the mountain, her eyes locking on to movement in the distance. It was so far away that she couldn't be sure, but the more she looked, the more certain she became—a company of soldiers was headed toward them.

"Looks like we have company."

Anatoly stood, spinning his axe into his hands. "How close and how many?"

"Looks like all of them, but they're at least two hours away."

"Oh," he said, sitting back down.

"Shouldn't we prepare?" Magda said.

"I'm not sure we need to," Anatoly said. "I suspect Ixabrax is getting hungry right about now."

"True," the dragon said, "but not hungry enough to eat a hundred men. Besides, I believe you're all now well enough to ride, so I suggest we leave this place in favor of a closer position, say the crevasse. That way we'll be in a better position to make our attack when the illusionary wizard returns with his battle plan."

"Fair enough," Abigail said.

"We should share the remaining two vials of dragon draught," Magda said. "Otherwise we could easily suffer injury from exposure over such a long flight in this cold."

They packed their belongings and donned their fur cloaks. Then Ixabrax squeezed out of the cave and unfurled his wings, stretching them wide before lowering his neck and allowing the three of them to climb aboard.

Abigail couldn't help smiling at the exhilaration of flight when the dragon lifted off the ground. He flew straight for the company of soldiers marching across the snow field toward the cave, roaring as he passed overhead. Most of the men scattered in terror but one man caught Abigail's eye. Haldir was leading them to the cave, his arms bound to a stout limb resting across his shoulders and tied to his neck. His torso was bare, red from the cold and from the blood oozing out of dozens of shallow slices cut across his chest. He slumped to his knees as he watched Ixabrax soar overhead with a mixture of vindication and awe.

Several hours later, Ixabrax arrived at the crevasse where Alexander had first found him. They made camp, waiting for Alexander to return and help them plan their attack. After several days, they ran out of food and firewood. Ixabrax left them to hunt. He was gone for nearly a day before he returned with a stag and a fallen log.

"Now I'm really worried about Alexander," Abigail said while they prepared their first hot meal in days.

Anatoly nodded. "This isn't like him. Something must have happened."

"Have faith. He'll return," Magda said.

"My patience grows thin," Ixabrax said. "I have delivered on my part of the bargain, yet your brother is nowhere to be seen."

"Maybe we should think about making our move without him," Abigail said.

"We've already been over this," Anatoly said. "Our best chance for success is to wait. Without Alexander, we'd be going in blind."

"I know the layout of the aerie," Ixabrax said.

"What about the rest of the keep?" Anatoly said. "The best chance your family has is to wait for Alexander to guide us."

"I agree," Magda said. "We'll free your family, Ixabrax … just not today."

Several more days passed, everyone growing more restless and uncertain by the hour before Alexander finally appeared.

"Where have you been, Human?" Ixabrax demanded.

"Searching for my wife," he said. "She's buried under a mountain and I can't find her."

Abigail, Anatoly, and Magda surged to their feet, but no one knew what to say.

"I'm still hoping she's alive but I can't know for certain."

"I don't understand, why can't you go to her as you have to us?" Ixabrax asked.

"She went after the bones of an ancient creature that won't allow magic to work anywhere nearby. Every time I get close, I wind up back in my body on Tyr."

"I'm sorry, Alex," Abigail said. "I wish I could give you a hug."

"Me too," he said, closing off his emotions and focusing on the task at hand. "I've already spent too much time looking for her, knowing full well that the same thing's going to happen whenever I get close, no matter which angle I approach from. It's time to focus my efforts where I can be useful and hope she can dig her way out."

"So you have a plan then?" Ixabrax said.

"I do. Unfortunately, the book I sent Zuhl didn't kill him. I'm not sure why, but he survived, so I plan to distract him while you enter the aerie and free the dragons."

He gestured to the ground beside their fire pit and a scale model of the enormous white marble fortress appeared, rotating until the section in question was facing them. It was a huge dome with a hole wide enough for a dragon to fly through in the center of the roof. Six towers rose from the edges of the dome, each culminating in a battlement, and each manned by two soldiers.

The entire domed building was surrounded by the main walls of the keep, which also featured manned watchtowers at even increments. The main building, Zuhl's manor, butted up against one side of the dome with many towers rising high overhead, offering a commanding view of the entire city and keep.

"As you can see, the place is a literal fortress. His men are vigilant, never hesitating to sound the alarm, so going over the walls is out of the question. They'd spot you before you even got close."

"That doesn't sound like a very optimistic assessment," Anatoly said.

"Notice here," Alexander said, pointing to a point in the outer wall where a small stream flowed through a grate and into the keep. "This stream feeds the main cistern, which in turn feeds the dragon aerie. The grate is stout enough to stop an angry bull, but the Thinblade will make short work of it. Once you're in, you'll be up to your armpits in freezing water, so we need to find a way to keep you warm. I was hoping you might have a spell, Magda."

"I'm afraid I don't, at least not until we're out of the water. Dragon draught would be our best bet."

"Where can we get some?"

"Zuhl's soldiers were carrying the last vials we got our hands on," Anatoly said.

"All right, so the first step will be to get some more dragon draught. Now, there's a guard tower manned by two men overlooking the stream."

"I do have a spell that can deal with them," Magda said.

"Good," Alexander said, gesturing to his illusionary model. It became transparent, revealing the path they would have to follow through the underground waterways. "There's a magical field here," he pointed to a place several dozen feet inside the keep. "I'm not sure what it does, but you should be able to cut your way around it."

"That's going to take some time," Abigail said.

"I know, but I'm afraid the field might warn Zuhl of intruders. We can't afford that."

"Your plan is starting to sound pretty complicated," Anatoly said.

"I know, but I've explored this part of Whitehall extensively and I've never seen such defenses. Zuhl takes his security as seriously as you would expect from a man who plans to live forever."

"All right, so once we're past the guards and through the grate and around the magical field, all up to our armpits in freezing water, then what?" Anatoly asked.

"There's another grate at the spillway into the cistern. Once you're through that, you can get out of the water and follow the access pathways that run alongside the waterways. This one," he pointed to one of five passages leading from the main cistern, "leads straight to the dragon aerie. Unfortunately, the access path stops where water flows under the wall into a large pool on the side of the aerie. That passage is grated as well."

"So we cut that grate and swim inside," Abigail said. "Then what?"

"Then you'll be in a giant room with six, hopefully sleeping dragons and possibly a number of human handlers. Pick the largest dragon and cut his collar before he wakes while avoiding or eliminating the handlers."

"Is that all?" Abigail said.

"The largest will be my sire, Izzulft," said Ixabrax. "He is a very light sleeper."

"Wonderful," Abigail said, "so we do this very quietly."

"That would be wise," Ixabrax said. Then he broke off a tooth and handed it to Abigail. "Show him this … he will know it comes from me and hesitate before eating you. Explain your intentions quickly and concisely. He has very little patience for humans, but he will do whatever he can to free our family. Once he understands your purpose, I have every confidence he will assist you."

"That's reassuring," Anatoly grumbled.

"I need you to help me understand the nature of Zuhl's control over your family," Alexander said to Ixabrax. "When you were in the aerie, how much influence did Zuhl have over you?"

"We were instructed to remain within the aerie without harming his servants or damaging the building."

"Good, I was afraid he might leave you with a command to attack any intruders."

"I was born into slavery in that aerie and in all my years, he never left such a command, but then there was never a single incident of an intruder entering the aerie either."

"Not terribly surprising," Anatoly muttered.

"What is my part in this?" Ixabrax asked.

"I need you to deliver us near the fortress and wait in case there's trouble," Alexander said.

"I would do more."

"I know, but you aren't exactly inconspicuous. We can't approach from the sky, or Zuhl will be alerted and then you'd have to face your whole family at once. This is the only way."

"Very well, Human, if I had a better plan I would offer it."

"Once the dragons are free, then what?" Abigail asked.

"You fly away and regroup at the crevasse," Alexander said.

"And then what? We're still stuck on this cursed frozen rock of an island."

"If you free my family, I will carry you back to Fellenden myself," Ixabrax said.

"Now that sounds like a plan," Abigail said.

"Good. See about getting some dragon draught and I'll check back tomorrow," Alexander said, fading from sight.

Back on Tyr, he opened his eyes and groaned softly from the throbbing pain behind his forehead. He'd been pushing too hard lately … with Isabel missing and Abigail preparing to attack Whitehall, there was just so much to do and all of it required his attention.

Anja was sitting in a chair next to his bed, transformed by a shapeshift spell into a young woman of about sixteen years old with shoulder-length, coppery red hair that flared out just over the shoulders, bright golden-brown eyes, and a swath of freckles across her nose and cheeks. She smiled brightly.

"Mother has agreed to let me spend more time with you. I still have a thousand questions. If you're feeling well enough, that is." She added the last when she noticed his pain and exhaustion.

"Of course, I'm always happy to see you."

"You need to rest," she said, frowning, "and not the kind of rest where your mind is off wandering around the whole Seven Isles. Lay back and close your eyes. I'll make you some tea."

Alexander looked over at Jack, who was sitting at the little table he used for a desk, but all the bard had to offer him was a smile and a shrug. He just nodded and lay back, closing his eyes and resting his mind. There was still so much to do, but he knew that his best chance of success was to pace himself. He wouldn't do anyone any good if he was too exhausted to use his magic when he needed it.

He spent the rest of the day talking with Anja, or more to the point, answering her seemingly endless questions. She was insatiably curious, her quick mind seizing on any new questions that Alexander's answers raised. By late evening he was exhausted. Sleep came easily and he woke the following morning with a clear head and a long list of things to do.

Chapter 41

First, he went to the site of the cave-in on Karth, carefully approaching the section of collapsed ceiling within the passage, manifesting only as a floating ball of light. What he saw caused him to snap back into his own body and sit bolt upright, breathing heavily.

Along the top corner of the cave-in, where debris filled the corridor the least, was a three-foot-by-three-foot tunnel dug through the dirt and rock, shorn up with pieces of stone pulled from the floor of the Goiri's crypt and used to form a ceiling and walls for twenty feet.

"She's alive," he said when Jack looked up.

"Did you see her?" Jack asked.

"No. But they dug out from under the cave-in. They're probably trying to escape the island. I need to find her."

Jack just smiled as Alexander lay back down and cleared his mind. After several failed attempts to find Isabel by focusing on her, Alexander returned to the crypt passage just outside the cave-in and quickly moved his awareness up the passage to the black-and-white room. From there, he followed the passage leading to the ghidora, moving more quickly than any person could run but maintaining clear awareness of his surroundings. Finding the ghidora frozen in place and the remains of Horace where they'd left them, Alexander blinked back to the black-and-white room where he took the passage leading to the crystal chambers.

Floating down the hallway, he saw Isabel a few feet inside the threshold of the chamber beyond. She was saying something to Trajan, but Alexander couldn't make it out. Once he got within ten feet of Isabel, he suddenly found himself back in his body on Tyr.

"She's alive and she has the Goiri bone," Alexander said, sitting up and smiling to himself. Of all the decisions he'd ever made, marrying Isabel was by far the best.

"Impressive," Jack said. "What's her plan?"

"I'm afraid she plans to stab Phane," Alexander said, his smile fading into a frown. "Without magic, she thinks he'll be vulnerable enough to kill."

"She could be right," Jack said.

"I'd rather she didn't bet her life on it."

"What would you do in her place?"

Alexander hesitated, taking a deep breath and letting it out slowly. "I'd kill Phane."

"Of course you would, given the chance. Isabel has that chance. And she knows it. More to the point, she's the one on the battlefield, in harm's way. Doesn't it have to be her call?"

"Of course it does, but I don't have to like it," Alexander said, lying back and closing his eyes.

It took some time to find the calm necessary to once again escape his body. After a brief conversation with Abigail, he appeared in Lucky's workshop.

"Ah, there you are," Lucky said, smiling amiably and getting up from the table and an early lunch. "I've prepared the material according to your specifications and I've begun to process a second batch."

"Good. Once you learn the entire process, you'll need to start production. That means you need a place with better security."

"Kelvin suggested the same thing," Lucky said. "We've begun construction of a suitable workshop with adjacent quarters in the subbasement of the new Wizard's Guild Lodge."

"Remember, only you and Kelvin know this is happening. Keep it that way."

"Absolutely," Lucky said. "We are both extraordinarily cautious when discussing this matter."

"Good, so you have orange-red granules ..." Alexander spent several minutes explaining the next few steps, detailing how each step should unfold, how the result should look, what failure looked like and how to recover. When Lucky could recite every step, Alexander said his goodbyes and vanished.

The process of making Wizard's Dust was long and complex—it would require several more visits with detailed instructions before Lucky learned the entire formula, and even then, the most difficult and delicate parts were yet to come ... Lucky would have to apply his magic in just the right way at just the right time. If he failed, the batch would be useless. There was still a long way to go, but they were making good progress.

Alexander lingered on the firmament, listening to the song of creation, but also listening for any hint of Siduri. Memories of his brief encounter with the strange little man intruded into his mind with maddening frequency. The ramifications of his story were terrifying and breathtaking all at once. Alexander couldn't help but wonder if Siduri was the key to it all, so he searched for him and listened for him and called out to him every time he visited the firmament, but all he ever received in return was silence.

He opened his eyes to find Anja sitting in the chair beside his bed, watching him intently.

"You're staring," Alexander said.

"Is that wrong?"

"Not wrong, just impolite."

"I wanted to make sure I remember what you look like."

"You'll remember," Alexander said, reaching for her hand.

She looked down. "Will you teach me how to fight with a sword?"

"Huh?"

"I want to learn how to fight with a sword."

"Anja, you're a dragon, why would you need to fight with a sword?"

She shrugged, shaking her head, still looking down. "I just want to learn."

"Ask your mother. I'll teach you if she agrees."

She smiled excitedly and raced out of the Wizard's Den, looking for her mother. It wasn't long before Alexander felt the approach of Bragador just moments before she appeared in the doorway of the Wizard's Den, Anja trailing behind her.

"May I?"

"Of course, please come in," Alexander said.

Bragador took the chair next to the bed. Anja stood at her side, struggling not to smile.

"Anja tells me you would teach her to fight with a sword. Is this wise?"

"I don't see how it's unwise, even if it is pretty unnecessary."

"Please, Mother," Anja said. "I really want to learn."

"Very well," Bragador said, "but do not aggravate his injury, Anja."

"She won't," Alexander said. "Jack will play the part of her opponent while I talk them through the steps."

Jack looked up from his papers, his eyes slightly wider than usual, but he recovered quickly, standing and then bowing with a flourish to Anja. "My Lady, it will be my honor to serve as your practice mannequin."

Anja giggled. Bragador frowned, but made no move to leave. "Perhaps you should close the door," she said.

Alexander nodded, willing the door to the Wizard's Den to close.

"I have word from Tasia. The Regency ship is a week from the northern coast of Karth."

"I've looked at that ship. The shade is aboard and he still has Aedan," Alexander said, holding Bragador's gaze. "We don't have a move right now."

"Very well, I will instruct Tasia to remain with your Captain Wyatt and provide him what assistance she can for the time being."

"Good. Wyatt's going to have his work cut out for him," Alexander said. "On another matter, my leg has healed well enough for me to walk without a cane, not far, mind you, but well enough that I think it's time to begin making preparations for my departure. I'd like to call a ship to come pick me up, but I wanted your permission first."

"Of course, but just a single vessel and tell them to fly the Reishi flag when they enter the Spires."

"I'll make sure they follow your instructions," Alexander said.

Bragador said her goodbyes and Anja came to Alexander's bed.

"Can we start?"

"All right, but we'll start with a knife, you're probably not strong enough to wield a sword."

Anja frowned, shaking her head. "Alexander, I'm a dragon. I'm plenty strong enough to handle a sword. In fact, I want to learn to use a really big sword."

Alexander chuckled. "Fair enough, but let's start with a knife. Many of the principles are the same, but a knife can be easily concealed where a really big sword can't."

"All right, if you say so," Anja said.

After a brief hunt for adequate pieces of driftwood and some minor modifications, Anja had produced two wooden knives. In the session that followed, both Jack and Alexander learned that she was not only stronger than a full-grown man, but faster and far more aggressive in a fight than most soldiers.

There was a visceral quality to her total immersion in the moment, all of her attention, focus, and intention narrowed down to the present. She moved like an animal, instinctually searching for an opening, an opportunity to strike, lashing out with blinding quickness and spontaneity when an opening presented itself.

After a bit of instruction and practice, Anja was an equal for Jack one-on-one. Her speed and strength matched his skill and experience. With time and practice, she would be formidable with a blade.

"That's enough for today," Alexander said.

"Oh, thank the Maker," Jack said, collapsing onto the ground, lying completely splayed out on the cold stone floor.

Anja giggled.

"You did well," Alexander said. "Think about the things you learned today and we'll practice more tomorrow."

Anja bent down and kissed him on the cheek before skipping out of the Wizard's Den, humming a tune to herself.

"Just think, Jack, you'll be able to tell the story about the time you got into a knife fight with a dragon and lived to tell about it."

Jack chuckled, shaking his head. "It would be unbecoming of a bard to tell such a tale about himself, so I rather suspect you will be the hero of this story."

"I'm still laid up in bed," Alexander said.

"Which makes your role in the story all the more heroic," Jack said, smiling with mirth and mischief.

Several days passed. Alexander checked in with Abigail every day, but they hadn't yet obtained the dragon draught they needed to enter Whitehall. Isabel was still cloaked by the Goiri bone, so Alexander couldn't find her, a fact that was both a source of worry and solace—worry because he wanted to see her, talk to her, know that she was all right, and solace because he knew she was still alive and Phane wouldn't be able to find her either.

He checked in on Lucky every day as well, watching his progress without disturbing him. Once he'd done his daily clairvoyant reconnaissance, Alexander spent the rest of the day with Anja, teaching her to fight. After a few days of training with the knife, she carved a small log into a giant broadsword and asked to start using it instead.

Alexander agreed, more than anything because he wanted to see this little waif of a girl wielding a sword that most full-grown men wouldn't be able to handle … and he wasn't disappointed.

Anja brought every bit of the strength and speed to wielding the broadsword that she had to the knife, but she was even more aggressive and forceful in her attacks. Jack was no longer her sparring partner—he'd sustained too many bruises and cuts to continue—so Anja practiced by herself against imaginary targets.

Alexander walked her through each engagement, presenting the imaginary enemies she faced, their locations, armament and actions, then had her explain how she would defend against each attack. Once she outlined her battle plan, Alexander walked her through it, examining how well each step would work, then she would drill her plan.

She worked tirelessly and relentlessly. She demonstrated a kind of single-minded determination rarely matched by human beings.

That evening, Alexander went to bed tired but unable to sleep, so he projected into the firmament instead. He went to Lucky first and found him sitting in front of the fire.

"Ah, Alexander, it's so good to see you," Lucky said, standing up. "I'm ready to proceed. I've processed the compound through the bright green liquid state you told me of and boiled the mixture down to black, brittle pellets."

"Good, this next step will require your magic," Alexander said. "You must dissolve the black pellets into one pint of muriatic acid and boil the mixture, adding more acid every time the mixture falls below half a pint. This process will take ten hours, during that time you must focus your magic on the mixture each time you add acid. As the solution comes to a boil, visualize the gold particles floating in the solution and see them spinning."

"Spinning?" Lucky asked.

"Yes, spinning very quickly," Alexander said. "I don't understand it either, but the sovereigns tell me it's a necessary step for the process to work."

"Very well. And once the ten hours have elapsed?"

"Boil it down till just dry—it should be white as new-fallen snow. I'll come back for the next step. If the product isn't white, you'll have to start over at step one."

"Then I shall focus intently on seeing the gold spinning," Lucky said. "On another matter, Kelvin would like to speak with you."

"I'll go see him now," Alexander said, fading away and reappearing in Kelvin's workshop, which was still under construction.

"Alexander, it's good to see you," Kelvin said, turning away from his supervisory role. "I have things to show you. Come."

He followed Kelvin into a well-locked and magically protected vault. It contained all manner of items, from weapons to clothes to jewelry, and everything was enchanted to one degree or another. Kelvin selected a staff from a rack of other staves and held it up for Alexander. It was about six feet long, shod in silver on either end, and carved with runes over every part of its surface. It was well-made and potently enchanted, but its bright, pure white colors told a greater story—this staff was made from the vitalwood tree, a conduit to the realm of light itself.

"I call her Luminescence," Kelvin said proudly. "Isabel gave me the idea in her fight with the scourgling. The staff will produce ordinary light in varying intensity from a dim glow to sunlight bright, but that's not where its real power lies. Every few hours, you can call forth the Maker's light. Near as I can tell, it's just as powerful as Isabel's light—it makes people want to stop fighting, disrupts spell casting for both wizards and witches, and it banishes most demons outright."

"Sounds like a potent weapon," Alexander said. "I'm impressed."

"The truth is, the wood itself wanted to be what she became," Kelvin said. "I had a number of other ideas, but every time I picked up the branch, none of those ideas felt right and this one always did."

"Then it's exactly what it's supposed to be."

"I hope so," Kelvin said, replacing the staff and picking up a finely crafted, though slightly undersized dagger. "I call this Demonrend. It will banish any demon it draws blood from. Commander P'Tal tells me it's balanced perfectly for throwing, but still long enough to wield effectively by hand. I made her from a fallen star I found decades ago. I've been waiting for just the right project for that hunk of metal and this seemed perfect."

"Thank you, Kelvin. I was going to head straight to Karth from Tyr, but I think I'll come to you first."

"I hoped you would, as does Commander P'Tal. His wound is all but healed and he's anxious to resume his duties."

"I'll bet," Alexander said. "Is Lita still following him around?"

"All the way here to Glen Morillian," Kelvin said with a chuckle.

"He doesn't know it yet, but he's going to miss her when he's mended."

"I suspect you're right," Kelvin said.

"I hope to see you soon," Alexander said, fading into the firmament.

He found Lacy sleeping fitfully aboard the Regency warship. Her quarters were comfortable, but there was a guard at the door.

Alexander slipped into her dreams, but not as himself. Instead, he conjured an image of Lacy's father in the distance, beckoning to her.

"You must go to Ithilian," he said, in a forlorn, desperate way. "You're going the wrong way." With that, he withdrew from her dreams, while she continued to toss and turn. It would be so much easier just to talk to her in person, but Alexander didn't want to risk her safety by putting her in a position to tell lies she wasn't able to sell.

***

"Dissolve the material in a quart of distilled water, then add a dilute solution of caustic soda in small amounts, stirring constantly until balance between acid and base is achieved—do you know what that means?"

"I do," Lucky said, chuckling. "Any alchemist worth his salt would."

"All right, boil the mixture down until it's just dry, then add another quart of distilled water. Boil it down again until you have black granules."

"And then?"

"Then you'll need an oven that isn't made out of metal, capable of producing high heat over long periods of time."

"I'll consult Kelvin on the matter," Lucky said.

Alexander faded away and returned to Tyr. He'd started sparring with Anja himself, though at slower speeds than she was capable of due to his injury. His leg was mending well, but it was still sore, especially when he put his full weight on it, so he took it easy while working with Anja to improve her technique.

During these sessions, he discovered that his new precognition was related to threats. If something dangerous was coming his way, he just knew. It first manifested with Anja when she got carried away and forgot they were sparring at half speed. She whirled with her wooden broadsword, bringing the blade around in an arc that would have probably brained Alexander, but he saw it coming a moment before it reached him and was able to duck. Had he been relying on just his all around sight, he might not have been quick enough, given Anja's extraordinary speed.

She'd proven to be a quick study, rapidly learning basic knife and sword techniques. She still lacked the nuance and deep understanding that came from experience but she was quite proficient at a variety of attacks, blocks, parries, and feints, having practiced them diligently.

Alexander started to feel a pang of loss every time he thought about leaving her, but he knew it was the right thing to do, no matter how bad it felt. He sparred with her daily and his leg grew stronger. Captain Kalderson's ship was coming to get him and he knew there would be no waiting once it arrived. He needed to be in fighting form by then.

He visited Lacy nightly, sowing the seeds of resistance within her mind, reinforcing her father's dying command in her dreams: *Take the box to Ithilian. Never open it.*

He checked with both Abigail and Lucky every day to see if they were ready to proceed and he worried constantly about Isabel. She was beyond his reach, immune to magic, unfindable.

After being cooped up in his bed for so long, he started to venture out to the island, walking and exploring with Anja in tow, asking a thousand questions. If felt good to walk again. Even if he wasn't fully healed, he could still cover some distance before needing to rest.

***

Finally, Lucky reported that an oven fashioned of crystal was complete and ready to use.

"Place the black crystals in an annealing boat and bake them at high heat for two hours. While they bake, visualize all of the impurities burning away, leaving only spinning particles of gold. After two hours, you should have a fine white powder with almost no weight at all ... Wizard's Dust. One ounce of gold will produce enough for one mana fast."

Lucky swallowed hard, looking at the tray of black pellets, realization of what he was about to do sinking in. "We're about to change the world," he whispered.

"Let's hope for the better," Alexander said. "You have the whole formula now. Produce enough to meet the needs of the Ruathan and Ithilian Wizards Guilds and the Reishi Coven, but no more. Don't stockpile any. Make only what you need for each mana fast and only once a candidate is selected. Spread the rumor that another cache of Wizard's Dust was found in the Reishi Keep."

"I understand," Lucky said. "I'll protect this sacred charge with my life."

Alexander smiled at his old mentor. Lucky wasn't one for such talk unless he was deadly serious ... or afraid. Alexander imagined it was a bit of both. Lucky had just become the most important man alive, the only man in the world who could actually make Wizard's Dust, the one man with both the necessary power and the requisite knowledge ... and that made him the biggest target in all of the Seven Isles. Phane or Zuhl would gleefully kill him to prevent him from producing Wizard's Dust, or just as happily capture him and torture him for the formula. Either way, his best defense was secrecy.

"I know you will. I'll see you soon," Alexander said, fading out of sight and returning to Tyr and Anja who was waiting not so patiently in the chair beside his bed.

Chapter 42

Ixabrax flew low and fast, skimming over the treetops, ducking into valleys and skirting around hills to remain unseen by the soldiers manning Zuhl's watchtowers. Abigail reveled in the intensity of flight, savoring the cold air on her face and exulting in the falling sensation she felt every time Ixabrax dipped into a low spot. All too soon, he flared his wings and brought the harrowing ride to an abrupt halt, delivering Abigail, Anatoly, and Magda to a secluded clearing boxed in on three sides by steep cliffs. Ixabrax worked his way under the trees to remain as inconspicuous as possible while he waited for Abigail to free his family.

They approached along the stream that fed into Whitehall's cistern, moving cautiously, maintaining a keen sense of awareness with every step. Magda tapped both Abigail and Anatoly on the shoulder, signaling that they were close enough for her to disable the guards on the nearest tower.

After a few moments, two scything pinwheels of faintly glowing magical force appeared over her head for just an instant before they shot forth, decapitating each soldier without a sound.

"Nice," Anatoly said … just a moment too soon.

A horn blew from the topmost tower of the keep, followed by a blindingly bright light emanating from the same tower and illuminating the spot where they stood, alerting the entire fortress to their exact location.

"How did he see us?" Anatoly asked, spinning his axe into his hands.

"Magic," Magda said. "If I had to guess, I'd say a sensitivity spell."

"So much for that plan," Abigail said, heading toward the grate.

She slipped into the frigid water, bracing for the sting of cold that never came, thanks to the dragon draught. The grate was made of stout steel bars that fell to the Thinblade without resistance.

Anatoly entered the passage first, followed by Abigail and then Magda. It was narrow and dark and they were up to their armpits in water so cold they would have already succumbed were it not for the magical protection of the dragon draught.

Not three steps into the passage, the water several feet in front of Anatoly erupted, spraying everywhere. He ducked his head, shielding his eyes from the sudden spray as an explosion rocked the passage. Fine steel darts flew in every direction, emanating from a device that had sprung out of the water and detonated in a deadly shower of well-honed steel. Anatoly's armor protected him and shielded Abigail and Magda behind him as well, but he had no doubt that normal armor would have been no match for the force behind each needle-sharp dart.

"What was that?" Abigail asked, working her jaw to pop her ears.

"A trap spell," Magda said. "I know similar magic … it's called a porcupine spell. It's cast upon a specially prepared item, which is then placed and activated. From then on, anyone who approaches the spell will trigger it."

"Can you tell if there are any more?" Anatoly asked.

"Yes, but it may trigger the security field."

"I don't think that matters now," Abigail said.

"Fair enough," Magda said, working her way past Anatoly in the narrow passage. After nearly a minute of whispering to herself, a wave of hazy blue energy emanated from her hands and spread out down the passage. As it passed over two spots in the water, hidden objects pulsed blue, as did the security field.

"Looks like two more," Anatoly said. "I'll trigger them while you two stay back."

Anatoly approached the devices with his arms raised across his face and his head down so his armor would take the entire attack. Once the danger had passed, Magda came forward and dispelled the security field. As they pushed through the water, they heard shouting from behind them—soldiers had discovered their point of entry.

The sound of the soldiers' voices faded before they reached the second grate barring the way into the main cistern. Abigail cut it open in seconds and then they were struggling to swim to the ledge surrounding the majority of the cistern.

After they reached the ledge and helped one another out of the water, they heard the muted roar of a drakini. The water was far too cold for the soldiers to survive, but the drakini had no such weakness.

Alexander appeared next to them. "All of Zuhl's forces are either moving to engage you or falling back to the main manor house to reinforce its defenses."

"Zuhl thinks we're after him," Anatoly said, chuckling.

"If you'd ever had a conversation with the man, you'd understand," Abigail said. "Which one of these passages leads to his manor?"

Alexander smiled, pointing to one of five large grated passages leading out of the cistern that fed the entire keep with water.

"Watch for the drakini," Abigail said, drawing the Thinblade. She made her way to each grate, cutting it into pieces with a few well-placed slices. She cut through the last of the five when the first drakini reached the entrance and launched into the air.

A light-blue magical rope leapt forth from Magda's hand, wrapping itself around the drakini, binding its wings and sending it tumbling into the water. Abigail calmly drew an arrow and killed the creature with one well-placed shot before leading the way into the passage to the dragon's aerie. It was long and straight with a six-foot-deep, four-foot-wide trench filled with water bordered on one side by a two-foot-wide walkway. They moved as quickly as possible under Magda's conjured light.

The walkway ended abruptly, but the water-filled trench continued under the wall, through a grate and into the watering pond for Zuhl's dragons.

Alexander appeared. "There are two handlers in the aerie right now. All six dragons are asleep. I'm going to distract Zuhl and find out why my book didn't kill him. Oh, and your ruse worked. The rest of the drakini went toward the main keep."

"Thanks, Alex," Abigail said as her brother disappeared.

She let herself down into the water very gently, Thinblade in hand, and carefully cut the grate from the walls while Anatoly held it to ensure it didn't make any noise. Abigail went through first, carefully breaking the surface and gently floating to the edge of the water. Peering over the side of the stone-lined pool, she saw a giant room lit only by daylight streaming through a large hole in the exact center of the dome.

Around the walls lay sleeping dragons.

Abigail took a deep breath and pulled herself out of the water, crouching down in the shadows near the pond while she schooled her breathing and calmed her pounding heart, water streaming out of her armor and boots.

Anatoly and Magda pulled themselves from the water on either side of Abigail while she searched the aerie for the two handlers. Seeing no sign of them, she scanned for the largest dragon. He was curled up next to the wall on the far side.

Carefully, cautiously, painstakingly, they moved through the shadows, choosing each step with care. When they drew to within thirty feet of the dragon, Abigail motioned for Anatoly and Magda to stop while she continued toward Izzulft, Thinblade drawn and at the ready, Ixabrax's tooth held high in the other hand.

"Hey, who are you?" a handler said, stepping through the threshold of one of the man-sized doors leading out of the aerie.

Izzulft opened his eyes and reared up, poised to strike. Anatoly faced the handler while Magda muttered under her breath.

"I'm here to help you … Ixabrax is waiting outside," Abigail whispered loudly. "I can cut that collar off of your neck."

"He gave you a tooth?"

Magda launched a handful of smoking pellets at the handler that burned out before they hit the ground but left a cloud of thick blue smoke surrounding him. A moment later, he wavered on his feet and then slumped to the ground.

"Yes," Abigail said, waving the tooth at Izzulft, bringing his attention back from Magda's spell. "We have to hurry. Bring that collar closer and I'll cut it off."

"Do not deceive me, Human," Izzulft said, lowering his neck slowly and tentatively.

Abigail didn't hesitate. As soon as he was close enough, she slipped the blade through the collar and cut it open with one smooth stroke. He reared back in surprise and then looked at Abigail as if seeing her for the very first time. Before she could blink, he snatched her up and launched into a low glide across the aerie toward the next largest dragon.

***

Alexander floated into a large, well-appointed but lifeless and impersonal chamber. He found Zuhl standing on a balcony in the cold, looking out over his vast army in the distance. Without a word, Alexander appeared beside him.

If Zuhl was startled he didn't show it, instead simply looking at Alexander and nodding respectfully.

"Hello, Lord Reishi. I must congratulate you on your ruse and on discovering mine so quickly. You're proving to be a more worthy adversary than I ever imagined."

"Did you think I wouldn't see through an imposter posing as my own sister?"

"I expected you would, but there was a chance you wouldn't—easily worth the risk, considering the paltry cost of a single priestess weighed against the potential reward. While I didn't really expect you to give me the lich book, I was quite surprised by what you did give me. It killed Mage Harkness, you know—a victory in your column by any account, yet also a potential defeat. You see, I have a few ideas for how to use the magic in that book, ideas that probably never even occurred to you, ideas that only a necromancer would conceive of. You may have done yourself grave harm, though I do applaud your initiative. Defeating worthy adversaries such as you and your rather resourceful sister will make my ultimate conquest all the more sweet."

"You're broken in the head, Zuhl. You're going to die, permanently, before this is all over. See, while I was looking for you, I actually found the chamber where you keep your real body. I know," Alexander said, holding up his hands to forestall Zuhl's protest, "your chamber is warded, I shouldn't be able to see inside, but I can. I figured out how to circumvent those kinds of magical defenses a few weeks ago. In short, I know where you sleep, and one of these days, I'm going to walk into that room and cut you in half."

"And yet today, here you stand, nothing but a projection, impotent. Even if you do manage to kill me, how will you defeat them?" Zuhl asked, presenting his army with an outstretched hand. "Face it, you're doomed, it's just a matter of time ... and I'm very patient."

"Without you, your soldiers will lose interest in the rest of the world and go back to fighting each other."

"So kill me then, if you can," Zuhl said, then held up his hand with a look of confusion mixed with concern as he examined a ring on his middle finger that was glowing brightly.

"How can this be?" Zuhl said, looking out at the giant dragon aerie and seeing nothing to indicate any trouble, then walking quickly out the door, his guards falling in behind him without a word.

Alexander shifted to the clearing where Ixabrax was hiding.

"Zuhl knows what we're doing—they might need your help."

"Understood," Ixabrax said, unfurling his wings and stretching them before launching into the sky.

Chapter 43

"We haven't much time," Izzulft said, midflight. "Zuhl will know I'm free and he'll order the others to fight or flee."

He landed briefly, carefully depositing Abigail on the floor, but leaving her off-balance just the same, before leaping on top of Nix, his mate, and pinning her head to the ground, exposing the collar to Abigail.

"Quickly," Izzulft hissed.

In the same moment that Abigail cut Nix's collar, all four of Ixabrax's siblings came awake, roaring in unison. Rather than fight, they launched into the sky, one after the other, flying from the aerie into the night.

Izzulft didn't hesitate, he snatched Abigail up again, ignoring the threat the Thinblade posed to him, or perhaps trusting Abigail to avoid harming him, and launched into the sky toward the nearest of his children attempting to escape.

If felt like time slowed down for Abigail as she watched events unfold, helpless as she was, clutched in a dragon's claw. Soldiers poured into the aerie from three different entrances while drakini floated into the aerie from above. Izzulft gained with each stroke of his powerful wings, reaching his child just before he reached the opening atop the dome-shaped aerie. With his free foreclaw, Izzulft grabbed his child's leg and dragged him back into the aerie, bringing him down hard, protecting Abigail, though not gently, while subduing his son and holding his head still so Abigail could cut his collar.

The collar came free easily. She looked up to see soldiers everywhere, then the turmoil was interrupted by Ixabrax, roaring in challenge as he descended into the aerie, savagely attacking the drakini before landing in front of Abigail and Izzulft.

"You have done well, Ixabrax," Izzulft said, "but we still have family to free."

"These humans are necessary," Ixabrax said. "We must preserve them."

"Agreed," Izzulft said, turning toward a troop of soldiers fanning out to surround Anatoly, who was already battling three men. The huge dragon belched forth a great cloud of super-cold air that billowed out, engulfing the entire platoon, freezing them solid to a man in moments.

"Gather your human friends and we will make our escape," Izzulft said, turning back toward another platoon of soldiers and freezing them solid as well. Frozen statues spread out in a battle line, terribly lifelike, terribly still.

Ixabrax moved to surround Abigail with his body and wings while dealing fatal damage with his tail and teeth to any drakini that ventured too close.

"Call your friends to you," Ixabrax commanded.

Abigail climbed up onto his neck and settled into a space between two of his back bone spikes, drawing an arrow and taking careful aim, letting it fly just a moment after she sat down, killing a soldier circling around behind Anatoly without anyone's notice.

The big man-at-arms and Magda were squared off against twelve of
Zuhl's palace guard, brutish soldiers, most of them bigger than Anatoly and they
were fanning out to surround the two of them.

Magda raised her hand and fired nine light-blue darts formed of magical
energy, targeting three of the soldiers that had gotten closest. Each took three to
the chest in rapid succession, Magda calmly selecting her targets and unleashing
her magic at them, one right after the other. Each collapsed in turn, sputtering
blood and groaning in pain.

The remaining men rushed them, raising a terrible battle cry as they
charged. Anatoly hurled forward to meet them, stretching out with his axe, and
bringing it down on the nearest soldier as quickly as possible, sacrificing balance
for first blood. The blade cleaved into the man's shoulder, driving him to his
knees, wounding him seriously but not fatally. Anatoly nearly stumbled, going to
one knee, bringing his axe in and then thrusting out into the midsection of the next
nearest soldier, stabbing the top spike through his belly and out his back.

Soldiers collapsed in on him from all sides. A battle axe across the right
shoulder turned him away from his attacker. A sword thrust into his left side
staggered him, knocking the wind out of him despite the protection of his armor.
Another sword thrust to the back drove him forward, opening his guard and
slightly stunning him. A giant of a man stepped up in front of him with a war
hammer held high. All Anatoly could do as the hammer fell was lean into it, take
the blow on his dragon-scale helm, and hope to remain conscious.

He was driven to his hands and knees, his axe clattering to the floor
beneath him, his head swimming in confusion and pain. The man with the hammer
smiled down on him, raising his hammer for a second blow … but then he
stopped, the war hammer slipping from his grasp and clattering to the ground
behind him as he staggered to his knees, an arrow through the neck. Another fell a
moment later with a shaft through the head to the feathers. He'd made the fatal
mistake of separating from the group attacking Anatoly just enough for Abigail to
feel certain of her shot.

Magda completed her spell, brandishing a longsword of blue-white
magical energy and charging into the fray. She circled just behind the nearest
soldier attacking Anatoly and stabbed him through the heart, drawing the attention
of the man Anatoly had first wounded. Holding the wounded man's eyes, she
casually circled another soldier and killed him with one stroke of her conjured
sword.

A soldier grabbed Anatoly, ignoring the commotion taking place in the
background, and pulled his head back, exposing his face to two soldiers standing
before him. Anatoly came up on his knees, bringing a knife up in each hand,
stabbing under each man's breastplate into the soft flesh of their lower bellies.
Both men shrieked in sudden agony, spasming backward and collapsing to the
ground in writhing pain.

The man behind him raised a knife but fell with an arrow through the
skull. Anatoly staggered to his feet, war axe in hand, and scanned the battleground.
Magda killed the last of the men confronting them with a well-placed trust to the

heart. Seeing the enemy dispatched, she let go of her blade and it fell to the ground, vanishing before it hit.

Abigail beckoned to them.

The aerie was now home to a confused, mostly aerial battle with the drakini trying to attack the soft membranes between the bone struts on the dragons' wings. Unfortunately for the drakini, the dragons were very good at killing them when they got anywhere close. All four dragons stood, back to back, in the center of the aerie and fought the drakini and any soldiers that were fool enough to charge into a dragons' lair.

Anatoly was wounded, Abigail could tell from his gait, but he was still alert and deadly. A drakini made a run at them, attempting to latch on to Anatoly with its hind claws and carry him into the air. Anatoly kept walking like he didn't notice the impending attack until the last moment, when he ducked under its feet, flipped his axe up and hooked it over the drakini's wing, dragging it to the ground and stabbing it in the back of the head with a dagger before retrieving his axe from the corpse.

Another drakini dropped straight down on top of Abigail, crushing her into Ixabrax's back spikes and cutting through her armor where his talons dug into her shoulders. She felt the warmth of her own blood soaking into her undershirt as the drakini launched into the air, dragging her with it. The pain was so sudden, so unexpected, that Abigail didn't fully comprehend what was happening until she was a good twenty feet in the air. She dropped her bow, a magical gift that had served her so well for so long—it was useless in this moment.

She drew the Thinblade. Even grasping for it in a moment of desperation, when she couldn't get a good hold on the hilt, the Sword of Kings still felt like it was made for her hand. The drakini's legs came free of the rest of its body just below the knees.

Abigail fell.

She hit the ground hard, breaking her left leg with a loud snap, sending a jolt of pain so intense that she forgot to breathe. Anatoly hobbled up, scooping up her bow along the way, kneeling next to her, looking into her eyes and nodding.

"She's hurt, help me get her onto the dragon."

Magda took his instruction without question or debate, stabilizing Abigail while Anatoly maneuvered her onto Ixabrax's neck.

The remaining drakini were fleeing the aerie in the face of the four furious dragons. Ixabrax launched into the night sky with a roar and his family followed him. He flew low and steady toward the crevasse, landing near the edge and letting Anatoly and Magda go to work on Abigail while waiting for the rest of his family to arrive.

Alexander appeared, standing over his sister while Anatoly fashioned a splint.

"You all right?" he asked.

"Been better," Abigail said through gritted teeth. Then she passed out, overwhelmed by pain when Anatoly set the bone and fastened the splint in place. He worked quickly and efficiently, with a mixture of great care and emotional detachment.

With her leg set, Magda broke some pungent flower buds open under Abigail's nose and roused her from her pain-induced unconsciousness. She woke stunned from the pain, but managed to accept it and take it into her, mastering the hold it had over her and regaining some control over her body.

Magda cast what limited healing magic she had over the leg, but it was a small remedy next to the kind of magic contained in a healing draught. Next, Magda cast a spell that numbed the pain, not removing it exactly, just making it feel like it was far away and unimportant. Abigail began to relax and clear her head.

Once his family had landed, Ixabrax introduced them to Alexander and Abigail.

Izzulft stepped forward. "I speak for my family. I will hear what you wish to say."

"My name is Alexander Reishi. I am at war with Zuhl, and he's using your family against my soldiers. Help me free your remaining children so he can never use dragons against us again."

"Motives that I understand," Izzulft said, regarding Alexander intently. "Bargain struck. What is your plan?"

"I'll tell you where they are, you hold them down, and Abigail cuts their collars."

"Simple, direct, and effective," Izzulft said. "I like it. Proceed."

Alexander vanished for a minute or so and then reappeared. "All three just launched from the aerie and they're headed this way, backed up by a hundred drakini or more. All three dragons have riders ... one of them looks like Zuhl."

"I'm not ready to fight yet," Abigail said. "My leg is broken. I can't even stand."

"No, but you could ride," Alexander said. "Tie on to Ixabrax's neck and he'll get you close enough to cut the collar while Izzulft holds the dragon down and everyone else watches your back. Go from one to the next, taking the rider first, then freeing the dragon."

Abigail grimaced in pain, nodding nonetheless.

"I know it hurts, Abby. I wish there was another way."

"Me too," she said, turning to Anatoly. "Help me tie on to Ixabrax. If we're going to do this, I need Magda riding another dragon to attack the enemy riders."

"I will allow it," Nix said.

Magda bowed formally with the utmost respect to Ixabrax's mother.

"You will ride my youngest, Human," Izzulft said to Anatoly. "This battle is liable to stretch out across leagues ... we wouldn't want to misplace you."

Anatoly grumbled to himself but held his tongue.

Abigail was relieved that the agony of getting mounted atop Ixabrax was finally over, that her pain had subsided into a low throb, but she knew it wouldn't last. The battle would be an exercise in agony. Flight required using your arms and legs to remain stable in your saddle ... more so when you didn't have a saddle.

Abigail closed her eyes and focused on her breathing while she waited for the enemy to draw near. Magda mounted, as did Anatoly, riding Ixabrax's youngest brother, Khazad. At the sound of the enemy's approach floating on the cold night air, all three quaffed dragon draught, the last of their supply. Coldness flowed into Abigail's veins.

The enemy crested a rise and formed up for an attack run. All four dragons leapt into the air, scattering in different directions. Abigail gasped in pain, willing her mind to focus on the fight and not on her injury, but was still distracted by the pulsating agony in her broken leg. Zuhl's trio of young dragons remained in formation, targeting Izzulft. The elder dragon roared in defiance and gained altitude, easily outpacing his children.

Nix carried Magda into the sky, following her mate in a wide orbit, waiting for a chance to strike. Her youngest son, Khazad flew at her wing, carrying Anatoly. Ixabrax waited off to the side, orbiting in wider circles.

Spells from the three riders fell short. Izzulft tipped over and fell into a dive, gaining terrible speed and closing the distance to the dragon on the right of the formation in seconds. He crashed into his daughter and grappled her wings tight against her chest, falling with her while his tail snaked around and cut the man riding her in half.

As they plummeted to the ground, Ixabrax altered course to glide toward the spot where Izzulft intended to land. "Be ready, I'll get you as close as possible."

Abigail slipped her hand through the thong on the Thinblade. Izzulft continued to fall with the other two dragons in tight dives behind him. Ixabrax altered course to intercept one of his sisters.

All Abigail could do was hold on and endure the pain, waiting to cut a collar while dragons battled around her. She started laughing at the insanity of it all.

Nix made a run at the lagging dragon that was chasing Izzulft to the ground, breathing frost in a great cloud, icing the wings of her daughter and collapsing the shield of the priest riding her. Magda waited until they had passed before unleashing her spell, a dozen shards of magical force, one after the next, leapt from her hand, streaking to the target and hitting the priest in the back with unerring precision. He slumped forward against the dragon's neck.

Izzulft broke their fall at the last moment, sparing his daughter a crushing death but dropping her hard enough to stun her, while remaining aloft and banking sharply toward the dragon still diving toward him. Zuhl loosed his spell. An orb of amber, tinted with blackness, shot toward Izzulft, transforming into a wide circular net at the last moment and collapsing around him, midair. Izzulft lost strength and folded his wings, falling nearly a hundred feet to the ground.

He hit hard.

Rolling to a stop on the glacier, the elder dragon groaned but didn't try to get back up. Zuhl pressed the attack, crash-landing on top of Izzulft and dismounting with a collar in hand, while Izzulft's daughter held him down. The moment Zuhl's foot touched the ground, Izzulft thrust into the air, carrying his daughter with him. He flew in an arc that brought them down near Ixabrax, landing on top of his daughter and holding her head down to expose the collar.

Ixabrax extended his head and neck close to his struggling sister, so Abigail could reach out with the Thinblade. She clenched her teeth in pain but managed to cut the collar cleanly and quickly. A moment later, Ixabrax's sister stopped struggling and Izzulft let her up. When Ixabrax launched into the air again, Abigail gasped in agony, fighting to remain conscious.

All at once the cacophony of battle was interrupted by the roar of a hundred drakini pouring over the nearest ridge. They split evenly between the now five free dragons and fanned out to attack en masse. One of the two remaining collared dragons circled in protection of Zuhl, while he removed the corpse in the saddle of the other and fastened himself in. A few moments later, he was airborne again with the second dragon riding his right wing.

Abigail felt sudden, stabbing pain with each thrust as Ixabrax struggled to gain altitude and distance from the twenty drakini pursuing him. Once he leveled off and started to glide in a wide circle, Abigail managed to wrest her focus from the insistent claim of such intense pain. She scanned the enemy below, all of them struggling to reach such a height, a few coming close, but none succeeding.

Calmly, Abigail nocked an arrow and took aim. The arrow sailed out and down, rapidly gaining speed, but falling well short. She adjusted her aim and fired again, this time scoring a direct hit in the back of a drakini circling below. It tried to glide to the ground but lost control, crashing in a jumble of broken bones.

Izzulft flew straight at the twenty drakini targeting him, crashing into several, claw, fang, and tail thrashing about in a whirl, dead drakini spinning off of him as he passed through their formation and spread his wings to gain altitude for another attack. The wave of drakini, now half their original number, turned to meet the dragon's next charge.

Magda, riding Nix, was working to get an angle on Zuhl and the remaining two dragons under his control. Anatoly, riding Khazad, was floating along behind her, attacking any drakini that got too close. Ixabrax adjusted his course to be as close to his collared siblings as possible should he need to deliver Abigail and the Thinblade.

Zuhl banked sharply, turning into Magda and unleashing an ice spike six feet long and a foot wide and moving fast enough to cut a man in two. Magda stretched out, reaching past Nix's neck, and projected a force wall below them. It manifested as an opaque, grey pane of energy and it only lasted for a few seconds, but the ice spike exploded into vapor on impact.

Nix breathed a cloud of frost at Zuhl, but his shield pulsed red and the frost blew past him as steam. She banked up and to the left, circling away from Zuhl, gaining altitude. Zuhl broke away to the right and circled around on Izzulft, who was nearly finished slaughtering all twenty of the drakini that had attacked him. Zuhl got around behind him and cast another paralysis net, the amber orb expanding into a fine mesh that started to settle over Izzulft's wings. This time he lifted his wings straight up and fell, escaping from under the net and avoiding the paralyzing effect of its touch.

Breaking his fall perilously close to the ground, Izzulft landed hard, crouching low for just a moment before thrusting into the air again. He gained altitude quickly, closing on Zuhl with each stroke. Zuhl cast an ice spike, Izzulft ducked and the six-foot-long shard of ice ricocheted off his back, shattering into pieces. He renewed his pursuit, clawing his way through the air toward his daughter and the mage that had enslaved them for so long.

Floating overhead on Nix, Magda loosed her spell. She knew it wouldn't penetrate Zuhl's shield, but that wasn't her purpose—she meant to distract him just long enough for Izzulft to close the distance. A dozen shards of magical force slammed into Zuhl's shield, one after the next. It wasn't a complicated spell, but it was quick and effective, two qualities that Magda favored for combat spells.

Zuhl looked up for just a moment before returning his full attention to Izzulft. As the elder dragon closed the gap, Zuhl removed a ring he was wearing and held it out toward Izzulft. Holding the dragon's eyes, he pronounced an ancient word and tossed the ring into the air. It vanished in a flare of total blackness. A moment later the two remaining collars flared the same black, and the dragons' heads came free in midair, two of Izzulft's children dead in an instant and plunging to the ground.

Zuhl leapt free of his saddle and fell toward the ground, slowing to a manageable speed and landing lightly. All of the dragons howled in fury and pain—two of their family were dead. The man responsible stood in open defiance below them. All eyes fell on him.

He stood in the snow, his white battle armor and long flowing snow-fox cloak blending into the surroundings. He didn't run or hide or flinch when the dragons roared. He stood his ground and began preparing a spell, while the remaining twenty or so drakini flocked to him, surrounding him in a complete cordon.

Khazad flew over him, breathing a cloud of frigid air as he passed. Anatoly watched as some of the drakini were forced to the ground, their wings iced up, but Zuhl was unfazed, his shield completely absorbing the cold of the attack and countering it with heat while he focused on the words of his spell. An arrow bounced off his shield a moment later. Abigail cursed.

Magda cast a small blue orb at him. It hit his shield, depleting it in a few seconds, leaving Zuhl completely vulnerable, but still, he focused on the words of his spell.

Abigail loosed another arrow. She was a long way away but her aim was true, she knew she had him the moment the shaft left the bow. She held her breath while the arrow sailed through the air in a graceful arc, counting her heartbeats until it hit.

Zuhl looked up, spreading his arms wide, an orb of utter blackness materializing above him. A moment later it pulsed, sending out a rapidly expanding shell of darkness. When the darkness passed over each dragon, a black tether linked them from their chest to the orb floating over Zuhl's head. Ixabrax was the only one spared, too far away for the spell to reach him.

Zuhl pronounced the final word loudly and defiantly. Abigail's arrow buried in his chest to the feathers only the briefest moment later. Magda's light-lance was next, burning a hole through the simulacrum where his heart was supposed to be. Zuhl slumped to the ground, dead.

In the span of the following three seconds, all of the darkness contained within the orb floating over Zuhl's head drained into the four dragons. Each became stiff almost instantly, frozen in place, the pure blackness of Zuhl's magic running its course. All four fell from the sky, their wings becoming so brittle that they shattered and broke off during the fall. Each hit the ground, exploding into a pile of blackened remains.

Anatoly hit hard, falling from Khazad and winding up nearly buried in the broken, desiccated remains of the murdered dragon. Magda leapt free of Nix and landed lightly in the snow nearby, watching in horror as all four dragons crashed to the ground and shattered into mounds of broken black, leaving terrible stains in the snow where they fell.

Ixabrax howled in a low wail, a death knell that carried on the wind for miles. Abigail felt such desperate sorrow in his cry. The pain of his loss was palpable, emanating from him in waves and all but overwhelming. She didn't say anything, choosing instead to cry silently. And not just for Ixabrax's loss, but for the guilt she felt for her part in it.

In retrospect, she should have known, she chided herself. Of course Zuhl would have a contingency plan, of course he would never allow the dragons he'd controlled for so long to roam free.

Ixabrax landed amid the lifeless ash of his family, falling silent and still. Abigail held her breath. Magda was moving toward Anatoly, but otherwise, the place was as still as a tomb.

"What have I done?" Ixabrax said. "My whole family ... dead."

"You didn't do this. Zuhl did," Abigail said.

Quicker than a cat, Ixabrax reached around, snatched her off his back and tossed her into the snow. Pain exploded from her leg. She gasped, tried to scream but couldn't. She rolled to a stop and lay still, gathering her wits and struggling to focus her mind on the angry dragon instead of on her broken leg.

"Listen well, Human," Ixabrax said. "Our business is done. You have failed to deliver my family and so my obligations to you end here. Do not seek me out again." His anger melted into sadness as if he'd forgotten Abigail's very existence and all that was left surrounding him were the remains of his family. With a howl of anguish, Ixabrax launched into the sky, turning north, away from Zuhl, away from his past ... and away from humanity.

Chapter 44

"Trajan, you have to come out of there for this to work," Isabel said, standing in the hallway leading to the crystal chamber. Ayela and Hazel, both bound and gagged, were each sitting in the center of one chamber, though Hazel, in Ayela's body, was struggling mightily to squirm out of the circle.

"She's trying to get free again," Trajan said.

"I know. Let one of your men handle it so they can use that thing and make this right," Isabel said. "As long as you and that bone are anywhere near this room, it won't work."

Trajan looked down at the femur he'd taken from the chamber. The bone was solid and sturdy with a large knot on each end, perfect for use as a club. He'd wrapped a leather thong around the end with the smaller knot. Isabel had selected a finger bone and tied a thong around it to make a necklace, concealing it underneath her tunic.

Trajan nodded and followed Isabel into the passage.

"All right, Hector, we should be far enough away," she said.

It had taken days for Trajan's men to dig them free of the Goiri's crypt, but they worked methodically with the air of men who knew that they were working toward a successful outcome. Isabel and Trajan spent a lot of time talking during those days. He was furious about the Sin'Rath and vowed to hunt them to extinction, exactly the reaction Isabel had hoped for.

After significant convincing, he accepted that his sister was living within an old woman's body and spent some time threatening Hazel with a variety of very painful ways to die. Hazel was, of course, gagged and bound, so it was a very one-sided conversation.

There were a number of smaller rooms at even intervals surrounding the main chamber where the Goiri had died, all accessible through large archways. The remains of furniture, glassware, and books littered the floors, but it looked as if the whole place had been destroyed in a mad rage a long time ago.

Isabel had gone to one room after the next, peering inside, hoping to find something useful and being disappointed, until she came to a very unusual room. It was rectangular, longer than it was wide. The walls, floor, and ceiling were made of stone in the first part of the room but gradually transformed into crystal shot through with gold near the far end. A low bench ran the width of the room along the far wall, carved from the same crystal and gold as the rest of that end of the room, with a large crystal bowl in the center of the bench. She peered into the bowl, expecting to find some kind of treasure, but found only dust. Still the room caught her imagination and set her mind to wondering.

During the days that Trajan's men worked to dig them free, Isabel found ample time to read the two spellbooks she'd taken from Hazel.

The charm spell was powerful and insidious, relying not on anger or love for the distracting emotion, but hate. At first, Isabel was surprised and confused by the nature of the spell, but soon came to understand the level of contempt toward another person one must feel in order to deprive them of their free will through such magic. That kind of contempt could only be the product of hate. Isabel got the impression that this charm spell was a variation of a more basic spell, one that relied on love, but she couldn't be sure. In any event, she didn't think she'd be making use of this spell anytime soon.

The shapeshift spell was another matter. It could be powered by either love or anger and it had a wide range of applications. Changing into something of similar weight and size was the most basic form of the spell, allowing the caster to assume another person's appearance, but the spell was much more potent for witches with the power and talent to make use of it. A High Witch could transform into a creature or object a hundred times her size or a hundred times smaller. At that level, the shapeshift spell became incredibly versatile. Isabel spent most of her time studying the spell, though she couldn't actually learn it since the Goiri bones prevented her from practicing. That didn't stop her from committing the spell to memory so she could practice it when she had the chance.

After they'd freed themselves from the Goiri's crypt, they went straight to the crystal chamber. Hazel resisted, of course, so two of Trajan's men had to bodily carry her. The same two tied a rope under her knees and looped it behind her neck. With her hands tied behind her back, she was unable to move out of the magic circle.

Hector pushed the large emerald in the center of the panel. Nothing happened.

Several seconds passed before the crystal began to glow, increasing in intensity very quickly, until it was so bright that even Isabel and Trajan down the hall were blinded.

The light subsided as quickly as it had come, plunging the chamber into relative darkness with only two torches for light.

Isabel approached Ayela and untied her legs, then removed her gag. "Convince me," she said.

Ayela proceeded to answer questions from both Isabel and Trajan for several minutes until both were satisfied that she was herself again. Hector stood back and watched until the verdict was determined, then roughly picked Hazel up and tossed her frail old body over his shoulder like a sack of potatoes.

"It's time," he said, handing Ayela Hazel's bag of potions and powders.

"Are you sure you want to go through with this?" Isabel asked.

For some reason she was torn. She knew at a very fundamental level that working with the darkness, even in the smallest way, always had a downside, but ... for reasons she couldn't quite explain, she wanted to see the ghidora summoned, she wanted Hector to send it to kill Phane. Even if he survived the attack, it was an attack that he just about had to meet in person. The satisfaction of bringing the war to his doorstep was very alluring. For far too long, he'd sent his minions after them. The chance to retaliate in kind was compelling. Yet ... where darkness was involved ... darkness was involved.

"Yes."

"It could have consequences," Isabel said.

"I know," Hector said, stepping around her as he carried Hazel toward the black-and-white room.

Isabel followed him, trying to come up with an argument that might reach him, some string of words that would change the loss he felt or undo his implacable need for vengeance. Nothing came to her. Hazel deserved to die, but Isabel was far more worried about the consequences of involving a demon in the process.

Hector didn't waver. He carried Hazel over his shoulder like so much produce until he was before the altar, looking at the remains of his brother. He set Hazel aside and very carefully picked up Horace's corpse, carrying him to the far side of the room and gently laying him on the floor next to the wall.

"I wish I could do more for you, Brother," Hector whispered.

He strode up to a wide-eyed Hazel and stopped, looking down on her, his expression a condemnation. Then he picked her up and put her on the altar. When she struggled, he sat her up and slapped her across the face so hard that her head lolled to the side. Hector laid her down and started chanting the words engraved on the altar without any hesitation.

"You don't have to do this," Isabel said.

Hector ignored her, chanting more forcefully, his voice filling the large chamber. Hazel came to her senses and started to get up when she was seized by wisps of black smoke suddenly appearing all around her. She froze in place, paralyzed by her life essence draining away from her and into the ghidora.

Streamers of energy, most dark and muddy, flowed from Hazel to the stalker-demon until she shriveled up and died, the beast coming alive, its eyes and tail blades glowing with power and murder. It leapt from its circle and ran down the large corridor to the opening in the side of the mountain ... and then it was gone.

Hector slumped to his knees, crying with his head in his hands. Isabel left him to his grief, but Trajan and his men were alarmed by the turn of events. The prince started to approach Hector, when Isabel intercepted him, pulling him aside.

"What just happened?"

"Hector just avenged his brother by sacrificing Hazel in exactly the same way she sacrificed Horace."

Trajan looked at the platform, then at Horace's corpse and nodded. "I accept Hector's motives, but what of the demon? Such a thing cannot be allowed to roam free."

"It won't. Hector sent it to kill Phane," Isabel said. "Then it will come back here."

"Do you think it will succeed?"

"No," Isabel said. "But at least Phane will know we're thinking about him, and that's worth something."

"I have never seen such a monstrous thing," Trajan said. "How could anyone stand against it, even Phane?"

"Magic," Isabel said.

Trajan hefted his club and looked at it intently. "If magic can defeat such a thing, and if this bone can resist magic, then this club makes me the equal of any wizard or witch."

"Perhaps, but all it takes is one well-placed blade and you'll fall just the same as anyone else," Isabel said. "Don't let the power of that club go to your head."

"How can I not?" Trajan said. "With this, I can finally rid my house of the Sin'Rath and kill Phane as well."

"One thing at a time," Isabel said. "Just remember, you can still die from an arrow, or a sword, or a dagger, or a jaguar, or from those horrible leeches in the swamp or ..."

"I get your point," Trajan said, forestalling her with a hand held up in surrender. "Where would you go from here?"

"After the Sin'Rath," Isabel said. "I don't know how many there were in the first place, but Phane killed one, and I watched a wraithkin kill one, and Hazel sent the ghidora after another."

"That would mean there are ten left at the most," Trajan said. "We won't be able to track the two that traveled with us through the swamp, so I recommend we return to our fortress and see if we can figure out where they went from there."

"I agree," Isabel said. "Do you know another way out of here?"

"I was hoping you did," Trajan said. "We came in through the top of the mountain and were set upon by gargoyles, dozens of them. I arrived here with twenty-four men, I have seven left."

Isabel looked down the tunnel leading to the opening used by the ghidora and weighed her options.

"It's worth a look," Trajan said, motioning for two of his men to go investigate. They returned half an hour later, describing a thousand-foot cliff marred by claw marks. It was sheer, smooth, and nearly perfectly vertical.

They returned to the black-and-white room, then went up the spiral stairs to the barracks level, through the dining hall to the staircase on the opposite end, and up. After several flights, they came to another barracks level identical to the one below. Two more levels followed as they corkscrewed up through the heart rock of the mountain. The stair came to an end in a nondescript stone room.

Beyond that room, they found themselves in a partially collapsed basement. Trajan led them on a path through the debris, following markers he'd laid down as he entered, climbing a partially caved in ceiling to the level above and eventually to an exit.

"Gargoyles line the walls," he said, pointing up at the inanimate guardian statues. There were dozens of them. Isabel was acutely aware of her limitations without magic. She would have to fight creatures made of stone with nothing but swords.

"I don't like those odds," Isabel said.

"Nor do I," Trajan said, "but I know of no other way out."

"Do we know if the bones do anything to them?"

Trajan looked at the femur he'd transformed into a club. The hilt was wrapped with a leather thong that ended in a lanyard, and he'd begun to carve symbols into the bone.

"I will go alone," he said, "draw them out and flee if they're able to overcome the bones. Remain hidden."

Trajan stepped out into the daylight, took three strides and stopped, waiting for the gargoyles to react. He didn't have long to wait. Seconds later, three woke and leapt off the wall, spreading their wings and diving toward him. The Prince of Karth held his ground, his club ready to strike, preparing to hit the first that got close to him. They lined up, one behind the next. Each evened out into a graceful dive that would bring it down on top of Trajan, one after another.

He waited.

When the first reached a range of about thirty feet, it very suddenly transformed into fine sand and scattered to the ground. The next in line disintegrated as well when it got too close, but the final of the three pulled up and returned to the wall, eyeing Trajan with menace.

Isabel and her party escaped the walls of the ruins under the watchful eyes of two dozen gargoyles, all awake but all remaining on the wall, thwarted by the Goiri's bones. When they entered the jungle, momentary relief at avoiding a fight with the gargoyles was quickly replaced with fear of jungle predators. Keenly aware of the dangers surrounding them, they moved slowly through the brush to avoid making too much noise. Trajan assigned one of his men to teach Isabel stealth in the jungle. Using nothing but hand signals, he guided Isabel until she'd learned to move quietly.

Nearly halfway down the mountain, Trajan stopped and went to a knee, signaling to the man behind him—there were three raptors ahead. Isabel was impressed with how disciplined his men were. She watched and obeyed as well as she could, going to a knee and relaying the hand signal to the man behind her. Within seconds, the entire group was low and quiet while Trajan formulated a plan.

He waved three of his men to him as he produced a small box and opened it carefully. Each of the three men carefully dipped a blowgun dart into the goop inside the box. Once armed, they melted into the jungle, circling the raptors while remaining downwind, flanking the predators until they could get the shot. Time stretched out. The jungle was silent. Isabel started to wonder. She would be watching through Slyder were it not for the cursed bone hanging around her neck.

Her anxiety started to build, worry transforming into fear and nearly spiking into panic when the three men finally returned and Trajan motioned for everyone to proceed quietly.

Isabel's sudden panic faded away as quickly as it had assailed her. She pondered it while she walked. She'd never experienced anything like it in her life, debilitating fear in the face of … nothing. It was unnerving.

All three raptors were down and unconscious, felled by poisoned darts delivering venom powerful enough to overcome even them. They moved past them and reached the edge of the swamp by late afternoon. Trajan cursed when they arrived at the spot where they'd left their rafts. All of them were gone, simply vanished.

"I have a boat farther south," Isabel offered.

"How many will it hold?"

"Probably seven, plus I have a raft that can hold the other four."

It didn't take long to reach Isabel's hiding place, load everybody into the boats and cast off. Isabel was more than happy to be leaving the mountain. She had what she'd come for … and the place had been less than welcoming.

Trajan set a grueling pace for his men, rowing the boat and poling the raft as fast as they could go, without interruption, one team of rowers taking over for the previous team, ensuring that forward motion never stopped. They reached the inner band of high ground late the following day with just enough time before dark to build a fire.

Trajan sat in front of the fire, the Goiri bone heavy end down between his feet, his hands resting on the pommel. "With this, I could rid Karth of magic once and for all."

His men nodded, murmuring their agreement.

"I could eliminate it from all the Seven Isles."

His men stopped nodding and started looking at each other.

"Magic is not evil, Trajan," Ayela said. She'd been very quiet since Hazel had been sacrificed. "It can be used for good as well."

"It's too much power to be entrusted to any one person," Trajan said. "Magic can do terrible things. Look what it did to our family—even to the Regency command staff."

"Bad people did those things," Ayela said. "They just used magic to make them happen."

"My point exactly," Trajan said. "If they didn't have magic in the first place, they wouldn't be able to do such things. Eliminate magic and preserve the world."

"And how do you plan to eliminate magic?" Ayela asked. "Are you going to start murdering people just because they have magic?"

Trajan frowned, his state of mind suddenly shifted by the slap-in-the-face tone of his sister's rebuke. He shook his head slightly as if facing his own statements for the first time and finding them abhorrent. "I'm not sure why I said that," he muttered, still shaking his head.

Isabel absentmindedly played with the Goiri bone hanging around her neck while she watched the exchange. She needed Trajan, both in the short term to get where she was going and in the long term as an ally, but his behavior was starting to worry her.

He quietly excused himself and slipped off into the mist. Not a minute later, he cried out for help.

Everyone came to their feet, drawing weapons and moving toward his voice. He wasn't forty steps outside the camp, just beyond the range of sight, and he was completely wrapped up by a giant snake, lying on his side, one arm free, struggling to breathe. The black-scaled monster was easily forty feet long and it had a good eight feet of itself wavering threateningly over Trajan's head, six coils wrapped around his body and the rest trailing out behind him into the mist.

Trajan's men spread out, surrounding the snake, but it hissed and struck, driving them back a step or two. Isabel tossed Trajan her dagger. He clawed around in the dirt blindly until his hand found steel, then came up with the blade and plunged it into the first coil of the snake. The snake flinched, loosening its grip, giving Trajan a precious gulp of air, before tightening around him again.

He stabbed again, and again. Each time, the snake recoiled but not enough for him to get free. One of his men got too close, jabbing at the snake with a spear. It dodged right and struck, four-inch fangs piercing into the man's chest in a blink, then recoiling just as fast, leaving the man still standing for just a moment before he realized he was dead and fell over.

Trajan buried the knife to the hilt and started sawing across the snake's body. It started to unwind, but Trajan held on, cutting crosswise, trying to cut it in half, until it tore free and vanished into the swamp. He got to his feet and handed Isabel her dagger with a nod of thanks before retrieving his club and turning toward the fire. He made it just one step before he collapsed, coughing up blood.

Chapter 45

They carried him to the fire and laid him down, but that only seemed to make things worse. He seized up in pain, gasping in short breaths, rolling on his side and curling into a ball. His men looked from one to the other and shook their heads in resignation. He'd been crushed by a giant snake. Most people didn't survive such a thing.

Isabel walked over and picked up the club, Ayela forestalling any protest from Trajan's men with a withering glare while standing over her wounded brother. Isabel walked away into the swamp, far enough for Hector's last healing potion to work. Without it, Trajan would die. With it, he'd be on his feet in a couple of days. When she asked Ayela if they should use it, given Trajan's feelings about magic, Ayela insisted they use it immediately.

When Isabel and the Goiri bone were far enough away, Ayela administered the potion, much to the consternation of Trajan's men. They protested loudly but she ignored them as she tipped her brother's head back. After swallowing the draught, he fell into a fitful sleep, becoming feverish in the night and waking frequently.

By morning, he was sleeping soundly and it looked like the worst of his injuries were mended. Isabel kept the club away from him while the potion did its work. She didn't know if the Goiri bone would stop the potion from working at this point, but she didn't want to take the risk.

By evening, he was up and mended well enough to walk. Isabel gave him back his club.

"Ayela tells me she demanded magic be used to heal me."

"Yes," Isabel said.

He nodded, frowning. "Thank you," he muttered, turning away from her.

They set out the following morning on a maddening journey through a maze of high ground that didn't often connect. Without Slyder, Isabel felt blind. She'd always taken him for granted, or at least the power he gave her ... now she recognized just what a blessing he really was.

They reached the far side of the high ground several frustrating days later. Tensions were high. The mist was starting to bear down on them, pressing in from all sides like it meant them harm, creating anxiety, fear, even panic. They'd had to backtrack dozens of times and they'd gotten turned around several times, but they'd finally reached deep water. One last stretch and they would be free of the insistent desolation all around them.

It took a day to harvest the wood for the two rafts they would need and another day to build them. They set out at dawn the following morning, poling across the water with two men working together on each raft to move them at best speed. By dark, they'd traversed the majority of the band of water circling the outskirts of the gloaming swamp, but they chose to tie off to a tree and wait for dawn before proceeding.

By dark the following day, they were several leagues into the jungle and feeling much better for it. Spirits were high when they stopped to make camp. The chittering, burbling, singing life all around was a stark and welcome contrast to the lifeless desolation of the swamp. Isabel was buoyed by the abundance surrounding her, wishing she could share it with Alexander as she drifted off to sleep.

The journey to the hidden keep took several days along a path selected by Trajan to be both direct and little used. What it turned out to be was an overgrown game trail. On the second day, two dozen tree rats attacked by surprise, but they all targeted the last man in line, swarming over him, driving him to his knees and killing him in a matter of seconds.

Everyone watched with a mixture of fear and revulsion, stunned by the sudden speed and overwhelming violence of the attack, until a number of tree rats turned toward them and hissed in challenge, guarding their next meal.

They moved with more care from then on which slowed them down but also prevented them from blundering into the clearing in front of the cave mouth leading to the fortress entrance.

Trajan signaled—four Regency soldiers—everyone went to a knee. He pointed to three of his men and signaled for them to circle the clearing and attack from a different angle, then waited for them to reach their position before silently ordering his remaining two men to follow him into battle.

All six charged into the clearing without a word, closing the distance to the four soldiers before they could fully process what was happening. Overwhelming force, coupled with the element of total surprise produced predictable results. Trajan reached his intended target first, swinging his bone club up and under the side of the soldier's jaw, lifting her up off the ground and twisting her head around with such force that her neck snapped, killing her before the blood spray from her shattered jaw could reach the ground. The remaining three died almost as quickly, two managing to get their swords half drawn before Trajan's men reached them.

Trajan and his companions entered the fortress cautiously, but the place was dead and still. At the main entrance, Isabel saw the remains of a battle she'd fought in days past. Four corpses lay crumpled around the entrance, decomposing just enough to lend a sickly scent to the musty air, all dead by Isabel's hand. Several more killed by others were scattered about, left to rot where they fell. In the center of the room was one of the witches, the greatest stench of decay coming from her corpse.

"So this one is definitely dead," Isabel said. "If we assume the ghidora killed the one Hazel sent it after and Phane killed Clotus, that leaves ten."

"We should make a thorough search of this place," Trajan said. "If more of the witches fell here, I want to know of it."

"You know this place better than anyone," Isabel said. "I recommend we stick together in case we run into more soldiers."

"Agreed," Trajan said.

The place was surprisingly large and Trajan did indeed know it well. He led them through an exhaustive search of the entire fortress, which proved to be a heart-wrenching experience for both him and Ayela. Hundreds of Trajan's soldiers were dead, killed in pitched battles that took place in the halls and barracks. Soldiers fought without full armor, sometimes even without boots because the attack had been so sudden, the enemy had breached the gates so quickly and poured into the fortress in such force that the defenders didn't have time to mount anything but the most hasty of defenses.

From the carnage, it was clear that the Regency soldiers had been ordered to leave no one alive. The dead had suffered various types of wounds, but each and every one of the fallen had another wound, a narrow-bladed dagger puncture to the heart. Even their own dead had been stabbed in the heart and left to rot.

The corpses were piled highest near the outer door of the king's chambers. Isabel had to watch her footing as she climbed over the four-foot pile of bodies. Within, they found more dead, including one of the Sin'Rath who had fallen just inside the king's door and died from a cut to her throat.

The king's chambers were large, cold, and dark. It took nearly an hour of searching to discover the three hidden doors leading out. They would have stopped long before finding the first one, were it not for Trajan's insistence that they keep looking.

"I know my father well enough to know that he has at least two hidden passages," he said. "Keep looking until you find them."

The first passage they found led to a series of more passages that seemed to permeate the entire fortress, shadowing the main passages and allowing access or a view into many important rooms. As well as Ayela knew the secret passages in the fortress, she had to admit she'd never been in these passages.

The second hidden door led to a long tunnel leading into the dark, a cool breeze picking up the moment they opened the door.

The third passage was locked from the inside, an oddity that made Isabel wonder. Further inspection revealed a peephole looking into the room from the hidden passage beyond.

"We should see what's behind there," she said.

"Agreed," Trajan said, motioning to two of his men. They picked up a table and used it as a battering ram to break the door open, thunderous echoes rolling away into the passages of the fortress with each strike. It took some effort, but they eventually succeeded, breaching the door and pulling it apart.

Beyond was a passage that led deeper into the mountain. After a few hundred feet, they came to a wide spot with a fifty-foot-deep pit barring their way. On the far side was a drawbridge operated by a winch with a hand crank.

"If you and Prince Trajan would stand back, I can cross and lower the bridge," Hector said.

Trajan frowned but followed Isabel back the way they'd come far enough for Hector's magic to work. By the time they returned, the bridge was in place. The corridor, roughly hewn from the mountain and having only rudimentary supports, continued for another hundred feet, opening into a small round cave with three hallways leading out. Two led back toward the part of the fortress occupied by the House of Karth, but the one directly across from them led farther into the mountain.

Another fifty feet and they entered a large irregular cavern lit by a vein of naturally luminescent crystals running through the ceiling. The place was a scene of squalor and filth. At least a dozen creatures had lived here, sharing this single living space, wallowing in each other's excrement. The stench was nauseating. The flies, revolting.

"This is where the Sin'Rath slept," Ayela said.

Trajan turned away from the room. Two of his men vomited.

"I've seen enough," Isabel said, covering her mouth and nose.

"There may still be a witch here," Trajan said. "We must search these chambers, no matter how distasteful it is."

"Well then, let's be quick about it," Isabel said, drawing her sword and heading to one of the exits, with Hector falling in behind her.

They searched for over an hour, covering an extensive network of passages and rooms, some locked, some open, others without doors. From this network, the Sin'Rath could view and hear most of the important rooms in the fortress and had access to many of the more important areas via secret passages that connected with the other networks of passages but that locked from the inside.

Isabel was especially interested in one room they found. It opened onto a balcony encircling a pit below. On one wall of the pit was a stout door locked from the outside. A hole in the ceiling of the cave allowed a stream of daylight to fill the well of the pit while plunging the rest of the room into shadow. It looked very different from here, Isabel thought.

They found a few passages leading to the surface but they were all still locked and barred from within, so they decided to keep looking, reasoning that the Sin'Rath had escaped by some other route.

While the search revealed nothing new, it did serve to reinforce the absolute nature of the Sin'Rath's treachery. For Trajan and Ayela, it felt like mockery. The Sin'Rath had been in control of everything … for their whole lives. They'd been watching, waiting … planning how they would use each member of the Karth line in their schemes.

Having completely searched the fortress, they left through the secret escape tunnel from Severine's chamber, walking into the cool breeze toward the surface. It opened behind a boulder inside a cave with a natural underground river surfacing in a rushing torrent and cascading out of the cave mouth and down the hillside.

Isabel knelt down, Trajan right beside her, examining footprints in the soft riverbank soil.

"Many people came this way," Trajan said.

"They'll be easy enough to follow," Isabel said. "The hard part will be spotting when the witches break away from the refugees."

"Not with all of us looking," Trajan said, motioning for one of his men to take point. They followed the trail from the cave and into the jungle for several hours before they came to a clearing littered with bodies, some were fallen soldiers from both the Regency and Karth, others were just people fleeing the Regency; some died by the blade, others were killed with magic.

The many paths leading from the clearing were all filled with carnage as if the refugees fleeing the fortress had scattered into the jungle the moment the Regency soldiers ambushed them. Trajan and his men began the painstaking process of following each path for a small distance and discovered that they all circled around to the same place, behind and to the left of the spot where they got ambushed. From there, the survivors of the ambush circled around and continued on into the jungle.

Their path took them over a small mountain pass and down to a major road that intersected two other major roads within a few leagues in each direction. Those who had escaped the fortress had camped by the road for the night and then gone in different directions, melting away into the jungle. Isabel looked at the trampled roadside where several dozen people had camped along it all at the same time and shook her head.

"Any idea how we can track the Sin'Rath from here?" she asked. "They could be anywhere by now."

"I was thinking the same thing," Trajan said, then smiling suddenly and pointing before taking off at a dead run down the road. Some distance away, another man scrambled out of the jungle, running away from Trajan down the middle of the road. Trajan stopped and returned, smiling and schooling his breath.

"Now we have something to track," he said.

"Who was that?"

"One of my father's men, a watcher assigned to wait here and see if anyone showed up. He will run back to my father and report our arrival."

"So the witches will know we're still tracking them," Isabel said. "We might not want to just follow that guy blindly back to them."

Trajan hefted his club. "The witches have no power."

"Maybe not," Isabel said, "but they can always give bows to the hundred men they have working for them. A hundred arrows may not be magic, but they will kill you just the same, club or not."

"I'll send two men ahead to scout," Trajan said.

"Fair enough," Isabel said. "Let's go ... but carefully." It was becoming painfully clear that Trajan was going to do what he was going to do, regardless of Isabel's suggestions. She turned her thoughts to figuring out how she was going to get close to Phane, and exactly what she was going to do once she did.

The man's tracks doubled back and looped around the other direction, meeting up with a set of almost forty older tracks marching two by two along a narrow jungle path away from the road. The scouts continued to range out ahead of them, searching out the path taken by the watcher, marking the trail and pressing forward.

After several hours of steady movement, the scouts were waiting alongside the path for them. They were in a rough part of the jungle. Cliffs, sudden steep hills and rocky outcroppings were the norm, with all manner of vegetation clinging to every surface possible. Travel was treacherous and slow.

"They left the trail up ahead," Trajan whispered, as his scouts followed the trail farther. Everyone was quiet, waiting for word from the two men, but time passed and they didn't return.

While they waited, Isabel started to worry that the Sin'Rath had captured them and were sending soldiers. Her idle worry seemed to take on a life of its own within her mind, expanding into fear and full-blown panic within the space of a few moments. She crouched with the rest of Trajan's men, shivering in fear of some imagined threat. Ayela noticed something was wrong and touched her arm with an inquiring look.

Isabel nearly leapt out of her skin at the sudden contact, her panic breaking and fading away like water. She shook her head to Ayela and went back to her own thoughts. Never before had she experienced such sudden and irrational fear. It couldn't be Azugorath, or the darkness, or anything else magical.

That left two possibilities: either she was becoming a coward … or it was the bone.

Chapter 46

After it had become painfully clear that something had happened to the scouts, Trajan led everyone along the path they'd taken and were relieved to meet them returning to make their report. They'd found a cave with a door at the back of it about ten minutes away. Had the Sin'Rath and House of Karth not left so many footprints, the cave would have remained completely hidden.

"So that's one way in," Trajan said.

"You think there might be another?" Isabel asked.

"I'm certain of it. There will be at least one escape passage and probably another entrance as well."

"If we could find the escape tunnel, I bet it would lead straight to the king's chambers. We could get behind them," Isabel said, "and avoid fighting your men altogether."

"That may be more difficult than you imagine," Trajan said. "Escape tunnels are often deliberately unfinished, with three or four feet left to dig so the exit point can't be easily found."

The rear guard raced up, low and quiet, and whispered something to Trajan, then returned to his post.

"Regency soldiers are coming this way," Trajan said. "They're about ten minutes out."

"We could always hide and let them fight it out," Isabel said.

"If my father weren't inside, I would agree with you. As it stands, we have little choice." He signaled to his point man and they started toward the cave.

The entrance was covered over with hanging vines. Once inside, they found a small cave, measuring ten feet deep, four feet wide, and almost five feet high. The back wall was occupied by a large, stout door. Trajan tried to open it, nodding to himself when it didn't budge.

"If you give me the space I need to use my magic, I can open that door," Hector said.

His tone was monotonous, void of passion or feeling, simply conveying information. Isabel made a mental note of his mood. She'd been worried about him since Horace died, but things had really changed with him after he woke the ghidora. His mood was dark, devoid of passion or humor or desire, as if some essential part of him had gone missing.

Trajan and Isabel withdrew about forty feet from the cave and waited for one of his men to signal. They returned to find the door open and two freshly killed men on the floor—both of them Karth house guard. Hector was cleaning one of his swords.

"What have you done?" Trajan said. "These men were of my house. Why did you kill them?"

"So they wouldn't raise the alarm," Hector said slowly without looking up from cleaning his sword.

Trajan started to take a step toward him, but Ayela stopped him with a hand on his arm.

Isabel went to Hector and stood in front of him, waiting until he looked up at her. She saw so much desolation in his eyes … it worried her.

"Don't kill any more of the Karth guards if you can help it," she said quietly but intently.

He nodded and went back to his sword, checking the sheen by looking along the length of the blade, then carefully, deliberately, sheathing it.

They filed inside, bolting the door behind them, and moved deeper into the underground stronghold with Trajan in the lead. He stopped at a corner, peering around momentarily before quickly pulling his head back.

With hand signals, he indicated three targets, one witch and two house guards. He selected two of his men to attack with him. Then he motioned for everyone else to remain where they were.

Isabel looked around the corner a moment after they moved, watching them race toward the trio without saying a word, weapons up and at the ready. They got within twelve feet before the three turned around. The witch tried to throw some kind of spell at Trajan. The expression on her demonically contorted face transformed from confusion to horror as his club whistled through the air, catching her on the side of the head just above the ear and caving her skull in with one stroke. She slumped to the ground. Trajan's men grappled with the house guard until they could be shown the truth of the Sin'Rath. Once they saw her true form, they both agreed to work with Trajan to kill the rest.

He questioned the two guards intensely for several minutes, gaining a basic understanding of the stronghold's layout and learning where his father and the Sin'Rath were likely to be, then assigned them to lead the way.

They quietly passed many doors, some with muffled sounds of snoring behind them. These people had just fled the Regency in the dead of night, narrowly escaping with their lives. Isabel suspected they were all exhausted; the emptiness of the corridors bore that out. The two guards led them ever deeper, winding through some levels and bypassing others entirely. Where they saw guards, they were able to pass without arousing suspicion because of their uniforms and bearing … until they got close to the witches and Severine.

They came upon two guards at the bottom of several flights of stairs. The guards seemed willing to hear them out, waiting patiently as they approached, until they saw Trajan and Ayela and immediately cried out an alarm, drawing weapons. Their two fellow guards that had joined Trajan attacked them with clubs, knocking their swords aside and lunging into them, followed by two of Trajan's men who took their weapons when they went down.

Isabel smiled as she approached the two men. They stood, held from behind, and looked past her like she wasn't even there. She casually tossed a pinch of sleeping powder into each guard's face. They fell in turn.

Trajan nodded his approval. Isabel knew it was about to become much more difficult to survive without killing. At least a dozen men were coming, footfalls in the distance, but getting closer, and quickly. Trajan deployed his men in a line, each loading a dart into his blowtube and facing the end of the hall. They waited patiently until ten soldiers and two witches stormed around the corner into the wide hallway.

Five blowdarts found five men, each of them toppling to the ground moments later from the potent paralysis poison coating the darts. Both witches raised their hands to cast spells over the fallen van of their guard force, but nothing happened.

"Look at what you serve," Trajan said, pointing his club at the witches. "See the truth of them and strike them down!"

One glimpse of the true form of the Sin'Rath, coupled with the elimination of their magical charms, and the five men bringing up the rear of the witches' guard set upon them with a kind of frenzied ferocity, as if killing them quickly might bring some measure of atonement for ever serving such loathsome creatures.

Two more of the Sin'Rath Coven fell screaming and cursing. That left seven.

After a brief conversation, the guards swore loyalty to Trajan and agreed to help locate Severine Karth and kill the remaining Sin'Rath. He sent one man to the upper levels to warn of the Regency's approach, and instructed another to attend to the seven men left sleeping in the hall. He took the remaining three men with him, expanding the number of soldiers under his command to eight.

The wide corridor turned right without any change in size, then ran straight for fifty feet, ending at a large set of stoutly banded doors, closed and barred from the inside.

"Can you open those doors?" Trajan asked Hector.

"Not if the witches are on the other side."

"They are, I'm certain of it," said one of the guards.

They started to hear the muted sounds of fighting coming from levels above. Isabel felt helpless. Alexander would be able to see through the door, then open it with ease, but then, he wouldn't be able to do anything without his magic. She was helpless because of the Goiri bone. With magic, she could burn a hole through the door.

"Hold this, Ayela," Isabel said, handing her the Goiri bone. Ayela took it, nodding ever so slightly.

Isabel marched off toward the door ... and then it hit her. When she stepped out of the null magic field, Azugorath slammed back into her mind. Isabel crumpled to her knees with a scream that filtered through the entire subterranean complex. Azugorath pushed harder and in several different ways than ever before, trying to capitalize on the first few moments of the attack to overwhelm Isabel ... and it was working. She felt her control slipping. Azugorath was making inroads, moment by moment, worming her way into Isabel's mind.

Then the psychic onslaught was gone ... vanished in an instant.

Ayela raced up to Isabel, kneeling next to her.

"Are you all right?"

Isabel nodded, taking the cursed bone back from her and smiling sadly.

"I'll be fine, but I can't open that door."

The muffled sound of the bar being thrown stopped them all, every eye on the doors as the bolt slid aside. The doors came open in a rush, twenty soldiers standing ready to charge any intruder. Seven witches stood behind them along with Severine Karth and several of his attendants, his man-at-arms, Erastus, among them.

Trajan stepped forth, his hands held wide, club held high.

"I am Trajan Karth, heir to the House of Karth, and I will be heard!"

The soldiers faltered … Trajan got closer.

"I only seek an audience with my father."

"Attack!" one of the witches shrieked.

The commander looked to Severine for the order but the king hesitated. Trajan reached the line of soldiers and the men parted. With sudden quickness, he raced through the men and straight to his father.

The witches howled in fury, but they were too late. Trajan got close enough to his father for the witches' magic to fail, revealing their true nature.

"Behold, Father," Trajan said, pointing with his club, "the true form of the witches you have served for so long."

Peti cried out to her sisters from one of the passages leading out of the room. "Come, we must flee!" Only two heeded her warning quickly enough.

With the spell over Severine Karth and his men broken, the witches looked around frantically for a way to escape. The battle turned very suddenly after that. Trajan marched up to the witch nearest his father and brained her with a stroke of his club, a line of black blood-splatter running diagonally across his face.

Then the soldiers set on the remaining witches, killing another three in moments before turning to pursue the three who had fled into the hidden passage. Isabel was still in the hallway. She'd withdrawn to the corner where she could hear the sounds of battle getting closer by the minute. The Regency was here and they were winning.

An explosion rocked the corridor, dust billowing from a room adjacent to the main room. The three surviving witches had collapsed the ceiling of the escape tunnel.

Isabel raced to the main room.

"Trajan, is there another way out? Regency soldiers are coming fast."

Severine looked old and haggard, like something within him had broken when he learned the truth of the Sin'Rath, but his eyes cleared slightly at Isabel's question.

"One level up is another escape route," he said.

"Lead the way," Isabel said, "we don't have much time."

They reached the level above and found a pitched battle taking place between two squads. The Regency were faring better, employing group tactics, fighting in a formation that took advantage of the limited area of the battlefield, using shields in conjunction with spears to present a united front.

The Karth guards were trying to breach their defensive line but only had numerous injuries to show for their trouble. Unfortunately for the Regency, Trajan and his men came up behind their shield line and attacked without warning or mercy. The battle ended very quickly.

Severine led them to a storeroom, everyone filing inside, when soldiers started pouring into the other end of the hallway from the staircase. First dozens, then scores, of female soldiers, all trained and equipped as well as any soldier ever fielded.

"Hector, I want you to go with Ayela," Isabel said. "Protect her and be ready because at some point I'm going to need you."

"What are you planning, Lady Reishi?" Hector said.

"I'm going to buy you the time you need to escape," Isabel said. "Ayela, Trajan, thank you."

With that she turned and ran down the hallway shouting, "Help!"

Behind her she heard Hector and Ayela yell her name but she ignored them, focusing on her plan.

The lead soldiers fanned out and formed up as Isabel approached.

"Halt! Who are you?"

"My name is Isabel Reishi. Go fetch your commander."

The soldiers looked back and forth at each other, unsure what to do when a wraithkin pushed his way past the battle line and approached Isabel confidently, a devious smile spreading across his lips.

"Hello, Sister," he said.

Isabel drew her dagger and slashed his throat in a stroke. His expression was one of stunned shock when he tried to blink and couldn't, slumping to the ground, bleeding out in a pool of red. The hall fell deadly quiet, all of the soldiers eyeing Isabel with a mixture of fear and awe.

"I'm not your sister," Isabel said to the dying wraithkin, then looked at the soldiers. "Someone go get your commander or I'll start killing you," she said, casually cleaning off her dagger. A few moments later, a woman with emblems of rank pushed through the soldiers arrayed before Isabel.

"What is the meaning of this?" she demanded, a look of alarm ghosting across her face when she saw the dead wraithkin.

"Are you the commander of this unit?" asked Isabel.

"Yes, I'm Commander Henna of the Regency Army. And who are you?"

"I'm Lady Isabel Reishi. Take me to Prince Phane."

Chapter 47

Alexander appeared next to his sister. She was lying still in the snow, focusing on her breathing. He could see from her colors that she was in great pain and from the unnatural angle of her leg, he could understand why.

Ixabrax howled in misery, his mighty voice fading into the distance.

"How bad is it?" Alexander asked.

Abigail opened her eyes and blinked a few times to focus. "Bad. I can't walk."

"Hang on, I'll be right back." He vanished and appeared next to Anatoly. Magda was there, carefully helping him disentangle himself from the charred remains of a dragon. She finally worked him free and both of them fell into the snow.

"How bad?"

"Been better," Anatoly said.

"Magda, can you keep them alive for a week?"

"If I can keep Zuhl off our trail, then yes."

"Good, stay alive. Help is on the way," Alexander said, vanishing.

***

Abigail smiled with satisfaction as she flew over Zuhl's naval yard and saw two giant ships and the docks surrounding them completely destroyed by fire, smoke still marring the horizon.

She'd spent nearly a week in a cramped snow cave with Anatoly and Magda. By the time the Sky Knights arrived, she was delirious from the pain of her injury, and Anatoly had slipped into a fever and was nearly gone. Several hours after the Knights gave each of them a healing draught, they were both strong enough to fly.

Alexander had organized a rescue mission disguised as an all-out attack. The combined forces of two flights, nearly two hundred Sky Knights had made the journey. With Zuhl's dragons gone, wyverns ruled the air.

The main thrust of the attack had been the docks in Zuhl's Crescent Bay. Over a hundred Sky Knights, armed with self-igniting firepots set the entire port ablaze. Even though the ships were all protected with shields, the fire was able to spread along the dock to two of the giant vessels, completely destroying both of them.

While the attack was taking place, a wing of Sky Knights found Abigail, Anatoly, and Magda, bringing with them the healing draughts and a witch who knew a few healing spells. Within a few hours, Abigail was in the air, bundled tightly in several fur coats and blankets.

The channel crossing was cold and painful, her leg still aching, though not nearly as badly as it had the previous week. Abigail smiled again when she saw the bombed-out remains of the Irondale port. Five vessels, all nearly complete, destroyed in their berths, each the target of one of Mage Gamaliel's explosive weapons. The third prong to the attack. One wing had delivered five explosive weapons, one to a ship. While they were protected by shields as well, the strategy was to allow the weapons to sink into the water beside the ships before detonating them … and it had worked.

Each berth was nothing but a crater blasted into the shoreline, debris littering the water in every direction.

***

Alexander watched the ship gracefully slip into the cave and drop anchor. A few moments later, a gangplank bridged the gap between the stone shelf where he stood and the deck of the ship. Captain Kalderson came ashore.

Bragador, Anja, Jack, and, of course, Chloe were all there to greet the captain. Alexander's leg still hurt and he couldn't run for more than a few dozen steps, but he'd given up his cane and was anxious to be on his way, even if that meant a painful goodbye.

"Hello, Captain," Alexander said.

"Lord Reishi, it's so good to see you alive," Kalderson said, nervously. "I'd have never of left you if I'd known you weren't dead, I swear it."

"I know, don't give it another thought."

Kalderson drew himself up and nodded. "Right then, I can be ready to sail with the morning tide."

"Very good, please make the preparations," Alexander said. "We'll be leaving tomorrow."

"Please don't go," Anja said, starting to cry.

"Anja, we've been through this. You know I have to … I have responsibilities."

"But I love you," she said, breaking down in tears.

"Child, this is for the best," Bragador said softly.

"No, it's not," Anja shouted. For a moment it looked like she wanted to run away but wasn't sure which direction to go, then she hugged Alexander fiercely.

"I love you and I will miss you every moment of every day," she said through her sobs. "This is too hard. I can't do it anymore. Goodbye, Alexander."

He swallowed the lump in his throat as she turned away and ran for the cave entrance, jumping off into the surf and transforming into her true form midflight, roaring in anguish as she took to wing.

"I love you, too," Alexander whispered, wiping a tear from his cheek.

***

The journey was long, almost two weeks, traversing nearly half the Isle of Karth. Isabel had insisted that the entire force accompany her back to the Regency fortress, ostensibly to provide her with adequate security, but actually to prevent them from pursuing Trajan and Ayela. The jungles of northern Karth gave way to a vast savanna stretching across the isle, home to many range animals and a variety of large hunting cats.

South of the savanna, the jungle resumed, blanketing the island for leagues in every direction. The south was less rugged territory, with several cities cut out of the jungle, though they all had stout walls surrounding them to ward against predators.

Isabel played her plan over and over in her mind, testing it for flaws, looking for ways that it could go wrong, knowing that she would never see them all but at least she could plan for some of the problems that might arise. Her plan was solid. She was determined to carry it out and her determination only intensified as the journey dragged on.

The soldiers treated her like glass, afraid that any comment might give sufficient offense to warrant a swift death. That suited Isabel just fine. She couldn't afford to think of these soldiers as people; she might need to kill them in the very near future, best not to be on a first-name basis.

At long last they reached the fortress. Isabel felt the all-too-familiar flutter of fear in her belly. The time had nearly arrived. She saw her plan unfold in her mind's eye yet again.

None of the walls surrounding any of the cities of Karth was a match for the wall around the Reishi Army Regency fortress. Isabel was actually impressed, even after growing up in Glen Morillian, even after Blackstone Keep, the Regency fortress looked impregnable.

The wall was a hundred feet high and a hundred feet thick, stretching around the entire fortress complex, easily half a league on a side. Atop the massive walls were all manner of battlements, from catapults, to ballistae, to banks of raised platforms where multiple archers could stand and fire all at once. The wall was surrounded by a moat nearly forty feet across and filled with all sorts of dangerous fish and snakes.

A drawbridge lowered and the gate opened, then a trumpet sounded when Isabel entered the fortress. She hoped Phane was waiting for her.

Beyond the gate was a twenty-foot square tunnel cut through the wall, lined with arrow slits and murder holes. Inside the walls was a small city, stone buildings marching away from a large square in front of the gate.

A lone figure stood several dozen feet from the gate when Isabel entered the square. He was tall, well-built, perfectly proportioned and had shoulder-length wavy brown hair and golden eyes. He smiled so disarmingly that Isabel felt her resolve falter. He was boyish, exuberant and full of innocent joy, genuinely happy to see her.

Prince Phane ... murderer ... tyrant.

She schooled her breathing and calmed her mind, using the time it took to dismount her horse to regain her composure and fortify her determination. He was the enemy. He deserved to die. She meant to kill him—right now.

"My dear Isabel, I have so looked forward to this moment."

"Prince Phane, I beg your forgiveness for my initial resistance," Isabel said, looking down as he approached.

"Oh, nonsense," Phane said amiably. "You're here now, that's what's important."

"I've brought you a gift, My Prince," Isabel said, holding up a leather bag with her left hand as she went to her knee. "I beg your forgiveness that I could only bring you the Sovereign Stone and not my husband's head."

Phane stopped, midstride, breathing sharply, and then approached much more slowly, looking at the little bag held out in Isabel's trembling hand as if he couldn't believe it was possible. He swallowed hard, reaching out very slowly, savoring the moment.

Isabel waited until he took the bag. The moment the weight lifted, she grabbed his wrist and lunged forward, bringing her knife up in a fluid arc, driving it up under his ribcage—her knife that had three coatings of blackwort baked onto the blade. For days during her journey, she'd stared at this blade, seeing it plunge into Phane's heart, seeing his eyes go dark.

The blade hit home, stabbing into his belly, penetrating up toward his heart. Isabel put all of her strength, all of her rage, all of her pent-up fear into her attack. The blade was just inches from reaching its target ... Phane's black heart ... when he stopped her. Faster than she could have imagined, stronger than she might have ever suspected, he grabbed her wrist, pushing down hard, pulling the blade free of his belly before it could reach his heart and end him for good.

Isabel felt a sharp stabbing pain where Phane had grabbed her ... a needle puncture. She could feel numbing coldness spreading from the tiny wound.

Phane frowned at her in confusion, stumbling backward, looking at the blood on his hand and then looking back at her and smiling with such triumphant glee that Isabel thought she saw madness.

"Well done, Isabel," he said, coughing up blood, while still backing away from her. "Not to worry, you'll just be paralyzed for an hour or so." He held up his ring so she could see the little dart that had punctured her. "Glow-worm venom ... you can't be too careful, you know."

She slumped to the ground, losing control of her body but not of her senses.

Phane stumbled backward and fell, blood soaking the front of his tunic and frothing from his mouth.

"You got me good, Isabel," he sputtered, still crawling backward. "No one has ever stabbed me before ... really hurts."

Commander Henna strode up to Phane, looking down at him with contempt and slowly drawing her sword.

"Perhaps our lord and master isn't so all-powerful after all," Henna said loudly enough for her entire unit to hear. Nervous laughter rippled through the ranks.

"Ah, that's a pity," Phane said, the door to his Wizard's Den opening behind him. "I actually liked you."

With a gesture, he picked her up with his magic, lifting her several feet off the ground, then with a flick of his hand, sent her flying into the air ... she landed somewhere in the jungle several thousand feet outside the walls of the fortress.

The laughter in the ranks stopped.

Phane crawled backward into his Wizard's Den with great effort, trailing blood across the flagstones, stopping only when he was entirely inside. His soldiers stood stock-still, watching with a mixture of fascination and fear while Phane struggled with the pain of his wound just like any other human being would.

"Take Lady Reishi to a circle cell," he commanded. "She belongs to me now." He broke into a fit of coughing, bright red blood splattering the hand he used to cover his mouth.

Once he composed himself, he waved at Isabel with his bloody hand, smiling his boyish smile, blood smeared across his teeth and face, as the door to his Wizard's Den closed.

A few moments later, Isabel's world went black.

Here Ends Cursed Bones
Sovereign of the Seven Isles: Book Five

www.SovereignOfTheSevenIsles.com

The Story Continues…

Made in the USA
Middletown, DE
07 August 2021

45591803R00166